Book 1
The Raining Thorns Series

Donna Shannon

To the Squid Squad, the greatest writing group that ever grouped, who read the first draft and told me it was good, even when it wasn't.

To Vera, my nan. Sorry about the swearing.

Last but not least, to my Uncle Steve – be good. And if you can't be good, don't get caught.

X

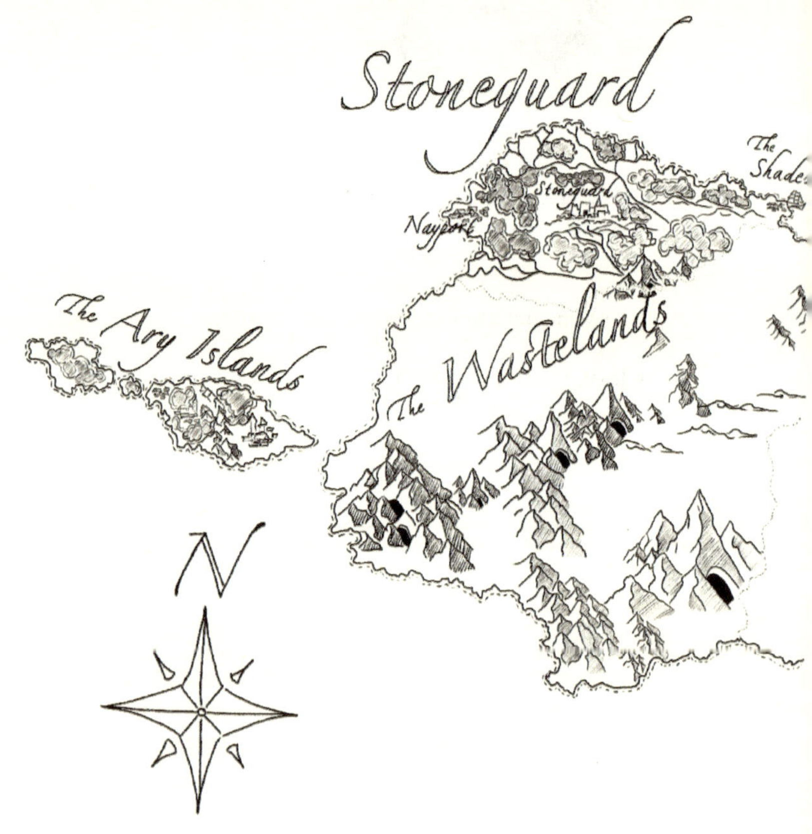

Stoneguard
The Shade
Stoneguard
Nayport
The Ary Islands
The Wastelands
N

Truphoria

PROLOGUE

The continent of Truphoria, the third week of summer on the 1345th Year of Mortality.

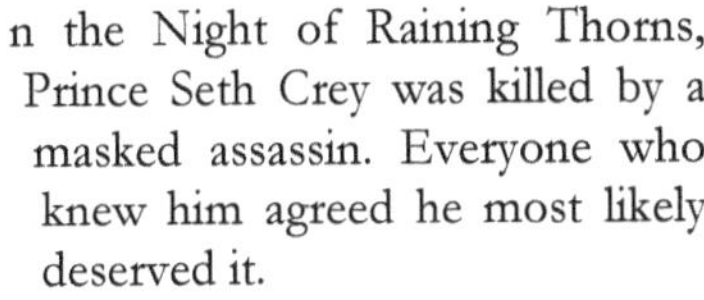

n the Night of Raining Thorns, Prince Seth Crey was killed by a masked assassin. Everyone who knew him agreed he most likely deserved it.

But hours earlier, public dislike of the adolescent had been placed aside. Dusk fell over the heart of Adem as the nobility of the world, plus a few opportunistic stragglers, flocked into Creys' Keep. Any concern about masked assassins had, unfortunately, fallen by the wayside. There was a far greater matter at hand.

There was a wedding due to start.

This was to be no normal wedding. It was a royal wedding, in the kingdom of Adem, no less. There would be romance, and love, and drinking and fighting in liberal amounts and, more importantly, cold feet…

Thirteen was a young age for one's youth to die.

Or so Seth considered, sitting on his throne beside his father. He glared down at his Portabellan guests, or, rather, King Theo's future investment.

The family of three plus their enormous entourage were recognisable purely by the sheer amount of gold coating their clothes and adorning their wrists and throats. Seth's father had laughed himself sick when he clapped eyes on them.

Best day of my life? Best day of his, more like.

Seth was far from having a good day. His mother had gifted him a ridiculous outfit she appeared to have fashioned out of an old dress, his shoulder-length hair was itching up a storm inside the collar and his Uncle Osney had forced him into a bath that left him smelling like a first-prize flowerbed and feeling a prize twit to match.

He was quite used to fragrant baths and ill-designed clothing of his mother's making. Thirteen years of being crown prince of Adem had well equipped him for that. It was the *hair*. Truphorian men kept it short and out of the way. Portabella had a fetish for long, luscious locks. He'd been growing it out on his mother's command since the betrothal was finalised a year ago. Queen Eleanor had curled it into tight coils with a pungent oil. It was hideous in every sense.

It's all for the sake of the alliance, his father had told him.

As far as Seth was concerned, he could stick his alliance up his arse. No Portabellan stick insect was going to have *his* babies anytime soon. He'd heard rumours about the procedure. It seemed ludicrously unhygienic.

King Theo Crey reached an elbow out to nudge his son's arm.

'Pretty little thing, isn't she?' he said over the din of the celebration.

'Dunno. The mother's in the way.'

The mother was a mishmash of wig and petticoat. Seth couldn't decipher the woman from the accoutrement.

'The girl, over there, look.'

Theo pointed.

Seth looked her up and down.

Cienne Fleurelle stood between her parents, her skinny form trembling within what must have been six tailors' worth of silk petticoats. She peered up at Seth over the top of a gilded fan and gave him a tiny, tentative smile, which he pointedly ignored.

'She's very… small,' he drawled. 'Lilly's bigger than her. Is she three years old as well? I don't think I feel comfortable seeing someone a full decade younger than I am.'

'Don't be stupid, she's of an age with yourself. You can't afford to be fussy, you know. You're a man now, or as good as at this age. You must spread your seed now that you're still young.'

Seth's face screwed up in disdain.

'That's disgusting,' he said with a shiver. 'Imagine sticking yourself into a *girl*. Ew.'

'It must be done. You are my heir, young Seth, and heirs must procreate. Why don't you show her around? Get to know her a bit before the ceremony?'

Seth threw his eyes towards the heavens and rose from his throne.

'And remember,' his father reminded him.

Seth pivoted with a dull expression.

His father flourished his right hand.

'Polite, chivalrous…'

'And complimenting,' Seth finished. 'The exact opposite of

what you're like to Mother.'

'Be gone, Seth,' Theo told him irritably, 'and heed my words or else!'

Seth stormed away, trying not to think of what 'or else' meant as the King of Portabella beckoned him over eagerly.

His matchstick of a daughter had taken heed of Seth's hostility and cowered behind his broad build, her silver-blond head scarcely visible.

Seth approached the family and bowed.

'Welcome, your majesty. My father and I are pleased to receive you.'

'And we are as pleased to be received,' the king said, his voice thick and jolly. 'Your highness, may I introduce Princess Cienne, my daughter.'

He directed to Cienne a stream of nonsensical speediness that Seth wasn't sure was even a human language.

The princess emerged from behind him to drop a quick curtsy.

'Greetings, my prince,' she said in a small voice, a thick accent curling prettily between the words.

Seth recalled his earlier counselling with the Duke of Osney and knelt onto one knee to take her hand.

'Greetings, my lady.'

He pecked the back of her wrist.

Princess Cienne retracted her hand, smitten.

'Do not let me keep you, Prince Seth,' King Fleurelle said to Seth with a benevolent smile. 'I'm sure you have much to show your future wife.' He winked.

Seth inclined his head with a faint, fake smile.

Give us a chance to unpack the rings, you dirty bastard, he thought privately.

Seth offered an elbow to Cienne.

She beamed at him and took it.

They strolled to the courtyard together.

He walked her around the perimeter, through the dining hall, around the spiralling patterns of the back gardens, everywhere he could think of to postpone having to invent small talk to amuse the silly creature clinging to his arm. As rain began to pitter onto the transparent crust that had become of Seth's hair oils, he led her back indoors and commenced a tour of the castle before, finally and tentatively, showing her to his rooms.

Where the fragile door of common courtesy was, abruptly, shattered from both sides.

'Get off! Get off!'

Seth tried to scream through a mouthful of Portabellan tongue technique as Princess Cienne squeezed him to her as tightly as possible.

He wrenched himself away and wiped his mouth.

'Salator Crey's balls!' he gasped. 'What the hell was that?'

'A kiss, my prince,' she said timidly, assuming her previous saintly façade.

'Is that what you call it?'

'Was it not pleasing, my lord?'

'Pleasing?' Seth shuddered. 'It was more… torturously inexperienced. Don't they teach you these things before you get here? Honestly. It was like having a puppy in my mouth.'

Cienne's face fell. 'I apologise, my prince.' She reached forward with both arms. 'Let me try again—'

'No!'

He stumbled out of her reach.

'You're already nearly suffocated me to death, leave me be!'

Cienne stood back, a delicate frown between her brows.

'Death? How could I have kissed you to death? You still live.'

Seth rolled his eyes. 'No, love, that was a joke.'

'Juh-oke?' she said slowly. 'I am not familiar with this word. It is like the word "poke"?'

'No, it is most definitely *not* like the word "poke"!!'

Seth stepped back again for self-preservation.

'I meant it was an exaggeration—'

'Eggs?'

Cienne huffed into her cupped hands and sniffed them, worried.

'What have eggs to do with me kissing you to death?'

Seth dropped his head into his palm.

'No, you nitwit, visit a library. You haven't kissed me to death, I only meant—'

Cienne's expression turned stony.

'Nitwit. I think I'm aware of this phrase,' she said in a monotone. 'I beg your leave, Prince Seth. I feel a bit sick, I should like to get some air.'

'Sick,' Seth echoed. 'I like that, I think I'll use that. It will look more convincing if we're both unwell, won't it? We can blame it on the shrimp, put off the wedding for at least another—'

The door slammed behind her, to the concern of no one but a raven outside, which left a spatter-shaped indication of its disgust on

Seth's window.

Smiling faintly at his newfound excuse, Seth entered his bedroom and bolted the door behind him. Women, he had decided long ago, were not his speciality – except for Cousin Elyse, who was notoriously easy to please.

Cream cakes, however, he thought warmly, were very much his best friend. His mother was bound to bring him a platter or two once she heard he was 'sick'. Particularly if he dropped the good old 'growing pains' line.

Anyway, he was a prince of the realm. The next *king*, in fact. He would get married whenever he bloody well felt like it, and his father… well, Seth could think of what his father would do in the morning.

He climbed under the covers of his deluxe four-poster and, despite the imminent arrival of cream cakes, fell asleep within moments.

Six hours passed.

Seth awoke to the sound of a raven pecking on his window. He sat up to chase it away when a small hand shot out of the shadows to slit his right palm with a short dagger.

Seth screamed.

The shade slapped another hand over his mouth.

The hand held a cloth… a damp cloth…

A raven's squawk echoed in his ears. Blackness washed in from the edges of his awareness, like rolling waves on a shore. The last thing Seth remembered on the night of his murder was the assassin dripping blood into a vial from the wound on his right palm.

~

The second and considerably more consequential thing that happened on the Night of Raining Thorns concerned an actual egg.

The Queen of the Forest was pissed off. Very pissed off indeed.

Someone had made shit of her castle.

She sat on the landing of what used to be a full set of stairs. Red smog drifted around her from the ground floor, dissolving the flagstones. She peered down into the centre of a massive crater in the middle of what prior to a moment ago was her audience chamber.

A few remnants of eggshell lay scattered in the centre.

The Queen shook debris out of her hair.

She tried to recall the date.

Third week of summer. King Theo's kid was getting married

today. She hadn't been invited, but that was fine. Social ostracizing wasn't something she was unused to.

Having explosive dragon eggs thrown at her was a different story.

Of course he would form an alibi first. That was King Theo Crey down to a T.

He could at least have given her a bit of notice, she thought sourly. A hoard of Crey foot soldiers arriving at her gate, that would have been fine, but magic… that was a cheat. And she should know. Cheating with magic was *her* signature move.

The Queen examined her household from the foot of the stairs. Some were badly injured. A lot of them were dead. This was not good. Hosting a retaliation with half a house and a council of six cripples was like enrolling in a jousting match with no arms – she might as well go ahead and put a sword in her own throat.

Now she was *really* pissed.

She limped to the remains of her bedchamber, adjusting her dress, the cream silk stained a dull grey from the explosion. She brushed her dust-coated hair away from her face. A mass of smouldering splinters in the corner marked the remains of her bureau.

A red glint caught her eye.

She dug a hand into the wreckage.

The amulet felt cool under her fingers, despite the blast. It had sat inside the drawer for years, decades even. The amulet had never been used. She had never had the desire to use it.

Similarly, the Creys had never made shit of her castle either. And nothing on their part had ever meant war. This had changed a lot of things… and there were a lot of things still to change.

She clenched it tightly in her fist and closed her eyes.

15

PART ONE: THE CATALYST

I

Serpus, the capital of Adem on the continent of Truphoria, on the first week of spring, 1365 YM.

utside a chapel in Serpus, one mile southwest from the old keep, a priest sprinted down Ablyminded Street. This was strange: priests never ran if they could help it. They burned marijuana in the presence of children and sometimes giggled during funeral services, but they never _ran_. It simply wasn't _appropriate_.

This time however was going to be the exception.

He burst through the chapel doors, panting.

'The dragon? Are you certain?'

'Most certain, Father,' the monk said gravely.

'And the king is _definitely_ gone?'

'Most definitely, Father.'

He gave him a small scroll to prove it.

Father Hope paced around the small chapel, his black robes gathered in his hands.

King Samuel Horne is missing.

He had hoped against hope that something large and vicious would have eaten the large and vicious king before his arrival back from the Far Isles. Alas, King Theo was rumoured to be due in the city for a beheading tomorrow afternoon.

The priest took the scroll from the monk's hands.

A prophecy has come into effect in the unnamed capital of Stoneguard. The King is gone, the Knight has been sighted and the dragon's arrival is nigh. The Prophet was right and the Fathers must be warned.

The scroll then went on to describe the apocalypse in over-dramatic detail.

Hope had seen the dragon with his own two eyes before, passing through Serpus on the way to Creys' Keep – which could only mean it belonged to the Creys.

Go figure.

He wrung his hands, dropping the scroll to the floor.

'What does he want us to do?'

'He said to prepare sanctuary for the Prophet,' the monk supplied. 'And pass the letter on. The messenger said this is the only letter being sent to the chapels.'

'To all of them?'

'To lessen the chances of the Antichrist finding it.'

'To increase the chances of it being lost, you mean.' Father Hope sighed. There was no teaching logic to some people. 'Does word of mouth not suffice?'

'He may hear us.'

'Everyone hears us on a weekly basis, how many of them listen to a word we say?'

The monk sighed. He had a point.

Hope stared out of the chapel, to the hills where Creys' Keep could just be seen in the distance.

This did not bode well. Everyone suspected, surely, but he always thought King Theo's bark was worse than his bite. He was no Rubeous Crey – he had been the worst one. And as for King Theo's father, well, the Wastelands didn't create itself.

He turned to the monk. 'Who sent the letter?'

'It's from Stoneguard, but whether they are the original writers of the letter, we don't know.' He lowered his voice. 'It has always been thought that His Eminence brought the Prophet to Stoneguard when he was discovered.'

That was true, Hope realised.

'Send it on,' he ordered. 'The others must be warned, whether it's true or not. We cannot take any chances.'

He stared out at the keep again.

'If it's true, this Knight of Thorns will need all the help he can get. He has no chance up against a Crey.'

~

Everyone remembered the Night of Raining Thorns, although funnily enough only a handful of people recalled the notion that there were any thorns involved at all.

Everyone knew there had been an explosion. Several explosions, in fact: the first within the castle in the Forest commencing a trail of detonations in a path all the way to the edge of Serpus. The inhabitants saw that part.

The thorns, ashes and occasional rose petal that had rained over Adem's capital after, however, had gone very much unnoticed. It *was* Prince Seth's wedding day, after all. Most of Serpus had either been too blind-drunk to see them or too concerned with the gravel buried in their faces from their unceremonious exit from the local pub.

Everyone knew about the fighting it had caused a week later. As Father Hope of the Faith of Salator Crey reminisced in the chapel log, the Forest Queen's War *'wrought horror upon the residents of Serpus for many days to come, with flame, gore and bits of beast-flesh a common sight, thus making an unholy mess of the chapel façade for me to clean up on my own because SOMEBODY was in the pub, BROTHER DANIEL.'*

Two accounts of the Night had been quickly snuffed out. A man claiming to have spotted a dragon flying out of the Forest had shortly been beaten with a hammer, and a manuscript had been quickly disposed of from a priest's room, a manuscript detailing what appeared to be a war dated twenty-five years into the future…

Best not to dwell on that type of thing. As Father Hope cites in his records, *'blood be-eth a bugger to get out of lacquered doors'*. And blood was a common enough feature of Salator Crey's chapels as it was.

Everyone in Truphoria saw one thing. Everyone, from as close as Serpus to as far as the kingdom of Stoneguard beyond the mountains of the Wastelands, saw the blinding white light of the Queen's fortress exploding. Yes, they all remembered the Flash.

But no one remembered the Hole. And nobody *would* remember the Hole because the Hole could make damn sure the Hole would be well and truly forgotten about by the next night. And it did.

Almost.

But that would be telling.

Which literary academics call foreshadowing.

Which is a fancy word for cheating.

And speaking of cheating…

~

Creys' Keep, on the hills north of Serpus, on the second week of spring, 1365 YM.

It was getting stressful in the palace of Adem.

The Queen of the Forest was rumoured to be planning another strike to push the borders and Stoneguard's king was on his way to discuss an alliance between Lilly-Anna and his runt Ronald. Theo was away to discuss trade deals with allies abroad, leaving Cienne in the lurch.

And why wasn't the next heir himself in charge of affairs?

Because he was dead.

And yet still alive.

To the misfortune of everyone involved, the assassination attempt on Seth Crey had failed – yet this knowledge remained unbeknownst to the prince himself. Seth's account of the whole ordeal included a description of the moment he departed his body and became a spectral poltergeist and *that was it*.

It never mentioned where the body went if he wasn't still in it or why he never ascended to the realm of Salator Crey like all Creys did in the legends of old –

But he was fine. So the matter was never raised again.

No one crossed Seth's beliefs because he had the scar to prove it. A small slit on his right palm, made by the knife of a man widely dismissed as a disappointment. There *were* standards to uphold, after all. If you're going to kill the prince of the realm, you might as well do it right.

But that didn't matter.

Twenty years later, through force feeding and manipulation, the 'Ghost of Adem' still lived – in a casket on the floor of his exasperated wife's bedchamber as time slid past for Cienne *very slowly*.

'Darling,' she coaxed.

She sat cross-legged, leaning an elbow on the lip of his open casket. She dangled an apple under his nose with her free hand.

'Please eat the apple. The physician says you need it, darling. Please…'

'Can't,' Seth said serenely. 'I'm dead.'

She sighed angrily.

She was thirty-three years of age, same as him. She should have six children by now, not some 'dead' man in a box. What made it worse was that force-feeding him was her only hobby – bar changing her Portabellan accent to a Truphorian one and researching every synonym to the word 'exaggeration'.

'Please,' she begged

'I'm dead,' he said, with a shrug. 'Sorry.'

Cienne dropped the apple onto her lap in frustration.

'Seth,' she said sharply, 'you are not a ghost, you never died, you are not thirteen, you are thirty-three, and if you do not take me to bed this instant, you shall feel what death really is like!'

Seth shrugged. 'I'm already dead. Your words mean nothing to me.'

Cienne clenched her teeth. 'Eat your apple!'

She shoved it into his mouth, slamming the coffin shut in his face.

Seth removed the apple, rubbing the joint of his jaw.

If Seth were alive, which unfortunately he was not *at all*, he would have thought of his wife Cienne Crey nee Fleurelle as a desperate woman. But dead men didn't think, they just remembered.

For instance, he recalled the night before, when Cienne decided to take out her frustrations on her late husband. This resulted in Seth being dragged mercilessly from his casket, thrown onto their bed and forced to perform an act of vulgarity before he escaped at a sprint, screaming for his mother.

That was not a good day, or so Seth remembered.

Then there was the week before, with the psychiatrist. The man swung a chain with a spiral-patterned disk on it back and forth in front of his eyes, intoning something about love and duty to the kingdom and a proper diet until Seth's mind went fuzzy.

Seth recalled in unfelt wonder how, as if controlled by an outside force, Seth had rushed into the pantry, eaten the entire contents and climbed into Cienne's bed to throw up in her mouth.

That was also not a good day, Seth reminisced, particularly for Cienne.

He also reflected on his daily routine – his force-feeding sessions with the lovely maid Anna. It was a pity he was dead. He remembered her being quite taken with him indeed.

If Seth had an opinion – which dead men cannot have – he would have thought his family to be very imbecilic indeed. Imagine forcing yourself on a dead man! The atrocity! And force-feeding him! What was the point? And as for Anna… well, she had better hope Cienne doesn't catch her soon. She took respect for the dead a little *too* far.

If Seth could feel wonder, he would amaze at the power of the human belief system for the way his family kept his position in the household alive using nothing but the sheer force of denial to assist them – but, as a ghost, he could not feel, or think. Just remember.

Seth would always remember the last person who saw him 'alive'.

He raised a hand idly and gazed at the scar running across his right palm. His memory of the assassination was fuzzy, but the scar proved it had happened, without a doubt.

Seth's Great Illness had lasted twenty years and counting. He smiled faintly in the privacy of his little refuge. He wondered if he could push it a little more… before his method acting reminded him that he was supposed to be remembering, not wondering.

Seth settled down into the maroon velvet lining. Now that Cienne had been left in charge, he could perhaps have some peace and quiet.

Seth rested his eyes, because dead men couldn't sleep.

~

Archibald Hart's Carpentry Shop, Stoneguard, the self-named capital of the kingdom of Stoneguard on the continent of Truphoria.

Things were about to change in the Hart household – or rather, the carpentry workshop where Archibald Hart was about to be confronted by his apprentice and his new hairstyle. There had never been anything like a hairstyle before. Stoneguard's residents opined that hair was nothing to be worried about and happened to everyone.

But Howie was breaking the mould – and how broken it looked, too.

'Who tried to skin you, then?' Archie asked.

Howie emerged from the market with his sandy hair chopped to half an inch long.

'A hair stylist from Serpus,' he said, running a hand through his short-back-and-sides. 'Reckons I look like the Prince of Adem now. Nice lady. Didn't try to kill me or eat me or anything. I told you all that rubbish about Serpus wasn't true.'

'She was from Serpus?' asked Archie in horror. 'I wouldn't go near someone from Serpus with a barge pole. Their king eats children!'

'She said there were plenty of children when she was last over. I took a risk. Could be worse because I could look like you.'

Archie scowled at that remark. To his mind, there was nothing wrong with long hair that resembled a grizzled knot of yarn sprinkled with icing sugar, so long as it was kept away from the lathe *at all costs*. But the problem with Archie was that he was, as Howie put it, an old biddy. This new-fangled 'style' thing was beyond him and would no longer be any use to him in any case: unless he somehow reverted back to twenty and grew a bit.

Archie shook his head and turned to the church bench legs he was working on.

Howie meandered around the debris.

Archie tried to ignore him as the boy tripped over chairs and stools, sending sawdust into the light of the sun and half-made furnishings flying across the room. Fine sawdust soared into his throat and nose, sending Archie into a fit of coughing.

He forever warned Howie about disturbing the delicate

balance of the workplace, but he never listened. At least he knocked over his own lopsided handiwork as opposed to Archie's masterpieces.

'Adrienne back yet?'

Howie picked up a trinket box Archie had great contempt for, turning it this way and that.

'No, but your annual newsletter came for you from your Aunty Doo-Dah from the orphanage. Why?'

'I made her a birthday present,' he said with pride, holding up the offending article.

Archie gave it a withering glance.

The dovetail joints quivered, as if in response.

'Hmm,' Archie said cynically. 'Getting ahead of the program, aren't you? Adrienne's birthday is in the spring.'

Howie glanced out of the door, lifting an eyebrow.

'It *is* the spring, Archie.'

Archie frowned and consulted his diary, unrolling the end of the parchment tacked on the back wall of the shop.

'Oh,' he said faintly.

'You'd notice this if you weren't cooped up in here all day long.'

Archie shot the window an apprehensive squint.

'You'd coop yourself up all day too if you saw the things I've seen.'

Howie rolled his eyes, anticipating the old lament.

'I didn't ship you and Adrienne over here for nothing,' he said in earnest. 'There are savages out there, you know. The war normalised it, all the things they do to people. I'll never forget what they tried to do to you when I first got you—'

'Yeah, they tried to eat me in the night. I know the story. Still pretty sure you dreamt it, though. I think I'd remember being tied up by a bloke with a knife.'

Archie pointed a finger at him.

'That was no dream,' he said sharply. 'They tried to kidnap you and sell you to a woman who eats kids for eternal youth. They drug you so you don't remember anything, they do it all the time. Look it up in a library.'

Howie's eyes lifted to the rafters again.

'Anyway, she's not back yet,' said Archie. 'She's still on her apprenticeship at the apothecary in the Shades, although whoever gave her that idea ought to have been killed. A woman's place is in front of the stove.'

'Don't let her hear that, she knows every poison in the world now,' Howie said in amusement. 'Anyway, she's independent. It's a good thing. Having women in the workplace is all the rage these days.'

'I expect the husbands will be enraged, yes. That's hardly a good thing, we have far too much violence as it is.'

'Er, no, Archie, I meant—'

'Anyway, cooking's less dangerous. Carrots don't try and rape you when you're changing its dressing.'

'She's fine,' Howie brushed off.

Archie hoped so.

'Alright, enough chit-chat, we have a large order to fill for the clergy,' he said, changing the subject. 'And try not to bugger up the pews like you buggered up that present, eh?'

Howie pulled a face at him and put the box down delicately.

Archie averted his eyes from the wonky joints. They were physically hurting his brain.

He regarded Howie as they got to work. He was, despite his faults in the woodwork department, a great kid. Possibly the best kid Archie had ever met, in fact, bar a young boy he apprenticed before him who became famous for curing lemurs. Or was it lepers? He could never remember.

People often said he had the Crey profile. Archie didn't see it, but he sometimes wondered if he wasn't related in some way. He had a strange kind of charisma – the kind that borders on hypnotism, pushes the borders on manipulation and downright conquers on indoctrination. Archie supposed that must have been why he kept him on. He did strange things to people's minds, even Archie's at times. It was a pity about his carpentry skills. It didn't matter how charismatic the boy was: as far as Archie was concerned, if he couldn't use wood properly, he wasn't a real man.

A knock interrupted him.

Archie looked up.

Adrienne beamed at them, laden with rucksacks from her time away.

'Hi, Archie,' she said brightly.

Archie grinned.

He had a great many nieces – so many in fact he kept a logbook for them to sign at each visit, just so he could remember their names. Many were so awful he often threatened to give them away free with any table and chair set, just so he could be rid of them.

But Adrienne was his favourite.

Her auburn hair shone in the morning sun, parts of it turning gold in the light. Her round face was flushed from the weight of her belongings, and her silver eyes – her mother's eyes – glinted happily as she stood in front of her makeshift family, dressed in an apron that could only be described as the muddied-and-bloodied hand-me-down of a surgeon with as little sanitation as a dung beetle's basement. Archie encouraged her to wear it to ward off predators. She was too pretty for his peace of mind. Just like her mother had been.

She had been with Archie since birth, and he had loved her like a daughter ever since.

Archie rose to greet her with a rare grin. 'How did you get on?'

'Great! They recommended I start up here after I sewed a Serpus man's finger back on. They even offered to lend me some money!' She beamed with pride.

'Oh, brilliant, well done. Oi, Howie, take her stuff upstairs, will you? Oof,' he gasped, dropping a rucksack, 'what's in here? You bring back a dead body as a souvenir?'

Adrienne giggled.

Howie skipped to the door.

'Happy birthday,' Howie said, handing her the little homemade box.

Her face lit up at the dreadful artefact, despite the chunks he'd hacked out of the lid beside the letter 'A'.

She opened the lid.

'Oh, Howie, it's lovely—'

The joints gave way, causing it to flatten.

She pulled them back into place and closed the lid in one fluid motion.

'Thank you!'

She threw her arms around his neck.

'You don't have to go to so much effort!'

'It's nuffin,' he said modestly.

Archie lifted an eyebrow. He decided to make her a better trinket box that might in fact have the capacity to *actually* hold trinkets. Partly for her birthday and mostly as a reward for being too polite for her own good.

The boy was a threat to society with his disgustingly heart-warming personality. Or a threat to the female populace, at any rate. Adrienne worshipped him. She'd be married to him by now were it not for the fact that, in terms of The Hint, Howie was as dense as a fortress wall.

Howie hefted her luggage onto one shoulder and trudged upstairs, to where the three of them lived.

Adrienne followed at his heels, clutching the box to her chest fondly.

It took Archie a moment before all feelings of unexplained paternal affection for Howie could be pushed out, to be replaced by his usual grouchy demeanour as the thought *slacker* slid into consciousness once more.

~

II

Lilly-Anna stood inside the entrance to the throne room as Cienne entered.

Cienne scowled with contempt at the highly decorated hall. Stone statues of Crey kings of old and emerald-coloured banners alternated along the walls, lining the pale stone behind them. The banners bore the Crey family motif: two snakes, emerald and gold, entwined in a knot to represent the intimate bond between Adem's king and god – with the added bonus of showing what traitors would look like on the way home.

Cienne directed her trail of thought *away* from that note.

She turned to face her sister-in-law, whose blue eyes – so like Seth's – were fixated to a huge crate outside the doors. Her brother's untouched riding clothes hung in folds over her small form.

There was something about Lilly-Anna that deeply unsettled Cienne, but it was difficult to say what it could be *specifically*.

It could have been the fact that she often carried a mace, like she was doing now. She twirled it in one hand as she circled the box.

Without warning, she swung it an inch from the guard's nose.

He flinched violently, a bead of sweat dropping down his temple.

Lilly cackled.

Similarly, it could be that she frightened the living daylights out of men six times her size. This Cienne pondered as the guard excused himself to walk to the outhouse stiffly and quickly.

But the most likely reason was probably the way Lilly stared at her sister-in-law the way one would stare at food. Which would have been fine were she, say, admiring her clothing. Cienne knew what she was doing and resented it. Bad enough for a man to hungrily ogle a married woman without the public's most prominent women's rights representative hopping on the bandwagon.

Lilly approached Cienne with a smile.

Cienne plastered the most stoic smile she could manage,

quickly asserting a boundary.

'Morning,' Lilly said, in a high-pitched voice grossly ill-fitting to her personality. 'Any joy with Seth?'

Cienne sighed. 'I wish.'

'Oh. Well, the old man's bought a new toy,' she said brightly.

She skipped to the crate, her mace swinging idly at her side.

'Come and see!'

Cienne approached the crate warily.

The thing about crates like this arriving on the Creys' doorstep was that they were frequently very dangerous – which was probably the point. She missed Portabella and its frilliness. At least it was genuine and didn't have a couple of knives hidden anywhere.

Lilly-Anna (what a terrible name that was for her, Cienne thought) grasped a handful of the cloak covering the crate and thrust it away grandly.

The dragon blinked in the sudden light and screamed, sending smoke billowing from its great nostrils.

Cienne gasped, stumbling backwards into the middle of the hall.

The cage stood ten feet wide and tall, and it was packed with furious muscle. The dragon's long neck hunched beneath the top bars of the cage. Its discomfort was evident in the beast's wriggling and jerking. Scales shimmered with every movement, turning from crimson to jade green to every colour in between. It had Crey written all over it.

'*That's* his "new toy"?' Cienne gaped, unable to blink for fear of missing a single movement. 'I, I thought he would get a, a dog or something, not a, a—'

'Dragon.' Lilly beamed. 'Isn't it brilliant? We've always wanted one, ever since we were little, me and—Seth! We should bring him out, he'd love it, come on!'

She tugged on Cienne's sleeve and pulled her to the stairs.

They panted up every step, Lilly in her ill-fitting breeches and jerkin, Cienne struggling to gather her masses of petticoats, until they reached the third and highest floor of the palace and burst into Seth's private quarters.

Lilly threw the coffin door open and shook Seth by the arm.

He snorted awake.

'Seth, Seth, wake up, look! He got a dragon! Come down and see!'

Seth bolted upright. 'A *dragon*?!'

'Yes, a dragon! Come on!'

She pulled him upright and dragged him downstairs.

Cienne followed close behind.

She knew, deep down, that no one could get Seth to do anything except for his tomboyish baby sister and her insistent enthusiasm. Not even his mother, or his wife – especially his wife. And it wouldn't even bother Cienne all that much were it not for the fact that she loved him, indefinitely and inexplicably.

And he knew it. He knew it from the day they first met… and he hated it.

They arrived back to the imposing animal's cage. As Cienne predicted, all memory of Seth's 'death' had temporarily dissipated, to be replaced by awe.

'Mine!' he proclaimed in a hushed voice, staring up with wide eyes.

'No hogging it, brov, it's mine too,' Lilly said with a smile.

Seth reached between the bars to brush its scales.

It hissed smoke into the air.

'What do we name it?'

Cienne approached and brushed a tentative hand against his, thinking he wouldn't notice.

He edged away, fixated to the dragon.

'What about Smokey?' Lilly said.

Seth burst out laughing.

'Smokey? What kind of a name is that? Why don't we call *you* Smokey since you have smoke for an imagination?'

'Oh, alright then,' she said mildly. 'How about—'

'Lyseria,' Cienne said.

Seth turned to her in surprise.

Cienne's heart skipped a beat as their eyes met, a seldom occurrence.

'I like it,' he said. 'Where did you pull that from?'

'It's the name of Salator Crey's companion,' she said meekly. 'I figure the king would approve, since she's a religious figure. She's a deity in her own right in my parts.'

'Oh, the dragon lady,' Lilly said in recognition.

The dragon released a puff of approval.

'Lyseria it is,' Seth said with a grin – the first she'd seen in a long time.

'Is it a girl?' Lilly wondered.

Seth tilted his head to the side and bent his knees.

'It's either that or a eunuch.'

A messenger entered the hall and they turned to face him as he bowed theatrically.

'Your highnesses,' he said, touching his forelock, 'I come from Stoneguard with a message. The king cannot attend today's discussion on the betrothal.'

Lilly breathed a sigh of relief.

'Why not this time?' said Cienne sharply.

There's always an excuse, she thought irritably. *The king has man-flu, the prince is violently hung-over…*

'The king is missing, your highness,' said the messenger. 'He's presumed dead.'

~

The gods proclaimed to anyone who would listen that all things happened for a reason.

When Adrienne's father was killed by a lunatic and her mother died in childbirth, Adrienne believed this had to happen in order for her to live with her beloved uncle Archie.

And when Archie brought a mysterious orphan born on the Night of Raining Thorns to live with them as his apprentice and made them move to a strange country, Adrienne believed this had to happen in order for her to fall in love with Howie.

And Adrienne reckoned that one day quite soon, something else would happen in order for her to marry Howard Rosethorn and have a lot of children. Or at the very least treat Howie for an injury and examine him *very closely*.

At the moment, the two were in Adrienne's tiny bedroom, unpacking her things. She waited for the catalyst for her aforementioned fate. She'd been waiting for eight years. It was bound to happen sometime.

Her room was half the size of Howie's, but she forgave him for that. It was littered with Howie's definition of art – little boxes with 'Adrienne' carved on top clumsily and frames for her sketches that were more like wonky diamonds than squares. Half of her charcoal drawings were of Howie, much to his approval: the rest were landscapes and still life drawings with him in there somewhere, usually bent at a ninety-degree angle for reasons only an artiste can justify.

The only part of the room that showed no hint of Howie's existence was where the straw bed consumed most of the floor space. Even the dangerously lopsided chest of drawers stood in the corner as a mark of Adrienne's reluctance to part with his good-intentioned yet poorly crafted efforts for her.

'So what's working with the dreaded Serpus-folk like?' asked

Howie, listlessly scanning the junk mail from his Aunty Philippina.

'It doesn't end,' she said with a sigh, sitting on her bed beside him. 'It would probably be fine if they weren't all sailors. Not only do you have to monitor those nearly on the croak, you have to keep the rest from fighting each other and throwing knives at people. They're lunatics.'

Howie laughed. 'You're better off setting up here, then. Worst you have to deal with is that rash going around. Speaking of,' he added mischievously, twitching ominously. 'Think I might have a touch of it down there. You wouldn't mind taking a look, would you?'

The image appeared in her head in total clarity.

'Of course,' she said evenly. 'I am a professional.'

Howie snorted and dropped the pretence. He flopped onto his back to gaze at the ceiling.

'So what have you been up to in my absence?' she said, diverting her attention to cleaner territory. 'Anything interesting?'

'Got my hair cut—'

'Looks great.'

'Thank you!' he said with a smile. 'That's about it, though. Talking to Archie doesn't beat our little chats, you know.'

'You missed me, then?' she said with a grin.

'Of course I did,' he said, sitting upright to meet her gaze. 'You're my favourite person.'

A pink sensation blossomed in her chest, spreading out in a glorious wave.

'Oh,' she said faintly.

She dropped her head on his shoulder.

She turned her face upward and her head spun at the mere smell of him. It was funny how the sawdust wasn't as appealing on Uncle Archie. His skin was coated in it, the fine substance settling in the folds of his shirt and even in his ears. He reminded her of the seaside on a sunny day with his sandy hair and eyes the colour of a summer sky. His hair really looked like sand, especially cut short, and his arm was warm around her shoulders, like the sun.

She felt immensely happy. Any minute now, the catalyst was going to occur. She could already hear wedding bells from the near future. Or maybe cow bells from the market outside, one or the other.

'Adrienne?'

'Mmm?' she murmured happily.

'I know you're tired from your trip back, but can I have my shoulder back? It's gone numb.'

She opened her eyes. 'Oh, sorry.' She sat up awkwardly.

Archie's voice floated up the stairs.

'Oi! When are you getting started on those pews?'

'In a minute!' Howie called.

He glanced at Adrienne with a wink.

'I'll manipulate Archie into letting me off and I'll be right back.'

'Okay,' Adrienne said, beaming.

He pecked her cheek.

It grew warm and reddened profusely.

'Happy birthday,' he said, rising. 'I've missed you!'

Adrienne smiled.

I've missed you too, she thought privately.

~

'Have you searched the Forest?'

'Yes, your highness. We've also searched the city, to no avail.'

'Maybe yusshould check the booze cabinet, 'e migh' be'n there,' slurred Ron in amusement.

In the upper level of the Stonekeep, Stoneguard's only tourist destination, two princes stood in the drawing room of the elder prince's quarters. One was considerably wobblier than the other as the elder, a narrow man with a pointed face, folded his arms impatiently, his brown hair hanging over his bloodshot green eyes.

'Did he arrive in Adem?'

'There have been no sightings in the ports of King Samuel—'

'King Stuffs 'Is Face, more like,' snorted Ron. 'Have you tried the pantry? Probably stuck in the sweetie cabinet, the shtupi' bah—'

After twenty minutes of pithy remarks, Prince Vladimir, finally, snapped.

'Be gone, you utter wretch!' he screamed at Prince Ronald, shoving him backward.

Ron stumbled on the flagstones, waving his wineglass in the air.

'Ooh, somebody's got all his feathers in a clump,' he trilled, with a pronounced 'P'. 'All summer roun' the lower regions, where even the tumbleweed's bin avoid—'

'GET! OUT!!'

Vladimir grabbed the scuff of his neck and threw him bodily into the corridor.

The man was a menace. At the tender age of twenty-one, Ron had gained the maturity of a six-year-old and a drinking problem that resulted in him looking physically ten years his own senior. Except that his hair, Vladimir mused hatefully, had managed to stay black while Vladimir's wasn't staying anywhere at all.

Ronald was the last thing the Hornes needed right now.

Ron slammed into the wall opposite.

'Watch out, you mis'rubble git!' he barked.

'Get out of my sight! I have more significant issues to deal with than your DRUNKEN BUMBLING!'

Ron pulled a face at him and stumbled out, cackling.

One of the most unfathomable mysteries of the continent of Truphoria was the condition of Ronald Horne's psyche. The trouble was that he had the mind of a ten-year-old – until he started drinking. It was incredibly difficult not to wonder how a man with such a passion for daisy-chains, climbing trees, leapfrog and the weekly game of snakes and ladders every Tuesday could have a tendency towards alcohol.

As if his childish imagination and energy weren't exhausting enough, Vladimir had Ron's drunken hallucinations to contend with, not forgetting a vulgar interpretation of life's little details that, once sobriety hit, seemed to disappear without a trace. This double-personality was aging Vladimir so badly he reckoned he'd die of old age before he hit thirty-five.

Vladimir dismissed the messenger with a wave and glared out at the morning sun.

King Samuel was missing, presumed dead by the authorities. Which was Vladimir, his successor, but that was beside the point. King Samuel dead wasn't such a bad thing. King Samuel dead meant good things.

King Samuel and the crown of Stoneguard missing, however, did not.

The crown of Stoneguard was a hideously important factor of Vladimir's life. Without the crown, the king was not a king, and without a king the kingdom was not a kingdom, making the War for the Orchard over fifty years ago – the Hornes' greatest victory – void. Without that awful, jagged crown-shaped lump of rock, Vladimir was nothing, and Stoneguard was a joke.

Needless to say, the safety of the crown was a damn sight more important to him than that 'shtupi' bastard'.

Vladimir narrowed his eyes to the south, to where the black mountains of the Wastelands framed the distant horizon.

He suspected *her*, of course. Who didn't? The nameless Queen was a madwoman, which was perfectly fine compared to her people. Vladimir didn't dare contemplate what the king might have gotten himself into with *them*.

Because in actual fact, despite being well-liked in general, King Samuel of Stoneguard was a fool. A *big* fool. And Prince Ronald was inheriting that foolishness in every respect.

A knock came to the door.

Vladimir spun on one heel, his jewellery clanging.

A monk stood just outside the door, twiddling his thumbs with the sheepish little smile his people favoured. A steel cross hung from his neck, adorned with five buttons down the spine and one more on the end of each centred arm – the motif of the Faith of the Seven.

Vladimir heaved a sigh. 'I take it my mother summoned you?'

'Um, no, your highness,' he said in a quiet voice.

Vladimir shot the Cross of the Seven a scathing glance.

What the Seven actually *were* was disputed – their faith thought they were gods, the Faith of Salator Crey thought they were devils, and most of the higher class thought they were imaginary.

But they definitely existed – Vladimir had seen the proof of that, twenty years ago, when his mother had deposited him on the altar, and they had bestowed upon him the Sword of Thorns.

Apparently. His eyes were closed at the time in prayer, so he couldn't be sure.

But they definitely existed – the chapel in Stoneguard's capital of the same name often saw food donations vanish without a trace. And on very rare occasion, some small folk swore blind that family members of a sinful persuasion sometimes disappeared as well.

Vladimir wished they had the decency to take Ronald with them.

'Go on,' he said. 'What is it?'

The monk bowed in his filthy grey robe, his bald and badly sunburned head reflecting the light of the sun. 'Majesty, there is a matter of great importance we need to discuss with you. It is a prophecy concerning the king's disappearance.'

Vladimir glared at him in disdain. 'Of course there is.'

The monk nodded. 'Indeed.' They never were very good at comprehending sarcasm. 'My lord, it is finally time to wield the Crystal Sword. The Knight of Thorns has been summoned by law of the Testament.'

Vladimir's eyes rolled upward.

'The Prophet has confirmed it,' the monk continued, 'and the texts of the Testament have illuminated in light of the Catalyst—'

Vladimir opened his mouth and, with great volume, yawned.

The monk looked taken aback. 'Am I boring you, your highness?'

Vladimir closed his mouth.

'Oh. Yes,' he said mildly. 'You rather are.'

The monk spluttered. 'But—the Prophet—he said—it's the day we've been waiting for, your highness. Your time to defeat the Antichrist is come.'

'*Has* come,' Vladimir corrected. 'Using proper grammar isn't a sin, you know.'

He eyed the monk's defeated expression with a mild sense of pity.

'Look, I grew out of this religious hero lark a very long time ago,' he drawled. 'But if it entertains you lot to pander to the call of a group of tricksters, by all means have fun with this new charade. Just keep me out of it. You can tell my mother I have handed in my notice as resident Knight of Raining Thorns, or *whatever* it is. Hers is the east wing, by the way.'

He waved a dismissive hand.

'But your highness—'

'Oh, "but your highness" what? "The world is coming to an end"? "A traitor is among you"?' Vladimir mocked shrilly, waving his arms about. 'Oh, what about "the holy flying", I dunno, "*cat* has descended from the heavens to proclaim the Chosen One"!'

'My lord, that is something the Crey religion would come up with,' the monk said in a hurt tone.

Ronald's re-entrance to the hall interrupted them.

He stood before them, his eyes wide and bloodshot.

'A cat just *flew* right past my bedroom window!'

Vladimir gave him a withering glance. 'Have you been at the incense again?'

'A flying cat?' the monk cut in.

'Glowing, too,' Ron added.

'Don't encourage him,' Vladimir scolded the monk, 'he was just eavesdropping at the door—'

'See? Look! Look out there!'

Ron pointed out of the window, bouncing on his heels.

Vladimir pivoted lazily.

And leapt back at the sight.

A scruffy grey tabby cat glared at them through beady eyes. It *hovered* behind the glass and hissed at them through an ethereal glow.

Vladimir trembled, his back pressed to Ron's shoulder.

'Th-this is highly irregular,' he stammered.

The cat launched himself at a robin and slammed it into the glass.

'Quite,' said the monk. 'Usually the Seven aren't quite so receptive to idle mockery outside of mass.'

'You were blaming it on the Creys a minute ago,' Vladimir drawled.

'The ethereal glow, your highness,' the monk said, gesturing with splayed fingers. 'The Seven do this all the time at the chapel, usually when someone questions their existence. Religious artefacts fly about the place every odd Sunday. Keeps the patrons coming in.'

'Do I get a reward for finding the Holy Flying Cat?'

'The only reward you'll get,' Vladimir sneered at Ron, 'will be a sharp shove down a long flight of stairs if you don't sober up sharpish.'

Ron cowered. 'Can I have the cat?'

'No, you can't have the cat. Honestly, your father's presumed dead and the entire kingdom dangles by a thread, and you're stood here going on about a stupid cat—'

'Behold!' exclaimed the monk.

The cat had disappeared.

The three rushed to the window to see it soar into the chapel after the robin.

Ron bolted outside, curious.

Vladimir's eyes flitted back to the window.

The local carpenter carried three benches into the chapel, assisted by a young fair-haired apprentice.

Vladimir blinked and looked closer at the youth, who promptly dropped all three benches on his master's foot with a wince.

'The boy,' Vladimir said. 'Who is he?'

'An orphan, your highness. Comes from Serpus originally.' The monk lowered his voice. 'There is a rumour he was found in the Queen's Forest on the Night of Raining Thorns. He may be an instrumental part of the prophecy if the rumours are true.'

Vladimir cracked a smile.

The monk shivered. A smile from the elder prince of Stoneguard never boded well.

'Of course he is,' he said. 'He's Seth Crey's double.'

~

III

'Can you walk?' Father Toffer asked anxiously.

''Course I can't bloody walk!' shrieked Archie. 'I've just had three oak pews dropped on all my toes! *All of them!*'

'Sorry,' said Howie in a small voice.

'Oh, that's alright, mate, it was an accident,' Archie said kindly.

He turned to the priest to screech, 'What are you just standing there for? I can't carry your benches now!'

The priest gathered his robes. 'Yes, I'll fetch somebody.'

'Hurry up!'

'Y-yes, sir!' stammered the priest.

He ran to the chapel, his garments tripping him up on the way.

A gentle breeze drifted across the centre of Castlegate Lane, bathing Howie in some much-needed cool air. He stood sheepishly at the step of the chapel, his shadow falling over Archie, who clutched his feet in both hands, his back against the chapel doorframe.

'Bloody priests,' Archie grumbled. 'Hate priests, bloody hate them!'

He glanced up at Howie.

'What you looking at?'

Howie blinked, his eyes locked to the open doorway. 'I… don't know.'

Something grey and furry zipped from one end of the chapel to the other and appeared to be wearing a full-body halo.

Howie quickly decided to ignore it. He helped Archie to his feet again.

Father Toffer emerged from the chapel to trip over his robes again.

Archie glanced around him. 'Well? Where are your helpers?'

Father Toffer ignored him. His gaze was locked to Howie.

Howie, tentatively, took a step back.

'You,' said Toffer. He pointed at him. 'What's your name?'

Howie frowned, blinking rapidly. 'Howard.'

Toffer squinted at him.

Within seconds, he had fled back into the chapel.

Howie and Archie stared after him for a moment.

'Odd,' said Howie.

Toffer reappeared at a sprint.

And thrust himself onto his knees at Howie's feet.

'My lord, I am honoured by your presence,' he said, head bowed.

Howie frowned at him, then the street behind him, then at Archie.

Archie lifted an eyebrow.

'"My lord"?' he said, shifting his weight to wiggle his right foot. 'Since when were teenage carpentry apprentices styled as "lord"?'

Toffer ignored him and took Howie's hand to kiss it.

Howie's nose wrinkled.

A stream of dribble led from his knuckle to the man's salt-and-pepper goatee.

'The Seven have sent us a sign. They have chosen you, Howard… uh…'

'Rosethorn,' Archie assisted helpfully.

'… Rosethorn,' he said seamlessly, 'to seek out his majesty, King Samuel Horne of Stoneguard. My lord, I implore you to follow us into the chapel to accept your quest.'

Archie snatched Howie's wrist and, to Howie's relief, jerked it away.

'He's overage,' Archie snarled.

Toffer made a disgusted clucking sound. 'Give me strength. He's not even my type.'

Nevertheless, he clutched Howie's hand again, pressing the back of the knuckles to his forehead.

Howie stared at his hand, stricken.

'Could you just… let go… thanks…'

He wiped his hand on the bottom of his shirt.

'… what do you mean, they've chosen me? How do you know it's me?'

'There's a picture,' an acolyte said helpfully.

Toffer glowered at him and continued, intoning grandly.

'You are the Knight of Raining Thorns, as stated in the prophecy. You are the Knight of Roses, beholder of the crystal sword and wearer of the very tight but extremely holy breeches.'

Howie glanced at his trousers self-consciously.

Father Toffer followed his gaze.

'We had it translated from the old language of Adem,' he said sheepishly. 'The nuns tend to get carried away with the details.'

'Right. Look, I'd better be off,' Howie said, backing off.

'But you are Howard Rosethorn!' cried the priest, snatching his hand again.

'I'm aware of that,' Howie said in a pained voice, 'please let go of my hand.'

'You must save his majesty King Samuel Horne, vanquish the Antichrist and defeat him—'

'Why would he possibly want to fulfil the demented ramblings of a depraved nun when he's got work to be getting on with?' Archie barked. 'I've a retirement to make out of him, no holy animals are depriving me of that yet!'

As if in response, the robin launched itself at Howie.

He ducked and was promptly hit in the face with the Holy Cat.

'Looks like they are,' Toffer said coyly.

Howie collapsed with a shriek. He rolled on the dusty ground, wrestling with the spitting ball of fur and its livid assault.

'Bloody hell!'

With a screech, the cat landed heavily against a stall a yard away.

Howie sat upright, his boyish face covered in hairline scratches.

'Oi!'

They pivoted to the east, the direction of the castle.

A young man with jet-black hair threw himself in the cat's direction.

'You threw him! How could you? That's animal cruelty, that is! Unbelievable!'

He picked up the cat and brushed it off.

'He started it,' Howie said sulkily.

Then he froze.

The newcomer was a nobleman, Howie realised in astonishment – his grey silk clothing gathered dust as he crouched beside the stall, cradling the cat. He looked up at everyone staring down at him and frowned, his face beatific above the unearthly glow.

'Oh, sorry,' he said quickly. 'I'm Ronald Horne.'

Archie's mouth hung ajar.

The cat gave a pitiful yowl.

'This day can't get any weirder,' Howie said, his jaw similarly open.

'Behold!' Toffer exclaimed.

'Hold that thought,' Archie said.

White beams of light lanced out of the chapel doors in every direction.

Toffer seized Howie by the shoulders and ushered him inside.

The glare clawed at his eyes.

Howie held out a hand, shielding them. With an arm over his brow, he glanced around as he was quickly ushered down the aisle. A handful of heavily vandalised pews faced the altar. A stone basin sat above, holding various produce: cabbages, fruit, wrapped meats – all of which, to Howie's alarm, vanished into thin air before his eyes.

Toffer prompted him to the altar, paying no notice.

The yellow glare came from the left side of the basin, leading them to a small podium.

Howie was thrust against it.

A book appeared to be the unlikely source of the light.

He glanced around helplessly at the men gathering around him and squinted into the pages, his hands curled around his eyes.

The gilded pages of the Testament gleamed in bright colours: red, orange, blue, green, violet. Howie had seen books before – from afar. But none had ever borne as bright a hue as in any of these pages.

One illustration was outlined in white to stand out the most.

A man with blond hair, brandishing a sparkly sword and, indeed, wearing what looked to be particularly tight trousers, stood in battle stance at the head of a hoard of soldiers. The profile looked familiar… too familiar.

Howie eyed the long nose with unease.

'That's me, isn't it?'

'Observe your opponent, my lord,' Toffer said with reverence.

Howie returned his gaze to the parchment, avoiding the nose in distaste.

Rearing up at him from the opposite page was a snake. A *large* snake. Roses and thorns strangled it, coiled tightly around its entire body.

Toffer knelt at the steps once more.

'This is a sign from the gods that you, Howard Rosethorn, must travel to the royal family of Adem in search of King Samuel Horne. You must identify the Antichrist among the Crey household and, at all costs, annihilate him.'

Howie made a face. 'Why can't I just help him? He looks like he's in pain.'

Archie limped up to the dais.

'Anyone want to tell me why we're faffing over a book instead of paying me for these pews?' he asked plaintively. He nodded at Howie. 'What's it say?'

'Think they want me to kill King Theo Crey,' Howie said, swallowing.

'Not right away!' Toffer exclaimed. 'We must first establish who the Antichrist is in the family. It might not be him.'

'I hope not,' said Archie, 'he's a cannibal by all accounts.'

'We think,' Toffer said, ignoring Archie, 'it may be a pretender at court. We will need to be delicate in our interrogations and discreet, and, if possible, curry as much favour with the Creys as we can.'

'"We" meaning "him", you mean,' Archie said, pointing at Howie.

Toffer tilted his head from side to side before, finally, relenting.

'Yeah, pretty much.'

'Yeah, no thank you!' Archie trilled.

He stormed up to Howie, hooked a hand under his elbow and hauled him through the group of acolytes.

Protests rose to a dull roar.

'Forget it!' Archie howled over them. 'I've already lost one good apprentice to, to lepers or lemurs or whatever. I'm not losing another one to the church. I might hand him over in six months if his dove-tail joints don't improve,' he added as an afterthought, 'but until then, you can find someone else. Good luck!'

'But—'

'The prophecy—'

'The book said—'

'The carpentry apprentice?'

Howie and Archie bolted to attention.

A guard stood at the door. Steel plate gleamed in sections from the light of the book, the rest marred by rust and dirt. He held a scroll up for Howie, one gauntlet shining.

'You have been summoned to attend his highness Prince Vladimir Horne at the Stonekeep.'

Archie lifted his upper lip. 'What for? Injuring the cat?'

'Archie,' Howie hissed. It was one thing to be pithy to a man of the cloth. Palace guards were a tad more dangerous.

Howie heaved a sigh and met the guard's gaze. 'When? I seem to have a lot on all of a sudden.'

The man twirled the scroll in his fingertips and unrolled it.

'Now,' he said. 'Or *else*.'

~

A skinny man covered in mud lurked in the city of Serpus.

Being the capital of Adem, Serpus was as its name's translation decreed – a dwelling of snake-like streets covered in the flea-like masses that were the city's population. But it wasn't Serpus itself that was worrying Amish.

He'd been a very bad woodsman.

But he'd had an excuse.

He slipped into the nearest mob – Serpus had dozens – and followed it towards the head of Arthur Stibbons' Street.

In amongst the horde of people, a chopping block stood in the centre of a semi-circle of armoured knights bearing the shield of the Creys: two snakes, one gold, one green, entwined in an elaborate knot. The chopping block was ominously empty.

Amish turned around nervously, or as best as he could while locked in the embrace of a nosy mob. Thankfully, there was nobody watching him… yet.

The crowd shifted outwards, leaving him some breathing space. He turned to watch the show the hoards had obviously come to see—

And screamed at the top of his lungs.

King Theo Crey stood an inch away from his face, wearing a slight smile.

Amish gulped furtively. He eyed the large beard in particular.

'Muh-my-muh-my-my liege!'

He tried to bow without head-butting him. The best he could manage was a little bob. His eyes flicked around.

The mob was suddenly pointing several spears at him.

'Amish Murdogh?' King Theo asked.

His deep voice reverberated across the square.

'Yuh-yur-yur—'

'Just nod, boy.'

He nodded.

The king folded his arms. 'I'm told you were loitering in… dangerous territory?'

He simply swallowed in reply.

'Territory that might be banned from entry on pain of *death?*'

He gulped again. 'P-possibly.'

'And tell me,' King Theo said pleasantly, 'what, pray, were you doing in said *dangerous territory?*'

'F-f-fuh-fuh—'

'—ing Faeries, yes,' King Theo finished. 'Now remind me: is that not a criminal offense?'

'Not if you don't get caught, my liege,' he quoted his father.

He froze in horror.

King Theo stared at him for a long, long moment.

Then he burst into laughter.

After a short moment, the crowd laughed with him.

The square echoed with mirth.

Amish also laughed, albeit uncomfortably.

Almost as soon as Amish began laughing, the king abruptly stopped.

So did the crowd, leaving Amish chuckling hoarsely.

He quickly shut up.

'Come with me,' Theo said darkly.

Silence smothered the square like a thick quilt. King Theo

strode into Arthur Stibbons' Head, the street's main square. Amish shuffled in his wake. The crowd parted to let them pass.

A darkly stained wooden block came into view.

King Theo pointed at the round space carved into the middle. Black splodges around its edges sent a chill through Amish's entire torso.

Trembling, Amish circled the block and knelt as instructed.

'As you know,' King Theo addressed the crowd, 'I am a man of simple beliefs. One belief is that people littler than us are vulnerable. Is that not so?'

The crowd murmured its agreement.

'A second belief is that people bigger than us are there to teach us a lesson.' He shot Amish a distasteful glance. 'And my third belief is that when a king goes away for a while, he is entitled to return to his dinner and a friendly hello *without having to cut anyone's head off first*!'

His voice rebounded against the cobbles and houses. The crowd recoiled at the force of it.

Amish whimpered.

King Theo cast a livid gaze across the square.

'The lesson I am here to teach today is that *I* am the big man here. And when the big man says, "do not enter the Queen's Forest and bugger the Faeries on *pain of death*", the "death" part was *not optional*!'

He paused to glare down at the accused.

'Have you anything to say?'

Amish finally cracked. 'I only did it for comfort, my liege! I was scared!'

'Scared?' he sneered, bending down to look him in the face. 'Scared of what? The Queen of the Forest? You should be, after what you've been doing!'

'No, I wasn't scared of that!' Amish's wails rose to the sound of laughter. 'I'm from the church.'

King Theo snorted loudly. 'Well, that explains it.'

The crowd tittered again.

'It was a letter!' Amish tried again. 'I was given a letter to send to the Churches of Salator Crey, and I read it, I know I shouldn't have, but I did, and it... it said horrible things, my liege...'

'About the Faeries? Wouldn't that have put you off?'

The crowd laughed again.

'NO! Listen, my liege, the letter, it was about a prophecy, my liege!'

King Theo gasped theatrically.

'My liege, it said horrible things, people are going to die, it said, holes will appear in the realm itself, and a dragon will burn us alive—'

'Dragon?' he asked, suddenly serious.

'Yes, my liege! Our only hope is a boy, my liege, for if a king dies, the rest of us is soon to follow!' He heaved a sigh, dropping his head. 'I only went to the Forest for solace, my liege. We're doomed! The dragon will kill us all.'

The king paused for a moment.

The crowd watched as Amish pulled a grubby piece of parchment from his pocket, handing it to King Theo. The king accepted it, pulling the string from around it and unrolling it carefully.

'The dragon belongs to the Antichrist,' he said. 'Well, well, what a coincidence.'

He stuck the letter in his shirt and signalled to one of his men.

Who handed him an axe.

Amish shrieked in terror.

'No, NO! My liege, it's all true, I swear to you!'

'I don't doubt it!' King Theo shifted his grip on the axe with both hands. 'Rest your head on the block there and I'll finish the story.'

Amish lowered his head over the chopping block in dread.

'The dragon you read about? It should have arrived at my palace about an hour ago, to be received by its new owner: *me*. And the Antichrist?'

He lifted the axe over his head.

'We all knew it would be me in the first place, didn't we?'

The crowd cheered in agreement.

King Theo clenched his teeth. He dropped the axe on the back of Amish's neck.

'Oh,' Theo said, shaking his head. 'Got quite a thick neck there, haven't you? Once more should do it!'

He hacked it again.

And again.

And again and again and again…

Fifteen minutes later, as the crowd dispersed in varying degrees of horror, King Theo returned to his coach coated in a thick layer of blood, holding Amish's letter.

'A prophecy, eh?' he said to a passing guard. 'I'll believe *that* when I see it.'

~

IV

Vladimir snatched Howie's chin and turned it this way and that.

'Seth Crey's double. There's no doubt about it – I'd remember that little shit's face anywhere.'

'You always were talented at making a good first impression,' Ron said dully.

They stood in the Great Hall of the Stonekeep. A long charcoal-coloured carpet yawned down the length of the hall, from the double doors to the dais. The throne was solid basalt, untouched by a human backside directly since the coronation of King Janus who was so dedicated to the imagery of his newly forged kingdom that he ate from stone, went to the bathroom in a stone chamber pot and even had a stone mattress.

The room had no other distinguishing features apart from a surprisingly colourful snakes and ladders board in the corner of the room and a yellowing stained-glass window depicting King Janus's coronation.

Sunlight poured through this window, casting shades of beige onto a disgruntled Prince Vladimir as they gathered around the throne, which was currently being occupied by Ron's new pet cat.

Vladimir released Howie to shove the cat off. Piling some cushions down, he sank into the throne with an imperious squint. By the premature lines cracking out from the corners of his eyes, Howie sensed a character trait.

'So,' said Vladimir. 'You fancy yourself a prophetic saviour, do you?'

Howie gulped.

'Was gonna leave it, actually,' he squeaked.

Vladimir regarded him critically.

'Just as well,' he said. 'I dare say even a "dead" Antichrist would cause you trouble.'

Archie stood against the back wall on one leg, rubbing his left foot as the two remaining heirs to Stoneguard examined their 'hero' intently. It must have taken Vladimir a lifetime to hate every living soul in existence, Archie observed as he shifted his weight onto the left. It wasn't easy hating someone who could indoctrinate a nation with an offhanded opinion such as a favourite food.

Mind you, Vladimir Horne was never thought of as part of the nation.

'Why are you here?' Vladimir demanded, unfazed by Howie's usually appealing underdog expression.

Howie swallowed. 'You summoned me here, sir.'

Vladimir scowled at him. 'Not in the *room*,' he said scathingly. 'Here. In Stoneguard. You're clearly a relation of the Creys, what business have you here?'

Howie glanced around and proffered, 'Carpentry?'

Vladimir narrowed his eyes to slits.

Ron got onto all fours and crawled towards the cat, who flopped onto the carpet, bathing in a ray of sun.

'Here, kitty-kitty-kitty,' he trilled, holding a hand towards the cat.

Vladimir aimed a kick at him.

The toe of his boot connected with Ron's shoulder.

Ron flinched onto his haunches, reddening.

Teeth gritted, Vladimir met Archie's gaze.

'He's yours, I believe?'

'Yes,' Archie said dubiously.

Vladimir rose and walked around to Archie, his three gold chains jingling.

'And what do you think of him?'

'He's a pleasant lad with good prospects, actually,' he snapped in reply before frowning.

That was strange. He'd been about to say, 'he's a bone-idle shit', but then he'd spied the infamous underdog expression.

Vladimir blinked. 'You seem very… vehement about that, don't you?'

Archie gulped. 'Just fond of him, is all.' He flung Vladimir a defensive frown.

'Hmm.'

Vladimir paced around the room, his ringed hands behind his back.

'Prince Death Crey's image, inexplicable charisma and a famously questionable existence, all manifested to us on the day of my father's disappearance. How quaint.'

Ron rose to his feet, scowling.

'Don't mind him, he's just getting arsy because he isn't the Knight of Wotsit anymore.'

Vladimir flung him a harsh glare.

'Oh, what do you know? You're loath to leave your beer tankard long enough to pass water.'

'And you're the vampire prince who recoils at the sight of the sun,' Ron spat back.

'Shut up!'

'You shut up!' Ron howled in indignation.

Vladimir punched him in the face.

Ron threw himself at him.

Howie and Archie watched in utter bewilderment as the two grappled at each other.

'Shall we just leave?' Archie asked.

'Don't move!' Vladimir screamed.

He held Ron in a headlock.

'Twenty years ago,' he gritted, straining to hold Ron still, 'when you were but a quickening of the womb, I was brought upon the Seven Gods and bequeathed the Crystal Sword. *I* am the Knight of Raining Thorns. You, Mister Rosethorn, are a charlatan!'

'Alright,' said Howie, hands raised.

'You will denounce all claim to the title of—stop it, STOP IT, get your claws out of my leg!!—and inform the clergy that their *real* Knight of Thorns will request their presence moment— HOOAAOOW, YOU BASTARD!!'

Ron had wrapped his teeth around Vladimir's wrist.

'Will do,' Howie said mildly, sliding backwards. He grimaced at the pair. 'Permission to leave, your highnesses?'

'NO!'

Vladimir threw Ron bodily onto the flagstones.

Ron landed on his knees and elbows, wincing.

'I want an explanation,' Vladimir said, breathing heavily, 'for why Seth Crey's doppelganger lives in my city. Who are you? A bastard brother? That sounds like it, I'm sure his parents have a couple knocking around between them. No doubt you're trying to claw back some kind of worth by pretending to be the Knight, I'm sure they were very eager to get rid of another Seth Crey.'

Archie's nostrils flared. 'What's your problem? He hasn't done anything to you!'

'As much of a "pleasant lad" as he is,' Vladimir mimicked, 'he comes from bad stock. I'm not having him steal my glory and covet my throne. *I* will find my father, as soon as court affairs are settled here. No Crey is depriving me of my crown, do you understand?'

Ron hauled himself to his feet in front of Howie and Archie.

'All I understand,' he seethed, 'is that you're angry at him because he looks a bit like the bloke that nicked your girly-girlfriend.' Ron lowered his voice to a whisper. 'Think it's time you let that one go, brov.'

Vladimir bared his teeth and launched himself at them with a screech.

Ron skittered behind Howie.

Howie flung his hands out in self-defence, his eyes squeezed shut.

When he opened them, Vladimir lay sprawled across the floor.

Vladimir lifted his chin from the flagstones. He spat blood and rifled in his mouth.

A tooth came away in his hand.

There was a brief silence in which Archie's thought processes consisted of profanities in different font sizes.

Howie eyed the prince and stood back.

Vladimir's face looked like thunder.

Ron bolted for the double doors.

'Traitor!' Vladimir howled. 'He assaulted me! Guards, arrest them! GUARDS!'

Two huge men who embodied the name 'Stoneguard' in every sense appeared in the open doorway, bolting forward to grasp Howie and Archie by the elbows. The two squealed as their shoulder joints creaked.

Vladimir rose slowly, hissing through the weeping gap in his top teeth.

His gaze locked to Howie's.

'Take them to Fred's shed,' he snarled.

~

Night fell on the city of Stoneguard.

The Stonekeep lurked over the dissipating crowd to cast a deep shadow over the minute city. Beside it the chapel stood twice its height to block out the light of the moon.

Pacing outside of said chapel, with one hand behind his back and the other clutching the crucifix around his neck, was Toffer, becoming increasing exasperated as his monks hovered inside the huge entrance. The order dared not move a muscle for fear of disrupting the priest's furious ponderings.

In the dank regions of the priest's rather small mind, much pondering was travelling in figures of eight, punctuated by excessive amounts of impressive swearing.

The Hornes had Howard Rosethorn and his smelly uncle in their custody since morning. Dusk had fallen about an hour ago, and the third turn of the clock was well underway. Toffer doubted the batty prince had simply invited them to a late dinner.

Toffer was just pondering the likelihood of appealing to the good nature of the savage Queen Aaliyaa when a small voice pierced the silence.

'Father?'

'What? What is it? In the name of the gods, can't a man think for five… min… utes…'

A young woman visibly shook in front of him.

Toffer planted a hand over his mouth and glanced at the monks, who were trying their very hardest not to give him the look of disdain they had mastered in his order.

'Father,' she said, fumbling with a small wooden box in her hands. 'I was wondering if you'd seen my friend and uncle anywhere recently? Sandy hair, five foot ten, blue eyes?' Her eyes welled up. 'I wouldn't bother you, only they've been gone all day and I'm worried about them, and I thought to ask you because they were supposed to be here—'

'Figured I had nothing better to do, is it?' he barked. 'Send a search party! I've better things to do!'

Adrienne wiped her nose and hurried away, blinking back tears.

A nun stormed up to him, indignant.

'Father, that was ghastly to the highest degree!'

'So,' he snarled, 'is capturing the Chosen One after I had given him all our money! You think I ought to be nice to everyone merely because I work in a church? You obviously haven't met Father Giery of the Creys' Keep, have you? It's not me that's horrible! I only wanted to help the boy on his way and perhaps get a bit of a name for ourselves, but no. The only way to make anything of yourself in this world is to be a dirty piece of pond scum with the morals of a common, a common…'

His eyes widened.

'Criminal.'

A light ignited in the depths of his eyes.

'I think,' he said, 'I have an idea.'

The monks, plus one nun, gulped

'Oh dear,' one of them said.

~

A figure shuffled itself out of the tallest tower of the Stonekeep and, clinging to the windowsill, tiptoed into two footholds a foot below the window.

Pitch black darkness lay in silence over the city, but a handful of soldiers stood guard outside the palace regardless, armed in chainmail and long spears. They leaned heavily on the spears and their snores soon reverberated down the empty street.

Thankfully, their backs were turned away from Ronald Horne as he painstakingly traversed each gap in the stonework, flinging a wary glance at the portcullis with every move.

Ron may not have been the sharpest spear in the armoury, but he knew a bad atmosphere when he saw one. He lived with Vladimir, after all. The man had bad atmosphere coming out of his backside, and if Ron had learned anything from his twenty-one years of experience, it was to avoid a bout of atmospheric diarrhoea like the plague.

However.

Howard Rosethorn was in captivity.

Ron glanced below him. His foot halted, distrustful of the tiny notch below it, and he climbed up a bit, lurching to the left in the direction of the arrow slots just visible in the gloom.

Despite his father being the most powerful man in the country with him being second to that, Vladimir had not known about Howard Rosethorn prior to their first meeting. But Ron did. He was all anyone could talk about for the last five years – at least among the servants.

As far as Ron could gather, he was an enigma, an anomaly. That he was the bastard son of a Crey was undisputed: the question was which one. Seth Crey had locked himself in a casket since he was thirteen and King Theo was, as King Samuel had put it, 'a prude'. Some said he was an immaculate conception of Seth's wife that had been wrongly discarded at birth. Some said he was trueborn and put into hiding after his brother's assassination attempt. One man claimed he emerged from a litter of kittens – but then he sold narcotics for a living, so he couldn't really be trusted.

People didn't make up stories like that about Vladimir, who was just pale and sulky. It was the *charisma* that did that. People loved him.

Even Ron liked him.

He didn't know why. Objectively, Howie came across to Ron as quite ordinary, just a kid doing carpentry for the local craftsman. But Ron didn't have many friends and beggars couldn't be choosers and so, that made him Ron's friend.

Although, he added mentally, the piteous underdog expression probably helped.

He glanced down as the familiar gravel came closer and suppressed the urge to leap off from a foot above. He couldn't risk a heavy landing: the grounds were so empty at this hour, the sound would bounce from wall to wall and wake the entire household. As soon as Ron's left foot brushed the gravel, he touched down gently.

The ground crunched slightly underfoot.

He flinched, casting the gate a cursory glance.

The guards didn't so much as stir.

Ron crept around to the back of the keep, wrapping his dark green cloak tightly around him.

At the rear wall of the keep stood an old garden shed, in which lived the castle groundskeeper amongst his equipment. Ron peered into the tiny, rippled window of the decrepit stone shack to see an equally decrepit old man curled up in a stitched woollen armchair, asleep.

Dropped on top of each other in careless piles around the chair were woodchopping axes, shovels, trowels and picks, all blurred into obscurity by the warped windowpane. He'd carefully arranged his gardening tools into a subtle booby-trap, Ron knew, which left a trapdoor to the dungeons blatant next to the door.

Ron paused to think.

The trap was set by a cunning bastard. This could only mean it was set for an *equally* cunning bastard to fall into.

There was only one approach to this kind of intellect.

Brute, stupid force.

Ron glanced around, turning about. His gaze lingered on a bull paddock twenty yards behind the keep. His eyes narrowed as he scanned the farm for any other signs of life.

He swept across the gardens noiselessly.

In the shed, old Fred the groundskeeper slid into bleary consciousness and sank comfortably back into the warm regions of sub-sleep.

Shortly after, chaos erupted.

Fred jolted awake to the overlapping sounds of a very angry bull and the front wall of his shack collapsing behind him.

He bolted backwards.

Heavy debris launched across his armchair, burying it beneath stone, mortar and the second heir to Stoneguard.

'Sorry, royal business. LOOK OUT!'

The bull bolted free of the reins.

Fred screamed, scrambling into the corner.

The bull launched himself at him.

A ceiling beam collapsed a hand's breadth away from the old man, landing between him and the offended bull.

'Help,' squeaked Fred.

He poked his head out from behind the wreckage.

'Sorry, can't, as I say, royal matters,' Ron said quickly.

He leaped from the small coach he had hurriedly lashed onto the bull. Scrambling over bricks and debris, Ron laboured his way to the trapdoor in the corner.

'Er,' he paused, turning to face Fred, 'where's the key?'

Fred, trembling, pointed over the rubble.

Ron swung his gaze around and up a bit.

'Oh,' he said with a laugh, smacking his forehead. 'Trust me to walk around with my eyes closed. Thanks.'

'But,' said Fred.

Ron lifted the door up with both hands and let it drop back against the wall. Squinting into the darkness, he quickly found the stairs and hunched down to lower himself into the pit.

'But… what about me?'

Ron didn't hear, or else he didn't respond.

The bull, on the other hand, turned around and released a call of nature right in the spot where Fred had flung an outstretched hand.

Fred felt the heavy yellow stream engulf his palm and began to cry.

~

The dungeons of the Stonekeep made up one of the largest prisons in the realm. The immense city of cells, built one mile down into the earth's crust, was lit by a mere five lanterns on each level, fuelled by a gas link sourced at the surface of Stoneguard.

These lanterns gave off the only light in the dungeons. The sparse illumination gave them an eerie atmosphere that, given enough time, tended to send prisoners mad.

And Archie would have found all of this incredibly fascinating were he and Howie not sitting in the middle of it all – or the lower middle, anyway.

Vladimir had banished them to the lowest level of the dungeons, into a damp cell slick with mildew and slug trails. One smell permeated the bottom of the keep: death, the damp, musty smell of decay and neglect.

The whole atmosphere disconcerted Archie. He blinked and blinked, struggling to adjust to the dim light of the lanterns and the snoozing cat thrown in with them, possibly for spite.

In the tiny cell with him, Howie hunched in the corner, miserable. Archie felt sorry for the lad. He hadn't done anything wrong. It was the prince's dentistry Archie blamed. He clearly wasn't looking after his teeth very well if a mild knock on the floor had dislodged one.

Something Ronald Horne had said returned to Archie suddenly.

The bloke who nicked your girly-girlfriend.

He meant Seth Crey, of course – Howie's rumoured heritage didn't come from nowhere, he was the spitting image of him. And Seth Crey's wife was that girl from the east – Sienna something, Archie thought.

Archie found that strange. How did the pale, spidery Vladimir Horne get away with an affair with King Theo Crey's daughter-in-law? Surely it was against the law to get off with the future queen.

Unless Ron just meant he had a crush on her. That probably made more sense, Archie thought. And it fit with the delusions of grandeur. He clearly thought very much of himself if he thought he was a prophetic hero.

Howie's head shot up.

'I can hear something.'

Straining his ears, Archie leaned against the bars of their cell.

Sure enough, he could hear the subtle creaking of the lift's cog mechanism.

It shrieked to a halt.

The sound woke the guard, who scrambled to his feet.

'Excuse me, sir, but Prince Vladimir has orders to forbid—'

Thunk.

'Urgh…'

Thud.

Footsteps sounded on the flagstones, the only sound to be heard after the guard's collapse. Archie held his breath as another sound manifested in the darkness… the sound of a spinning ring of keys.

'Sorry I took so long,' a familiar voice echoed down the corridor.

Archie blinked in disbelief.

Howie joined him in front of the bars.

'Prince Ronald,' Archie said in disbelief.

'Just Ron will do, thanks,' said Ron with a grimace.

He looked the worse for wear. His hair was matted with dust and mortar, as if he'd thrown himself through a wall, wearing the worn garb of the caretaker, by the look of it.

Ron caught Archie's bemused stare and self-consciously brushed some of the dust lingering in the folds of his shirt.

He glanced up at them and grinned.

'What the bloody hell do you want?' Archie snarled.

Ron lifted an eyebrow.

'Well, if you're going to take that tone, I'll take my ring of keys elsewhere—'

'No, don't do that!' Howie said hastily.

Ron's chin rose in disdain. Nevertheless, he returned his foot to the floor.

'He's sorry, now look. I'm sorry for pushing your brother, it was self-defence! He threw himself at me, you can't lock us up for that!'

'Well, I *was* going to let you out,' Ron said haughtily, 'before *he* decided to snap at me.'

'Sorry, *your highness*, it's a side-effect of being locked in a *dungeon*.'

Howie stomped on his foot.

Archie bit back a howl. He'd just trod on his broken toe.

'What changed your tune?' he squeaked, hanging from his grip on the bars. 'You were eager to leave earlier, so I recall.'

Ron shrugged. 'I got to thinking. Being on the run with a bloke with a magic cat sounds a lot more fun than staying here with my scary older brother.'

Ron shot Archie a malevolent squint.

'However, that was before you were rude. I could go for a bit of family unity after that.'

He stalked back to the lift.

'Oh,' Archie groaned, 'come on, look, I'll make it up to you, look, we, we'll, we will—'

'Find your father,' Howie said.

Ron froze in his tracks.

Archie grimaced.

'Make you a cabinet free of charge...' he finished in a pained voice.

Ron pivoted.

'You'll find my father?'

Howie grimaced, then nodded. 'Promise.'

Ron thought about this.

'We'll throw in the magic cat,' Archie added.

'Deal,' Ron said brightly.

He scrambled to the lock and fumbled with the keys.

'How are we getting past the guards?' Howie asked.

Ron swung the door open.

'They'll be asleep, we'll worry about them later. I've a plan.'

Ron glanced at the cat, sleeping contentedly in the corner.

'I think we'll have to leave the cat here for this one…'

Moments after their swift ascent in the lift, the cat awoke and stretched with a yawn.

After establishing that it was alone, it curled back into a ball, shone like a beacon… and disappeared.

~

Meanwhile, a mile above them, Fred's right hand crawled beneath the rubble in agonising silence.

The bull snorted directly above his head, but he was used to that at this stage.

His arthritis-riddled fingers squirmed beneath the rocks. Something thin and long slid beneath his thumbnail. The booby trap.

Old Fred Turpentine was, he was wont to admit, not the best groundskeeper in the world. You didn't get sent to King Horne-Half-Empty for talent. The Stonekeep was the lowest rung in the caretaking business and possessing a tendency to dig for buried treasure didn't get you up the promotion ladder.

But Fred's kleptomania had its uses. His knowledge of every booby trap in the known universe was what ultimately kept him in employment.

He snatched the wire tightly in his fist and, shying away from the bull, tugged gently, listening for the atmosphere to change.

The rug moved slightly under the influence of the chicken wire.

It pulled the pike with it.

Strapped to the handle, a piece of flint skidded off the floorboards.

A flame appeared.

It multiplied by two upon contact with a splinter in the floorboards, and a sliver of smoke began to rise.

Fred waited patiently for the shed to burst into flames and, hopefully, engulf the bastards who caused the bull to piss on his head.

~

V

Outside, Sadie waited. The moon shone above him, two-dimensional.

Everyone knew the moon wasn't real. It didn't even look real. It was slightly elliptical, suspended in mid-air and travelling in one direction: left. It never moved up or down or went away. As the stars pirouetted in the sky, the moon remained static, watching the world permanently and only seeming to shine on default. The world turned, but the moon watched, an oversized fresco on the great wall that was the sky, sort of like the petrifying portrait of Great Aunt Matilda on the great wall that was Sadie's mother's living room.

Gravel crunched behind the gate.

Sadie turned, one leather-covered hand clenching a torch.

He squinted at his oppressor. The figure was small, or so Sadie hoped.

Small meant he wasn't a guard, and Sadie was not getting along with the guards at the moment due to the much-discussed matter of the unspeakable fact about "Sade" – "Sade" being the pseudonym for the little boy whose parents had wanted a girl.

He didn't want to delve into his mother's intent on changing her son's gender by force of denial. He was fifty-five: he had bigger issues than a name that didn't suit him. Besides, so many others had delved into this issue that, had it been an abyss with the depth of a hundred leagues, the delvers would have suffocated from a lack of air.

Sadie Marbrand diverted his attention from the matter and concentrated on the steadily approaching figure, hoping the need to kick someone's ball-sack could wait until the morning.

As the figure entered the moonlight, Marbrand saw it swerve from side to side, as if lost. Marbrand stepped forward to find it was Prince Ronald, holding a black dog collar and lead.

'Lost a dog, your highness?' he called pleasantly.

Ron swung to him and flinched.

'Uh, um, yes, exactly!' he jumped in with potent enthusiasm.

Marbrand noted the prince was smoking slightly from the rear and filed this offhandedly in a mental file labelled simply as 'Ron'.

'Have you seen him?'

'What does he look like, your highness?'

'He's…'

Ron paused, curling his upper lip inward.

'Black. With white spots,' he added as a slow afterthought, 'on his… regions in the rear. Yeah.'

Ron shot Marbrand a wide grin. Then a slight frown.

'Can you smell roast beef?'

'Um, no, sir. Black with white spots, is it?' he said, scratching his chin. 'Can't say I've seen him. I'll put the guards on the lookout and call you when they've found him, yes? Allow me to walk you to your quarters and the lads, they—Sir!'

'What?' Ron said.

A plume of white flame flickered around Ron's waistband, stark in the twilight.

Marbrand shoved him onto the grass behind him and rolled him back and forth.

Two figures dashed past his peripheral vision.

Marbrand jolted his attention from the extinguished Ron.

Plumes of a similar nature roared across the roof of Fred's shed.

'Crap!'

He guided Ron to his feet before jogging to Fred's aid.

~

Ron watched the guard race out of sight. He dusted himself off, glanced at the shed to make sure that, yes, Fred and the bull were out safely and, regaining posture, made for the direction of the palace orchard.

'Now, that wasn't so hard, was it?'

Archie doubled over, massaging his shins.

Howie flapped his sleeve, which was aflame.

'Please tell me there's no more running,' Archie panted. 'My shins are on fire!'

'Are they, Archie?' Howie shrilled. 'Are they really?'

Archie snatched his shoulder and ripped the sleeve off at the seams.

Howie flung it to the ground and stomped it into the path, his arm prickling.

'What now?'

Ron smiled faintly into the distance for a moment.

'Oh, yeah, the plan,' he said with a start. 'We climb the tree by the wall, go over the wall and onto a flat roof sloping down to the back alley.'

'Then what?'

Ron sucked his top lip. 'Didn't think that far ahead.'

'I thought not,' Howie said dully.

'First thing I'm doing is picking up Adrienne,' Archie said, 'before someone hears she's at the shop unattended. Point us to the tree.'

'We don't have time,' Howie said. 'He's gonna send guards after us, they know this city like the back of their hand. We need to leave the city as soon as we've over that wall. We can send her a letter once we're somewhere safe.'

'Oh yes, a letter. The best-known defence for armed robbers

in the night.'

'She's a surgeon-in-training,' Howie said in exasperation. 'She collects tiny knives and knows where main arteries are. She'll be fine.'

'Oh, is she your girlfriend?' Ron said in interest.

Howie glared at him.

Archie glared at Howie. 'She'd better not be.'

'She isn't!' Howie said firmly.

Ron shrugged and guided them to the tree closest to the wall.

Archie pointed two fingers at his own eyes and then at Howie's.

'She isn't!' Howie hissed at him.

They wound off the gravel pathway and ducked under hanging branches. Thin ones, Howie noted with unease.

'They're very spindly,' he said.

'This one's fine, I've climbed it loads of times,' Ron said. 'And there's footholds on the upper part of the wall. I made them.'

They came to the tree and looked up. And up.

Archie swung his gaze from the summit of the wall to the top of the tree. There was a considerable distance between the tree and the wall – at least twice the length of the tree by itself.

Archie made unintelligible noises. He simply flung his hands in demonstration.

'I've done it loads of times,' Ron said flippantly.

Archie thrust his hand to Ron's face, fingers first.

'You're twenty-one!' he screamed at him. 'I'm twice your age, how the hell am I gonna—'

Howie shushed him violently, covering his face with both hands.

'We'll manage!' he hissed at him. 'Now keep your voice down!'

Shuffling footsteps urged them towards the tree.

~

Sixteen buckets of water and twelve bottles of brandy later, Marbrand stood outside the charred remains of Fred's shed as its owner wobbled in blissfully medicinal drunkenness.

'The two prisoners have escaped, you say?' Marbrand asked to clarify.

'Hyeah, dah lackhwit prince helped them to hescape, sir,' slurred Fred, nursing the last of his dozen bottles closely to his chest in case it might run off. 'Sheems like he's hup to something shushpishishousousous...'

He paused with a frown.

'… ous,' he finished with a smile.

'I quite agree with you,' said Marbrand.

He recognised the curling of the upper lip anywhere. Anyone subject to Ron's drunken and/or sober pranks knew the signs of fabrication when they saw them. And while sending guards chasing off after imaginary dogs could be deemed a suitable prank, it wasn't half as imaginative as the antics Ron got up to and what's more, it was done in a hurry.

'I'll have a guard posted at the trapdoor tonight, Fred. You find an inn and take the day off tomorrow. We'll cover the expenses.'

'O' course, shir, couldun impee on your doo-tees, not at all,' he said, grinning at the prospect of a day off. He paused conspiratorially. 'Any chance of some more—'

Marbrand strategically ignored him.

'Ankovich?' he called behind him. 'Inform the crown prince of the captives' exit, will you?'

He paused and added an afterthought.

'And check on Spotty-Balls, will you? Just in case he *is* missing?'

'Of course, sir.' The soldier saluted, turning to leave.

Marbrand followed close behind, his mind on Ron.

He couldn't think why he would want to release two prisoners. An unfortunate side-effect of a mother like Aaliyaa Horne was that friends were a rare occurrence.

But perhaps that was the idea?

What if Ron had taken a night-time jaunt to the dungeons and they nabbed him there? Offered to take him on an adventure?

'Let us out,' he pictured them saying. 'We'll be your friends.'

It seemed feasible. He ought to go after them and bring him back. At least to get away from the silly 'Sadie' jokes for a while.

As if on cue, Fred trilled behind him.

'Goo-bye, Sadie! S'always nice to have you call down!'

Sniggers followed Marbrand's hand as it rose to rub his temple tiredly.

~

'My shins!' Archie squealed.

'We get it, you're old!' Howie hissed down at him. 'Now be quiet!'

The branch teetered against the flat of the wall. A conveniently placed oil lamp illuminated their way from directly above them. Howie decided that the task of meandering it could wait until the very last minute to plan. Stress, plus Archie's numerous shin-related complaints, held Howie's brain in a pincer-grip.

Quiet rustling ahead marked Ron's self-assured climb.

'Got it!' he said softly. 'I'm on the wall. Let me know once you're here and I'll help with the footholds.'

Howie made to surge ahead.

A strangled yelp.

'I'm stuck.'

'Oh, for Christs' sake,' Howie spat at the wall.

The branch wavered beneath him.

'Stop shaking the tree!' he scolded Archie. 'I'm not gonna be able to help you up if I fall off!'

'Stay there!' Ron called down in a soft voice. 'I'll help Howie up and come back for you.'

Archie flapped frantically; his limbs were contained in a layer of foliage.

Howie squirmed ahead, his stomach flat against the branch. He gave a short yelp as it tilted downwards.

'You'll be fine, keep going,' Ron assured him. 'It's a good branch, I've used it loads of times.'

Howie grimaced, straining a hand outward.

Rough stone brushed his fingertips, to his immense relief.

'Go easy,' Ron said.

The branch scraped against the blocks.

Howie scooted closer to the wall, fingers locked into two footholds. This was clearly a well-worn route, he saw: small gaps stood out in clusters spanning a yard in every direction, black holes in the gentle yellow light.

His knees clattered into the rock. He pulled himself up, elbows trembling to the bone. Glancing between his knees, he slid the toes of his boots down the wall tentatively until they were swallowed by a hole. His limbs smarting but with a firmer grasp of the wall, he slowly straightened up.

'My arms are killing me,' he groused.

'Stretch them out and hang for a bit if you're feeling tired,' Ron advised. 'Trust your feet. You have a good grip on the wall now.'

Howie leaned back from the wall, elbows creaking. The ache relieved itself, but not by much. He heard Ron climb back onto the tree.

Howie negotiated the footholds, feet and hands taking turns with each other, working in silence broken only by shifting leaves and his own shallow breath. His armpits hurt, of all places. This was *not* what he signed up for eight years ago. Not by a *long* shot.

His fingers slipped on the bricks.

A small animal shriek escaped from him involuntarily.

'You alright?' Ron called.

'Yep, just nearly fell to my death,' Howie said in a strangled whimper.

'You'll be fine, there's shrubbery just below us.'

'Great,' Howie whined. 'That's very reassuring.'

He groped upward again, hoisting himself up. His shoulders were beginning to smart: his entire body was tensed with fear, which didn't help the exertion pains.

'Archie, you alright?'

'No,' floated up from within the foliage.

'He's fine,' Ron called.

Howie's foot clanged on the edge of the brazier. He hissed, stepping up with haste and thrusting his body weight ahead of his grasping right arm.

His hand flailed in mid-air for a moment.

Howie yelped and threw his hand down.

It slammed onto the edge with an audible *clap*.

He had reached the top.

He shuffled upward until both hands gripped the top edge and scrambled up the final footholds, shuffling from his palms to his elbows. The wall was as thick as he was tall, which was a relief. He pulled his knees under himself, shuffling a safe distance from the edge. He glanced down into darkness for a moment before, with a shudder, directing his gaze to the battlements.

'I'm at the top.'

'Great!' Ron said brightly. 'Go on, up you get.'

'No!' Archie squeaked. 'I'm going back to the dungeon.'

Howie ignored him. Pivoting, he hopped off the short dip to the narrow corridor of the battlements and faced the city of Stoneguard, peering out between two crenulations.

A vast collection of terraced roofs and disjointed chimneys greeted him from below. For as far as the eye could see, tiny bursts of yellow light illuminated the narrow streets and close-knit houses beyond. Faint laughter sounded from Howie's far left, a small group of men exiting a bar.

Howie followed the winding streets back to his home, the tiny, terraced house where they and Archibald Hart's Carpentry Shop lived. He eyed the street longingly, the dirt road, the small tavern, the empty stalls. The road he called home since he was twelve years old.

'Get your ass over here, Howard! I need a hand up!'

Howie obediently obliged.

He heaved Archie up, Ron assisting from behind.

'There,' Ron said in annoyance. 'Wasn't so hard, was it?'

Archie squealed unintelligibly.

Howie ignored them. A glint outside the carpentry shop caught his eye.

'And how are we supposed to get back down?' Archie shrieked. 'Magic? If you'd told me we were supposed to fly down, I'd have brought the cat!'

'There's a flat roof sloping down onto the street,' Ron said, crossly. 'Don't you listen?'

'There's guards outside the shop,' Howie said quickly.

'What?'

Archie bolted forward, hands clasped to the edge.

A shining brass breastplate paced outside the shop, waiting access.

'Shit, Adrienne,' Archie whispered in horror.

'As long as we're not there, she'll be fine,' Howie said.

'What? No, we have to go get her—'

'No, we can't,' Howie insisted, 'otherwise she'll be harbouring escaped criminals. We're no use to her up here in any case.'

'Not now she's opened the door,' Ron said.

Sure enough, the faint outline of Adrienne's head came into view in the light from the carpentry shop door. A brief exchange occurred between her and the guard before, with a curtsy, she closed the door.

'See, he's leaving,' Howie said. 'She's fine where she is.'

Archie looked defeated for a moment before blazing pure indignance.

'If I should return to find her missing a limb,' he threatened, pointing a finger at the space between Howie's eyes, 'or an eye or her maidenhead or so much as a frigging *eyelash*, I will skin you alive.'

'That's fair,' Howie said. 'Can we leave now before we get caught?'

Ron hopped up onto the wall between the crenulations. *Hopped*, Howie observed in horror, watching the toe of Ron's left boot hang over the edge.

'So the flat roof is by the cake shop,' he announced to the wall at large.

Archie flung fleeting glances across the street below. 'Which is…'

Ron tilted his head down. And around.

'… on the… other side… of the castle,' he said. He flung them a sheepish glance. 'Sorry.'

They watched the wall yawn out in a broad circle, rising and falling in gentle slopes. Howie guesstimated at least a hundred feet of walking distance.

'I hate you,' Archie seethed.

~

VI

Morning broke over the unfamiliar road to the Shades in a warm wave. The sky brightened from royal to cobalt blue, stopping the trio of outlaws in their tracks. The early morning sun had not quite risen yet, but Howie wished he could see it now so he could flick it a two-finger salute.

'You hide behind a cloud of acid rain for my eighteenth birthday, but you come out to cause my execution, don't you?' he seethed quietly.

'What are you blithering on about?' Archie said in a wilting tone.

'Just talking to the sun,' Howie said meekly, scowling up at it.

He eyed his miniscule entourage, stretching stiff shoulders.

Archie was limping a few yards behind him, which was nothing new. What was new was the layer of thick muck coating him all down one side.

They all had it. Their descent from the castle battlements went smoothly – as in they slipped smoothly on the slick roof slanting down to deposit them into the smooth wet slurry pooling outside a handful of terraced houses to the rear of the Stonekeep.

Ron was once again preoccupied with a butterfly that had decided to follow them. Presumably because of all the flowers he spent the morning gathering, 'in case we bump into any mad queens'. Apparently Adem was full of them.

Howie heaved a sigh and blew out through pursed lips.

'What are you huffing at?' Archie spat at him.

Howie stomped to a halt in the middle of the narrow dirt road and flung Archie a withering glance.

'Where do I start? We'll start small, shall we? It'd be nice to walk at a reasonable speed without stopping every two minutes to wait for a grouchy old codger to catch up!'

'I'm not old!' Archie said hotly. 'I have flat arches!'

Howie turned from him in disgust, his hands on his hips. Flakes of dried mud peeled from his brow as it furrowed into a hard line.

'What are we going to Adem for anyway?' he demanded. 'I thought you hated it there?'

'I do,' said Archie. 'Funnily enough, mortal danger makes it seem like a carnival.'

'And it's the last place my dad was sighted,' Ron piped up.

Howie glanced at him.

Ron's backside glanced back, his head and arms currently rooting around in a ditch for an elusive bloom.

Archie halted at Howie's side and panted, his mouth ajar.

'Don't look at him like that, it's your fault.'

Howie flung his arms in the air.

'How is it my fault his dad's gone AWOL?' he whispered hysterically.

'Not that. Why'd you tell him we were gonna find his dad for?'

'We were locked in a dungeon, Archie! I had to say something!'

'If you'd shut up long enough for me to suggest my cabinet idea, we'd probably be home by now,' Archie seethed. 'I'd cheerfully labour for hours at a wooden likeness of slimy little Vladimir Horne if it meant not roaming around the countryside after you two.'

'Oh yeah,' Howie snorted, stalking off, 'because a bespoke cabinet will make *everything* better.'

'It does when I make it!' Archie snapped at him.

Howie clenched his fists at his sides, seething at Archie, the Hornes, God (or gods, according to Stoneguard), the sun, everyone. He knew he shouldn't have entered that church. Or maybe he should have attended a bit more beforehand. Everyone knows the gods shy away from regular churchgoers.

Archie took about a dozen steps before slowing to a halt again.

'Christs in heaven, my legs!' he wailed, clutching the back of his shins. 'I'll never make it there, my legs are about to split in half! How the hell did Adrienne walk all the way to the Shades?'

'She didn't, she got a lift with Keith,' Howie said.

He walked ahead for a couple yards before realising that Archie was frozen in place.

'She what?' Archie asked dangerously.

'We met Keith on the way out of the city,' Howie said, 'she got a lift with him.'

He glanced at Archie.

Whose face was twisted in pure fury.

Howie splayed his arms. 'What's wrong with you now?'

'You let my niece,' Archie simmered, 'get into a coach with the proprietor of a countrywide chain of knocking shops and you *don't see the issue here?*'

'He's your mate.'

'That doesn't matter!' Archie exploded. 'He picks up waifs and strays and plonks them in his hellhole in the Shades! He can't tell either of you from the Christs themselves! What the hell were you thinking?!'

'Archie, it's a hundred and fifty miles away! She was hardly going to walk it on her own, was she? Anyway, she's fine, isn't she?'

Archie, red-faced, opened his mouth to scream.

Howie cut across him. 'Did she look like she'd been plonked into a brothel for three months? Don't you think she would have *mentioned* it? She's never set foot near a brothel in her life, she's a prude! If he'd taken her near, we'd never have heard the end of it!'

Archie opened and closed his mouth a few times, at a loss.

'She's never leaving the house again,' he muttered to himself instead. 'I can't risk it. He won't let her go a second time.'

Howie rolled his eyes and strode on ahead.

'Get off the road,' Archie barked at him. 'You can't stride along in the middle of the road like that, he'll have sent men out.'

'We wouldn't have to *be* in the middle of the road if you'd just ordered a coach like a normal person.'

'Normal people don't order coaches at twat o'clock in the morning! It would look dodgy.'

'And cowering in the ditch doesn't, is it?' Howie snapped. 'We might as well keep moving until we get to the village. You can rest your precious arches in the afternoon.'

'Afternoon?' Ron moaned. 'I can't stay up that late!'

Archie glanced at him.

'You mean to say you're actually nocturnal? I thought that was a propaganda rumour.'

'It was,' Ron muttered. 'My brother started it.'

'You really don't like him, do you?' Archie commented.

'Does anyone?' Howie muttered.

'I tried to,' Ron said. 'He doesn't make it easy. My father's brilliant, though. We built a treehouse in the orchard together, just the two of us, a few years ago. It was great.'

'Where was he going last?' Howie asked, softening.

'Helping King Theo Crey with the midnight patrols.'

'Patrols? What are they patrolling for?'

'Faeries,' Archie said. 'In case they creep out of their

woodland.’

Howie pulled a face. ‘What, titchy little things with wings?’

‘They aren’t like in children’s books, Howie,’ Archie said with a shudder. ‘Not in the real world.’

Howie lifted an eyebrow and added ‘Faeries’ to an internal list marked ‘Archie’s Irrational Phobias’.

‘Don’t they have a queen?’ Ron said.

‘Queen Wosserface? She’s better off staying away from them, with her anger management issues.’

‘How d’you mean?’ asked Howie.

Archie pointed.

To the right, over a panorama of high green hills, Howie could see the grey void on the far horizon and the black mountains jutting out from it.

‘She did that,’ Archie said.

Howie glanced at him. ‘She made the Wastelands?’

‘That was her mother, fifty years ago,’ Ron said.

They continued down the considerably more colourful country road, the city of Stoneguard far behind.

‘King Theo’s father hired her to do it in this war ’bout fifty years ago, back when King Theo was just a kid.’

‘They used to own the whole continent,’ Archie said. ‘The Hornes started a rebellion and declared half of it theirs after Theo Crey started nicking apples out of the Hornes’ orchard.’

‘Are you joking?’ Howie exclaimed.

‘Nope,’ Ron said. ‘Granddad got very worked up about his apples.’

‘He started a war because a little boy nicked off his apple tree?’

‘It was more to do with the kid’s dad copping off with half of Janus Horne’s mistresses,’ Archie said.

‘Oh, *that* makes more sense,’ said Howie.

‘Between Seb Crey cuckolding half the nobility and his predecessor being a cannibal, the Hornes thought “sod this, I’ve had enough” and they rebelled. They were just divvying out the mainland when the Forest Queen burned most of it into the ground. Stoneguard would have been one of three new kingdoms if it weren’t for her. Only Stoneguard left of it now. Half the continent’s useless because of her.’

His voice lowered.

‘People say she *enjoyed* burning the place up. Say they saw her dancing that day, between her purple demon flames, spinning around and *laughing*.’

He twirled his index finger in mid-air in demonstration.

'Purple demon flames?' Howie asked with a frown. 'What, she's a witch?'

Archie and Ron shrugged in unison.

'No idea,' Ron said. 'No one's seen hide nor hair of her since. No one even knows her name anymore. Everyone was too afraid to utter it.'

Howie pictured a woman of Faerie description, with blue skin and violet hair to match the flames dancing with her across the continent of Truphoria, and would probably have understood the horror were she not about five inches tall in his imagination.

Before he could say as much, rattling sounded from behind them.

A pair of horses pulling a small carriage appeared, atop of which sat a man with his sparse amount of grey hair arranged in a spectacularly bad comb-over.

Howie and Ron lowered their heads and stepped off the road.

Archie, however, walked into the centre of the road and shouted, 'OI! Dickhead!'

The horses slowed and the carriage trundled to a halt.

'Wanna explain why my niece was in your custody last winter?'

The driver craned his neck.

'Damsel in distress, innit,' he called. 'Said her uncle was too busy conked at his lathe to escort her to her first job. Had to step in as honorary godfather and protect her virtue for you. You owe me for twelve hundred dissatisfied customers, by the way. Broke my heart, having to turn their money away like that.'

Archie grinned from ear to ear.

Howie and Ron emerged from the ditch, peering out at him.

The man was portly, his rubbish comb-over clean and freshly combed. He wore a black cloak with a garish turquoise shirt underneath. *Not a farmer, then*, Howie thought with a wince. Farmers generally had better taste.

A young woman in a straw hat perched next to him, a flowery linen dress fluttering in the breeze.

'Oh God,' Howie said, closing his eyes. 'Not him!'

'Who is he?'

'Keith,' Archie said.

Keith dismounted from the coach and stood in front of Archie, looking him up and down.

'You're covered in shit, mate, you know that? I take it the carpentry shop's gone belly-up?'

'Let's just say the gods have it in for me as usual,' Archie said.

'Any chance of a lift for an old mate?'

'Well, alright. On condition you lot get yourselves a bath when we hit the village. Just don't touch the young lady, not unless you're paying.'

He glanced at Howie and tilted his head to one side.

'Who are you, then?' he asked in a pleasant timbre.

'Howard,' Howie said patiently. 'The apprentice. We've met, like, a thousand times?'

Keith's bulbous eyes widened.

'Ah, Howard!' he exclaimed, clapping a hand on his shoulder. 'You were my first customer!'

Archie shot Howie a sideways glance. 'First customer?'

Howie buried his face in his palms.

'Yep,' Keith grinned. 'My first client in the new shop in the village, when he was dropping Adrienne off to Thingy Wotsit's place. Nothing but the best for the Knight of Raining Thorns, eh?'

'News travels fast, then,' Archie said in a flat tone.

Howie cleared his throat daintily. 'Yep. So, the coach—'

'What is it you do for a living?' Ron asked Keith in interest.

'That… doesn't matter,' Howie said. 'Come on, let's get going.'

'Where you headed, anyway?' Keith asked.

'The Shades,' said Archie. 'Long story short, we had an altercation with Vladimir Horne, so now we're on the run. Take it you heard about the king going missing?'

'Oh yeah, we've searched the house in case he's hiding for a freebee. No sign yet.'

He climbed aboard and gave Howie a hand up.

'Half expected to find you there,' he joked to Howie, 'after you attacked the prince like that. Knocked his teeth out, I heard. That's not like you.'

'One, I didn't attack him, it was self-defence. And two…'

He shrugged Keith's elbow away.

'… I only went that once because *she* was special.'

'Yeah, she's special alright. Locked you in the pantry, wasn't it? Because you wanted to get to know her first!'

Archie laughed.

Howie's eyes narrowed.

'She said he refused to bum her until she told him her favourite colour!'

'Do you have to phrase it like that?' Howie asked in a pained voice.

They piled in together like sardines.

The young woman clung to Howie's arm to keep balance, to his distinct unease.

'I didn't know she was a…' he glanced at Ron, '… an employee, I just liked her and wanted to get to know her.'

'So does everyone, but the poor girl's got a quota to fill,' said Keith, squirming into the middle to take the reins. 'She can't sit around chatting and leave the Duke of Osney waiting outside, can she? Everyone on?'

He eased the horses into a trot, and they trundled uphill.

Hot breath landed in Howie's right ear, making him flinch away. He had hoped the layer of human shit across his face might have dissuaded her, but apparently not.

'My favourite colour is yellow,' the girl whispered in his ear.

Howie pointedly turned his face to the left, to her disappointment.

~

Elliot Maynard entered the tavern and swiftly approached an occupied table in the corner. He waded through the dense crowd of drinkers and narrowed his eyes in the dim candlelight, his sights set on the glint of flame on metal in the far corner.

The armoured man glanced up lazily and backed up against the wall.

Elliot slid in beside him. The sheer girth of the man conquered every inch of free space. He was built like a fort, with a large brown beard pouring down his neck. He propped an elbow on the table, which creaked.

'Alright?' Elliot said idly.

The man gave him a sideways glance. 'Hello.'

Sat next to Elliot, he looked like a pencil nub placed beside a brick.

'I hear you're off to the Shades on palace business,' Elliot said. 'Need a hand?'

The man regarded him.

'Could do with one,' he said, giving him a cursory glance. 'You'll have to purchase your own supplies, mind. I haven't the money for enough steel to cover all of your…'

He shot the thick muscle across Elliot's shoulders a bitter look.

'… you,' he grunted.

Elliot rolled his shoulders, as if in response. 'As you wish.'

The man regarded him again, his brows furrowed. 'What are your thoughts on travelling through the Wastelands?'

'If it's necessary,' he said.

'Long journeys?'

'Not a problem.'

'Night duty?'

'Can't stand the daytime.'

The man smiled faintly. 'What's your name, sir?'

'Elliot Maynard,' he said. 'And yourself?'

The man's smile faded. 'Er… Sadie.'

Elliot's eyes narrowed slightly. 'Oh yeah?'

'Yes.'

Elliot lifted an eyebrow and shrugged. 'Alright.'

Marbrand blinked. 'You haven't got a problem with my name?'

'Something to call you, innit?'

Marbrand paused. Then he held out a hand. 'Welcome aboard.'

~

VII

A salty wind drifted lazily over the ship, the air lukewarm against the thick sails.

Howie leaned on the rail, gazing out over a clear blue ocean. Too clear, he noticed: it was littered with miscellaneous debris from the ship, various specimens of dead marine life and what could only be described as incredibly ominous shadows beneath the surface.

The first mate stood beside him, facing the opposite direction to watch the crew.

Sam was a waif and visibly recoiled in the presence of Ron, Howie and even Dora, Keith's new 'employee'. But when it came to working with the sea, he was a cog in a well-oiled machine.

Which was just as well. Captain 'Legless' Hopkins was as useful as a chocolate teapot. He – somehow! – suffered a recurring case of seasickness in *every single journey*, rarely exiting his cabin except to open the door a crack and holler for a drink. Sam, an actual *double amputee*, had gifted him the nickname after outstripping him in every competence.

Howie heaved a sigh.

It was approximately 6,750 miles between the Shades and Adem's nearest available port, Breaker's Hold. According to Sam, the entire journey would take between twelve and fourteen weeks, provided the weather remained fair and nothing caused them to suddenly travel backwards.

Halfway into the voyage, the vessel seemed to be holding out well.

The same couldn't be said for Howie. He hoped they would speed up soon. Meeting a king who hunted peasants as well as wildlife was preferable to spending time with the crew. Two jokers named Silas and Tully Beult had gifted them a squid-filled cake two weeks prior. The level of suffering involved in meeting King Crey would be marginally less unpleasant.

As though called by the thought of his name, Silas Beult himself left Captain Legless's cabin and walked up to the deck. He gave Howie a genial nod before strolling to the other side of the deck to watch the horizon.

Howie nudged Sam, earning a violent flinch.

'What's he doing in there?'

'Legless summoned him, probably,' Sam scoffed. His accent had a wavering cadence, a mishmash of different dialects folded into one, marking him to be pure sailor born. 'Useless bastard. Only got the ship because his dad's some lord's second son. Sooner he pukes himself to death, the better. We'd a casualty the other year there, one of the hands had lost a finger, and this bastard wouldn't let him leave until he'd cured his *tummy ache*. Imagine! Keeping Two Finger Si on nursemaid duty while some poor kid's bleeding to death!'

'Why's he called that? Did he lose half a hand as well?'

'*He* didn't. He got into a fight, before he joined the crew, and maimed the poor bugger by removing one finger from each hand and keeping the bones in his pocket out of spite. He made him dinner afterwards, though, so he's largely considered an alright bloke.'

Howie recoiled at the thought of the bones. 'Sounds it.'

Si's gaze was locked onto the coast as the Faerie Forest came into view, his grimy, dull hair rustling in the breeze. Howie couldn't tell if it was grey or fair: he didn't look past his mid-thirties. He looked familiar somehow, as though he was related to someone Howie knew, but Howie couldn't place it.

Howie's attention wandered to the horizon, where the Forest sat in all its glory. Birdsong chirped from the foliage clinging to the piers, below long grass rippling in the wind.

He once again pictured the Forest Queen dancing through the flames. He wondered how the owner of such a beautiful place could turn half a continent into the grey, dusty wasteland that had been their only view of the continent for weeks. He couldn't imagine it. He himself cringed at the thought of rolling his eyes at someone, never mind setting them on fire.

The wind picked up, pulling the ship along with it.

Sam grinned and started yelling orders as they surged ahead.

Howie pushed himself from the railing and headed belowdecks.

'We're speeding up again, aren't we?' Archie all but howled.

Howie shut the cabin door behind him, dodging a low-hanging beam on his way in.

A lantern swung back and forth from a beam in the middle of the ceiling, illuminating the table and hammocks grappling for space. Archie lay in a foetal position in one of the hammocks, wincing as the corner of the table burrowed itself into the small of his back.

Ron sat on a stool opposite, pouring over a map weighted across the table with empty beer tankards.

'Calm down, if we were going to die, we'd have done by now,' Ron said, rolling his eyes. 'Honestly, you'd think you never spent a moment away from your workbench, the way you harp on.'

'He hasn't,' said Howie with a smile, falling into his own hammock behind Ron. 'So what's the plan of action once we're off the ship?'

'Burn it,' Archie seethed.

Ron consulted a map the captain had given them.

'Once we make port in Adem, there's a main road going west to Serpus.'

'How far?'

'Roughly three hundred miles.'

'Three hundred miles?' Howie exclaimed in disbelief. 'We're gonna be on this boat for six weeks and counting and there's still another three hundred miles to go?'

'Told you we should have gone through the Wastelands,' Archie said. 'Would've been faster.'

'Not much faster,' Keith said from the door.

He poked his head in and waggled a bag of coins in the air.

'Girl's making a bloody killing here,' he said in delight. 'She'll do well in Serpus. Silas Beult's had her three times this week alone, and it's only Wednesday.'

'You've set up in Serpus now, is it?' Archie said, before he could go into details about Silas Beult's carnal preferences.

'Yeah, Petty's running things there while I'm checking up on our country properties. What's this about the Wastelands again? I told you, we're better off on the ship.'

'Have you seen this map?' Archie demanded, flinging a hand back at it. 'We're gonna be about eighty by the time we reach Serpus at this rate! If we'd cut through the mountains like I said—'

'Then we'd still be in the Wastelands, only without any food or beer,' Keith said with a snort, leaning against the doorframe. 'We've a cushy journey on here, you know. I've been through the Wastelands before, you know. Bloodthirsty animals would have killed us within hours. They've nothing else to eat there: even the herbivores wouldn't say no to hot flesh passing through. You've got dogs, feral Orchardfolk, venomous snakes, ghosts, not a dog's turd to be seen, never mind food. Would have been fine taking the old kings' road if that witch hadn't burned it up, but a week passes like a year in the Wastelands. Me, I was one of the lucky ones.'

He held out his arm to reveal two dark spots on his forearm.

'Bit by a venomous snake,' he said proudly, 'and lived to tell the tale.'

'Keith, those are freckles,' Archie said.

'No, they ain't, they're scars,' Keith said sharply. 'Twelve days I spent in that cesspit. Scared off my tits, I was.' He caught Howie's eye. 'Well, not too scared, you understand. I was brave, me, in the wilderness, on my own.'

'Like with yesterday's incident with the trout?' Howie asked with a smirk.

Keith scowled at him, giving his trousers a wipe just above where a dark stain marred the fabric.

'How long a journey is three hundred miles, exactly?' Archie asked.

'Ages,' Ron groaned. 'Breaker's Hold drops out in the sticks. It'll take two days to reach the nearest inn by coach, and that's assuming we don't stop for food in between rest periods for the horses. The next city's fifty miles from that.'

'Should've gone to Maketon,' Keith said. 'Would've taken you to Nayport in the south. Longer boat trip, but the river goes straight up to Osney and Serpus is a couple days' ride from that.'

'Nice to know that *now*,' Howie spat at him. 'So we'll be camping out for the next decade, then. Unless a dragon comes along and we can tame it.'

Archie laughed shortly. 'You're supposed to be killing dragons, mate, not taming them.'

The ship surged, sending their hammocks sharply left.

Archie clung to the sides with a yelp.

'I hate ships!' he wailed. 'Nothing's worse than ships, nothing!'

Black smog wafted through the open doorway.

Howie coughed violently, wafting it away with one hand.

'Is that smoke?' he said in a strangled voice.

Boots thundered down the corridor of the ship's underbelly.

'I'll take that as a yes,' Howie said uneasily.

~

Out on the deck, Sam scolded a deck hand on the proper procedure for tying an anchor bend. It was simple. Even a *child* could do it.

'Look,' he snapped, pointing at the mess of threads, 'you make two turns around the shackle, leave them open, pass the free end behind the standing line, feed the free end through the first turns before tying a half hitch around the standing line, then take the free end and tie a backup knot with the tie end around the standing part. Is that *too much to ask?*'

'No, sir,' the boy trembled. 'But… what came after the shackle part?'

Sam groaned and threw his arms to the heavens, turning to remedy the abomination before him. He felt a hot wind wash over him and ignored it as something heavy splashed overboard.

'Now,' he said, straightening up to observe his handiwork, 'did that look so hard?'

The boy had vanished.

He frowned, leaning over the edge.

There was one extra ominous shadow beneath the surface.

'Oh,' he said in surprise. 'Didn't know I'd been so hard on him.'

A huge, winged mass soared over the ship.

He ducked.

The creature curved over his head in an arc, dodging the mast by millimetres. It soared vertically into the air, a trail of hot smoke in its wake as its twenty-foot wingspan shrunk into the clouds.

Sam stared in its wake in horror, his eyes wide.

'A dragon?' he exclaimed in disbelief.

Screams erupted from the other side of the ship – and Lyseria burst through the sails.

~

Howie rushed out from below decks.

He turned on his heel and, stumbling, rushed back down again.

The mast collapsed with a great crash behind him.

The four peered up the stairs.

'You had to say it,' Archie said hoarsely, peering over his shoulder. 'You just *had* to say it!'

The dragon stood on the wreckage, rearing its head into the

sky in an imperial pose. Its red scales shimmered orange in the bright light of the sun. One gold-specked pupil flickered to the stairs and the head darted towards them.

They retreated with a wail of unison, clutching each other.

A massive paw groped into the bowels of the ship, all claws and muscle.

'This can't be real,' gasped Howie, bulging eyes locked on the dragon.

Nails as long as Howie's hand scored deep lines into the floorboards.

'We're gonna die,' Archie whined, sweat pouring down his temples.

'No, we're not,' Ron said.

They looked at him in incredulous silence for a moment.

'Have you been drinking again or what?' Archie asked suspiciously.

'No,' Ron said, glaring at him. 'It doesn't want to kill us. It would have breathed fire on us by now if it did. It wouldn't reach for us unless it wanted its owner.'

Everyone looked at Howie.

'It's hardly me!'

'You summoned it!' Archie shrieked.

'It was a turn of phrase! It's not like I whistled for it and called it for its dinner!'

'Why don't we pet it and see?' said Ron.

'See what? Our lives flash before our eyes?' Keith shouted. 'Mine's too filthy for that! You can pet him since you're so keen.'

Ron eyed the paw. He grabbed Howie's hand without warning and pulled it forward.

'Ron, get off me, what d'you think you're doing—'

He pressed Howie's palm onto the top of the paw.

Heat coursed out of it like a furnace. Howie winced, but the heat thankfully didn't rise above mild discomfort.

Howie's shoulder muscles clenched in anticipation and, tentatively, he gave the creature a rub.

The paw vanished out.

Quickly replaced by a head.

The other three hastily retreated, leaving Howie alone.

Howie swallowed with difficulty. His mouth had gone dry.

All he saw were nostrils, steaming and wide. They flexed and contracted, roving over Howie's torso, taking in his scent.

Howie stood bolt upright, his entire face scrunched as tightly as possible.

He felt the nose brush his chest and whimpered involuntarily.

Then it nuzzled him.

Howie prised an eye open.

It was *nuzzling* him, like a purring cat. Only it wasn't purring as such – more like rumbling in a sort of contentment, like a happy little pet… avalanche.

Howie lifted one hand in a wide arc and, carefully, rubbed behind its ears.

The head was roughly the size of his own torso, with small ears protruding out of the back at odd angles. He found a soft spot of leather-ish skin and tickled it.

A little trill escaped the beast, which wriggled happily.

Its shoulders collided with the top of the deck. Painfully, Howie thought.

Very, very tentatively, Howie manoeuvred past the dragon.

'Come on,' he said gently. 'Let's get out of here, eh?'

They felt the ship thud and shudder underfoot as the dragon retreated. The head slowly slipped out.

Howie followed it upstairs, hands held out in front of him.

Archie, Ron and Keith watched him in silence.

And then Howie screamed.

Archie, Ron and Keith ran out to the deck.

Howie's shirt was *gripped* in its teeth.

With a sharp thrust upwards, it fired Howie into the sky and bolted after him.

'It's killed him,' Ron said levelly.

'Bollocks!' Archie screamed.

The dragon swept overhead with a screech.

Archie bolted to the wreckage. He plucked a sliver of wood from the ruins of the mast and groped his way up the mountain of splintered wood, wielding his stick firmly.

'What the bloody hell are you doing?' Keith shrieked.

'I'm getting my boy back,' Archie said in determination – albeit a squeaky kind of determination.

'How?' Ron asked in exasperation.

'By shoving this pointy stick up its nose,' he said. 'He might live if it drops him into the water. It can't be hard to aim at a nostril half a foot wide.'

'But you're a withered toad fossil,' Ron said.

'Well, you're no beauty queen!!'

Phwoom!!

The dragon swept him up.

'Oh, bollocks!' shrieked Keith.

Archie screeched his way through the clouds.

The dragon soared into an upwards arc, the back of Archie's jerkin gripped tightly in its teeth. As its course straightened, the beast flung its head back, arching its long neck to drop Archie onto its back.

Archie screamed, fingers scrabbling on the dragon's scales for purchase. He slid from its back with a defeated whimper.

A hand snatched his elbow.

'Mind your step!' a voice called in a giddy timbre. 'It's a long one!'

Archie howled. 'HOWIE??!'

Howie grinned maniacally at him. With one elbow hooked around the dragon's neck, he heaved Archie up.

One hand around a bulging wing muscle and the other on Howie's shoulder, Archie anchored a foot into the dragon's ribs and swung a leg over, as if mounting a horse.

Archie flung both arms around Howie's ribs, sobbing.

Below, on the deck, Keith had taken Archie's place on the rubble. He was straightening his aim with the stick when two voices shrieked at him from above.

'GET OUT OF THE WAY!!!'

Keith skittered off the debris.

The dragon's claws slammed into the remains of the mast, sending splinters flying in all directions.

Archie laughed shrilly, his elbows hooked firmly under Howie's armpits.

'He's not attacking,' he said in a high voice. 'He wasn't trying to kill us, he was only playing! We're alive! We're alive!!'

'He's a she,' Keith said, bent in half to crane his neck underneath.

'Who cares? We're alive...'

Archie dived off the dragon's back in a dead faint.

Ron caught him under the armpits, his gaze locked onto the beast.

Howie sat upright just behind the dragon's shoulder-blades, his hands on the joints of her wings. He was visibly trembling; his elbows wavered from side to side.

'That is so cool!' Ron said, beaming at them. 'How fast does she go?'

Howie whined and spluttered, trying to capture the power of speech.

'*F-fast*,' he said finally.

'That is so cool,' Ron said again. 'Can she carry four people?'

'You're not actually telling me,' Keith shrilled, 'you're thinking of riding that thing to Serpus?'

'Look at the size of her wings!!' Ron exclaimed, flinging a hand out at her. 'She has to fly at least, like, a hundred miles an hour! We'll be there in no time!'

'What if she gets hungry?' Keith squeaked. 'She'd have a four-course meal ready to go!'

'Do you see her eating people right now?' Ron pointed out.

'She-she's quite gentle in a horrifying sort of way,' Howie piped up weakly, folding his arms under his forehead.

'See?' Ron said, bouncing on his toes.

Keith was still arguing shrilly to Ron, but Howie had lost all comprehension. He lifted his head and squinted blearily at the back of the dragon's neck.

A leather band – man-made, by the looks of it – clung to her scales, polished to a deep brown.

Howie reached for it with both hands.

'She's got a collar,' he called.

Keith squinted up at him, his teeth bared. 'You which?'

'She's got a big dog collar. She's domesticated.'

Ron screwed his face up in bemusement. 'Who's rich enough to own a pet dragon? I sure as hell ain't.'

Howie tilted the band towards him.

'Lyseria,' he read.

On closer inspection, the clasp formed a snake's head.

'The Creys,' Howie said. 'What a coincidence.'

Ron hoisted Archie upright as he regained consciousness.

'Come on, let's go! We can drop her off at the castle, tell 'em she was lost!'

'Oh, and they're just going to take our word for it, are they?' Archie squeaked.

Ron jumped up Lyseria's ribs.

Howie took his wrists in his hands and pulled him up.

'Yeah, he's friends with my dad,' Ron said.

'That and this one is the spitting image of Prince Seth,' Keith said, pointing at Howie.

Howie released Ron, who slid in behind him.

'So I keep hearing,' he said in dread. He hoped this prince wouldn't turn out to be ugly.

Ron eyed Archie and Keith, standing around the dragon. 'You

coming then or what?'

Heaving a sigh, Archie climbed aboard behind Ron, Keith following close behind.

Lyseria leapt from the deck and spread her wings, pushing hard against the wind.

They clutched her and each other for dear life. Howie peered over the side.

The deck had caved in towards the centre, boards of timber standing upright in the air. Faint mumbles and shuffling from beneath the fallen sails appeared to be the only signs of life.

'We should probably help them.'

'Later,' Ron said. 'Royalty comes first, eh?'

Howie stared into space. 'Spoken like a true politician.'

Lyseria pressed down, guiding them higher and higher. Tilting her wings vertical, she surged ahead, curving in an arc towards the mainland. They bowed their heads against the thundering wind as the Forest raced beneath them.

~

Vladimir Horne reclined as best he could in the basalt throne, atop cushions of silk that slithered beneath him like fish in a net.

Princess Felicity stood at his side in the formal manner, her hand held loosely in his.

According to a reliably *late* source, a cargo ship bound for Adem had departed three weeks ago with five extra passengers, one of whom was a whore.

As uncharacteristic as this sounded of Ron, Vladimir was inclined to believe it of the two convicts. Gallivanting to the next kingdom and taking a prince with them for collateral? Classic degenerate behaviour. No doubt they would deliver him to the Creys for a ransom.

Felicity gazed at the ceiling. Her eyes locked onto a butterfly fluttering across the room. Her hand fell from Vladimir's to catch it, a childish grin spread across her stupid face.

Vladimir glowered at her. The vile Seth Crey managed to bag affluent parents, a beautiful wife, a wide net of connections and a claim to the kingdom of Portabella, and Vladimir was stuck with the leftovers.

Said leftover, a scion of Mellier named Felicity Emmett, appeared to have finished psychological development at age five. Her main concerns were the visible properties of her hair, the organisation of each meal into separate food sections that did not *under any circumstances* touch each other, and the protection of the butterflies that gathered around the buddleia bushes planted around the castle at her request. A very *expensive* request. She had no other interests or hobbies whatsoever. It was as if someone had built a wall around her mind to prevent it expanding and had stuck a pressed butterfly collection next to the door.

It was a pity, thought Vladimir. She was really quite pretty, at least compared to her horse-faced brother. If only she'd inherited her brother's mind. Vladimir would have killed to have someone like that at his side.

Felicity cupped the butterfly between her hands. 'Look.'

Vladimir avoided her gaze with a frown.

A man was shown into the throne room, bearing a cloth-covered item roughly proportionate to Vladimir's head.

Vladimir grinned.

The man knelt before the dais, unveiling the Stonecrown with a flourish.

Crafted from a similar stone as the throne, the coronet gleamed under a thick layer of polish. The circlet of charcoal-coloured basalt has been worked into a delicate swirling pattern, matching the smoky whirls of lighter blueish grey through the stone. The design was basic: seven points to mirror the seven points of the Seven's cross, with sweeping arches in between.

Vladimir licked his upper teeth in anticipation. The sharp taste of metal marked where steel replaced his missing tooth.

The crown was a copy, but a good one. King Samuel himself wouldn't have batted an eyelid at it.

'Sir, you may place it on my head,' he said imperiously.

'Right away, your highness!'

The man bowed. His beret flopped to the floor, revealing a rather bad comb-over.

Lifting the crown from the cushion he had delivered it on, he placed it, with care, on the top of Vladimir's head.

The moment of glory ended rather abruptly with a shriek of:

'AHH! AHH! TAKE IT OFF, TAKE IT OFF, IT'S HEAVY, IT'S CRUSHING MY BRAIN!!'

The man yanked it off hurriedly.

Vladimir exhaled shrilly, his head hunched between his shoulders.

'What the hell?' he squealed. He massaged his skull with his fingertips. 'Why is it so heavy?'

'It is the exact proportions and weight as the original artefact,' the man insisted, his voice small and injured. 'Chipped from the same quarry as the original crown and many other stately artefacts such as the Stonethrone—'

'And the Stone-chamber-pot and the Stone-winter-hat and the Stone-quilt and I'll just bet there's a Stone… butterfly-net in there too for Felicity,' Vladimir spat. 'I get the picture. Take it back and get them to shave a bit off the inside or something. I'll get a skull fracture if I have to wear that for an hour.'

'Of course, your highness,' he said hastily.

' "Majesty" from now on,' Vladimir corrected. 'Kings are addressed "your majesty".'

'Yes, your majesty,' he corrected himself, gathering the crown, the cushion and his hat in hasty movements and scrambling away.

'Can I play with it?' Felicity asked sweetly.

She skittered out of the hall after him, peering over his shoulder.

As soon as the doors slammed shut, Vladimir winced and stood up, rubbing his back.

He was fed up with stone now. Gold, though, was something Vladimir never tired of seeing.

He strolled to the window, thinking of his brother.

It wouldn't be prudent to bring Ronald back from Adem. If he knew that Vladimir had the Stonecrown forged (and he would if his little playmate Felicity had anything to do with it), the little worm would blab and the Hornes would be a joke forever.

If Ron stayed with his new friends in Adem and never came back, Vladimir's throne would be safe. And there was also the possibility that Ron wouldn't make it back alive once the convicts were finished with him.

Marbrand would soon confirm that. And perhaps he could send Marbrand on a little assassination assignment too, just to secure his claim a little more.

And now that Father is as good as dead, Mother and I can finally get down to business.

The biggest obstacle had been Samuel Horne. Vladimir flinched at the image of his disdainful face glaring down at him and shivered. Queen Aaliyaa Horne may be as batty as a dark cave at night-time, but her connections to the church were as sound as the throne behind him. They would do anything for the Knight of Raining Thorns and his saintly mother.

And Aaliyaa's plans aligned very nicely with Vladimir's deepest desires.

Sunlight lanced through the stained glass behind him. The yellow light put him in mind of the blond-haired beauty of his dreams, whose portrait hung in his room, a gift from his mother before King Samuel decided to intervene in their splendid fairy tale.

It might come to fruition yet, he told himself with a glimmer of hope.

Vladimir smiled to himself and leaned against the windowsill to feel the sun.

PART TWO: THE CREYS

I

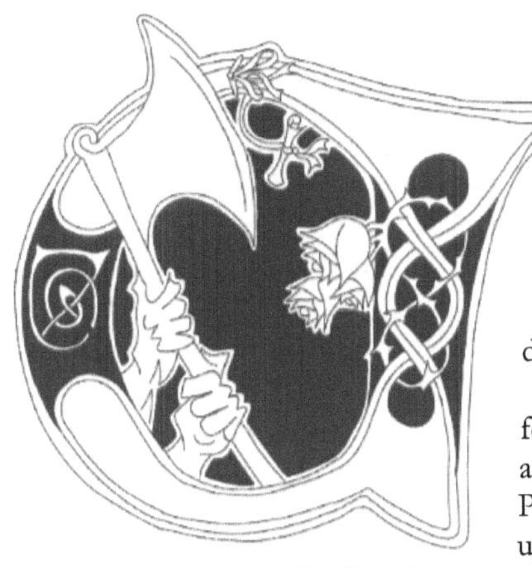

knife buried itself into the wall directly to the left of Ronald Horne's biggest fan.

Stan screeched deafeningly.

A battle cry shortly followed, along with a small armoury, as Serpus's famous Prince Death burst into uproar.

Stanley Carrot slid from his seat to cower beneath the table.

Bottles smashed overhead, showering him with shards of glass and droplets of beer. Barstools crashed against the walls and tables crumbled around him in the midst of axes, shovels and dog kennels.

Such was an average night in Prince Death, the tavern in Arthur Stibbons' Street.

As the years wore on, Prince Seth's mental health became less of a concern and more of a source of entertainment. Thus it was that the main tavern in the heart of Serpus was named Prince Death, in honour of the 'dead' Prince Seth.

It was better than the previous name, which was so filthy the only punters who came in were those looking for a two-silver backwards: the payment of two silver pounds in exchange for something Stan didn't dare contemplate in case his head might implode.

A familiar shriek of alarm sent his head spinning to the right.

Entering the front door of the tavern was his Aunt Petunia, the manager of Stan's uncle's... establishment. Who, upon spotting Stan's head level with the top of the table, yelped in indignation.

'Stan! What have I told you about coming in here after dark? It's bloody dangerous!'

She jerked him out by one armpit.

A wood-chopping axe landed blade-first in the back of his chair and stuck there.

'I didn't know a fight was going to break out!' Stan said shrilly. 'I only came in for a bacon sarnie and a cup of tea, honest!'

He let her drag him onto the cobble-lined Arthur Stibbons' Street by one elbow.

Eyes followed Petunia down the street, which was nothing new. She stood six feet tall and willowy, with a flowing gown of amber silk, matching nicely with her deep golden hair. Stan felt small and waif-like in her shadow, a little gargoyle of a youth with close-cropped chestnut hair that stuck up at odd angles.

'Yeah, that's what they all say before their eyes get replaced with bottle necks! Come in here, we don't want your uncle coming back to find you impaled!'

She led him to a grubby old building in the crook of a V-shaped junction. A building he knew all too well.

Stan squirmed out of her grasp. 'I ain't going in there!'

'Why not? It's only Keith's place!'

'That's me point!' he shrieked, flailing his arms above his head. 'I'd rather be murdered in the Prince Death than take me chances in there!'

'Don't be silly, I go in there every day for work, don't I?' she scoffed.

She snatched the scruff of his neck, roughly.

'It's disgusting, what you lot do in there! I'll catch diseases in there!'

'No, you won't! You're too much of a bloody prude to put out!'

'Those places should be outlawed! Gerroff my arm!'

Petunia clenched her teeth.

'Don't be a baby!' she snapped. 'It is just a brothel!'

'I'd rather be a baby then go in there and catch one of those… diseases going around!'

'They aren't airborne, Stanley,' Petunia said, giving him a withering glance. 'We'll leave you in a room by yourself if you insist!'

'I'll be on my own somewhere else, thank you! Imagine if Prince Ronald came to visit and spotted me coming out of there! I'd have to kill myself out of shame!'

'As if that halfwit would make it to Serpus alive—*what the hell is that?*'

'Don't think you can divert my attention whilst you ferry me into that cesspit, lady,' Stan accused speedily, 'I ain't brainless, me, I, I, I-I-I—'

He paused as a cloud of smog floated across Petunia's face.

He spun around. 'HOLY—!!'

The heavy foot traffic of Lower Stibbons' Street scattered.

Screams like that of Stan's erupted.

A twenty-foot-long silhouette glided down the navy blue sky to the road.

Petunia vanished soundlessly into the brothel.

Stan pressed his back as far against the doorframe as possible.

As the silhouette neared, its shape formed in the soft glow of the street lighting. The body of a lizard, talons like an eagle, a long neck six feet long at the end of which a broad snout blew hot air across the street. Black eyes with gold-coloured slits down the centre fixed themselves onto the cobble-lined dirt road. It skidded along it heavily, throwing clouds of dust at everyone in the vicinity, including Stan.

Stan coughed and spluttered, rubbing dirt from his eyes.

The dragon folded its bat-like wings onto itself and sat to gaze idly at the shocked crowd. It was then that Stan noticed four men astride it, shadowy waifs lingering along the spine.

They dismounted, stumbling on the cobbles.

One was his own uncle, Keith, who nodded at him in wide-eyed silence before promptly collapsing into the door beside him.

Two were new to him – a blond youth and a gaunt middle-aged man who threw up in a waste barrel across the road – but the fourth man, on closer inspection, was very familiar to Stan.

A hot flame swept up Stan's spine.

Prince Ronald Horne of Stoneguard, Stan's place of birth, stumbled away from the scarlet dragon and promptly toppled face-first into the cobbles.

Stan bolted forward to help him.

His bootlaces snuck under the heel of his other boot, sending him pitching forward onto his face, inches away from Ron's own.

His face flaming, Stan quickly unstuck it from the pavement and scrambled to his feet, hand outstretched.

'Evening, your highness, Stanley Carrot, Stan for short, big fan and that, great job you're doing, er, the princing and that,' he babbled.

Ron dragged himself to his feet via Stan's ecstatic handshake.

'Nice to meet you, your highness, sir, lot paler in real life, did anyone ever tell you that?'

'Er, no,' Ron said.

He paled further.

'Excuse me,' he grated with a wince before heaving a mixture of stomach acid and what smelled like fish onto Stan's waistcoat.

Stan's nose wrinkled.

A fisheye glared up at him from his knee.

'Sorry,' Ron gritted with a burp.

'Not a problem,' Stan said, his back stiffening.

He held out the end of his waistcoat for examination.

'Royal, fishy sick. An honour, really… and that…'

The older man finally pulled himself away from the barrel to face them.

'Oh, Stanley, Hilary's boy,' he said hoarsely, clapping a hand on Stan's shoulder. 'My, you've grown, haven't you? Only yay high last I saw… I saw'r… oh God.'

An upheaval of a new blend of fish-flavoured vomit interrupted the man, plastering itself on Stan's boots.

Stan glared at his newly decorated attire, then at the new arrival.

Who smiled sheepishly and added, 'Nice to see you again.'

'Yeah, real nice,' Stan said wryly. His face wrinkled and his eyes roved up and down the length of him. 'Who are you, anyway?'

'Archie Hart,' he said, propping himself upright with his hands on his knees. 'Friend of the family. Made your cot yonks ago, free on behest of your dear mother, but I'm sure you can repay me by giving us lot free beds for the night? Empty, obviously, we won't bankrupt your fine establishment.'

'This ain't mine!'

'Nah, this is mine!' Keith piped up, re-emerging from the building with Petunia in tow. 'Well, get in, then, before I reconsider letting you in for free!'

'I'll be along in a minute, I'd better get Lyseria back to her owner,' the young blond man said, leaning his forearms across the beast's shoulder-blades.

He seemed to have evaded the altitude sickness, Stan observed with a sigh of relief. He didn't think his clothes could withstand any more stomach acids.

'Castle's up yonder,' Petunia called, pointing north. 'Belongs to Lilly Crey. She's ridden it down here the past two weeks.'

'Thanks.'

The youth shot her a smirk.

'Nice to see you, Pet.'

'It will be once you've paid me, pet,' Petunia retorted cheekily. 'Whole night's worth of takings you owe me. Got me a husband to feed.'

The kid's face fell. 'Husband?'

'Me,' Keith grinned.

He slid an arm around Petunia's waist, which was about level in height with his ribcage.

The kid looked disgusted. 'You?!'

'Me,' he said happily. 'Happy to share my lady, the profit she rakes in. She's wasted on you, mate.'

'You're twice her age!'

'Makes no odds to me, sweetie,' Petunia said with a wink. 'Off you pop, then! Don't want to keep King Crey waiting, do we?'

The youth scowled and kicked his heels into the dragon's hide.

Lyseria spread her wings, crashing into a hanging sign and sending it clattering down a side alley.

'Oh,' Keith called after him, 'and Petty's favourite colour is blue, by the way!'

The faint sound of a raspberry being blown sounded from above as the dragon swept off.

Keith barked a good-natured laugh, pulling Petunia into the brothel.

'Good kid, him,' he commented as the others followed. 'Gormless, but good. Now, when you're finished being sick on my equally gormless nephew, there's a few beds empty inside, aren't there, love?'

'A few? Bloody whole building's empty, I should think,' snorted Petunia, 'bar the room with the Crey kid in it. Bought all our girls for the day and took 'em to the deluxe suite. We'll eat like the royal family for a week, I expect!'

Stan frowned. 'What, dead Prince Seth? In here?'

'No, the girl.'

Archie's nose wrinkled as he stood outside, still leaning on his knees. 'The *girl?*'

'I don't wanna know,' Stan said with a sigh.

He entered the house sullenly, plonking himself at a deserted dinner table in the main hall.

Ron and Archie followed suit, dropping miserably to either side of Stan.

The soft sounds of giggling and shifting furniture surrounded them from upstairs, to Stan's discomfort.

'I feel awful,' Archie moaned.

He dropped his forehead onto the table.

'Sea-sick, air-sick, dragon-sick…'

'Sick-sick,' Stan piped up.

'Sorry about that,' Ron winced.

He proffered a hand with a little, hopeful smile.

Stan took it sheepishly.

A slam startled them from upstairs and a small figure bounded down the stairs, giggling shrilly.

'I gotta go, ladies, sorree…'

Stan grimaced. 'Home-sick.'

A young woman crossed the room, grinning from ear to ear. Her mousy-blond hair was tied messily to the top of her head with several strands hanging down the back and on either side of a small round face bearing two big blue eyes.

However, those were about the only features that indicated her femininity. Her clothes appeared to belong to an older, taller brother and her leisure habits left a lot to be desired – in Stan's view, anyway.

He tried to ignore her.

She jogged out onto the street, only to skip back into the door with a frown.

'Has anyone seen my dragon?'

Ron's eyes narrowed.

'You mean the one that went all the way beyond the Forest to attack a ship heading to Breaker's Hold, quite possibly killing everyone on board bar a young good-looking prince and his small entourage?'

A delicate line creased the middle of her brow and quickly smoothed out.

'Oh,' she said slowly. She tutted. 'I leave her outside for *five minutes*—'

'You left her outside *all day*,' Petunia said. 'If she hadn't flown away this morning, she'd have scared away all our customers.'

Lilly-Anna Crey glanced out at the deep blue sky.

'Oh. Well, send her to me when you find her,' she said idly, swinging a cloak about her shoulders.

'Our friend's already on it,' Ron said. 'And he'd better get a substantial award for bringing it back with its head still on or there'll be war.'

'Whatever. Thanks!'

She slammed the door on her way out.

Ron glared after her.

'I don't like her,' he and Stan said in unison.

'She's a good kid,' Keith said, 'albeit in dire need of a scrub and a loan of a dress. Friendly, like.'

'Princesses are supposed to dress well, not reek of horse manure and say nice things to people, at least in front of their face,' Ron said. 'She just acts like a bloke.'

Stan laughed shortly. 'It ain't like that anymore, your highness. This is a new world.'

'At least she doesn't think she's dead,' Petunia said with a shrug.

Stan frowned in mid-air. 'Why does Prince Seth think he's dead, though? Surely there's a fundamental difference between life and death that doesn't take twenty years to figure out?'

'He had a near-death experience the night of his wedding,' Petunia said in reply. 'His father found him in his room, swearing blind he'd been murdered. Made him go along with the wedding anyway, having him think it was his funeral, and they've been having him force-fed for the last twenty years while he lies in his coffin, waiting to be buried. Hopeless case, if you ask me – won't have children, won't go to public outings, won't touch his wife…'

'Shame, too,' Keith added. 'Good looking girl is Princess Cienne. Found a dead ringer for her in Stoneguard, by the way. Made us a killing on… the… boat…'

His face fell.

'Oh bugger, I've left her on the boat… there goes our newest breadwinner.'

Ron shrugged. 'Anyway, do you really think Howie's related to them?'

'It does look like a stunning coincidence that the apparent hero of the realm happens to be Seth Crey's double,' said Archie.

Keith blinked in mid-air.

'Seth Crey's double,' he muttered to himself.

'What was that, love?' Petunia asked attentively.

Stan looked into his uncle's eyes to see, just beyond the pupils, the malignant cogs of ingenuity spinning at high speed.

'What time is it?' Keith asked suddenly.

Petunia glanced out of the window.

''Bout seven, I s'pose,' she guessed.

Keith grinned at her. 'I have an idea.'

'Oh, I was afraid you'd say that,' Stan moaned, his head in his hands.

~

Howard felt wonderful.

The wind ran through his hair, his cloak rippled behind him with a powerful swish, and he felt as light and free as air. A haggled night with Petunia was nothing compared to a flight on a dragon. Despite the sharp pinch of a dozen scales digging into each hand and an unfortunate chafing of the groin.

It had been a most eventful afternoon. The first afternoon, in fact, that Howie had ever seen a griffin – although Lyseria had cooked it alive before he got a good look at it.

In a humble act of kindness, the dragon had graciously shared the lightly charred meat between them – only for Ron, Archie and Keith to dismiss the delicacy in a lengthy bout of flight sickness that, strangely, Howie didn't seem to be affected by.

He observed the long neck yawning out ahead of him.

Judging by the stories, he hadn't expected to find dragons to be so… genial. A lot of Lyseria's mannerisms mirrored that of a house cat: she nuzzled him in affection he felt was as of yet unearned and puffed hot air in his face playfully. It was as if dragons found people… cute.

She had yet to grasp the fragility of the human form though, Howie reflected, nursing a bruised rib from when Lyseria had thrown him into a tree during horseplay.

He peered around Lyseria's shoulder.

The Creys' Keep approached at high speed. A ring of turrets glowed in the torchlight, giving each wall a golden gleam. From this height he could see the entire complex: the rooftops behind the high walls, the huge block in the centre of the inner ring of wall with a slim tower shortly behind it, followed by a large chapel ringed in elaborate spiral-patterned gardens.

Lyseria touched down before the gaping palace entrance.

The portcullis creaked up.

Howie slid from Lyseria's back and touched down heavily on the gravel. Lyseria sniffed his head, lifting his hair slightly. He rubbed the soft leather behind her ear as guards marched out to meet him. The guards parted to reveal King Theo Crey.

Howie swallowed. Theo Crey made Vladimir Horne look like a twiglet.

Crey was, for want of a better word, *huge*. Every aspect of him was big, especially the red beard streaked with grey beneath the thick gold coronet atop his head. But looking at the face in between, he saw benevolence in his eyes and the rosy cheeks gave off nothing but cheer.

Well. To first glances, anyway. The way Archie had it, not a lot of other people got to see this view of the king through the foot-wide execution axe he wielded during formal occasions. He was known as the Grim Reaper of Adem and was rarely seem by the average person more than once in a lifetime.

Howie was relieved to see the Grim Reaper had left his axe at home this evening.

Howie tilted his head down, bowing as best he could with

Lyseria's face pressed into his stomach.

'Your majesty,' he said.

King Theo inclined his head.

'I'm just returning the dragon,' Howie said carefully. 'She sort of… collided with our ship. My name is Howard Rosethorn. Sir.'

King Theo lifted an eyebrow.

'Howard Rosethorn,' he said, extending a hand.

Howie hesitated, unsure of whether to shake it or kiss it. He settled for a shake, which he seemed to approve of.

King Theo frowned slightly. Extending a hand gently, he laid a gentle touch under Howie's chin and guided his face this way and that.

'Extraordinary,' he said softly upon examination.

Quickly, he released him.

'Welcome!' he exclaimed, his voice suddenly booming. 'And thank you for returning Lyseria. You haven't seen my daughter on your travels, by any chance? The creature was waiting for her outside Arthur Stibbons' Groin, no doubt.'

Howie blinked. 'Beg pardon, your majesty?'

'Arthur Stibbons' Groin,' he repeated. 'The whorehouse on Arthur Stibbons' Street, called the Crook if I remember rightly. You know that road in Serpus in the shape of a man lying down?'

Oh, Keith's place, Howie thought with dread.

'I'm not familiar with it, I haven't visited Serpus before,' he lied strategically.

'Ah. You're better off, really. I'm sure you'll get to know the place, it's quite popular,' he said, 'particularly with my youngest child, strangely.'

He sighed and shook his head.

'Come! Let us take that beast off your hands and get you a drink. You could do with feeding, I imagine, after babysitting a dragon all day.'

A genuine smile crept over his face. Howie bowed, this time with feeling.

'She's a strange animal,' King Theo mused.

Lyseria launched herself over the high wall.

'Ordinarily, dragons are fairly indifferent of people, but she seems quite infatuated with you. She's the same with my son, actually. Must be the resemblance…'

Before Howie could reply, a ragged-looking old man jogged towards them and skidded to a halt. He snapped a badly aimed salute, nearly taking his own eye out.

He clapped a palm over his eye.

'Your majesty, there's an emergency in the courtyard.'

King Theo exhaled. 'That didn't take her long. Go on, who's the dragon flattened this time?'

'No, your majesty, it isn't her,' he said, still rubbing his eye. 'It's the prince, your majesty, he's had an accident.'

Theo Crey rolled his eyes towards Howie.

'I keep telling her to leave him get on with it, but she never listens,' he grumbled, as if Howie knew exactly what he was going on about.

King Theo turned to the old man with a look of annoyance.

'Go on, what's she done to him now?'

And the man told them…

~

II

A few minutes earlier…

Cienne stood in the courtyard of the castle, drinking in the silence while she still had the chance. Owls could be heard muttering in the trees above her and the night air felt damp against her skin. She stood facing the buddleia bushes impassively, due to the fact that the tailor had added three more petticoats to her ridiculous gown and now she couldn't move without pulling a muscle.

Portabella had a style unique to the noblewomen of the country – unique in that everyone else has the sense to wear clothes they can move around in. The idea was to remain as slim as possible and compensate their lack of weight with silk.

So much silk in Cienne's great-grandmother's case that it killed her, one fateful summer stroll as the weight of her dress caused her to drop twelve feet into a sinkhole and suffocate to death.

That was the extreme end of the scale, though Cienne felt her current attire wasn't much farther away. She brushed at the enormous skirts bursting out from the waist of her tight corset. It seemed to be a necessity. Men from Truphoria apparently found the style extremely attractive.

Most men, anyway.

She sighed heavily and shut her eyes to the sounds of crickets and owls and… footsteps.

Her eyes opened to meet those of her husband.

She blinked, startled.

'Are you alright?'

Seth froze, his eyes wide. 'What are you doing?'

Cienne lifted her eyebrows. 'Just getting some air.' She gestured at her corset. 'Quite hard to breathe in this unassisted, as you can imagine.' She tilted her head slightly. 'What are *you* doing?'

Seth stared deep into her eyes and lifted his shoulders. He furtively jerked his trousers *shut*.

'Just getting some air,' he repeated.

Cienne looked him up and down. She squinted at his trouser leg. 'What's that wet patch on your knee?'

Seth sucked in a breath, wide-eyed. His eyes flicked from the knee to Cienne and back again.

'Give me your hand,' he said instead.

'What? Why?'

'Just give me your hand,' he insisted, holding his palm out to her.

Cienne lifted her hand.

Seth grabbed it, pulling her along with haste.

'Where are we going?'

'Shed,' he said quickly.

'The shed? Why? What are we doing in there?'

'… something we should have done a long time ago.'

An image flashed in the back of Cienne's mind briefly.

She smiled faintly.

'Well, in that case,' she said, linking arms with him and walking much faster.

They arrived at the thatched shed in the corner of the courtyard.

Seth opened the door for her.

She shoved him inside ahead of her and shut the door behind her.

They stood face to face, grinning at each other.

'Uh, well,' Seth said, grinning a bit too widely.

'Well,' she echoed.

She took his hand in her own.

Seth gulped audibly, his gaze flicking helplessly around the room.

'What am I thinking?' she thought she saw him mouth, but quickly dismissed this as her imagination.

'Well?' she said softly, stroking his arm. 'What would you like me to do?'

He stared at her, stricken.

Before she knew it, Seth had pressed a shovel into Cienne's right hand.

The grin slid from her face. 'Um…'

'You dig the hole, and I'll get the coffin,' Seth said brightly, grinning again from ear to ear.

Her heart sank to her stomach. 'What?'

Seth laid a hand on each of her shoulders.

'Bury me. Today. I know you're not exactly wearing the correct mourning attire, but that doesn't matter!'

He circled her to open the door, joyous.

'I don't know why we waited so long!' he exclaimed at the world at large.

Cienne stared blankly at the back wall of the shed.

'We don't need a ceremony, or guests or anything! Just you, me and the hole, that's all I need!'

He swung back to observe her.

Cienne turned slowly, clenching the shovel in both hands. Her upper lip twitched.

'You're getting me to bury you?' she gritted through clenched teeth. 'Again? Do you think I'm an idiot?'

Seth lifted his eyebrows. 'Why? Are you?'

Cienne's mouth hung ajar. The blow was not a surprise, but it stung, nevertheless.

Seth lifted his tainted knee and, deliberately, wiped the moisture off with two fingers.

'How much longer,' Cienne said in a strangled voice, 'do I have to endure this charade? I saw Lilly spirit you away to that brothel. I know you don't care what I think about it, so why do you attempt to divert my attention from it?'

Seth toyed with the slick substance with his thumb and, demurely, sniffed it.

'You know I don't care about you,' he said, staring at her through heavy-lidded eyes. 'So why *do* we have to endure this charade?'

Cienne clenched her teeth shut, forcing back the tears.

'I love you,' she said.

Seth curled his upper lip, rubbing his thumb and fingers together in distaste.

'Whether you like it or not,' she went on, trembling. 'It is my duty.'

'To follow me about the castle grounds like a forlorn puppy taken too soon from the litter?'

He leaned in close, until they were nose to nose.

'Bury it,' he advised in a breezy tone. 'It's only hurting you.'

He coiled a section of her hair around his finger as he spoke and let it slip away.

Cienne exhaled, tremulous, through her nose.

'I'll bury it,' she said quietly. 'Of course I'll bury it. But I'll have to kill it first, won't I?'

Seth's brow furrowed slightly.

Cienne took a step back, hands twisting around the shovel.

'Because you're not actually dead, are you? You just *think* it! You think it on *purpose*, because what you *really* think is that we're all *stupid*, don't you?

'But we can change that, can't we? Just you, me and the hole, eh?'

She let out an abrasive giggle.

Seth stared blankly at her, his mouth ajar.

'I,' he said, 'may have taken this too far.'

The shovel *blurred*.

~

Tension coursed through the neurons of Howard Rosethorn three hours after King Theo had entered the palace keep. It appeared to be a permanent element of his mind at this point.

This wasn't helped by the sudden appearance of Keith, Stan and Ron.

'Why are you here?' hissed Howie in exasperation.

'Trust me, Howard, I'm looking after your future,' Keith assured him.

The trio jogged past, through the gaping portcullis.

Howie gaped after them and rolled his eyes. He turned fully from the inner portcullis and examined the perfectly kept flowerbeds and cultivated lawns. He briefly entertained the idea of following them inside, but quickly figured if a man's marital problems concerned a shovel, it was probably best for all parties if he stayed put.

Just as he thought this, the double doors opened behind him, bathing him in amber light.

A man in black stood inside.

'Howard is it?' he asked, extending a hand. 'I'm the butler. James de Vil, very nice to meet you.'

'I go by Howie. Mind if I call you Jimmy?' he asked jovially.

He grimaced. 'I'd rather you didn't.'

Howie stuck out his lower lip. 'Not even Jim?'

The butler ignored this and turned to the slowly opening

doors.

'His majesty requires your assistance inside, sir,' he said smoothly.

He gestured for Howie to enter.

Howie's eyes narrowed. 'Requires my assistance with what?'

~

'I assure you, the boy's a miracle worker!' Keith said in earnest. 'The prophesised Knight of Raining Thorns himself! Who better to heal your beloved son than the prodigal son of Salator Crey?'

'The child of Salator Crey?' Theo said dubiously.

'A Crey, anyway,' Stan said. 'That's a definite Crey-type profile if I ever saw one.'

Theo's eyebrow lifted. He mentally compared the youth outside to his first born again. They could almost be twins, bar the age difference. The hair and profile were the same – exactly the same. The only differences were minor alterations of the facial features and the fact that Howard's eyes weren't crossed like Seth's currently were.

'And you think he can revive him?'

'Better than that!' Keith said, grinning. 'He'll bring him to his senses. Make him stop thinking he's dead.'

King Theo swung around, making Keith flinch.

'You'd better not be lying, Keith Large, for I have been looking for an excuse to lob your head off for *years*.'

Keith looked offended.

'Lying? Moi?' he said, using a Portabellan word purposefully. 'Never. You wait until he gets here. *Absolute miracle* worker. You'll see.'

The king growled at him, turning away.

Stan nudged his uncle.

'I thought you said you were mates?' he hissed, shifting from foot to foot.

'I said we went way back.' Keith winced. 'Just not in a good way.'

Ron rolled his eyes.

The door to the throne room opened.

Howie entered, looking anxious.

'Is everything alright?'

'It will be!' Keith said in earnest. 'Once you've worked your magic on Prince, er, you know…'

'Seth!' hissed Stan.

'—Seth here,' Keith said seamlessly, 'everything will be fine. He's all yours!'

Howie blinked. 'All mine for what?'

'Reviving,' King Theo said. 'He claims you're a fully trained physician.'

'Keith, that's *Adrienne* that's the physician!' Howie all but screamed irately.

'Oh, I knew it was *one* of Archie's kids,' Keith said, flippant.

'Can you revive him?' King Theo asked.

Howie blew a sigh through pursed lips, his cheeks bulging.

'I suppose I could try,' he said doubtfully.

'That's my boy,' Keith grinned. 'Off you go!'

Howie gulped and knelt beside Prince Seth Crey.

The man was sprawled across the grass, the right side of his head swollen. The weapon lay a couple of yards away, stained with blood from a wound near the prince's hairline.

Focussing away from the wounds, Howie regarded his patient as a whole.

'We're like twins,' he said, puzzled.

King Theo cleared his throat.

The others followed suit.

Howie glanced around, at a loss. Simply on gut instinct, he slapped Seth across the left side of his head.

Keith, Stan and Ron flinched as one.

'He's gonna get us hanged!' whimpered Stan.

Seth blinked his eyes open and raised his head.

'Who're all of you?' he asked blearily.

His eyes met Howie's. The intensity of his stare gifted Howie with a shock of anxiety.

'Hello, gorgeous,' Seth said.

He leaned forward for a kiss.

Howie hit him again for self-preservation.

Seth collapsed back down with a grunt.

'What was the last one for?' Keith squeaked.

'Hush, man, the boy's at work,' snapped King Theo, fixated.

Seth slid onto his knees, grinning.

'Oh, playing hard to get, are we?'

He grunted.

The sides of Howie's fists had connected with his forehead.

'He's gone doo-lally,' observed King Theo. 'Hit him again, Howard!'

'Don't mind him, give me a kiss,' Seth coaxed.

'No,' Howie yelped, pressing his hands over Seth's face and squirming backward.

'Don't be a prude, come on, you'll like it—'

'No means NO!'

He forced Seth's face to turn to the side.

Stan and Ron began to back away from the carnage.

'Stay,' Keith ordered. He turned his attention to Howie. 'One more hit should do it!'

'How am I supposed to do that when he's—'

As if in response, the prince surged forward, trapping Howie between his elbows.

Seth tried to kiss Howie again.

A significant portion of tongue was already visible.

Howie suppressed a retch and thrust his knee upwards.

Seth's eyes bulged.

Howie shoved him off.

Seth rolled backwards until his head hit the discarded shovel. He flaked out across the gravel again, rubbing his eyes.

'Mummy,' he whined.

'Still doo-lally?' Keith asked in dread.

'No, this is what he's always like,' King Theo said with a sigh. 'Hitch him to his feet, we'd best take him inside. Well done, boy!'

He hoisted Howie to his feet by one hand and clapped the other on the back of his neck.

'You could be an excellent asset to the palace! There's always someone here needs a good slap now and again. Good job!'

Howie grinned, relief and utter bewilderment turning his knees to water.

Privately, he thought: *what the* fuck *just happened??*

Stan and Ron took an arm each and hefted Seth to his feet.

Music drifted into Howie's consciousness as faintly as mist. He spotted the players in a gallery high above the dining table as the king sank into a throne at the head of it, facing the double doors to the courtyard.

The minstrels played louder at a wave of King Theo's arm.

It was the gentle sound of stringed instruments that formed the backdrop to Seth's whimpering.

'I want my mother, let me go,' he said feebly.

He shrugged from Stan's grasp and fell onto the flagstones.

'She tried to kill me, you're all trying to kill me, I want my *mother*!!'

King Theo rubbed his eyes.

Two women entered the room from opposite ends.

A lady in, by Howie's estimations, her early fifties skittered down the spiral staircase to their right, her greying hair and blue skirts billowing. She skidded to a halt beside Seth, cradling his head, like a new-born.

The second, a girl of perhaps Howie's age, loitered by the courtyard entrance, dressed in worn leathers and looking rather guilty.

'Mum,' Seth wept, burying his face in his mother's shoulder, 'she hit me, my head's bleeding…'

'I know, lovey, I know,' she crooned, stroking his hair.

'… she told me she was going to kill me, she—'

He gasped loudly, the sound catching in his throat with a gurgle.

'She killed me for *real*.'

King Theo rolled his eyes again.

'Oh dear, never mind,' the lady trilled, giving Seth a squeeze. 'Will we get you a cream cake to make it all better?'

Seth sniffled. 'Yes.'

The queen helped Stan half-lead, half-drag Seth to the stairs.

The butler waited for the door to click shut behind them before giving it an odd glance.

'He's thirty-three, you say?'

King Theo threw his eyes to the ceiling in response.

Howie sank into a cushioned chair and took in his surroundings.

The room was filled with carvings of snakes. Over each arch and on each door, marble snakes curled around the edge to meet in an open-mouthed attack, their jaws propping a single torch between them. The chairs were a similar fashion, the snakes coiled on the back of the chairs and legs consisting of mahogany vipers entwined together in a savage embrace.

The biggest motif of all was on the double doors in front of them: two snakes, one encrusted with emeralds an inch wide, one fashioned out of pure gold, tied in an intricate, complex knot, each snake's head swallowing its companion's tail.

At the moment the image was split vertically in half. The girl hovered in front of the gap, looking sheepish.

Howie faced King Theo to find irritation glance past him to the girl.

'Lilly,' said King Theo in dark tones.

Lilly looked at him with startlingly wide eyes.

'Hi, Daddy,' she said in a high voice. She grinned at him, albeit falteringly. 'Everything alright?'

King Theo's eyes thinned.

'Where were you all day leaving the dragon to get bored and wander into a trading ship bound for Breaker's Hold?'

His voice, though not raised, boomed across the hall.

'Er, round town,' she said, not daring to break eye contact. 'And the dragon's called Lyseria.'

'I'm aware of that, I had a collar made at great expense, lest you forget,' King Theo snapped, 'which would have been for nothing had she not been returned by this gentleman!'

'Sorry,' she mumbled.

'You will be,' he said, leaning back, 'now that you are barred from your little daytrips to Arthur Stibbons' Arse Crack.'

'Eh?' Lilly whined in dismay.

'Don't think I don't see you sneaking your brother to the knocking shop when Cienne isn't looking!' he barked. 'I won't have you keeping *this cad*,' he jerked a thumb at Keith, 'in luxury when the boy has a perfectly good specimen of his own at home for free!'

'Man has to make a living,' Keith muttered.

Howie slammed a heel into Keith's foot.

'Speaking of whom, go and find Cienne in the council chamber and sit with her until she calms down. And do not *on pain of death*,' he emphasised, 'mention Seth or a spade.'

'Okay,' Lilly said, retreating out of the door.

She threw Howie an odd glance in passing.

He returned it in earnest. *That's a princess*, he thought in astonishment. By the way her vowels curled and the letter 'H' vanished in her dialect, he almost took her for a stable sweep.

An auburn-haired girl laden with a tray of beverages offered him a cup of beer.

Howie lifted one off the tray with a grateful smile.

The king knitted his fingers together and rested them on his stomach, reclining to observe Howie.

'He fakes it, you know,' he said idly.

Howie lifted his gaze. 'He's faking his Great Illness?'

'Oh, yes,' he said. 'It was his little trick as a child, feigning illness. By his account, he'd suffered everything from the common cold to the flux before he was ten. He was better at acting when he was a boy, but now he's cocky. See how his eyes gleamed when he told my wife he was "dead for real"?'

Howie had spotted it immediately. It was the gleam Keith's eyes had throughout the whole fiasco a moment ago. The gleam of a brilliant idea coming into being.

'I noticed,' said Howie.

King Theo grunted a laugh, shaking his head.

'His mother believes him, of course,' he said. He assumed a shrill impression of the queen, '"He wouldn't turn down a nice cream cake if he wasn't seriously ill", *yes*,' he returned to his deep tones, 'but the platter doesn't vanish from the counter of its own accord, does it?'

James de Vil snorted by the door, where he had stood since escorting Howie into the keep.

'If it did, it wouldn't break all the crockery on the way out.'

'Just so,' Theo agreed.

He frowned at Keith, who snatched a goblet from the maid thirstily.

It almost seemed to Howie that the king had telekinetically forced him to place it back on the tray.

Keith proffered a broad grin.

It withered as King Theo snapped, 'Why are you still here?'

'Just waiting on my nephew,' he said mildly. 'A halfwit, you understand, gets lost crossing the road, sort of thing.'

King Theo spotted the wistful glances Keith was shooting at the tray of drinks.

'Must run in the family,' he said nastily. 'He's at least Lilly's age. I'm sure he doesn't need his hand holding. You may leave at your pleasure.'

'As you wish, your majesty.'

He bowed deeply. Then he waved frantically at Ron and Howie.

'Come on then!' he hissed at them.

'No,' King Theo cut in, 'Prince Ronald will stay with us, and his manservant too. It's only fair that I accommodate these high-standing figures of society after such an arduous journey.'

Keith blinked.

'*That's* Ronald Horne?' he asked, bemused.

King Theo rolled his eyes. 'Your highness will wish for the nephew to stay as an extra servant?'

'You mean Stan…ley?' Ron asked. 'Yes, that would be best, yes.'

His gaze flitted to a hurt-looking Keith.

'There, he'll be perfectly looked-after. Safe journey!'

King Theo blithely waved him away.

'Yes, your majesty. Goodnight, your majesty—majesties,' he corrected.

He bowed and retreated out. Repeatedly.

King Theo gave the doors a withering glance as they slammed

behind him.

'Imbecile.'

'How did you know who I was?' Ron asked before he could stop himself. 'We've never met before.'

'That was a bluff to get rid of him,' he admitted.

The maid placed a goblet of wine into Ron's hand, unasked.

'In truth, any excuse would have gotten rid of that idiot, but I wanted you lot to stick around. I've been trying to get your father to wed you to my daughter, you see.'

'I see,' Ron said in a gravelly voice, peering uneasily into his cup.

'But what I really wanted rid of him for,' he said to Howie, 'was to ask you if you were aware that he's telling everyone about you being this "Knight of Raining Thorns"?'

'He's talking rubbish, your majesty,' Howie said in a pained voice.

King Theo laughed aloud. 'Indubitably!'

He took a goblet from the maid and gulped it down.

'I take it you're a follower of the Seven, is it?'

Howie thought back to his first day with Archie, when he asked if he'd have to go to church.

'You're too pretty to go to church,' Archie had said, aghast. 'The old bastards'd ruin you!'

Howie hadn't known what he meant by that and, eight years later, he didn't really want to.

'I was actually brought up to avoid religion in general, your majesty.'

King Theo chortled. 'You're better off than all of us, then. The Seven aren't even gods, anyway – they're just tricksters: powerful, no doubt about that, but no more than any cottage mage you'd find about the place. I once knew an extraordinary woman,' he added, 'who was a close friend of theirs and visited them as often as you'd visit your mother!'

'Really?' Ron asked in interest. 'Who is she?'

King Theo paused, almost sorrowfully.

'An old friend,' he said after a pause. 'A very old friend indeed.'

'Hmm,' Howie said, for want of a better response.

He eyed Ron from the corner of his eye.

Ron was sweating profusely, staring deep into his goblet.

'I assume you were pushed in our direction by one of their priests?' King Theo went on.

'That and my brother,' Ron said from the cup. 'He doesn't like us too much.'

'He… doesn't have much confidence in our quest to find King Samuel,' Howie corrected, trying to avoid the phrase 'escaped convict' as much as possible.

'Well, that is yet to be seen.'

Ron hid behind his cup and drained it, clicking his fingers for another before the last drop hit the back of his throat.

'But recent events seem to be in your favour,' King Theo said. 'They told you about the Antichrist, I imagine?'

'They… mentioned it,' Howie said. 'But the holy flying cat overshadowed the run-down on the quest, so…'

'Holy flying cat?' King Theo barked a laugh. 'They don't do things by half, do they?'

'They never said who he was, though,' Howie said.

'They seldom do. They like the theatrics of sending a teenager out to suss the details for them.' King Theo pulled a small scroll from his pocket. 'A trespasser into the Forest gave me this shortly before his execution.'

He handed Howie the missive.

He opened it and stared blankly at the words.

'What's the dragon got to do with it?'

'The dragon, I'm told,' King Theo said, 'is the demonic servant to the Antichrist.'

Howie looked at him.

King Theo simply grinned in response.

Howie delicately placed the note on the table. 'I resign.'

King Theo roared with laughter.

'Wise,' he said with a cackle. 'I'd take this prophecy lark with a pinch of salt, my boy. But by all means, use it to your advantage. King Sam will be more likely to follow the fourth Christ back to his castle rather than an *escaped convict* of his son's.'

He winked.

Pins and needles shot up Howie's spine. 'You won't send us back, will you?'

'So Prince Vladdy can kill you? Good God, no,' King Theo said, shaking his head. 'I have plans for you, my boy. *Big* plans.'

Howie frowned, confused.

Heels clicked on the staircase.

Seth's mother emerged, looking bedraggled.

'Is there a guard free?' she said breathlessly. 'I can't get Seth to settle, and he needs to eat.'

The maid headed for the queen. Howie saw her hand waving

for him to follow.

'Um,' he said, rising. 'I can help. If that's alright?'

'Go ahead, you can hardly do worse for him, can you?' King Theo said. 'Return when you're finished, least you deserve is a good meal before bed.'

Howie smiled honestly at the word 'meal'.

'Thank you, your majesty,' he said.

He followed the queen and her maid to the stairs.

Upon the slam of the door behind them, Ron grabbed every full goblet of wine within orbit and cradled them in both arms.

The king raised an eyebrow. 'Thirsty, are you?'

Ron nodded between cups.

King Theo blinked and simply shrugged. He held his own cup closer, just in case.

~

III

A day in the realm consists of three turns of a seven-hour clock, each turn representing daybreak, midday and nightfall. Stan was starting to think it was the wrong turn of the clock as he sat on the edge of the bed, cradling a bloody nose.

Prince Seth lay on his side on the duck-down quilt, shaking.

'I had the most horrible dream,' he whispered. 'I was being beaten to death by an imposter. And my father was there, cheering him on...'

His eyes widened.

'And you were there!' he breathed, pointing at Stan.

All things considered, Stan's night could have been a lot worse. At least Ron seemed normal enough. Stan didn't think he could have stood watching Ronald Horne have a public nervous breakdown.

A figure hovering in the corridor caught Stan's attention. He blinked fatigue from his eyes.

A woman's voice spoke gently from behind the door, which hung ajar.

'Your majesty, why don't you let us help the prince? I'm sure his majesty the king would like to see you.'

The queen – Eleanor, if Stan recalled correctly – sighed, presumably from behind her.

'If you say so,' Eleanor said. 'Call me if he asks for me, won't you?'

'Of course, your majesty,' said the maid, presumably.

Stan watched the figure's head bob up and down in a curtsy.

Footsteps padded down the corridor and dwindled as the figure – a young woman in her twenties – entered, followed by Howie. The maid pushed back her long reddish-brown hair to tie it back with a black ribbon as she approached Seth.

'Good evening, your highness,' she said softly, perching on the bed. 'Are you ready for something to eat?'

'No,' he said sullenly. 'Go away.'

She shrugged. 'Have it your way,' she said, rising to leave. 'I'll just inform Princess Cienne that her husband isn't eating *again*...'

'No, don't do that,' he whimpered.

'Are you going to sit up, then?'

'Mm-hmm.'

Seth dragged himself upright.

'That's better. I'll fetch your food and something to sort out that gash to your head.'

She peered at his temple, which still glistened.

'She had a right go at you with that, didn't she?'

Seth scowled at her sullenly.

The maid smiled faintly, brushing a hand over his shoulder.

She rose to leave, waving for Howie to follow.

The door slammed in front of poor Stan as he was about to leave, muffling an annoyed grunt.

'So what brings Mister Rosethorn to Adem of all places?'

Howie paused.

'I honestly have no idea,' he said.

The maid quirked a half-smile. 'People have been talking about you. I'm told you're the prodigal son of Salator Crey himself.'

'I dunno about that,' Howie said. 'But I'm guessing you didn't bring me up here for an introduction.'

'You're right,' she said.

She strode to the stairs, Howie in tow.

'That ship you were on may have had a man aboard by the name of Silas Beult. Do you know what became of him?'

Howie remembered him. One half of the infamous comedic duo, the Beult brothers.

'Honestly... no.'

'Hmm. Well, if you see him, let me know. My name's Anna, by the way,' she added as they reached the bottom step. 'Anna Beult.'

'A sister?' Now that he thought about it, she had a striking resemblance to Tully.

'Not technically,' she said. 'I married him.'

'Oh,' said Howie with a laugh. 'That didn't occur to me.'

'You thought I was available?' she teased.

What he actually thought of was the whore Silas Beult had spent the past week interfering with both above and below decks, but Howie wasn't about to tell *her* that.

'No, nothing like that,' he said with a smile. 'I don't do married women.'

'Don't knock it 'til you try it.'

She smirked at him and pushed open a door. Clouds of steam billowed out.

'I think I'll let you bring Lady Muck her dinner. She doesn't like peasants, but I think a prodigal son trumps us in that category.'

They stepped into the kitchens.

Granite flagstones and marble worktops surrounded them. Anna set the princess's dinner tray as Howie stood by the counter, taking everything in. Savoury food of every description was being pulled from spits and ovens: veal, poultry, boar, beef, bread, soup, pies.

Howie's stomach roared. He'd be eating some of that later, he realised. He would be sitting in front of all that food, beside the *king of Adem*. It made a night in with Archie's famous pork mush smell like poverty.

Incidentally, he wondered where all the leftovers went. He had an image of the dragon curled up at the foot of the table, having spare ribs thrown at her.

He inhaled wistfully and made a beeline for the tray once Anna had finished.

Leaving the kitchens behind him, he climbed the staircase with care, cradling the tray of bread, pork and soup in both elbows and sliding along the curved wall to prevent tipping over.

He followed Anna's directions to the third floor and counted three doors to his left. He knocked lightly and waited a moment before entering.

'Hello?' he said softly.

The princess's quarters were larger than the entire Hart home by itself. Howie stood in the drawing room as faint rustling sounded from a door standing ajar to his left. The place was very… curtain-y, he thought. Lots of peach silk surrounded him.

He edged to a small dining table in the centre, placing it on top before leaving.

He was halted by a voice hoarse from crying.

'Take it in here, please.'

Howie picked up the tray and took a left. He circled the huge four-poster and placed it on a bedside cabinet. He turned to the soft shuffling of silk sheets and halted in a daze.

Pale blond ringlets gathered haphazardly around a startlingly beautiful face. Princess Cienne sat up to face Howie, her slim form dressed in a shimmering nightgown. Her delicate features were set in a mournful droop – until she caught Howie's eye.

A white fog overcame him.

'Who are you?' she asked, staring at him.

Howie licked his lips. 'H-Howie.' He bowed his head.

'Why are you here?'

Howie gulped. And gulped again. His chest felt tight. What the hell was wrong with him?

'Brought you dinner,' he managed, gesturing.

Cienne shifted herself onto one elbow.

'How did you get to be in the castle?'

Howie blinked repeatedly.

'I… found the dragon,' he said. 'Brought me here… crashed into the, the boat, and…' Inspiration struck. 'Gonna fix Seth.'

Cienne blinked. 'Fix him?'

'Um…' He had the distinct feeling of floundering down a hole of his own creation, but he struggled on. 'Make him better, I mean. Make him… think… normal.'

His good intentions must have shown through. Thankfully, she smiled.

'That's very sweet of you,' she said.

Red heat swept up his neck and over his face. 'Thank you.' He began to back away.

'Will you join me?'

The pins and needles returned. 'Sorry?'

'I won't be able to eat all of this alone,' she said, gesturing to the tray. 'Come.'

She patted the bed in front of her.

Howie's mouth went dry.

Cienne watched him swallow ineffectively and handed him her drink.

He took a long swallow.

And coughed it back into the cup again.

His throat burned.

'It… there's whiskey in it.'

Cienne snorted and laughed.

'Anna,' she said fondly. 'She does this whenever I've had a bad day.'

Howie coughed again, his eyes watering.

Cienne pushed the bowl of soup towards him gently.

They sat in silence for a moment while he ate. She didn't appear to eat anything, he noticed. She held a slice of bread in her hands and picked it apart, more interested in mangling it rather than consuming it.

'Are you a relative of Seth's?' she asked.

Howie swallowed. 'I don't know. Maybe. I might be. I never knew my parents, so...'

She stared at him with wide eyes. 'Oh.'

His gaze flickered from her to the food and back again, unsure how to deal with the intense staring. He tried to think of something to say, but his mind had stopped working. All that seemed to register was the thought: *I wouldn't mind being hit by* her *with a spade...*

'What's it like being a princess?' he said instead.

Cienne smiled at him. 'Terrible.'

Howie smiled at her. He thought he saw a glow about her face at the sight of his smile, but quickly dismissed it as his imagination.

'Your entire existence,' she went on, 'revolves around begetting heirs for an insipid moron who hates you so much, he'll fake a mental illness in order to keep you away from him.' The melancholy look fell back over her face, erasing every hint of a smile.

'His loss,' Howie said. 'I think you're wonderful.'

He froze.

'That was way too forward, I'm really sorry,' he said quickly, ducking his head.

'No.'

She pinched his chin between her fingers and lifted it until their eyes met.

'Never be ashamed of what you think,' she said. 'Especially when you think such lovely things about people.'

His heart hammered rapidly, stuttering with every second beat. Howie looked at her face, too youthful for a woman in her thirties and with a paleness that suggested too much time spent indoors. He considered kissing her.

The image of King Theo with an axe quickly expelled that thought.

Cienne said nothing. She just gazed at him with blue eyes that were almost as pale as her hair.

A little voice deep inside niggled at him, the voice of a teenage boy just before his voice breaks. *Go on, she likes you... go for it...*

Logic retorted in the voice of Archie.

Don't even think about it! She's the savage king's daughter-in-law!

Teenage idealism brought pictures. Interesting pictures.

So did Logic. His concerned blood. Lots of it.

Logic won with flying colours.

'I have to go,' Howie said aloud, rising to his feet.

He gently placed the half-empty bowl of soup in her lap.

'The king's expecting me,' he explained.

'Of course,' she said with a faint smile. 'I look forward to meeting again. This was nice.'

'Yeah, it was.' He paused. 'Your highness,' he amended, bowing.

She held out a hand, palm-down.

He took it in his left hand and kissed it firmly. Then he left, red-faced.

Cienne examined her hand intently, deep in thought.

Left-handed, just like Seth, she thought. *Interesting.*

~

On the church door in the capital of Stoneguard, a large plank of timber was nailed over the arms of the iron cross emblazoned on its surface. It read 'closed'.

A middle-aged woman in a headscarf approached the door and pushed it to clarify that it was, in fact, closed. After some murmurings of confusion, the crowd outside the church door grew, then dwindled as the worshippers headed for the next best thing to religion: a pint in the neighbouring tavern, the Jolly Rotter.

One group chose to linger outside.

Each shrouded in a black hood, the four men snuck to the side of the church. They ensured that nobody was watching and, after much deliberation, kicked in the basement window.

To their alarm, a head poked its way out through the shards. 'Evening.'

They shrieked.

'No need to be alarmed, only the order here,' the head said jovially. 'Now tell me: you wouldn't need any criminal activity performed for you this fine evening, would you?'

The apparent ringleader frowned. 'Criminal what?'

'Activity,' the priest replied. 'Theft, murder, sort of thing.'

'Well, we were looking to have something of yours, as it happens,' said a man of the dimly opportunistic persuasion.

'Shush!' snapped the ringleader.

'For a reasonable price, I could save you a lot of bother and simply steal *someone else's* artefacts for you.'

The brow of the ringleader once again furrowed.

'You mean instead of us stealing yours for free, we pay you for someone else's tat?'

'Well, my terminology sounds a lot more reasonable.'

'Hmm, good point,' the ringleader said wryly. 'Let me just confer with my associates…'

After much crashing, smashing and the shriek of a passing stray cat, Father Toffer sat dejectedly under the basement window, now a lot poorer than he was five minutes previously.

'That didn't seem to work,' murmured a monk in the shadows.

'Hmm,' Father Toffer grunted. 'I think we'll limit ourselves to assassination, then. Might prove to be an effective stress-reliever.'

~

Seth's surroundings consisted of lots of green, the smell of outdoors and a wretched howling loudly in the distance. No, not the distance, he decided after brief observation. Quiet. And close, in all directions.

A normal man would simply have described this as a forest, but Seth was more observant than that. His method acting proclaimed that ghosts were hyper-aware of their surroundings, and far more appreciative of it thanks to the ironic contrast of death and its view into the attributes of life he was now missing out on. That and there was bugger all else to do.

Rustling interrupted Seth's appreciation of his surroundings. He swung around. There was nothing he hadn't already observed for the past hour.

Something like suspicion niggled at him, but it couldn't be actual suspicion because that was an instinct and ghosts have no instincts, his method acting reminded him, except for perhaps the sudden urge to shout 'BOO!!' in dark corridors.

In death there was no suspicion, his method acting reminded him. Just memories. And senses. And other-worldly thoughts, he'd just decided.

There it was again. That unidentified rustling.

He kicked himself away from the tree behind him and slowly approached the sound.

He grossly misjudged its direction.

As was evident by the strong arms wrapped around his elbows from behind.

'Oh, what now?' Seth exclaimed, squirming.

'Keep wriggling and we'll be gone before you can say reincarnation,' a voice hissed in his ear.

'And that's a bad thing, is it?'

'Shush!'

Seth was swung in the opposite direction and marched off.

Fear was not something his method acting got along well with. The sensation of cold steel being pressed between his lungs had evidently won their latest dispute.

He was flung unceremoniously into the rushes.

He held his hands up in defeat.

'Okay, alright,' he said shakily. 'I know what you want. Just get it over with.'

Seth rolled onto his hands and knees.

'Hurry up, you know how it goes.'

'What?' Howie squeaked. 'No! Get up!'

For the sake of his mental health, Archie picked Seth up by the scruff of his neck and hauled him to his feet.

He looked around to certify that there was no one around the woods behind the keep but Seth, his eyes squeezed shut, Howie, looking worried as usual, himself and Ron, whose expression indicated poor post-alcohol temperament, i.e., a bloody rotten hangover.

The whole farce was Keith's idea, but to nobody's surprise, he vanished the day the plot was to be executed. Howie was relieved. Hopefully, he would be gone for good.

'Who sent you?' Seth barked. He wriggled out of Archie's grasp. 'It was my father, wasn't it? I knew he tried to have me killed, now he's sent you to finish me off!'

'I thought you were already dead?' Archie said testily.

Seth froze.

The trio exchanged knowing side-glances.

'How much is your silence worth?' Seth relented.

'It *is* an act, then,' said Howie.

'Look,' said Seth, 'if your missus hit *you* with a shovel and tried to rape you every other night, *you'd* pretend to be dead as well. I'm not the one in the wrong here!'

'Think you could pretend to be *not* dead for us?' Archie said.

'Why should I do you any favours?'

'So we don't have to do this dodgy ritual Keith gave us?' said Archie, holding up a sheet of paper folded into quarters.

Seth gave it a withering glance and cleared his throat.

'You may perform any ritual you wish,' he intoned, 'for I am an otherworldly apparition and hold the knowledge that—'

'Fine, please yourself,' Archie cut in, opening the page.

Seth gave him a sideways glance, regarding him with a slight frown of confusion. 'What are you planning on doing?'

'Um…' Archie straightened the page. 'We have to…'

He squinted.

'"Find a squirrel, chant the special chant wot is writ here and send the dead soul to the body from oblivion",' he read in a deliberate monotone.

Seth's eyes narrowed.

'A squirrel,' he mouthed, frowning.

'A squirrel?' Howie echoed, perplexed. 'Did you read that right?'

He snatched the sheet and frowned at it.

Glancing over his shoulder, Ron read it and grabbed it to press closer to his face.

'A…' Seth said slowly, blinking and lifting his eyebrows, '…squirrel.'

'Yep,' Ron gritted through clenched teeth.

He flung the sheet into Archie's hands.

'"Because of the prince's soul climbing the tree of purpose, style of *fing*",' read Archie in disdain.

He let the sheet flutter to the ground.

'If he'd wiped his own faeces onto the page, it would have produced a better ritual than this.'

'This is starting to look incredibly silly,' Seth commented. 'Why don't you go off and find a real ritual? If I'm going to rise from the dead, I want it to look a bit authentic.'

'Can't you just pretend we did it?' asked Ron. 'You tell your father that, I dunno, a bolt of lightning fell from the sky and hit you in the face or summink, and then we can get down to finding my father and dropping the charges on Howie—'

Howie cleared his throat noisily.

'Oh, he's a criminal, is he?' Seth said with relish, grinning.

His teeth, Howie spotted, were prominently crooked at the canines. Howie ran a tongue over his overbite, pleased to note that at least his were straight.

'Too bad I can't help you,' Seth crooned. 'Have a nice execution, I hear Vladdy's ones are always fun.'

'I don't like you,' said Howie in dark tones.

'I don't like you either,' Seth said airily. 'Luckily for you, my father seems to. For the moment. Enjoy it while it lasts before he finds out about your criminal record.'

'I wanna hit him again,' said Howie with venom.

Seth tutted. 'I think your reputation's been soiled enough, sunshine—'

Archie punched Seth in the back of the head.

'*My* reputation can handle it,' he sneered. 'Now lie down and be quiet before I sully it again.'

Seth winced, rubbing his head.

'Right,' Archie said as Seth lay flat on his back. 'Now let's do something in case one of the king's mates comes along. I feel like there are eyes on the back of my head.'

'Do what, exactly?' Howie asked in annoyance.

'I dunno, you think of something! You're the Knight of Wotsit.'

'So?' Howie shrieked. 'What am I supposed to do, *magic* him normal?'

'You could *try*,' Archie said in disdain.

'I know some magic,' said Ron.

Archie snorted. 'You know a magic spell that can make this bastard act like a normal person?'

'Less of the "bastard" or I'll put you in the Tower,' Seth said.

'Dunno. I've heard Vladdy chant it a few times.'

Archie flailed his arms into the air.

'How do you get away with calling that man Vladdy?' he exclaimed. 'He chants heathen prayers and throws a fit at the drop of a hat and you call him *Vladdy*?'

'Just start chanting,' Howie said dully. 'And it had better be a good one. If we accidentally kill Seth Crey, I want it to be entertaining.'

Seth flicked an obscene hand gesture in his direction.

'Alright.' Ron coughed. 'Er… it's a bit difficult to pronounce, though…'

'I think we'll be fine,' Seth said wryly from flat on his back.

'Right… okay, here goes.'

Ron cleared his throat and began.

Difficult to pronounce was an understatement. The words were throaty and blustery in places, sounding like a dragon struggling to flame. Howie was wondering what kind of language this was when Ron finished, the last word fading.

A pause lingered.

The wind began to pick up, sending rushes hitting Seth across the face from beside him. It whistled in the trees, blowing leaves straight off the branches to rest on Prince Seth…

And then it stopped.

After a pause, Archie said, 'Does this a lot, does he?'

Then the lightning struck.

The bolt hit Seth full in the face, making his eyes bulge and his lungs heave.

He started to twitch and gasp loudly as tendrils of pure white light curled around his body, enveloping him.

All this occurred in a second. The next it was gone, leaving Seth motionless in its wake.

Howie craned his neck forward from a few paces away.

Soot covered Seth's face, which smoked slightly but was otherwise, incredibly, intact.

'Ron,' said Howie slowly. 'How many times have you heard your brother chant that?'

Ron paused. 'Nightly for the past twenty years?'

'You'd tell us if something like that had happened before, wouldn't you?' asked Archie, trembling.

'Well, yes,' he said, rolling his eyes. He peered at Seth. 'Is he alive?'

'Yes.'

The three of them started, shuffling backwards.

Seth blinked up at the morning sky. He sat up with a wince, rubbing his charcoal-covered face and the back of his neck. He glanced at the trio, his legs folded beneath him.

'None of you have anything to eat, have you?' he asked. 'I'm starving.'

Howie glanced at Ron. Who glanced back. Then they both looked at Archie.

Archie stuck out his lower lip and, simply, shrugged.

Howie and Ron followed suit.

Until Seth stuck both hands into his trousers.

They stared at him.

He rummaged with an expression of horror.

'You alright?' asked Howie.

'These were never like that before,' said Seth in a frightened whisper. 'Where did all this hair come from?'

The three exchanged glances.

Archie lifted a finger, signalling to wait. He approached Seth and bent double, leaning on his knees. He licked his lips.

'Seth?'

Seth met his gaze, wide-eyed.

'How old are you?'

'Thirteen,' he said.

Archie swallowed.

'As in one,' he held up an index finger, 'and then three?' he concluded, displaying the relevant digits.

'Well, yes,' Seth squeaked.

Archie craned his neck towards the others. 'This isn't good.'

Howie winced.

Ron rubbed his back.

'They won't kill you immediately, Howie,' he crooned.

'We've *broken* him,' Howie exclaimed, covering his face with both hands.

''S alright, I have an idea,' Archie said.

He turned back to Seth, who gazed up at him, childlike.

'Seth,' said Archie gently, 'do you remember the assassination?'

Seth nodded, whimpering. 'Did I die?'

Archie flung a thumbs-up and a *wink* at Howie and Ron before proceeding.

'You didn't die,' he planted a hand on Seth's shoulder, '… but you *thought* you did.'

Seth frowned at him, then at Howie and Ron.

They nodded eagerly.

Archie leaned one palm on his knee.

'You've been very ill…'

~

IV

Seth coughed through a mouthful of venison.

'… and suddenly, from the blue, a bolt of lightning shot down from the sky to hit Seth in the face, yes, but HOLD! He did not die but rose with a great cry: BRING MY DINNER THIS INSTANT!'

The guests roared with laughter, cutlery banging on the table.

'And so he was brought here, and WAS HE NOT FED WELL?!'

King Theo clapped a triumphant hand on Seth's back.

Seth choked and spluttered.

'CAREFUL, BOY!! Don't want you to croak it again, EH?'

The lords bellowed, laughing again.

Seth tried to laugh along and ceased after he nearly gagged.

Howie sat quietly two seats away from Seth at what was undisputedly the world's longest dinner table. At a table spanning the length of the dining hall, over a dozen lords and their wives sat around them, barely half-filling the table, with the king at the head of it, Queen

Eleanor at his right and Seth at his left.

His daughter was nowhere to be seen. 'Probably sulking,' were the king's words, though Howie suspected 'throwing a sharp weapon at something king-shaped' was a more accurate term. She had taken the brothel ban rather badly for someone with the right to execute anyone rejecting her advances.

But at the moment, he wasn't too concerned with any of that.

Seated between him and Prince Seth, dressed in finery worth the cost of the entire Stonekeep, was Cienne Fleurelle, picking politely at her food and wincing at the king's bawdy jokes. Her gaze flitted to Seth occasionally, who returned it with a small salute and the uncomfortable expression one has with someone they want to avoid.

This angered Howie. He would show him, one day.

He'd show Cienne too, show her a real gentleman, whisk her away to somewhere romantic, show her sunsets, write her poetry once he'd grasped the fundamentals of spelling, write a *book* about her, once he'd grasped spelling, about how lovely she was and ram it down Seth's throat, with the king's permission. That's it. That's what he'd do.

And after he'd taken her into the sunset, he added internally, he'd ask her to get rid of that *awful* perfume before he started hallucinating. Yes. That's what he'd do. He had it *planned*.

So had Seth, after slowing down on the eating so the food actually *reached* his stomach. He'd lost twenty years of his life – and he had a lot to do.

First, he'd learn how to train his dragon so she didn't crash into him again like she had that morning, nearly killing him in the process. If Howard Woss-His-Face could do it, so could he.

Then he was having a chat with Lilly-Anna about her staring problem. She always had been a strange kid. He wouldn't be wholly surprised if she fancied him, to be judged by the way she was drooling at the moment.

Speaking of women, he wondered where his wife was. He'd heard she was a goddess, or so Howie said with the dreamy gaze that indicated love was in the air and self-preservation was in the chamber pot. Seth would enjoy his marriage, if only to see the look of anguish on Rose-Prick's face.

And lastly, he would have all ravens killed. That was important.

He was vaguely aware of the doors slamming as he returned to daydreaming about this glorious wife of his. Just as Rose-Prick entered a mental rendering of Seth's bedchamber at the opportune moment, his fantasising was cut short by two wiry arms strangling him from behind.

'Seth!' shrieked a piercing voice, apparently in delight. 'Are you back to normal, then?'

The unknown beholder of affection squeezed him tighter, blocking his airways.

'Who... you...' he rasped.

'Your sister, duh!' she said, rubbing his head. 'Had your memory blown out or something?'

He frowned.

Another sister? He wracked his brains, trying to remember. The girl's pungent odour of horse manure wasn't helping.

Except that it was as clarity washed over him.

'Lilly!' he exclaimed, turning to face her. 'I knew that smell was familiar!'

'Ha, ha, funny as ever,' she sneered, strangle-hugging him again.

Seth grinned broadly and swung her back and forth. Despite the body odour, he was fond of her. She was like a little brother to him.

He blinked and turned to whom he had mistaken for Lilly. His daydreams suddenly had a face.

'Ah,' he breathed, smiling faintly.

Cienne caught his expression and beamed at him.

'Ain't she pretty?' said Lilly, an arm draped around his neck.

'Definitely,' said Seth, transfixed.

Cienne grinned and returned to moving her dinner aimlessly around her plate with a smirk.

Seth continued to stare at her as Lilly moved along the table. Something bothered him about her, something important. He shook this off with a shrug. He doubted it would bother him for long. She was damn attractive.

He turned back to the feast, throwing an idle glance at a scar on his right palm.

Realisation bloomed. He looked at Cienne, then back at the scar, then at Cienne again... and a twelve-year-old girl smothered him in a torturous embrace and the raven was at the window, pecking incessantly, and the killer, he was there too...

'Eek,' Seth whimpered.

Theo thumped his tankard on the table loudly, signalling for silence.

'Call the messenger! I want people called for, tournaments organised, parades, feasts, celebrations for all!' he bellowed. 'My son, the next king, has returned, and he shall be welcomed! Send for all the major families and tell them the festivities begin on the third week of summer! Send for them all…'

His eyes narrowed.

'Except for *her*,' he said, his voice dark. 'She stays where she is.'

'Who?' asked Seth.

'Third week of summer!' Queen Eleanor changed the subject. 'What a wonderful idea! The Night of Raining Thorns, no less! Howard's birthday!'

'Yay,' Lilly trilled happily, 'a double party! Double the drink and double the whore—food,' she amended at her father's glare.

'I was also killed that day if you'll recall,' Seth said sourly.

'You're better now, that cancels it out,' said Lilly. 'Only you do look a bit green. You alright?'

'Not really,' he winced.

History was making him ill, rushing into the present like a child into a sweet shop and bringing that sickening kiss along with it…

And the assassination, the raven at his window, the numbness of whatever drug had knocked him unconscious, the knife at his hand and the blood dripping to the floor, all converging into a dizzying heap of terror—

He threw up.

A pureed selection of fine meats landed on Seth's plate, his parents' meals and on the clothes of the Duke of Osney.

Seth's throat burned.

'Oh, he's gotten carried away with himself,' tutted Queen Eleanor. 'I told him, eat too much meat and your body will reject it. Take him to his rooms to rest, Anna, we'll continue without him.'

Anna left a tray of wine goblets in front of Ron and hurried to obey.

Ron stared torturously at the tray.

Seth shrugged out of Anna's grasp and wobbled to the stairs, not before shooting a foul glare at his father.

Howie too had noticed the short exchange between King Theo and Cienne a minute earlier: their eyes meeting in mutual understanding as King Theo mouthed 'tomorrow' with a meaningful wink.

'So what's the plan for tomorrow, your majesty?' the Duke of Osney asked brightly, ignoring Seth's donation to his current look. 'Time to introduce his highness to the woods, I take it?'

'Of course, a hunting trip!' exclaimed King Theo. 'That'll put some colour on the boy, no mistake! We'll wean him back onto proper food if it kill us, eh?'

He glanced slyly at Cienne.

'Nothing gets the appetite going like a good hunt, isn't that so?'

Cienne smiled. 'We can only hope, your majesty.'

King Theo's grin faltered as his gaze fell on Ron.

'Speaking of appetites, we'd better bring him as well before he drinks us dry,' he said. 'He hasn't stopped guzzling our booze since he entered the palace, and I don't reckon his mother will appreciate him coming back with liver failure. Deals with the occult, apparently,' he said knowingly.

Sure enough, Ron had already inhaled the contents of the discarded tray and was laughing hysterically at the space between himself and the floor.

Howie excused himself, got up and hitched Ron to his feet by the armpits.

'What d'you think you're playing at? I was having a laugh in there!'

Howie dragged him into the courtyard by one arm and slammed the door behind him.

Ron staggered, regaining enough composure to glower at him.

'I've helped Prince Seth now,' Howie said in a low voice. 'I think it's our cue to leave.'

'What about my ole man?' said Ron. 'You 'aven't helped him yet, and 'e's a king. Much more 'fluential than a measly *prince.*'

'Well, he isn't here, is he?' Howie snapped. 'And he certainly isn't in the bottom of their wine cellar! You just wanna stay here and get drunk!'

Ron blinked repeatedly.

'So?' he said finally. 'Anyway, thought you liked it here. I heard you were getting on very well with the princess.'

Howie shushed him violently, flapping a hand up and down.

'Nothing happened!' he hissed. 'You'd better not be telling people either! Last thing I need is to be beheaded for suspected adultery!'

'No one's gonna find out,' Ron scoffed, 'you're Howard Rosethorn!'

'Oh, don't call me by my full name, I hate it,' Howie wailed, visibly cringing. 'It makes me sound like a knob.'

'You're s'posed to sound like a knob, you're the Knight of Raining Thorns! You're a prophecy! Holy trousers and all that!'

Howie snorted. 'Says who? The deprived nuns?'

'Uh, the… glowing cat, the tamed dragon, the bolt of lightning from the *sky*—'

'Fine,' Howie said. 'Just… shut up about the princess, alright? She doesn't even like me, anyway. She's too busy making eyes at Prince Shitface in there.'

'As if Prince Woss-'Is-Face 'as 'alf a chance anyway. He's got a lazy eye.'

'She *gave him* that lazy eye,' said Howie with a dull expression. 'With a *shovel*.'

'Exactly! She didn't hit you with a shovel, did she?'

'Yet,' said Howie.

'Look,' said Ron, placing a compassionate hand on his shoulder. 'Go for a sleep. Things will look much better in the morning, is what my ole man used to say. That's why the sun comes out!'

'I bet you won't be so cheerful about that come morning,' said Howie. 'I'm telling you, hair of the dog does not make a hangover better.'

'I know that,' said Ron with a snort, stumbling back into the great hall. 'That's why I just keep drinking instead.'

Howie threw his eyes to the heavens and shook his head.

~

Back in the great hall, King Theo's guests were wandering off, leaving the king's council behind to discuss the celebration arrangements. They gawked at Howie as he passed to meet King Theo, who was beckoning him with one finger.

King Theo placed a hand on Howie's shoulder.

'Strange story, that is,' he said.

'I wouldn't believe it either if I weren't stood right there, your majesty,' said Howie, wringing his hands.

'Oh, I believe you,' said King Theo, clapping his back in reassurance.

They made their way to the staircase to the left.

'That crop of forest is very close to the Forest border: many a strange thing has happened there, trust me. But never mind that! We have a clean slate with the boy once more! See how he ate back there? He hasn't eaten like that in nigh on twenty years! There's hope for him yet, eh?'

'He's lost a lot of his memory, though,' said Howie.

'Yes, very quick thinking on Archie's part,' said Theo in admiration. 'Clever, that man. With any luck, the boy might turn out alright. But on to you. How would you feel about staying with us permanently?'

Howie met his gaze. 'Really?'

'Of course! We'll have you as a guard, or a squire, perhaps,' he said in earnest. 'We might have to fabricate a noble house for you to be a squire, but we'll keep you here somehow!'

Howie nodded. 'That would be great. I kind of promised Prince Ron I'd help find his father, though.'

'Oh, we'll sort that! No doubt he's languishing in a bar someplace, he had a very similar temperament to young Ronald in that respect. Go to the council tomorrow morning, we'll arrange for some notices to be put out. For the moment, I have a little job for you.'

They trudged upstairs.

'I have some visitors in my quarters that need my attention this evening, and I need you to guard the door. Make sure no one enters or leaves without my permission, is that clear?'

Howie nodded.

They arrived outside King Theo's quarters on the third floor. The corridor's white walls dimmed to yellow in the torchlight, and the heavy oak door to King Theo's drawing room was slightly ajar.

Howie peered in curiously.

King Theo slammed it shut.

'This isn't for your eyes, lad,' he said sharply. 'You just guard the door and I'll let you know when you're excused.'

'What's going on in there?'

'Just seeing some young couples whose marriages were unaccounted for.'

Howie gulped. He had a feeling that referred more to the wives than the husbands.

'You won't… hurt them, will you?'

'Goodness, no. I'll just scare them a little bit.'

You'll do that alright, thought Howie.

'As I say, no one is to enter,' King Theo said.

He entered his quarters rather eagerly.

Howie recoiled where he stood.

'Oh God,' he whispered.

A moment later, booming laughter came from the room, along with the occasional shifting of furniture.

Howie was scared. He really didn't want to be here.

He wrung his hands, wondering why on earth King Theo had placed him in this horrific position.

Seth shuffled down the corridor wearily, still looking unwell. He spotted Howie standing guard and frowned.

'Is there a reason why you're loitering there?' he drawled.

Howie swallowed. 'The… king wanted me to guard the door…'

Seth heard the laughter. His face cleared.

'Ah,' he said in realisation. 'He's with some newlyweds, I take it?'

'Yep,' said Howie, squirming.

'Oh.'

Seth went for the door.

Howie stepped in front of him.

'Are you sure you want to go in there?'

Seth flung him a withering glance. 'It might be a bit much for your delicate constitution, but I'm quite used to it. I've joined in to the likes of this since I was nine.'

Howie gaped at him. '*Nine?*'

'Nine.' Seth paused as a woman's giggle sounded from inside. 'That's a fake laugh if ever I heard one.'

Howie's stomach contracted. 'Can't you make him stop?'

'He is who he is,' said Seth with a shrug.

He tried to enter.

Howie stopped him again.

'He said no one was to enter.'

'Not even me?' he said, rolling his eyes.

'Why would you want to go in there anyway?' Howie asked in despair. 'He's clearly—'

The door opened a crack.

'Seth? Is that you, boy? Come in! Have some fun with us!'

Seth glanced wryly at Howie and patted his face before entering.

Moments passed before Seth's laughter joined that of the others. There were other men in there also, by the sounds of it.

Howie glanced around nervously. Then he noticed the door was ajar again.

He gulped again and, bracing himself, peered into the crack.

He pulled his head back with a frown. *What the…?*

He peered in again in disbelief.

All of the women were standing by the far wall and, contrary to Howie's assumption, were fully clothed.

King Theo stood in the centre of the drawing room, at the head of a circle of men including Seth… who were juggling severed heads.

Howie blinked.

The Creys were the only men having any kind of fun with the grotesque game – the others were the husbands who failed to receive the king's consent, judging by the apprehensive looks they were giving the king.

Howie turned away from the spectacle.

So that was what he meant by scaring them. Somehow, what Howie had thought of earlier seemed much, much worse.

~

V

'Why,' said Ron angrily, 'is that git screaming so loud?'

He threw his covers off and swung out of bed with a wince.

There was nothing like waking to a wine-poisoned brain and a terrified scream at dawn. The combined efforts of hangover and Seth's voice cut strips from Ron's brain.

He trudged sullenly to the stairs.

His guest quarters were on the third floor's east wing. The west wing held the royal apartments, along with the floor's only staircase. A length of corridor running around the keep separated the rooms from a series of verandas viewing the courtyard from all angles.

Ron cursed the verandas as they spilled sunlight onto the gleaming white block walls. It made walking the width of the keep an ordeal for one with a splitting migraine.

He crossed the keep, his hands over his eyes, to find the source of the screaming perched on the edge of his bed, pointing at the window.

Ron barged into Seth's bedroom, slamming the door behind him and flinching at the noise.

'What is it?' he hissed.

'That,' said Seth, pointing.

Ron faced the window.

'There's nothing there but a raven,' he said.

'Get rid of it!'

Ron flung him a withering glance. 'You're afraid of birds?'

'Just get rid of it!' shrieked Seth, tear stricken.

Ron stepped to the window and gave the glass a tap.

The bird bolted for the clouds.

'There,' said Ron as though to a small child. 'All gone.'

Seth visibly deflated.

'Thank you,' he said more calmly.

Ron sighed and turned to leave when Seth screamed again.

A boot hit the window.

The returning bird flew off again.

Ron folded his arms, observing Seth Crey.

His fair hair bedraggled and his bedclothes askew, Seth sat with his knees tucked under his chin and his second boot raised in defence, trembling.

'You could do with a drink,' Ron said.

~

Howie awoke with the warmth of the mid-morning sun on his face and the smell of the elderly clinging to him from all sides. He bathed in a warm sea of silk in the king-sized four-poster, in an apartment usually reserved for Seth's grandmother. The grandmother in question lived in the old castle in the middle of Serpus, but the room still held lingering scents of lavender.

Two days had passed, punctuated by feasts and celebrations. Howie and Ron had spent them exploring the many sights and wonders of Serpus, each day ending with a grand feast in which he ate so much food he would lose consciousness in half an hour, not to wake until the next day's second turn.

The council had become a great source of help. The Duke of Osney, Ron had been pleased to see, had arranged for large notices to be displayed all over the city, offering a sum of money to anyone with information about King Samuel's whereabouts.

Howie glanced to his left, to a bedside cabinet on top of which lay a daily stack of letters from lords all over Adem, citing updates on their own investigations. It was certainly a relief to know he wasn't expected to traipse around Adem on Lyseria like a berk.

The only area he didn't receive daily updates on was the Forest. King Theo and Queen… Something-or-other were on poor terms, it appeared.

Howie stretched his arms and legs out in front of him, lying on his side. He thought about getting up to scan the missives and yawned instead, reluctant to rise from the warmth embracing him.

He froze.

There was no warmth like *that* embracing him when he fell asleep.

He looked down to find, to his alarm, a slim, pale arm around his ribs and another curled under his shoulder. After some investigation, hair tickled the back of his neck.

He cleared his throat loudly, hoping it wasn't the grandmother.

The hugger jolted awake. The arm retracted.

'I'm so sorry, I think I must have wandered into the wrong room by mistake.'

Howie's mouth went dry.

'It's fine, your highness,' he said vaguely.

In actual fact it wasn't fine, he realised with dread. He wasn't wearing any clothes.

'Nothing happened, I assure you,' Cienne said defiantly.

He'd never been in a bed with so many silk sheets before. It was unbearably warm in there with anything besides his smallclothes on. Which didn't explain why he didn't have any smallclothes on either, he thought in cold terror.

Howie tugged his sheets closer, in particular around his midriff.

'U-u-u-uh, uhm…' he stammered.

'I'm so sorry,' Cienne said quickly. 'This is very embarrassing, isn't it?'

'Yee-y-yip,' Howie managed.

He heard her slide out from the sheets and kept his gaze placed firmly in the opposite direction.

'I must have had more to drink than I thought last night,' Cienne went on, unheeded. 'I could have sworn I turned into the west wing. I honestly thought you were Seth, you look ever so alike in the gloom. I'm very sorry, by the way, you must have got a fright just now.'

'It-s-s okay, your highness,' Howie faltered.

His heart hammered three beats for every second. He'd had a dream last night, he thought in terror, and he wasn't sure how much of it was a dream after all.

'You can turn to face me, my love, I am clothed,' Cienne said patiently.

Howie rolled over, tentative. Sure enough, she was sporting her shimmery nightgown.

She smiled at him. 'You're very sweet. A perfect gentleman.'

Howie struggled to speak for a moment before nodding.

He wondered how on earth she managed to evade looking like a troll in the mornings. Even her hair shone as though it had been combed through only a moment ago.

Cienne tilted her head to one side, letting a waterfall of fair hair tumble from her shoulder.

'Are you alright?' she asked softly. 'You look stricken.'

'I think I might be in love with you a little bit,' he let slip, Teenage Voice of Idealism apparently taking the helm in this conversation.

Her eyes widened perceptively.

'You'll be killed one day, with a mouth like that,' she said in amusement.

Howie tucked the top of his sheet under his chin. 'Will it be worth it?'

Cienne grinned in a manner that hinted it most certainly would *not*.

'I had better be going before my ladies-in-waiting discover I'm missing.'

She perched on the edge of the bed and, without warning, leaned across to kiss his cheek firmly.

'Have a good day,' she said, sweeping out.

Howie stared after her, transfixed.

Making sure she was definitely gone, he hesitated a moment before he licked his lips and, hastily, flung the sheets over his head.

Early afternoon broke in warm waves over the courtyard.

Howie strolled across the gravel an hour after his encounter with Cienne, feeling much more relaxed.

King Theo and a number of retainers had gone on a hunt in the woods, according to the butler, and a few guards had been sent out to look for a missing Prince Seth.

He'd left the morning's messages lying on the bedside table, forgotten, but Howie couldn't be bothered to worry about them today. Today was to be his day, despite the prophecy. Wherever King Samuel was, he could bloody well wait.

He heard the door behind him open and turned to face Lilly, also holding a pastry.

'Hello,' she said cheerfully. 'Good night?'

Howie jumped to attention and gave her a low bow.

Lilly frowned at it and waved her free hand up and down.

'Get up, get up, I'm hardly human, never mind royalty,' she said as he straightened up. She took a bite of her pastry and said with her mouth full, ''S Harold Rosethorn, isn't it?'

'Um, Howard, actually,' he said.

'Oh, right, sorry.' She swallowed. 'Thanks for bringing Lyseria back the other day, my old man would've killed me if I'd lost her. Lucky you weren't killed, though. Any other day she'd have burnt you to a crisp or sat on you.'

'That's good to know,' Howie said with a wince.

''Specially dislikes poor people,' said Lilly, to Howie's bemusement. 'You're lucky you look like Seth, or you'd be a goner.'

'I'm not poor as such,' he said, affronted.

'Seems to really like you, actually,' she went on, more to herself than to Howie. 'She don't take to people to haven't got "Crey" written on their underwear, but she rescued you from a sinking *ship*—'

'She *sank* the ship,' he said, beginning to get annoyed.

'... and my father really likes you, Harold—d'you mind if I call you Harry?'

'I'd rather you called me Howard,' he said.

'You could pass yourself off as my brother and I doubt he'd even care – probably kill him and have you replace him, actually...'

Howie zoned out at this point and turned his head to gaze at the flowers.

Lilly prattled on, too swept up in her own stream of consciousness to pay any notice.

Being the apprentice of an agoraphobic carpenter, the concept of flowers – or anything that wasn't brown or covered in sawdust – was a whole new experience for Howie. He quite liked the way they were arranged into alternating colours around the walls, all the way to the garden shed where he'd found Seth unconscious only a couple days before.

The rest of the courtyard was clear open space, a gravel circle with a beautiful marble fountain in the centre. The fountain depicted a huge snake rearing its head, water spilling from its jaws.

He thought of Adrienne at random. He missed her. She loved flowers. He could see her perched on the edge of the fountain, sketching away. The thought warmed him. He made a mental note to write her a letter. Maybe he'd pick her up on the dragon, just to see her face...

Lilly meanwhile was back on the subject of her father.

'... I'm hoping he'll think better of marrying me off to him now he knows he's a raging alcoholic. Might call off the betrothal if I'm lucky. I mean, imagine having the name Horne. Makes you think they're all constantly—'

'You mean Ron?' Howie cut in just in time.

'Yeah, that's him,' she said. 'Heard him in the hall this morning, talking about going for a drink.'

'What, this morning?' he asked with a frown. 'Isn't it a bit early?'

'Judging by the amount he necked last night, I imagine it's never too early for him,' she said with a snort. 'He'd wanna watch his liver. Here, maybe he took Seth with him. D'you hear him screeching at a bird outside his window this morning? And this was after him and the old man spent a night jugging *severed heads*.' She shook her head. 'He was better off "dead" if you ask me.'

Howie frowned again. 'Where's the nearest pub?'

'The inn in the market down the road doesn't serve booze 'til the third turn,' said Lilly. 'Nearest after that is the Prince Death in Arthur Stibbons' Street. Bit of a trek, though.'

Howie narrowed his eyes. 'Not if you have a dragon.'

~

Outside the Prince Death, Lyseria was curled up next to the door, asleep. Passers-by gave her a wide berth, trying very hard not to breath.

Inside, a crescendo had erupted consisting of two princes, a lot of falling over and a song about faeries. Fairies – a notably different spelling – were innocent, loving creatures of the forest – in storybooks. In real life, their unique biological survival instincts began to kick in: the kind that didn't stop kicking in until either they or their victim broke a pelvis.

Business was not going well thanks to Princes Ron and Seth, or so Howie judged by the dwindling number of lunch-goers in the building.

After a joyous refrain on the 'flames' of the Forest Queen, Lilly cut in with an irate, 'Really?'

Ron snorted loudly in reply. 'Not really, she'd murder us.'

'She eats blokes, so I've heard,' Seth piped up. 'And not in the way in which we prefer.'

He and Ron snorted loudly, leaning against each other on the floor beside a table turned over on its side.

'Ugh,' Lilly said, turning to Howie. 'Behold, the heirs to the continent of Truphoria.'

'We'll never last,' Howie commented.

'Ron,' Seth said suddenly, a look of alarm across his face. 'I've lost my arm.'

''S right here, mate,' Ron said, patting the arm across his shoulders.

'No, no, I had another one, I'm sure of it,' he said, searching the floor behind them. 'Sort of longish looking thing, with wriggly bits on the end, have you seen it…'

Howie squinted at them with his jaw hanging ajar.

Lilly grimaced.

Seth crawled under the table, still holding Ron in one arm while groping with his left for the apparent third arm. Ron tilted back in his grasp, seemingly unperturbed.

'Oh, he's actually being serious,' Howie said after a moment.

'Apparently,' Lilly said with a frown.

'Have you got it?' Seth demanded.

He emerged to glare at Ron.

'What do I want your arm for?' Ron scoffed. 'Got two of me own, see?'

He held them out proudly.

'That one's mine!'

'No it ain't!'

'What do we do now?' said Howie.

Seth tried to pull off one of Ron's arms at the shoulder.

'Hope my old man don't pop in for a pint and catch 'em,' said Lilly.

'It's attached to me!' Ron gritted, pulling his arm away from Seth.

'Liar!'

Howie rolled his eyes. He leaned forward and tugged Seth's arms out in front of him.

'Look,' he said, pointing to one arm. 'Here's your left one,' he tapped the other, 'and here's your right.'

Seth's expression cleared.

'Ah!' he exclaimed, grinning. 'Had it in my hand the whole time! Fancy that!'

'Yeah,' grunted Ron, rubbing his shoulder.

'Here,' said Seth.

He pulled Howie to the ground roughly.

''Cause you found my arm, I'm going to give you a reward,' he drawled with a burp.

'No thanks,' said Howie, wriggling.

'No, no,' said Seth, arms wrapped tightly around Howie's shoulders. 'I'm gonna let you have my leg.'

Howie grimaced in utter incomprehension.

'I think you should keep it, it's still attached,' he said finally.

'Nope,' Seth pressed.

He planted his left leg on Howie's lap.

'It's all yours!'

Lilly giggled. 'Is he putting the moves on you?'

'I hope not,' Howie gritted. He fought the urge to hit him. 'Please take your leg away, I don't want it.'

'You can have more if you like,' said Seth, his eyes roving over him.

'NO!!'

'Howie and Seth, sitting in a tree,' Ron sang. 'K-I—'

'Stop it!' Howie barked. 'You're giving him ideas!'

'Yes, I can come up with ideas all on my own!' said Seth.

He snatched Howie's wrist and forcibly planted his palm on Seth's knee.

Howie jerked away. 'Stop it!'

'Oh, you want me really,' Seth said with total conviction.

'No I don't, get off my arm!'

'Yes you do! I'm a prince, everyone wants a prince!'

He gagged slightly, to Howie's alarm, and swallowed down hard to continue.

'I'll buy you things, wonderful things, clothes and jewellery and castles—'

Howie shoved his hands out of his shirt.

'—we'll live in Serpus, nobody will look in there! We'll be together at last, just you and—'

He paled and was promptly sick on Howie's jerkin.

Howie's eye twitched.

'I'm so sorry,' said Lilly, cackling uncontrollably.

Seth turned a bleary eye on his doppelganger, who wore a deep scowl.

'How 'bout a kiss, then?' he said keenly.

Howie shoved Seth's forehead with his palm.

Seth tilted backwards, his head cracking a table leg on the way down.

'Ow!'

Howie wiped his front with the corner of a nearby tablecloth.

'I hate my life,' he seethed.

He rose to his feet and left.

Lilly nudged Seth with the toe of her boot.

He stirred.

'Where'd he go?' said Seth hoarsely. 'I thought we had a connection.'

'He's no good for you, Seth,' Lilly said gently, reaching down to pat his head.

~

VI

Cienne stabbed a potato moodily, the noise of the impact echoing down the empty hall. The faint sounds of Seth's retching could be heard from within the kitchens as his dinner sat cold and untouched beside her.

The sullen silence was soon broken by King Theo's entourage.

They crashed through the double doors, laden by a family of wild horses.

'To the kitchens!'

They hefted their spoils to the door on Cienne's left.

Behind her, Cienne fancied she could hear the retching increase in volume.

King Theo circled the table to sit at her side, starting Seth's dinner.

'The hunt fared well, I see,' she commented.

'Yes! Lost a boy, unfortunately, but it was to be expected. Sickly creature. Though at least he had a bit more spirit than my sorry excuse for a son.'

Cienne eyed him, sympathetic.

Seth had conveniently vanished just as King Theo summoned him for the hunt. The king hadn't even been angry when he learned this. Just disappointed.

Even now, several hours later, Theo was subdued and sullen, a far cry from his usual booming exuberance. His brow was set in annoyance as he gulped down a mouthful of mashed potato.

'How fares he, by the way?'

'Drank himself sick, your majesty,' Cienne said in a weary voice. 'He's currently in the kitchens, reacquainting himself with his breakfast.' She sighed heavily.

'Soon, my dear, soon,' he soothed, patting the top of her head. 'The boy still thinks he's ten. Give him some time and if all fails, we'll send Rosethorn back to deal with him, eh?'

Cienne smiled weakly.

James de Vil entered the hall laden with goblets of wine and the king's usual tankard of beer. He placed them on the table to clean a pool of something indescribable left by Seth.

'Don't we have a maid to do that, man?'

The butler winced at the volume of King Theo's voice.

'She's in the kitchen, your majesty, holding back the prince's hair, so to speak.'

'She's what?' he demanded, rising to his feet. 'That's your job! Send that harlot on her way and get Seth out here now, lest I give him something to really be sick about!'

'Yes, your majesty,' he drawled, rolling his eyes.

'One other thing.'

The butler pivoted lazily.

'Any more cheek from you, boy, and it's a demotion to washer woman for you.'

'What, again?'

Theo bared his teeth.

The butler's eyes widened. He quickly bowed and scurried off before said teeth could come any closer.

'Another fine decoration for the front entrance, methinks,' he growled.

Seth slouched out of the kitchen door and collapsed into the seat beside his father's. He cast a sceptical look at his father's plate. 'I'm not even going to ask if that's mine.'

King Theo pointedly ignored this.

'Seth, tell me,' he said with his mouth full once again, 'when were you planning to conceive our next heir?'

Cienne choked slightly, covering her mouth.

'Oh, not at the dinner table,' said Seth with a painful grimace.

'Why not?' he demanded, thumping down the last of Seth's dinner. 'It's past time you made use of yourself! You're halfway to your deathbed, boy! Best put those tools to good use before they wither and fall off!'

'Your analogies are as encouraging as ever,' Seth drawled.

Queen Eleanor entered from the courtyard in front of them, the ends of her skirts trailing behind her. She flung Seth a fond glance.

He returned it with a genuine smile.

'Your majesty, His Grace Henry Meyer of the Ary Islands has arrived early for the tournament. He heard of it on his way here to propose marriage between himself and Lilly, what should I tell him?'

King Theo bellowed with laughter.

'You mean the Earl of Herpes?' he said, to Seth's bewilderment. 'Recently widowed, isn't he? I wonder why. Tell him not to bother, we have the Horn-ee boy for that. Funny, spelling it with an "e" on the end,' he added 'Makes you think they're all constantly—'

'Oh, change the subject,' said Seth in disdain.

'Yes, well, he seems to have his heart set on our family,' Eleanor said, rolling her eyes. 'Perhaps we can send him to my mother. I hear my niece Elyse is still to be wed.'

Seth burst out laughing. It was the most enthusiastic laugh Cienne had heard from him ever.

'Rather him than me,' he said. 'She's a worse kisser than Cienne.'

King Theo looked up from his dinner.

Cienne froze.

Seth met each gaze in turn.

'We practised on each other when we were twelve,' he said. 'When we heard Cienne was coming.'

Queen Eleanor flung him another glance that was considerably less fond.

Seth lifted his shoulders meekly.

'It was her idea,' he said in a small voice.

King Theo shot him a withering glance. 'Cienne, you're good with these people. Why don't you head out and smooth things over while Seth and I have a little chat on our own?'

'About what?' asked Cienne, rising.

'Oh, bloke stuff, matters of the heart, sort of thing.'

'The over-rated art of making children,' muttered Seth.

'See if they can't ship over a griffin for the feast,' King Theo went on, ignoring Seth. 'Damn difficult to catch wild, but they make a mean pie. Taste like duck, don't you know?' he said to Seth idly.

Cienne curtsied before leaving, Eleanor at her heels.

'Talkative, isn't she?' said Seth as the door closed behind them. 'Couldn't get a word in edgeways. Remind me again why I'm married to that bag of bones?' He ran an index finger around the rim of his cup. 'Even Cousin Elyse at least had a bit of personal—'

He gasped.

A thick hand clenched a fistful of Seth's close-cropped hair and wrenched his head back. The beard obstructed Seth's view of his father's face as King Theo hissed down at him.

'You're married to that "bag of bones" because *I* said so. And don't forget, I can easily have her widowed and remarried to your Cousin Mortimer. If you'd prefer.'

'No, no,' Seth whimpered, 'be a waste, wouldn't it?' He paused. 'Who's Cousin Mortimer?'

'Do your duty and you need not know. Otherwise…'

King Theo ran an index finger across his own throat with a slitting sound.

'… it's the chopping block for you.'

Seth gulped. 'Alright then.'

Theo grinned. 'Good boy.'

He released Seth to pat the crown of his head.

'Take a walk. I gather Lilly's looking for you for a run around. Be back by nightfall, no excuses, or else.'

Seth nodded in silence and rose, rubbing his scalp.

'And stay away from your Cousin Elyse!' he bellowed after him as an afterthought.

Seth slammed the doors behind him, rolling his shoulders.

If I ever have kids, he thought with a snarl, striding across the courtyard, *I will never, ever, pull their hair like that.*

He strode past Queen Eleanor, Cienne and their guests without a second glance, threw the front entrance open and stalked into the bright sunlight.

He stopped dead as the door closed.

The face of Lyseria obstructed his view of the front gardens.

Seth gulped and, tentatively, patted her nose. 'Good dragon.'

She sat on her haunches half a foot away from him, crouching to get a good look at him.

Seth attempted to sidle past one of her massive wings.

Her head shot towards him.

He flinched, turning away from the flames… which didn't come.

Seth opened one eye to see a big red snout nuzzling the front of his jerkin, tucking itself underneath his armpit in content. He frowned down, baffled.

'You're just like a big dog, aren't you?' he said, rubbing a leathery eyebrow.

As if in response, a massive tongue ran up his face, jerking his head back with a crack.

'Nyaah!'

Seth froze, his throat and face hot and glistening. It was like being wiped with a freshly cooked ham.

Lyseria slid back from the door to recline on the grass, watching him expectantly. He wondered what she wanted. *Do dragons chase after sticks? What does one feed them? Biscuits?*

Seth ran various scenarios in his head concerning a dog lead before dropping cross-legged beside her, a hand clasped to the back of his neck.

The beast was bigger than a horse and built like a lizard, with a neck three feet in length and clawed feet currently hidden beneath a thick chest. A long, wiry wing curled protectively around Seth's back as he gazed up at the clouds, rubbing her head.

He paused.

A raven stared at him from the top of a nearby tree.

Lyseria sensed Seth's apprehension and watched it with a hiss.

Seth stared at the raven with a scowl, his eyes narrowed.

Note to self, he mused. *Carry a crossbow.*

It swivelled its head from side to side, getting a good look at him. It launched itself to the grass three yards away, making him jump.

A low growl surrounded him. Lyseria.

It jumped forward again, now barely a foot away.

Seth leapt to his feet and bolted to the castle wall.

Lyseria pounced on it, tearing it to pieces.

Just as Seth's heartbeat slowed, an entire flock burst out of the tree.

His blood pounded.

Black plumage sped over everything, obstructing the gardens and even Lyseria sitting in the grass.

Seth scrambled around the corner and barged through a handful of people outside the keep.

The ravens descended.

He ran out of the small back portcullis of the castle, tripped and stumbled his way to the castle farms a short distance away.

A burst of inspiration led Seth to a scarecrow in the centre of the wheat field. He yanked it to the ground and hid behind it for a moment in defence.

The ravens seemed unfazed.

Seth dropped it sheepishly, came to a fence and vaulted it. A crop of woods filled the horizon and he headed straight for it.

In his wake, the birds curved and arched over and around him, relentless.

Once at the forest, Seth leapt onto a branch.

His head levelled with the gaze of a raven.

He shrieked, releasing the branch.

His knees crashed into stony ground. Seth winced as they protested, but the sight of a black feather in the rushes drove him back to his feet. Cradling a stitch and sweating profusely at this point, he pressed on. Beams of sunlight peeled the back of his neck and sweat clung to his skin and clothes.

Ravens. They were everywhere, filling every blank space in the sky.

Fatigue washed over him, but he couldn't stop now – the ravens grew, expanded, bigger than Lyseria now and soaring over his head in formation, forming his father's beard...

'Seth!'

The flock scattered, leaving the forest bright in their wake.

Lilly stood in front of him, beaming, dressed in loose, airy linen and a straw hat.

Seth skidded to a halt, head thudding and stomach churning.

He wobbled in front of her, his vision wavering.

'I was looking for you,' she said brightly, taking a swig from a skin in her hand. 'We're all practising for the tournaments in the summer. You wanna come?'

Seth leaned on his knees with both palms.

'I feel sick,' he said faintly.

'Wuss,' she teased, pulling him by the arm regardless. 'Come on! I'll go easy on you!'

He squeezed his eyes shut and opened them again, trying to focus.

Everything looked awful. The trees were jagged and thin, with branches like bones. Skeletal creatures with beards of moss and foliage, with thin wooden fingers swiping across them in a slitting motion. *It's the chopping block for you…*

His vision rippled like water. The only detail he could pick out now was Lilly's water bottle…

'Can I have a drink?' he asked, panting.

'Oh, yeah,' she said easily, handing him the skin.

He drained it in one and handed it back.

Lilly upturned it with a blink. 'Surprised you even tasted that wine.'

'Wine?' he tried to say, only it came out 'whay'. He was sure it had been water. It hadn't tasted of anything.

'Come on,' Lilly pestered, tugging his arm. 'They'll tire out the horses if we don't get there now.'

'Nngh,' he groaned, his head aching.

It's the chopping block for you…

'Seth?' Lilly asked, lifting his chin to examine his face. 'How long have you been out in the sun? You're dressed way too heavily…'

Chopping block…

Squawk! echoed the raven on the Night of Raining Thorns, pecking on his window.

Chop

'Seth?'

Chopping…

Ssslit…

Seth flopped forward onto his face.

~

136

PART THREE: ADRIENNE

I

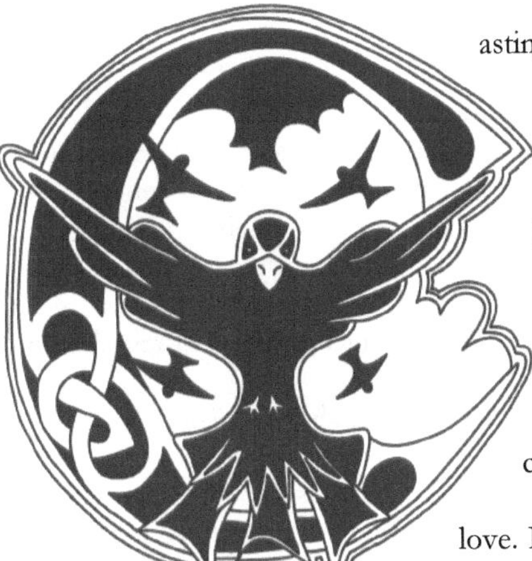

asting a thick black shadow over the barbican, the protruding gatehouse to the Creys' Keep hung at a dizzying height above Adrienne's head.

'Who goes there?' the guard called from the gatehouse.

'A friend of Howard Rosethorn,' she called up. 'Is he here?'

'Not at the moment, love. Probably in Arthur Stibbons' Groin, if I'd have to guess.'

Adrienne frowned and decided not to ask.

The castle loomed before her like a great beast, the tall walls casting a shadow over the bridge, where she loitered. In the depths of the palace stood the Tower, Adem's answer to the torture chambers beneath the Stonekeep.

From her left, a pig gazed at her lazily before wandering back to the farming grounds behind the palace. *Speaking of pigs*, she thought sourly, picturing Howie.

Howie. Her dear, beloved Howie, a thoughtless deserter. She wouldn't have thought it, but the evidence was clear: he'd gallivanted off to Adem with her Uncle Archie, leaving her to pay a king's ransom for a horse to find them, and not a very good horse at that.

What's more, she had to travel through the Wastelands by herself to do it.

Though it could have been worse, she thought back. The Old Kingsroad meandered between the blackened peaks in a wide path, curving down into a valley housing a deep river. It was an easy journey with the ample supplies she had gathered before crossing the border – helped in no small part by the lack of dodgy-looking men in the vicinity.

She shivered and gave her pouch of scalpels a grateful pat.

If she'd known they were enjoying the hospitality of the Creys as opposed to hiding from the wrath of Vladimir Horne, she would have stayed home, kept her savings for her apothecary as planned and, more importantly, *not* risked her virginity travelling through the dodgiest areas of Stoneguard and Adem alone. They were getting a smack for this one and no mistake.

'Oi! Miss!'

Adrienne jerked her gaze upward.

'Madmiss—Madmwa—Madam Cienne says you may enter and wait for Mister Rosethorn,' the guard called down to her.

Adrienne watched the portcullis winch open, creaking at it went. It shrieked to a halt, and she jogged underneath it, up the path to the keep entrance.

She halted at the double doors, which opened to reveal who could only be the princess herself.

'Thank you, your highness, for your kindness,' said Adrienne, with a low curtsy.

Cienne's hair fluttered over her face as she gave her a kind smile. The sunlight shone through it, giving her an ethereal look.

'Howard should be back soon enough,' she said, surprising Adrienne with her distinct lack of a Portabellan accent. 'He normally spends the afternoon in the city before returning for dinner. You're welcome to wait inside if you like?'

'Yes, your highness, thank you.'

Cienne turned to the butler behind her, her silvery curls swinging behind her.

'You may open the doors again, James.'

As the doors were pushed open, Adrienne turned to the butler as Cienne entered.

'Adrienne,' she introduced herself as they shook hands. 'Can I call you Jimmy?'

'Please don't.'

'Oh.'

She watched him enter before her and made a face at the back of his leotard.

'What is it you do for a living, Adrienne?' Cienne cut in.

He Who Shall Not Be Called Jimmy shut the doors behind them.

'I'm presuming you aren't married yet?'

'Not yet, no,' she said, thinking of Howie in spite of her anger.

Cienne locked eyes with her and smirked, as though reading her thoughts.

'He's a handsome boy, isn't he? Howie?'

'Yes, he is, very. I mean,' she amended, flushing, 'to answer your question, erm, I practise medicine for a living.'

Cienne grinned openly. 'We should employ you here.' She dropped back to Adrienne's side. 'My husband is forever getting himself unwell of late. If you're interested in a position with our chief physician Erik, I can arrange an audience for you with the king—'

At that instant, the doors were flung open with a bang.

A group of iron-clad men and a small woman carried someone into the hall, a fair-haired, blue-eyed—

'Howie!' said Adrienne in alarm.

'No, no, it's only Seth,' the girl said in reassurance.

She shifted her grip on Seth's armpits.

'He's had sunstroke. I've one of the lads over to fetch Erik, the guys said it could be fatal if—'

'It's okay, I can fix this,' said Adrienne firmly, striding to the prince's side. 'He just needs cooling down, can you put him on the floor? He needs water, lots of it, as cold as you can get it.'

'I'll get some wine—'

'No,' she snapped at the guard, who recoiled, 'that will make him worse, just get some cold water. Take off his shirt, too, get him some ventilation, and fan him…'

Cienne watched in fascination.

Servants rushed past with buckets of water. Adrienne tore his shirt open and gestured to the men, who poured a bucket over Seth's head and torso.

He spluttered, a small spray fountaining from his lips.

Adrienne helped him into a sitting position. Cupping a handful of water in her palm, she held it to Seth's lips.

'Here. Do you feel any better?'

'Mmm,' he said groggily.

'Sunburn ointment for his neck wouldn't hurt,' she said. 'Can you organise that?'

A knight nodded and ran out.

A man not much older than Adrienne bolted to Seth's side as she planted a wet cloth around his forehead.

She rose as Erik took over and faced Cienne, her trousers sopping at the knees and her expression sheepish.

'Apologies for being curt, your highness. I learned to act quickly in these situations. Many of the doctors I've worked with have a tendency towards killing patients and pinning it on apothecary houses to put them out of business.'

Erik flung her an affronted scowl. 'I beg your pardon?'

Adrienne carefully ignored him.

Cienne smiled. 'Now you *must* meet my father-in-law.'

~

The drawbridge creaked open under the gaze of the setting sun.

Howie entered, Stan and Ron at his heels.

Stan had been employed as Ron's manservant – mostly to keep him away from the Crook and stem the endless hideous complaints Stan had of the place. Thankfully, Stan seemed much happier with the position. Ron surprisingly didn't need that much looking-after for someone with the brain development of soft cheese.

'Wotcher,' greeted the guard from the battlements. 'Young lady called to see you, Mister Rosethorn. Goes by the name of Adrienne?'

Howie's face lit up. 'Really? She came all the way here on her own?'

'Oh, is that your girlfriend?' Stan asked in delight.

'No,' Howie laughed. 'We grew up together. She's Archie's niece. Let's go see her!'

He ran to the keep.

Adrienne sat at a small chair in front of King Theo in the dining hall as James de Vil allowed Howie access. Queen Eleanor flanked King Theo's left and Cienne had planted herself in Seth's seat.

At the moment, Cienne's captivating presence flew over Howie's head. His attention was fully upon Adrienne as she rose to meet him.

He extended his arms.

'Adrienne! When did you get here, how—'

She punched him in the nose.

His head jerked back, and he staggered, clutching his face.

King Theo roared with laughter.

'Good right hook, my gal!' he bellowed, slapping the arm of his chair.

A nostril dribbled worryingly. Howie didn't think it was broken – yet.

Adrienne grabbed the front of Howie's collar and pulled him forward until they were nose to bloodied nose.

'I waited,' she snarled, 'for *weeks* for you to return. *Bloody weeks!!*'

'I'm sorry, I kept meaning to send you a letter—'

'And I journey through the sodding *Wastelands*,' she emphasised, 'to find you and Archie, nearing getting mugged about five times along the way, and where do I find you? Living it up in a bloody castle, leaving me stuck on my trot worrying about you!'

'There was a situation,' said Howie feebly, 'I had to leave fast, I didn't think—'

'No. You didn't think,' snapped Adrienne. 'Where's Archie?'

'He's living in the… brothel…' he trailed off.

Her expression turned to ice.

'Nice of Keith to mention it at the market,' she seethed. 'Well, you can bring me to him, then, to *provide* for me. As is his duty as my guardian. In the meantime, I have a sick prince to attend to. If I don't find you at the inner portcullis in three hours' time with directions to this *brothel*, I'm going to be seriously *pissed* off!'

She slammed into Howie's shoulder on her way to the stairs behind him.

King Theo laughed hysterically.

Howie held both hands around his nose with a piteous frown.

'She's one of a kind, your young lady,' he teased.

'Er, not mine specifically,' he replied, visualising Archie's face if she was.

'Yet,' Theo said with a smile. 'That was no shallow punch, my lad. Not to worry, you'll be back in her good books by the weekend.' He winked.

Three stories up, Adrienne stood in front of an empty four-poster in bemusement. The bed lay devoid of sheets, pillows and princes, the two former having been hastily thrown in the empty fireplace in apparent disgust.

Two stories below her and slowly making it three, Seth Crey was feeling claustrophobic. Not because of the one-by-two-foot room he had stumbled down into whilst throwing his sweaty sheets into the fireplace, although that did contribute to the experience in a major way.

It was the girl. Seth didn't even know her name – he was certain whoever she was, she hadn't been around for long. Her eyes bore into his whenever they met, as though she found him familiar and couldn't place why. It was almost invasive – like she was rooting through a little room in the back of his mind, except there wasn't anything for her to root through because she and Seth were the only ones in the room. The room labelled Seth Crey's Attention Span.

Never mind that he had fallen down a secret chute hidden behind the fireplace. That sort of thing tended to happen often in a place run by Theo Crey. That sort of thing was *normal.*

What worried Seth were the *feelings.* The unexplainable symptoms he was suffering since he'd recovered from the sunstroke: the sweaty palms, high blood pressure, heartbeat irregularities and eye-twitching that followed the presence of *her*.

Although the eye-twitching probably wasn't a part of it, he reflected. Even if it was happening a lot recently. Incidentally, he couldn't remember having a big dent in his head either. No doubt Cienne had something to do with that.

But that wasn't important.

What was important was that this woman was giving him a fever beyond anything sunstroke could evoke, and he couldn't bloody understand *why*. She was feeding him cold water every twenty minutes and fanning him. It defied logic.

And there were other things too... strange things. He wondered if it was something he'd need to discuss with his mother.

The ground creaked again, as it had twice already. Then he dropped again, hitting the ground heavily, his fall cushioned by moss and decay.

As with the previous occurrences, the trapdoor swung back up again, the rebounding hinge twanging.

He was quite used to this now, apart from the throbbing tail bone.

He had a feeling this was one of the various hiding places King Theo used to make people 'disappear'. Though he couldn't understand the point of the cushioned trapdoors on each floor. Surely it would hurt more to fall once, a *long* way down.

Unless there was something worse underground he wanted them to be alive for.

The third trapdoor gave way quickly, depositing him onto a large basket full of clothing that smelled of decay.

He blinked in the near-darkness and grasped the wall to pull himself up.

A torch hung from the wall by a brass ring in the mortar. He clutched it tightly in his left hand and limped to the nearest oil light across the hall, lighting the canvas tip immediately.

The light revealed little, only that he was in a skinny corridor in front of a heavy oak door. He walked the length of the corridor, torch in hand, and counted four doors along one wall, along with either the boiling system for heating the keep or an elaborate torture instrument, or both.

Seth turned to the door nearest to the boilers, all thoughts of the girl aside.

Carved in high relief on the door was the Crey family emblem.

It suddenly occurred to him where he was. The castle vaults, where family valuables and secrets were kept hidden from all but the owner of the vault. This was the royal family's joint vault, the other three belonging to each member. Poor Queen Eleanor was left without one – the queen wasn't regarded as a member of the royal family since most kings married the daughters of their enemies, but she made up for it by taking full control of this one.

The door opened at the slightest touch.

A number of old portraits of Seth's ancestors stood in neat piles along the walls.

Seth shut it again in disinterest.

He figured there would be no gold in there. His father's stash tended to reside around his throat, where it was to stay if King Theo's axe had anything to do with it.

Interestingly, the next vault he faced was his own, judging by the engraving on the wood, possibly made on his father's request: a worm.

He snorted wryly and traced it with his finger.

The door unlocked and swung open, startling him.

He entered warily, acutely aware that his wife must have entrance inside.

After finding some oil lamps surrounding the entrance, Seth lit them, turned to face the vault – and gaped.

'Oh my God,' he said, each word in increasing levels of horror.

What had once been a treasure vault had been renovated since Seth's 'death' and had quite obviously been renovated by Cienne.

Now it was a *shrine*.

'SETH' shone on the back wall, written in stained glass reflecting the torchlight, illuminating a terrifying mural of Seth's face just below the letters. A replica of Seth's head sat in front of the monument, an object constructed of linen and rushes. It stared up at its real-life counterpart like a severed head.

Statues and busts of marble surrounded the head, bent and deformed as the sculptor had viewed his subject through a body of water. A bloodied shovel was held in a skewed elbow that appeared to have no visible owner. Seth found the garden implement familiar but couldn't place why.

The last detail was a thick roll of parchment laid neatly in front of the head.

Curiosity in its most suicidal form drove Seth to the parchment. After close inspection, it revealed things about the mindscape of Cienne Fleurelle that would make King Theo himself pass water out of sheer terror. Or possibly laughter.

After learning more about passion than his mind knew how to

deal with, Seth threw the parchment far out of sight.

At that moment, his eye caught a glint beneath the grass head's chin.

He reached underneath the head gingerly. A glass vial rolled beneath his fingertip, and he flicked out a tiny bottle the size of his thumb. Holding it up between his finger and thumb, he tilted his head to read the label.

'Last resort.'

His jaw dropped mid-shudder. He let it drop to the ground.

It smashed with a scarcely audible *ching.*

He hastily wiped his hands on his front.

He scrambled to his feet and escaped quickly, bolting for the stairs at the end of the boiler room.

At the back of the keep, James-Not-Jimmy de Vil leapt backwards as the basement door flew open.

Seth emerged from within, wide-eyed.

'Is everything alright, your highness?'

He dropped a washing basket containing Seth's sooty bedclothes and King Theo's drawers, both of which had to be boiled until they returned to the colour white again.

'Fine,' said Seth, looking traumatised. 'Just… fine…'

He wandered around the keep in a daze.

The butler watched him go and shrugged, picking up the discarded basket.

~

Half a mile away from the Stonekeep, in a secluded chamber of the chapel crypts, Father Toffer stood hesitantly in the near darkness. A small lantern hung from the ceiling and was the only thing to highlight the cloaked figure standing before him.

'Y-you wished to speak with me,' Toffer quavered.

'I did,' said the figure, little more than a darker form of darkness.

'I see.'

He shifted from foot to foot.

'You aren't from the palace, are you? Because we know the whole "thou shalt not kill" bit and all that, but we're doing it to support the church and anyway, it doesn't count if we haven't had any business yet—'

'I haven't come on behalf of the palace,' the visitor intoned. 'I have a contract for you.'

Toffer stood up straight, a look of euphoria sweeping over his face.

'A murder contract?' he asked eagerly.

'Less of a murder contract,' said the figure, handing him a small scroll. 'More of an execution order.'

Toffer accepted the scroll of parchment and unrolled it.

His face fell.

'This is a whole family tree,' he said in horror. 'You want all these people assassinated?'

'Yes. That is your profession, isn't it? Assassination?'

'Only part time,' Toffer pointed out.

'Only no time, considering nobody's hiring you.'

Toffer scowled.

'You do want to be hired, don't you, Mister Toffer?'

Toffer sighed. 'Well, yes, but I had hoped for something less… significant. You know, to gain some experience.'

'A whole royal family should be experience enough for you. You're also a priest, Mister Toffer – the gods look kindly on you.'

'I doubt they look kindly on a certified oath breaker,' he said to himself. 'The commandments deliberately state, "Thou shalt not murder foreign royalty with potentially open pockets"—'

'Do the commandments state anything about the fulfilment of prophecies? I think they do.'

'I read nothing in the prophecy regarding—'

'The Knight was sent to save the King and vanquish the Antichrist and his pet, the Dragon,' the figure announced. 'Who in the world owns a dragon, do you think?'

'The Creys,' Toffer said, 'but we can't just kill the whole family just because one of them might be the Antichrist! Suppose it's the next owner of the dragon after their assassination?'

'Well, that's easily solved,' the figure replied. 'You'll also be killing the dragon.'

Toffer gulped.

'But it breathes fire,' he whined shrilly.

'And so will you. You breathe the fiery will of the Seven Gods, which is stronger than dragon fire. And should you fail them, you'll find out what else is stronger than dragon fire…'

Toffer gulped.

'Oh… alright then, but only for the sake of the prophecy. How much is the contract worth?'

'The undying gratitude of the gods.'

'I thought as much,' he said bitterly. 'Anything else?'

'Yes.'

She pulled from the depths of her robe a letter with the seal of the Hornes on it and handed it to him.

'I want you to dispose of this.'

'I'm not a bin,' he said moodily.

'What else is stronger than dragon fire?'

'Not this letter, that's for sure.'

He snatched it and hid it in his robe.

'That all?'

'For now.'

'And your name?'

'Unimportant,' said the figure. 'I am simply an agent of the Knight of Raining Thorns.'

'Uh-huh. I'll send the bill to him, shall I, in case expenses exceed our agreed fee?'

~

II

Morning squinted through the thick curtains of Seth's bedroom, lancing in from the balcony doors opposite.

Something had evidently caught fire early that morning, Adrienne surmised. She sat in a soft chair inside, alone. She couldn't think of any other reason a technically unemployed person would arise at the crack of dawn to do absolutely nothing all day. Aristocracy was one of those things that remained a mystery to Adrienne – much like the room's sickly sweet interior design. If it were a cake, Adrienne decided, it would rot her teeth out just to look at it.

She knitted her fingers together in her lap and slouched back, recalling the last hour's events while staring up at the pointlessly decorated ceiling.

She'd started the day by following Howie's directions to Keith's brothel and pulling Archie out by his left ear, vowing to skin him and use his bones for medicine if she found him near the Crook again. Keith wasn't best pleased with the loss of free labour. However, he quickly retaliated at the sight of the Crey emblem on the emerald-green uniform King Theo had given her.

Howie was currently on a tour of the holiday destination that was Serpus and had pulled Ronald Horne along with him. She hadn't been invited, she thought scornfully. No doubt they were perusing the rest of the city's brothel industry. One day she'd ask King Theo if she could cure the ills of the city and burn the Crook to the ground. He might allow it.

Especially if he learned that his council thought (with glee) that he had representatives of the Crook working in the palace – i.e., Adrienne. If she worded it correctly he might demolish the place himself using some strong – and loud – words. Little more than his voice was needed to bring down a building, after all.

But that would have to wait until after the aforementioned lords had finished 'patrolling' the grounds and tired of following her around, meaning she had to stay in this putrid room with the excuse of tending to Seth. Who had vanished again, but that was beside the point.

Adrienne closed her eyes and began to doze off.

Four floors below her, Seth inspected the bowels of his home.

When I'm king, he mused, shining a torch up each shaft to ensure that, yes, a ladder was fixed securely to the back wall, *all of this stained-glass shit is coming down and I'm putting a proper castle up instead of a glorified greenhouse.*

He was surprised no one had thrown a rock at it yet. Surely King Theo had made enough enemies by *now...*

He manoeuvred the torchlight to Lilly's vault and smiled at the extremely apt dung beetle motif on the door. Noting it was ajar, he pushed it open and laughed out loud, his voice bouncing off each wall.

Every dress his mother had thoughtfully made for his little sister had been thrown unceremoniously inside in a big pile. Interestingly, all jewellery that would no doubt accompany them was nowhere to be seen.

Chuckling mirthfully, Seth closed the door and moved on to the final vault.

A bear stared out of the door like it was guarding it, making Seth shiver. The door was shut tight, but the key remained in the lock, a similar bear decoration looking down at the ground.

Seth turned it curiously, heard the lock creak and slide, and pushed the heavy door inwards with a gulp. There was no telling what would lurk in King Theo's vault.

He peered around the door, letting the bear guard him from the contents of...

... the empty vault.

Seth examined the room intently, without moving a muscle.

There was nothing but thin air and an uneasy atmosphere between the four walls. He'd left it empty on purpose, Seth realised. To all intents and purposes, it was an empty room, and if it had been filled with rotting corpses it would have scared the prince less.

He closed the door firmly and locked it, in case his father came down and left Seth in need of his medic again.

The medic.

Seth slid to the door, his back against the bear door.

The girl was doing something to him. His symptoms were getting worse and, according to an extremely certain James de Vil, none of it was on account of the sunstroke. It was her.

She was poisoning him.

It was the only explanation. She needed him to drink tainted water every twenty minutes, to 'keep him cool' – to keep him ill, more like. Only thing was, he couldn't understand why she wouldn't strike Theo first. Perhaps she could have been trying to weaken him with grief, but grief didn't seem to apply to him. It applied *thanks* to him, but not *to* him.

He considered telling Cienne, but quickly ruled that out. She'd probably lend the girl her shovel and replace the grass head with a real one.

I'll never be able to unsee that, he thought.

He stood up carefully, torch in hand. The whole development was depressing him, and he needed to sleep.

In his quarters, Adrienne jolted awake to the sound of a thump.

She turned to the fireplace and was alarmed to find Seth standing inside it, dusting himself off.

'Your highness?'

He swung to face her. 'How long have you been there?'

'About an hour. I was looking for you.'

Seth's eyes narrowed. He stepped out of the embellished fireplace.

Adrienne regarded him in silence.

He strode to his bedroom – a long walk due to the rooms being too big and mostly empty.

He was a relative of Howie's, no doubt about it. They looked alike, spoke alike, walked alike. He was Howie with crow's feet.

'How are you feeling, your highness?'

'Fine.'

He knelt on one knee and reached under the bed.

'No more hallucinations? Nausea? Dizziness?'

'No more than usual.'

Adrienne frowned, rising from the chair. 'What do you mean, usual?'

'Oh, you know…'

Seth rose to his feet.

'… since you started poisoning me.'

She blinked. 'Poisoning you?'

Seth turned, pointing a loaded crossbow in her direction.

Her eyes widened. Glancing around to certify he was aiming at her, she said, 'Who's been poisoning you?'

'You have,' he said, his voice wavering slightly. 'Clever, noticing I was unwell and coming to the rescue, very attentive.'

'I have no idea what you're talking about.'

He snorted with a smile very much like Howie's wry smirk.

'Very good, like the act a lot, thing is, the curtain's dropped, sweetheart. Now, you can either leave via the door behind you or the window behind me, I don't care which.'

Her pulse quickened. She didn't know where he got this poisoning rubbish from, but she didn't like the way she was speaking to her. The last thing she needed was to be kicked out onto the curb after everything that had happened on the way here.

What was even more upsetting was that it was like Howie was the one accusing her.

'I, I would never poison you, why would you think that? Are you getting symptoms of some kind?' she asked, stepping forward.

'Stay!' he barked.

She froze, stunned.

'Enough with the act, darling,' he said, approaching slowly. 'You know what symptoms I have, you've been causing them with whatever you've been putting in my drinks. Don't even bother with the tears, love,' he added, noticing her eyes shimmering, 'because it won't wash with me. Now leave my palace or I'll have to explain why the king's newest employee has a hole in her arm.'

Adrienne burst into tears.

Seth's eyes shifted from side to side, still wielding the crossbow.

This was an unwelcome predicament. She was bawling her eyes out far too convincingly, chest heaving, nose and eyes streaming, snorts… snorting. It wasn't an attractive sight. Her facial features reddened in the wake of her tears. It made her look younger – she was little more than a child really, at least ten, fifteen years younger than him.

'I just came here to find my family, I'm not here to hurt anyone,' she sobbed. 'I haven't done anything wrong, I just wanted to help you, that's all!'

Seth hesitated.

Then he sighed, dropping the crossbow on the floor.

It fired at a dress of Cienne's opposite, the quarrel vanishing into the petticoats.

'Look,' he said gently.

He walked to her side to stroke her hair.

'I'm clearly just very confused with all that's happened. I'm sorry I accused you.'

She pressed her face into his shoulder, much to Seth's discomfort, and the snorts subsided. He settled an arm around her shoulders until she calmed down. Before long, his shirt felt as though it had been attacked by an extremely isolated rain cloud.

'Umery,' she said.

'Sorry?'

She unstuck her face from his shirt and repeated, 'I'm sorry. I didn't mean to start blubbing like that. It's just been a really hard couple of weeks.'

'That's alright,' he said softly, brushing back her auburn hair. It was pretty, he noticed. 'I'm sorry I made you cry.'

She wiped her eyes and met his gaze.

'You look just like my friend Howie,' she said faintly. 'It's uncanny.'

'Is he as good-looking as me?' he teased.

She giggled. 'Almost.' Her face drooped. 'I miss him.'

'Where did he go?'

'The city, with Prince Ron. Any other time he would have asked me to come along. I suppose we're just not as close as we used to be.' Her voice grew thick with misery.

Seth thought of Rosethorn.

'Your friend is Rose-Prick?' he said without thinking.

Adrienne snorted. 'Is that what you call him? At least it's botanically correct.'

He smiled.

She smiled back.

Seth's smile faltered.

'Oh God,' he hissed.

'What's wrong?'

'The symptoms are back.'

'What symptoms?' she asked abruptly. She checked his pulse and listened to his chest. 'Describe them to me.'

'Um,' he faltered, flushing. 'Nausea. I get nauseous and hot, and… and sometimes when this happens, my… um, my, it gets…'

He blushed, feeling intensely aware of her proximity to him.

'It gets what?' she said, looking into his face.

Seth winced. He shifted his gaze downwards.

'It only ever happens when I'm around you,' he added despairingly.

Her eyes followed his. Her jaw dropped.

'Oh,' she said softly.

'What is it?' asked Seth, wiping sweaty palms on his shirt. 'Is it serious? How bad is it?'

'Bad?' she said, distracted. 'No, it's fine, it's, it's just... I think I, sort of, feel the same way.'

Seth's nose wrinkled.

'I doubt it, you're sort of lacking in the department that's giving me trouble, if you catch my drift—'

She kissed him.

The symptoms were back full force now. Cold sweat covered him, his face flushed deeper, and his insides tingled.

He *liked* it.

He tilted his head to the right and simply stood there, letting her do whatever she was doing, which was utterly unhygienic but not bad *at all...*

Until she pulled herself away.

Seth gaped at her, his mouth still ajar.

'I don't think I should be doing that,' she said.

Seth stared at her and, slowly, tilted his head.

She was beautiful.

But was she? She didn't have much of a figure, wore the dull green dress of palace servitude, had the remains of an acne problem, had a mouth like *silk...*

He swallowed again.

Cienne would kill him. And her. Brutally. With a *spade.*

Sod it.

~

Having ditched Ron in the throne room and gained permission from the lovely Cienne to check Seth's rooms, Howie reached the top of the stairs and found the next door on his right.

'Adrienne? Thought you might be feeling left out, so I came to see... oh.'

In the half-second it took for the two to notice his arrival, Howie had seen romance in an uncertain light.

In one sense it was quite sweet, the way they stood in each other's arms, lips locked, holding each other's hands and hair as opposed to somewhere indecent.

In another completely different sense, their heavy breathing foretold of a disconcerting future event that was thankfully postponed as they broke apart hurriedly.

'Oh, sorry,' said Howie, backing out. 'I didn't know you were, um, sorry, um, your highness…'

Seth gawked at him, his fingers still laced between Adrienne's.

Howie stared at them, his mouth hanging open. He felt unpleasant.

'I'll just leave,' he said, hurrying out.

'No, wait,' began Adrienne.

Howie closed the door carefully behind him.

Adrienne swore under her breath, jerking her hand from Seth's.

'Wait, don't go!' said Seth.

She left the door open for Anna and bounded for the stairs.

The maid frowned after her, clean bed sheets in hand.

'Someone's in a hurry,' Anna commented. She turned to Seth. 'Is everything alright?'

He stared at Anna with his mouth open.

'Your highness?'

He stared at her hair in particular. It was auburn.

'Your highness?' Anna pestered.

Adrienne's face flashed over hers. They were very similar looking.

Seth snatched her around the waist and slammed the door behind her.

~

Adrienne ran after Howie.

He walked hurriedly down the front gardens, Stan and Ron ahead of him.

'Howie!'

He turned.

'Oh, hi,' he said. He seemed subdued.

Adrienne skidded to a halt in the gravel. 'Are you alright?'

Howie's brows lifted. 'Yeah, yeah, I'm fine. Thought you were busy.'

'I… was a bit, yes,' she said after a pause.

'Mmm.' He licked his lips. 'Yeah, I just wanted to let you know we'll be in Castlefoot Market if you wanted to join us when you're finished with… with him. We reckon we can get free lunch if we bring Ron with us. Apparently it's royal prerogative to bum free stuff off people.'

'Oh,' said Adrienne. 'I can come now if you—'

'No hurry,' Howie said quickly. 'I'll see you later.'

He turned away and jogged for the gate.

Stan and Ron glanced at Adrienne with confused expressions before following him.

Adrienne stood where she was, stung.

~

'I'm really, *really* sorry about that.'

'Don't worry,' Anna said in a monotone. 'No harm done.'

'I don't know what came over me,' said Seth in despair.

'I've had worse, it's not a problem.'

'To lick someone's face? That sounds like a problem to me, I'm supposed to be a human being, not a dog!'

'At least you exercised some restraint. Most of your lords head straight for the skirt.'

Seth wrung his hands. 'You won't tell anyone, will you?'

'Not if I want to keep my head attached.'

'Alright then.' His face crumpled. 'I'm *really* sorry.'

Anna sighed. This was not part of the job description. Not by a *long* shot.

She wiped her face hastily and turned her attention to the bed covers.

Seth hesitated.

'Was I... you know... that bad? At kissing?'

Anna glanced at him critically. 'No.'

Seth smirked, leaning on the wall on the other side of the bed. 'For a dead man.'

'Oh,' he said, deflating.

'Maybe your wife would appreciate your efforts better.'

Seth winced, the grass head appearing behind his eyelids. 'You're probably right.'

He kicked himself from the wall and circled the bed to leave.

'I really am—'

'Yes! I know!'

~

The usual biweekly execution in Serpus meant the king would be out for the afternoon, leaving Jimmy to finally relax. The council scurried across the hall, getting arrangements ready for the upcoming festivities and largely ignoring him. He sat at the huge dining table with his feet up.

Seth bounced down the stairs.

'Slacking off, I see.'

Jimmy glanced up.

'Everyone is entitled to some slacking off once in a while,' he said. 'Especially me.'

Seth raised his eyebrows and sat at the table next to him, also with his feet up.

'My wife isn't around, is she?'

Jimmy eyed his anxious expression. 'You saw the shrine, didn't you?'

Seth shuddered in reply.

Jimmy smiled sympathetically. 'Don't worry, I'm pretty sure her brand of insanity is curable.'

'It is, Jimmy. I just don't like the method I'll need to apply to cure it.'

The double doors opened.

Adrienne walked in, glancing at the stairs.

'Do the stairs in here lead somewhere the ones in the throne room don't?'

'Throne room stairs lead to the east wing,' said Jimmy. 'These ones bypass the servants' floors and go straight to the west wing, where the royal apartments are. Why?'

'Nothing, I just wondered.'

She hovered by the door, smiling timidly at Seth, who smiled back.

Jimmy glanced from one to the other in open curiosity.

Seth rose, beckoning for her to follow him.

He walked her to the centre of the courtyard, to where the fountain stood in all its glory.

Adrienne was transfixed to said glory in horror.

'Why is the water fountain flowing blood?'

Seth glanced at the marble snake. Sure enough, it sprayed water that was slightly pinker than average.

'Bird must be trapped in the pump or something. It doesn't always do that. Anyway, look, I came to ask you something. Erm...'

He hesitated.

Adrienne sidled closer, gazing at him.

'What,' he said, 'is your... favourite... type of plant?'

Adrienne smiled brightly.

'Well, I like dock leaves. Because when I was little my uncle had nettles outside the back of the house, and I kept falling on them, and that was when I thought I would do herbalism because they don't just heal that, they help all sorts of things, and, and… you meant what's my favourite flower, didn't you?'

Seth nodded hastily, dismissing thoughts of giving her a bouquet of leaves.

'Um…'

She shrugged.

'I've never really thought about it. I always liked copying the pictures of flowers in storybooks.'

'Oh, you like to read?'

She nodded with a smile.

He clicked his fingers. 'I have it! Wait here!'

He vanished into the dining hall.

Adrienne waited patiently, hands clasped in front of her.

Lilly passed through the courtyard, flicking a knife in the air and catching it.

'Hello,' she greeted cheerfully.

'Hello,' said Adrienne with a curtsy, which Lilly waved away with distaste.

Seth exited the door as Lilly entered it, a wrapped package in his hands.

'I was given this years ago to give to Cienne at our wedding… but her "Seth Crey" shrine is full enough as it is.'

He held it out to her.

Adrienne accepted it, lifting the front cover.

It was a lavishly illustrated book of Adem mythology.

Adrienne poured over the table of contents in fascination, a finger tracing the knotwork around the border.

'I've never heard of these,' she said, head close to the page.

'Really?' Seth said in surprise.

'No, I grew up in Stoneguard mostly. And my uncle was never much of a reader.'

She looked up to meet his gaze. 'Are you sure you want me to have this?'

'Of course,' he said with a smile. 'You'll get more use of it than I will. My mother read them to me so often I know them better than the back of my hand.'

'Only… it's really nice…'

'It's yours. To show you how much I like you… and to apologise for, you know, threatening to shoot you with a crossbow.' He gave her a sheepish smile.

She examined the book avidly.

'Why would you like me?' she asked in bewilderment. 'I'm

nothing special. Princess Cienne is the most beautiful woman in the world. I'm just a girl from Stoneguard, not a princess or a lady or anything…'

Seth shook his head, leaning forward to stroke a section of her hair.

'You're special to me.'

Adrienne beamed shyly.

A messenger boy in green tiptoed over to them and hovered a couple of inches away.

Seth gave him a withering glance. 'Can I help you?'

'The king requests your presence, your highness,' he said, bowing his head.

He stood like this for a few moments as Seth scowled at him.

'I'll be with you in a moment,' he said. He waved him away with the backs of his hands.

The boy bowed and left.

Seth rolled his eyes and turned back to Adrienne.

'I'll see you later on,' he said, reaching out to her.

He cradled one cheek in his left hand and kissed the other, making her blush.

'Goodbye, your highness,' she said softly.

He sidled past.

'Seth,' he corrected, pivoting to face her. '"Your highness" is a term for people who are below me.'

She grinned as he left, clutching the book to her chest.

Jimmy and Lilly had their heads stuck in the crack between the dining hall doors.

'Sorry,' Lilly said, hastily moving out of the way. 'Couldn't help ourselves.'

'It's the most interesting thing he's done in the last twenty years,' Jimmy added. He peered at the book in her arms. 'Did he give you that?'

'He wanted me to have it,' she said, anxious. 'Should I give it back?'

Lilly shook her head. 'Nah, keep it. It'll only go in Cienne's "Seth Crey" shrine otherwise.'

'That's exactly what Prince Seth said.' She ran her fingers down the leather-bound cover. 'Do all princes give expensive things to people who work for them?'

'People, not often,' said Jimmy. 'Women, on the other hand…'

Adrienne winced.

'Mind you,' Lilly said, 'Seth isn't your typical prince. He doesn't have a whole lot going on between the ears, for a start.'

'I know that,' she said in a low voice, in case he was in earshot. 'He tried to shoot me earlier because he had a sexual attraction to me and thought I was poisoning him!'

'I told him not to do that,' said Jimmy, his eyes to the heavens.

'And then we kissed – which was actually rather nice,' she conceded coyly, 'and now he's giving me presents. You don't think he's asking me to be his mistress, do you?'

'I told him not to do that either,' said Jimmy.

'Yeah, that would be a bad idea,' Lilly said, wincing. 'Cienne isn't the most...'

She looked to Jimmy for assistance.

'She has anger management issues,' he said.

'Oh,' said Adrienne uneasily.

'And she's very easily jealous,' Lilly added. 'There was a whole spell there a few years ago when she had it out for me because she was convinced I was sleeping with him.' She grimaced. 'She can be *seriously* disturbed sometimes.'

'Shame,' said Jimmy. 'Otherwise she's a very pleasant woman. Stuff like that makes her look like a maniac.'

Adrienne could only agree there.

'And there's my dad's desire for grandchildren,' Lilly added. 'He can be very persuasive when he keeps a giant axe under the dinner table.'

Adrienne could only agree with *that* also.

'Anyway,' said Jimmy, 'you're better off with your Howard. He's not married for a start, or practically middle-aged. And he does carpentry,' he added with enthusiasm. 'Very useful.'

'I never thought he liked me that way,' said Adrienne glumly. 'At least, not until earlier. He walked in on me and Seth... you know, and he looked really upset about it.'

'And well he should,' said Jimmy firmly. 'You're a good-looking girl. I'd parade you around the city over Ronald Horne any day.'

Lilly shot him a look of deep disgust. 'I bet you would.'

'I'm speaking objectively,' he argued.

'Oh please, where a skirt is concerned, you rarely speak objectively,' Lilly scolded with a grin. She gave Adrienne a side-glance. 'Though if it helps, he does make a very good point.'

Adrienne smiled sheepishly.

'Right. Well in that case,' she said, lifting herself to her full height, 'I will buy something nice to wear and meet him in the city for lunch.'

'And I'll come and prod him with something sharp until he compliments you,' Lilly said brightly.

Adrienne grinned.

~

At the keep entrance, just inside the porch, the king was displeased.

'IN A MINUTE?!' he howled. 'When I give a summons, I expect him to be here IMMEDIATELY! Fetch him again this instant before I find and disembowel him!'

'Your majesty, I'm sure he means no offense,' Cienne said in a soothing voice. 'He's had a busy week, I'm sure he'll be along shortly—'

'Father!'

She swung at Seth's bark.

'Is it urgent?' he asked impatiently. 'I was just on my way out with Cienne.'

Cienne blinked. 'Were you?'

Seth halted at Cienne's side, dressed in the standard gold and green regalia.

'Where can I get a coach?' he demanded. 'Something pretty! And today would be nice, please!'

Servants scattered in search of horses and carriages.

'About time!' King Theo boomed. 'I trust you've recovered from your convenient ills of late?'

'Well enough,' said Seth.

A coach trundled into view.

'Come, Cienne,' he said sharply, striding to it.

'Boy!'

Seth turned with a sigh.

'Your mother and I will be out for the evening. The Earl of Herpes will be meeting us at the Old Fort, he has a daughter that would be a good match for Mortimer. We're sending Lilly to Osney's to befriend some women *without* a collection of diseases, so the keep is yours for the night. Should you need it.'

King Theo's gaze flickered to Cienne, and he winked.

Seth winked back. 'As you will, my liege.'

He pushed Cienne to the coach by her shoulders.

'Cienne,' he said as the doorman slammed the carriage shut behind them.

She perched demurely in front of him.

'It's been apparent to me lately that you might be a little bit…

annoyed with me.'

'No, no, not at all,' she lied.

'No, you have, I've noticed,' he said. 'And I've also noticed that I've been neglecting you. So,' he said as they trundled downhill, his back turned away from the horses, 'I want to rectify this by asking if you would like to spend the day with… me.'

He lifted his shoulders hopefully.

A smile crept up one side of her mouth. 'Really?'

'Yes,' Seth said with a smile.

'Of course I would,' she beamed. 'Where would you like to go?'

'The Crook in Arthur Stibbons' Street. I've reserved.'

She made a face. 'The knocking shop,' she said dully.

'Nah, not really,' he said jovially. 'Anywhere you like.'

He gestured to the countryside at large.

She smiled. 'Anywhere?'

He nodded once.

Cienne beamed. 'I know just the place.'

~

III

In the Head of Arthur Stibbons' Street, i.e., the square at the end of the street, where the late Arthur Stibbons' head was found, a play was being performed in the centre of a large ring of children. It was called 'Knighty-Knight Salamander', according to the bad grammar on the sign atop the horrifically painted backdrop.

Arthur Stibbons' Street was notoriously discovered after, a century ago, a group of the king's guards were sent in pursuit of an escaped convict named Arthur 'Salamander' Stibbons. What they found were several body parts situated in the respective parts of the street, designed in the shape of a giant stick man lying on his back by a street founder with acute precognition and a macabre sense of humour.

His macabre sense of humour was demonstrated in his celebrated comedy… apparently.

'Salamander, thy were a crafty fellow indeed,' intoned a man wrapped in tinfoil, 'but halt: aren't there thy limbs surrounding me? Lizard limbs to my right, lizard limbs to my left, a crown before my feet, laced in blood…'

'I thought this was a comedy?' asked Ron uncertainly.

'I expect the playwright thought it was very funny when he

looked into the future and saw how much money he made off it,' said Archie in a dull voice. 'I told you it would be crap, Howard.'

'I was told it was very good,' Howie said, embarrassed.

'It is, my hole,' Archie scoffed.

'Hark thee, thiefly poltergeist!' the actor exclaimed, flailing his arms in the air and jogging around the set, to everyone's bemusement.

He picked up a shard of wood that was supposed to be a lance and flailed that around too.

'Hark at the cries of the laughing dead, hark at the victims of your bloody reign, hark, hark, HARK AT YOUR—'

Ron snatched the lance irritably and smashed it over the actor's head.

He toppled face-first onto the cobbles, much to the cheering crowd's approval.

'Hark at that, mate,' Ron snarled at the back of his head, rubbing his bloodshot eyes.

Laughing the loudest in the centre of the audience was Lilly, standing doubled-over, nursing her ribs. Adrienne stood at her heels in a pale blue gown that set off her gleaming reddish-brown hair.

Howie half-smiled and made his way over.

'So much for socialising with the noblewomen of Osney,' he teased Lilly.

His gaze caught Adrienne. 'Oh, you look lovely.'

Adrienne flushed profusely.

Lilly straightened up to face him, wiping tears of mirth from her eyes.

'Yeah, I sent the chambermaid in my clothes and told everyone I was coming down with a cold. What my old man don't know won't hurt him. I thought I'd come here and have some *fun.*'

Ron joined them in the middle of the throng, wrinkling his nose at Lilly.

'So,' Lilly said, strolling out of the square with the group in tow. 'What brings you to the city's leading entertainment industry?'

'We were hunting out a good pie maker, and they were in our way,' said Archie.

They strode down the street's torso.

'Also we figured we ought to complete Howard's task from the gods before they confiscate his good luck.'

'I'd hardly call it good luck if he keeps being molested by my big brother,' Lilly said. 'What task's this, by the way?'

'Finding my father,' said Ron.

'Oh, King Sam,' Lilly said in realisation. 'My father used to talk about him. Said he was quite decent as the family goes and was lucky to exist that way.'

Ron waited patiently for the 'no offense', which didn't come.

'You tried asking the gossips yet? They know everything, between them. You should ask your man who runs the Prince Death, he'll have heard it. You should ask about your old lady,' she said to Howie, who looked bemused. 'She dumped you in the Forest, wasn't it? I'll bet whoever found you is from here, you know. You get all sorts in the city.'

'Right,' he said levelly.

'I mean, surely she's from here, right? Unless she got pregnant in the Forest. But then that would make you half Faerie, so you'd probably be blue. Wouldn't you?'

'Don't really wanna talk about it—'

'Oh, actually,' she said, pointing at Howie's nose, 'you know what, you're a dead ringer for my Uncle Fred. That might be it, I heard he was a right man-whore back in the day, he might have got your mum up the duff and pegged it back to Portabella—'

'Hygiene may be a challenge for you,' Ron cut in sharply, 'but he clearly said he didn't want to talk about it. Unless your hearing is as bad as your sense of smell?'

Lilly frowned at him as they moved ahead of her. She gave her armpit an experimental sniff.

'She might be on to something,' said Archie. 'Asking the gossips about the king, I mean.'

Lilly retched loudly, dropping her arm for reasons of safety.

The others paid her no notice.

'People would surely notice a king hanging around,' Archie continued.

'Particularly one with no concept of the word "inconspicuous",' Ron added.

'The pub's where they'd meet,' said Adrienne. 'It's like what a cauldron is to witches.'

'Or an armoury to a battle militia,' said Ron. 'Stan said they were throwing hatchets at him the other week.'

'That'd be because he's a thicky and goes in there in the evenings,' Lilly said with contempt. 'Afternoon's best, while the families are in for lunch and the drunks are still docile.'

Upon their entrance to the Prince Death, a great crescendo of a silence erupted. That is to say, most people abruptly stopped making noise and opted to converse in lower tones, inevitably leading to louder volume levels thanks to a large number of incredibly bad whisperers.

They stood in silence as the hissing noises hit them full in the face.

'I can see why they called the place Serpus,' said Archie.

'It's a Crey! Sure of it!'

'No, no he's just some orphan they took in.'

'He looks like a bastard son to me. Fink he's Seth's? He looks like Prince Seth.'

They made a beeline for the bar.

'D'you fink he's married?'

'What's it to you?' her companion asked sulkily, the first non-whisperer since they entered the bar.

'Bit too good-looking to waste, is all I'm saying,' the woman objected.

'I dunno, he looks shifty,' another said.

'Yeah, his eyes are too close together.'

'Can't trust a man whose eyes are too close together.'

'Sitting right here,' grumbled the non-whisperer, 'and my missus is ogling the upper classes.'

'And he's blond,' a voice pointed out. 'Blond men are evil. Common-known fact.'

'King Seb was blond, and we all know what he did…'

'*Hmm*,' they murmured.

'Sitting *right here*,' the non-whisperer continued, unperturbed. 'At this *very table.*'

Howie cleared his throat loudly.

A barman eyed him, his sleeve buttoned over the place where his arm had been severed above the elbow. 'We don't want no trouble here.'

Howie frowned at him. 'Why would there be trouble?'

The man didn't answer. He just looked at them through narrowed eyes.

Archie stepped up to the bar. 'We'll just have a drink, please.'

'Something strong,' Ron said. 'And noise cancelling.'

'Only allowed sell ale this time of day now,' he said, 'and weak ale at that. Wife's orders, on account of a song went round that wasn't to her taste.'

He eyeballed Howie and Ron in particular.

Howie was impressed by Ron's expression of utter bemusement. He then recalled that Ron had drunk himself into oblivion on the morning in question and was probably genuinely bemused.

'Shame,' he said to break the silence.

He reached for his coin purse.

'No, no need, sir,' the barman insisted, waving his hand. 'This round's on me, if it please you, your highness.'

'Um, thanks,' said Howie, 'but I'm not a highness.'

''Course you are,' he insisted. He plonked a large flagon of ale on the counter though, for the life of him, Howie couldn't recall him pouring it. 'Not for nothing you're our namesake, Prince Seth. Hope there's no offense taken by the nickname, your highness,' he said quickly. 'Only anything would do to replace "The Wet"—'

'I'm not Seth,' Howie cut in. 'Er, Prince Seth, that is. I'm the bloke that came in after,' he scowled at the memory, 'you know, the one he molested the other day.'

'Oh, right. Well, have it on me anyway. You could probably do with obliterating that memory away.'

Howie nodded in relief as the man turned away.

'On another note,' Archie said, leaning on the bar beside Howie, 'we actually came here for some information—'

'I don't know nuffin,' he said automatically.

'You sure?' Lilly said.

She dangled a sack of coins under his nose.

'I can make it worth your while,' she wheedled.

The barman gave her a withering glance.

'In one ear, out the other, you know how it is—'

Archie clapped the bag of coins away, irritated.

'We just want to know if King Samuel's been around at all?'

The barman's eyes narrowed. 'What for?'

'So I can hit him,' said Ron.

'What d'you mean, hit him?'

Ron glanced around. 'Like this?'

He cuffed Archie around the ear, earning an indignant yelp.

The barman relaxed. 'Oh, alright then.'

He leaned forward, as did they.

'I heard the Forest being mentioned,' he said. 'But I wouldn't go parroting that around Serpus too loudly. King Theo has a nasty habit of beheading anyone who crosses the border – reckons what they do to Faeries is animal cruelty.'

'Well, it is,' Archie said.

'I heard it's more two-sided than it looks, actually,' said Lilly.

'Anyway,' the barman went on.

Howie's eyes flickered from face to face during the exchange before he realised that no, he was not going to get an explanation, it seemed.

'Last thing we need is another hideous battle barely twenty years after the last one, so I'd keep shtum if you want King Samuel to live through the year.'

'He'd hardly execute another king just like that, would he?' asked Ron.

The barman shrugged. 'I'm not a king, mate, so I wouldn't know. I'd wait for King Sam to return of his own accord if I were you. I wouldn't call the place friendly. Only King Theo's ever set foot in there without being armed to the teeth.'

'I see. Cheers for that.'

They picked up their drinks and meandered around the tables to the beer garden out back.

Just as they were leaving, the whispering gained volume.

'What big ears that old bugger had.'

Archie's head jerked back into the room.

'Better to hear an awful attempt at whispering with,' he retorted with a scowl.

~

A sparrow soared over the centre of Serpus, the only speck of colour in a world of greys and browns. Colour never happened in the city of Serpus. Colour cost too much to be wasted.

The bird flew above the knotted streets and skinny alleys until it found its target and dived.

Fifteen feet below, Lilly and Ron had found a charitable patriot with a coach and were climbing aboard.

Adrienne nudged Howie.

'What did you mean earlier by "molested"?'

Howie made a face. 'You don't want to know and, frankly, I wish I didn't.'

The sparrow landed on his shoulder.

He swatted it off irritably.

'So we're headed for the Forest, then,' Ron said.

'Looks like it,' said Howie. 'After you, my lady.'

He bowed to Adrienne with a flourish, indicating for her to board the coach ahead of him.

She went a bit pink and smiled at him.

'Here's hoping he's just lost so we can finally go home.' Howie touched Adrienne's elbow lightly. 'Will you go with me? Might be a good idea to have a trained medic on hand in case the *fairies* attack.'

He wiggled his fingers in front of Archie's face.

Archie scowled. 'Go ahead and mock. It won't be me holding your hand after they violate you.'

Howie lifted a sceptical eyebrow.

The sparrow landed on his other shoulder. It tweeted in annoyance as it was brushed off again.

'Will the king be giving you some guards? 'Cause I'm not having her alone in the Forest with *you* as her only form of defence,' Archie went on.

'I'll ask if you insist. Will you bugger off?'

This last one was aimed at the persistent avian.

It answered a call of nature on Howie's collar in response.

Howie exclaimed in disgust, wiping the side of his neck.

'What does it want?'

'It dropped a scroll,' Ron said, pointing.

Adrienne knelt briefly to the cobbles to retrieve it.

Mission complete, the sparrow fluttered to the roof of the coach.

'I've heard of carrier pigeons, but this looks a bit silly,' said Lilly.

The group surrounded the note.

It read, in a spidery hand:

Her Majesty the Queen of the Forest requests your audience. It is of the greatest importance. Please await Her Majesty at the Sleeping Meadow as soon as possible.

A tiny map about an inch wide consumed the rest of the small slip of parchment, showing a lake and an 'X' indicating their proposed destination.

'Looks like we're starting here,' said Howie.

'Rule me out, the woman's a nutter,' said Archie.

'And that makes her different from anyone here… how?'

'Wastelands,' Archie said.

'Mother,' Ron reminded him.

'We might as well go, since we're headed that way anyway,' Lilly said brightly.

'Who said anything about you going?' said Howie.

'Me,' she said, as though that settled everything.

She glanced at the little bird, who was cleaning its feathers.

'Determined, innee? Flying all this way just to give us a bit of paper.'

The bird scratched at the coach roof with its feet. Shortly after, it inclined its head downwards.

Ron climbed up to read it aloud.

'"You would be too if your queen was a nutter".'

They blinked.

The bird tweeted again and gave what could almost have been a shrug.

~

Vladimir glared at the invitation in his hands.

King Crey's festivities were on the third week of summer. Unless he managed to *fly* there, he would have to cross the charred peaks of the Wastelands by horse to make it there in time.

What an unfortunate occurrence, Vladimir thought sourly. *I have to risk my life crossing the haunted Wastelands to celebrate the 'return' of 'dead' Seth Crey. Because King Crey would never have thought of that.*

He wasn't looking forward to this outing, and not just because of the suspicion of foul play. It was his first official trip out without Sir Marbrand, and he said as such to Lord Tetzel during a supper between them, a blank-faced Felicity and nobody else – because nobody else could hold a civil conversation with Vladimir Horne without getting a haunch of pork hocked at their head.

Queen Aaliyaa was nowhere to be seen. Just as well, Vladimir thought, or she really *would* get a haunch of pork hocked at her head. She had been going on non-stop about the 'imposter' Howard Rosethorn and about how she would secure her son's rightful position. Vladimir hoped she'd take her time with it. He was enjoying not having the fate of the realm plonked across his shoulders for a change.

'Any joy with the council's investigations?' Lord Tetzel asked.

He wiped his nose on his sleeve, spreading a thick streak of mucus over a moustache that could have been a pipe-cleaner in a previous life. Queen Aaliyaa's mother had drawn the short straw with her second husband. The Tetzels simply didn't have the gravitas and otherworldly aura Vladimir's grandfather had had to offer. Lord Leroy was no exception. He was more slime than anything else.

Vladimir tore his gaze away from the slug trail across his uncle's upper lip.

'Nothing,' he said in reply. 'Sir Marbrand has as many distinguishing features as a mud puddle, and nobody recognises the name "Sir Sadie Marbrand" as anything but a joke. Ten times I was referred to a house of ill repute. Ten! And this was *after* I had said it was a man!'

'Do not blame the council, I fear since they lost their lands to the Battle in the Orchard, they have become quite detached from the world beyond the council chamber. Not to worry. If anyone can persuade Ronald from his captors, it's old Marbrand. Never met a man with a better sense of honour and duty.'

'Certainly,' Vladimir muttered.

He wasn't so sure himself. An honourable knight wouldn't have snuck out in the dead of night, leaving a random guard to explain himself.

A cloud momentarily passed over the sunlight streaming into the window, dulling the room for a moment. Vladimir's face became a selection of shadows as he pondered aloud.

'Marbrand vanishes soon after my dearly departed brother. That makes three crucial members of the household missing in a matter of weeks, all before a dubious invitation's arrival…'

Tetzel raised an eyebrow. 'You think the Creys have a hand in this?'

'Perhaps. Although it does seem convenient that Marbrand was on duty at the time of the prisoners' escape.'

'Oh, he wouldn't have anything to do with that, your majesty,' Tetzel insisted. 'Trust me. Marbrand and I were thick as thieves back in the day.'

Vladimir recalled every instance of Tetzel and Marbrand's interactions, wherein Marbrand usually wore an expression that withered grass.

'Indeed.' Vladimir paused. 'Uncle, you are my sole remaining confidant save for my mother and my wife. I need your council on this: should I attend the Creys' celebrations?'

Tetzel stroked his moustache a moment in thought before quickly regretting it.

He wiped his hand on his front.

'It would be a sign of weakness to duck out of the event. Attend the festivities, my prince, but warily. I'll have my best men from Thintower escort you.' He opened a bottle of wine and poured himself a glass. 'How is the queen bearing up?'

Vladimir snorted. 'She doesn't seem bothered if I'm being frank. She never did like Ronald.'

'I assure you, your mother loves you both dearly,' he said with conviction. 'As her half-brother, our private exchanges, however short, provide for me an intensity of knowledge on my dear older sister.'

'Really?' said Vladimir. 'She talks to me non-stop, and I still have no idea what she's blathering on about. A pity, really. Her talents could have proved useful if she had any cognitive coherence.' He frowned into the ceiling. 'Should I bring her with me?'

'That would be going too far,' Tetzel warned. 'Bring Aaliyaa into contact with the pretender calling himself the Knight of Raining Thorns? Not a good idea, your majesty.'

'True.'

Felicity held a lock of her mousy hair under her nose and sniffed it. 'Am I coming to the party?'

'Of course, dear,' Tetzel assured her, patting her hand across from the table. 'Tell me, what will you wear? Bring us an outfit so we can see.'

'Alright,' she said with a tiny, triangular grin, bouncing to the stairs.

'What. A. Moron,' seethed Vladimir as she left. 'She has the mental capacity of an empty peapod. Bring me Cienne Fleurelle, I'd trade my crown and country to Seth Crey for that masterpiece.'

'Unwise,' said Tetzel.

'Don't I know it,' Vladimir said with a sigh. 'Let's just hope my current wife emerges with something half-tasteful to wear.'

A moment later, Felicity Emmett appeared with a large dress.

To Vladimir's annoyance, it was not the least bit tasteful by any stretch of the imagination.

~

IV

Jimmy strode in circles around the throne room. Waiting was one thing in life that did not appeal to him. He preferred to be busy. Marginally.

On the other hand, it did teach him to be observant, or so he thought as he spotted a giant ornamental shield trembling in the corner of the room.

Prince Seth was behind it, his hair standing at odd angles and his shirt askew, wielding a sword.

'Sir, you look like you've been attacked,' he stated in faint surprise. 'Who did this to you?'

'Wife,' he choked.

'Ah, I figured as much. I take it the romantic dinner is off?'

A knock landed on the door.

Lilly-Anna entered, flanked by her recently acquired entourage.

Jimmy gave her a nod. He could never bring himself to bow at something that smelled of a sunbathing compost pile.

'Good evening, your highness. Your father isn't here, but he's expected back in a few minutes, so I should hide, if I were you. There's a dinner for two going cold upstairs, if anyone fancies it,' he added as an afterthought.

'Nah,' she said swiftly. 'You're not my type. Small girls, big guys, that's my bracket.'

Jimmy frowned at her before giving his head a small, bemused shake.

Lilly peered over at the shield. 'You alright over there?'

'Alright?' Seth squeaked, shivering. 'It was horrible! Romantic? In a cornfield around the back of the palace? Maybe if I was with someone else! I'm no expert, but even I know you don't kiss with your teeth!'

'Ouch,' winced Jimmy. 'Nowhere delicate, I hope?'

'Don't answer that,' Lilly said in a pained voice.

'But no, that was fine, she got the hang of it in the end, we went home, had the apartment to ourselves, it was great,' Seth said rapidly, 'went upstairs, killed the lights – but then she wouldn't stop!'

'Lovely,' drawled Jimmy. 'Anyway—'

'It was awful!' Seth went on, completely unheeded. 'She wouldn't let go, I couldn't breathe! She wouldn't let me go to sleep, I was so tired—'

'ANYWAY,' Lilly cut in, 'just came to see the lads back, thanks for the tip-off, I'm off out.'

She exited the keep briskly.

Seth opened his mouth to continue.

'I'll get you a drink,' Jimmy said while he had the chance. 'Put down the weaponry, I'm sure she's done with you now.'

Seth lowered the shield with a shudder.

Howie, Adrienne, Ron and Archie lingered in the centre of the hall, where Lilly had left them.

Howie's eyes thinned.

There's no need to be harsh, he thought. *Enthusiasm is nothing to be ashamed of.*

He couldn't see what she saw in him anyway. His face was all nose and teeth, and his eyes were so close together they almost met in the middle. It was only part-exaggeration. Howie had spent the last ten years lamenting these details in his own face.

Seth pushed himself onto his feet and made for the three gilded thrones at the top of the hall.

Atop a three-step dais, the sturdy oak chairs gleamed, golden snakes spiralling against one another up and around the cushioned seats and backs. Two snake heads reared at each other open-mouthed over the head of Seth Crey as he slumped into the throne to the far right, his back to an embroidered 'S' stitched in gold to the emerald fabric.

Seth folded his arms behind his head, his eyes on Adrienne.

Howie turned to find her smiling at him coyly.

His thoughts wandered to the incident of before and quickly jumped back out.

Howie cleared his throat.

'When will the king be returning?'

Seth flung him a withering glance. 'How should I know? I'm not his keeper.' His eyes roved over Adrienne again, with a hunger. 'Why?'

'Need to speak to him about King Sam,' Howie mumbled, his neck growing hot.

There was a tense pause in which Jimmy returned, placed a drink in Seth's hand and stepped away in silence.

Archie broke it with a loud yawn.

'I'm knackered,' he announced. 'Any chance of me kipping here? I was gonna stay up and see the king, but I'm dead on my feet.'

Howie ignored him, his gaze fixed sullenly to Adrienne, whose eyes were fixed rather more earnestly on Seth.

'The butler will give you a room,' Adrienne said, absently.

Jimmy glared at her. 'Oh, will he?'

'Yes,' Seth barked, 'he will.'

'Right you are. This way,' Jimmy said swiftly, leading Archie to the stairs.

Ron followed, sensing a Vladdy-type bad atmosphere and striving to avoid it.

This left Howie and Adrienne alone with the prince, although, for a change, Howie was being totally ignored as an unfamiliar tension coursed through the room.

'Well,' Adrienne began, 'I take it you didn't have a very nice day.'

Seth breathed in.

'No,' he exhaled. 'Went awry the moment you left my room, actually. Shame, really. It started so well.'

She blushed. 'It wouldn't have been a good idea if I had stayed, would it?'

'Why would that be?' he asked, a picture of innocence.

'Well,' she said, 'there was an… atmosphere building…'

Seth smirked at her.

Howie rolled his eyes. 'She means you were gonna have sex.'

'Howie!' Adrienne snapped, reddening.

'Don't be embarrassed, my love,' said Seth, grinning at her. 'We're all adults here – except for him, maybe. I doubt he even knows the rudimentary procedure, really.'

'I got a good idea from the two occasions you tried to make love to *me*,' said Howie frostily.

They ignored him, each consumed with the presence of the other.

'Would we have?' Adrienne asked. 'If I hadn't left?'

Howie bristled. Why does she insist on talking about—

Seth tilted his head to one side.

'No, I couldn't do that to you,' he said softly. 'I'm not sure you could handle it.'

Howie fixed his gaze to the uppermost point in the vaulted ceiling, concentrating on his breathing.

Adrienne licked her lips.

'The sheer weight of the consequence,' Seth continued, 'would flatten us instantly.'

'Oh, you're not *that* fat, sir,' Howie commented with a friendly smile. A cheap barb, but an effective one.

Seth glowered at him, folding his arms self-consciously about his abdomen.

The doors swung open with a bang.

King Theo and Queen Eleanor entered, followed by their usual entourage.

'You never told me she was diseased, Osney,' grumbled King Theo.

He strode up the emerald carpet and dropped into his throne beside Seth.

'I could have married her to Mortimer and cleaned up.'

'Your majesty,' Osney said in a pained simper, 'Mortimer has been presumed dead for about twenty years now.'

'Oh, nonsense,' King Theo waved it off. 'Saw him the other day, on my way back from delegations. He's a good lad – much better than the heirs we usually end up with.'

'Cheers,' Seth said sourly.

'Seth!' he exclaimed, as though just realising he was there.

He clapped a hand on Seth's shoulder so hard his bones shuddered.

'How did it go? Did everything go to plan?'

'There was hardly much on the agenda, Father,' said Seth, massaging life back into his arm.

'How was it? Come on, out with it?'

Seth grimaced. 'Uh...'

'Well?'

'She weren't unwilling.'

'So you've consummated it, then?'

'Yep,' Seth replied, wincing at the memory.

'*Yes*,' said King Theo, rubbing his hands together. 'I give Fleurelle a year and all that good land will be *mine*.'

Seth's eyes thinned. 'You mean mine?'

'In name, yes, but it's still *mine*.' He wheezed a laugh under his breath. 'Where is she now?'

'Upstairs, asleep. I hope.'

'Is she with child?'

'Oh, I don't know! I didn't hear a bell ring to certify I'd hit the jackpot,' said Seth, rolling his eyes.

'The sooner, the better, I say,' Osney said. 'Good, solid proof of the affair is what's needed.'

'Yes, the shock might kill him faster,' King Theo said in anticipation.

Queen Eleanor leaned forward in her seat to beam at her son. 'I'm so proud of you, Seth.'

He smiled thinly.

'Why don't you have an early night? Cienne would love to see more of you!'

The smile slithered from his face.

Howie eagerly adopted it.

'Alright, then,' Seth said with a wince, rising.

'And do what she says!' Theo called after him. 'I want you milked dry by sunrise!'

'Oh for Christs' sake!' Seth exclaimed under his breath.

Howie tried vainly to suppress a smirk. It crept through regardless.

Seth glowered at it as he stalked to the doorway behind him.

King Theo cackled at his own wit.

'I assume he's in good working order?' he said to Adrienne.

Adrienne started.

'Er, oh, yes, your majesty. As far as I'm aware.'

'He hasn't come to you with plumbing issues or anything?'

'No, no, quite the opposite,' she blurted, 'I mean, he, um, he... actually said he was looking forward to... to spending time with the princess.'

I'll bet he did, Howie thought sourly.

'Excellent! Glad to hear it!' King Theo boomed. 'Keep your eye on Cienne, won't you? If anyone will get a child out of the boy, it'll be her.'

'That or his Cousin Elyse,' Eleanor muttered, unheard by everyone but Howie.

Adrienne curtsied and made for the stairs with a pained expression.

'You're a good omen, my lad!' he exclaimed to Howie. 'If it weren't for the two of you, the boy would be in his grave by now!'

Hold that thought, Howie mused.

Aloud he said, 'I appreciate your… appreciation, your majesty.'

'Speaking of graves, any news on poor old Sam?'

'Actually, yes,' Howie said, eager for a change of subject. 'We got a tip-off in the Prince—'

He stopped himself just in time.

'—in the pub on Arthur Stibbons' Street that he was spotted near the Forest. And,' he added, pulling out a slip of paper, 'we received this shortly after.'

He climbed to the stop step briefly to hand King Theo the missive.

Theo paused, eyes fixed to the slip of paper. 'I see.'

Howie hesitated, licking his lips.

'I was gonna meet her,' he said. 'To ask some questions. You don't think she's up to something, do you?'

Theo looked up.

'Oh, no, she could fell an army in her sleep,' he said nonchalantly. 'If she were up to something, we'd know about it. She's not exactly… subtle. No, I think you have the right idea.'

'Should I bring some guards with me?'

'… I don't think they would do you much good, my boy,' he said honestly. 'I'll send four of our palace guardsmen, for your own piece of mind. Bring your young lady with you, you may have need of her. And Ronald, that might help. And… wait here a moment.'

He rose and headed for the back corridor.

'I have something for you to show her, will help matters immensely. I won't be long.'

He vanished.

Howie waited with his hands behind his back. He smiled at Queen Eleanor, who smiled back.

Until the doors opened with a bang and Lilly strode in.

She froze under her mother's gaze.

'Lilly,' she said in dark tones.

'Hi, Mum,' said Lilly with a sweet smile. 'Dad isn't home, is he?'

'He is.'

'He is? Alright, I'll be back later, then,' she trilled, backing out.

'Lilly!'

The doors slammed.

Queen Eleanor sighed. 'He'll kill her one day, just you wait.'

A little while later, Theo returned, burdened by a long item covered in green cloth.

'This was a gift from her the day Seth was born,' he said, standing beside Howie and unwrapping it. 'The blade is unbreakable, I'm told. I've never had the gall to try it out – one of a kind, you see. You are to wear *this*,' he handed it to him, 'when you see *her*. That way, she'll know you're with me.'

Howie unsheathed the broadsword in his hands.

The usual snake motif was there: two silver serpents, one intertwined with the other, from one end of the blade to the ends of the guards, where the heads snarled in opposite directions. The hilt itself was wrapped in snake skin and comfortable to hold.

The blade itself was its true highlight.

Two slim shards of crystal had been flattened together, sparkling in the light of the braziers. Howie grasped the hilt and pointed the blade at the ceiling. It was the weight of a throwing knife – literally. A two-year-old could easily have wielded it.

'It's a magic sword,' Howie said in awe.

'In a way,' King Theo smiled.

Howie twirled it in his left hand and wielded it horizontally above one shoulder – making sure to point it at the door rather than King Theo's face.

'It's yours.'

Howie's head jerked up.

'What?' he asked in disbelief, a smile creeping across his face.

'I don't want the bloody thing, it's as thin as a sheet.' he said, flicking the flat of the blade and making it *ping*. 'I'll believe it's unbreakable when I see it.'

Howie brought the blade level with his eyes, gawking at it.

'Shouldn't Seth have it?'

'Nah, he doesn't deserve it. I'll give him something he can use when he gives me an heir, like a spoon or something. It's yours if you grant me one boon in return.'

Howie nodded, admiring the sword fondly.

King Theo put an arm around his shoulders.

'I need you to forge a truce with her,' he said. 'We've been warring for nigh on twenty years about her bloody borders, but I reckon if you do manage to get old Sam home, that slimy son of his will have a say, and as for Aaliyaa Horne…'

He shuddered.

'If we get the Forest on *our* side, *those two* can't get her first, understand?'

'Yes, sir.'

'Good man.' He patted Howie on the head. 'Take Seth with you, he can make himself useful for a change. Oh,' he added, 'and don't tell Seth where you got the sword. He's already jealous of you as it is, and I can't have him acting like a child in front of our friend in the Forest.'

'Don't see what he's jealous of,' Howie muttered. 'He's the one married to a frigging *goddess.*'

'Pardon?'

Howie jumped. 'Nothing,' he said in louder tones. 'Just thinking aloud.'

~

V

A knock came to the door.

'We're closed,' the barman called out.

'Imperial business,' a voice called back in.

The barman paused. Who the hell in Arthur Stibbons' Street used the word 'imperial'? Did the average alcoholic larcenist even know what 'imperial' meant?

He certainly didn't, so he decided to open the door – though only a smidge so that a mere sliver of him was visible from outside.

'Yes?'

A small man stood on the step, dressed in battered armour with his helm under one arm. Behind him loomed a great boulder of a man, blotting out the light of the sun – or the amount of natural sunlight you actually *got* from a sun that blatantly thought Arthur Stibbons' Street didn't deserve to be lit.

'Morning,' the smaller man greeted in a gruff voice, rubbing grey fuzz on his chin and looking like he hadn't slept in two days. 'I'm looking for three men. Two young lads, one dark-haired and one blond, and a middle-aged one with a limp. Have you seen them in the last few weeks?'

'Wossit to you?' the man asked.

'We fink the prince is a captive,' the bigger man replied.

He earned an elbow in the ribs from his companion.

'OW!'

'Prince?'

'The dark-haired individual,' said the small man with reluctance.

'Oh, Prince Ron? Yeah, bit of a regular, as it goes,' the barman said. 'Who's asking?'

'A guard of the Stonekeep,' said the first man.

'Who specifically, if he asks?'

The man looked as though he had been dreading this. 'Sadie Marbrand.'

'Oh, the missus is it?'

'No, it's him, actually,' corrected the larger man, jerking a thumb at his companion.

He received another dig in the ribs for his trouble. 'OW!'

The man looked bemused. 'Your name is Sadie?'

Marbrand rubbed his eyes.

The barman burst out laughing.

'Sadie?' he said with a chuckle. 'Yeah'r, I'll tell him. I'll tell you where he lives, in fact, since that name's too funny to be a lie. Lives north from here, in the castle. King Crey might let you in if you tell him Sadie's looking for him!'

He roared with laughter again.

Elliot Maynard barked a laugh. 'Oh yeah, good idea, actually! OW!'

'Thank you for your co-operation,' Marbrand said.

Elliot nursed his ribs.

'No problem, Sadie,' said the barman, testing the name out gleefully. 'Good luck, Sadie!'

Marbrand inclined his head wearily and rolled his eyes as the pub door slammed.

'So the Creys have him,' he muttered, strolling to the main thoroughfare. 'Excellent.'

'Thought that was bad?' said Elliot Maynard, who wasn't the sharpest spear in the armoury but made a pretty good battering ram all by himself.

Marbrand ignored this dim comment, the latest of many, as they made their way through the crowd.

'What's the plan now, then?'

'I say we apply for the job of night watchman and guard Ronald from afar. Then we'll slip out during the celebrations and bring him with us.'

'And the prisoners?'

'Leave them. If the Creys are holding him hostage and we escape, they're welcome to his wrath. Hopefully, we'll be long gone by then.'

'Right. You'll need to change your name, though.'

'Oh, you think?'

'Absolutely,' said Elliot firmly.

The wry edge to Marbrand's tone had, as ever, flown right over his head.

'They'll take the piss out of you with a name like that.'

'So what do you suggest?'

Elliot thought about it. 'Well, my ole man was called Russell, before he was mauled to death by dogs the other year. That's a good bloke's name.'

Marbrand paused, then nodded in approval.

'I suppose Russell sounds alright,' he said. 'Better than Sadie, at any rate.'

They strode down the road left of the Crook, called the Lame Leg Alley due to a funny turn at the knee.

~

'The lord of Nayport requests an invite to the festivities, your majesty.'

'Who?' King Theo asked.

He stood next to Howie and Jimmy in the throne room, surrounded by people milling about, preparing for Seth's adventure.

'Nayport, your majesty,' said Jimmy, pointing at a spot on the map in Howie's hands. 'Right there, a hundred leagues south of Shallowoak in the west. He's sent a gift as well, some book he's dedicated to you.'

He opened a leather-bound tome in his hands to show him.

'A book, you say?'

King Theo frowned, taking it in his hands and turning it this way and that.

'Literary fiction, I'm told. Very popular around court, but I don't see the attraction,' Jimmy said in disdain. 'A sheepdog could have produced a more interesting plot, in my opinion.'

He then digressed into an in-depth lecture on literary themes as King Theo chewed on the edge of the spine.

Howie turned his attention to the map.

The part of the Forest the Queen's scribble had indicated was over a hundred and fifty miles away, beyond the Silver Lake east of

Serpus and past what used to be a symbol marking a keep before it was hastily crossed out. Howie calculated five days' journey by horse, maybe more if Seth was joining them.

He flung a withering glance at the prince in question.

Seth flirted with a few eligible bachelorettes on the porch. They seemed to have shown up to catch Ron's eye and appeared utterly fed up with being lumbered with his bumbling older equivalent.

He wondered how Seth would cope without his mummy following him around. The poor woman was probably glad to have a break. Seth hadn't spoken to her since she'd wrestled his fluffy pink blanket from him that morning.

A loud rip tore Jimmy from his critique with a blink.

King Theo blew his nose on the table of contents.

Jimmy closed his eyes, praying for strength.

'So what shall I tell Nayport, your majesty?'

Theo weighed the book in one hand, deciding. He peered across the hall at his son with one eye shut and fired the book spine-first into the back of Seth's head.

It smacked the upside of his head with a satisfying thunk.

Seth howled, bending double with both hands holding his head.

King Theo bellowed with laughter.

'Excellent! Give him my blessing and have him bring more with him in some different sizes!'

Jimmy bowed and mouthed an apology to Seth, who scowled at them bitterly.

'Now,' King Theo said as he finished cackling. 'Are you clear on your route? Have everything you need?'

'Yessir.'

Howie rolled the map into a tube and slid it into his belt, alongside his new sword.

'Good. And don't forget our little plan,' he added, tapping the side of his nose.

'I won't.'

'Good lad. Make sure my boy doesn't get killed, don't go near the Faeries and good luck!'

Howie nodded with a smile and strode out, Ron and Adrienne in tow.

Seth followed them sullenly, still rubbing his head and snarling under his breath.

The four left the keep and walked to the inner portcullis, where their carriage awaited. Just as they prepared to climb aboard, a call stopped them in their tracks.

Seth released a pained sigh and faced his wife, flanked by the butler.

'Seth,' Cienne said. 'How long will you be gone?'

She held her hands out palms-down in front of her.

'Um, not sure,' he said. He glanced uneasily at her hands.

Cienne dropped them sheepishly at her sides.

'You'll be alright, won't you? It's nothing dangerous, is it?'

'Uh, no, no, not at all,' he said, scratching his nose. 'I'll be fine.'

He gave her a tiny smile and lifted his shoulders in what he assumed was reassurance.

'Good.'

They paused and, very hesitantly, pecked each other on the mouth.

'Bye,' he said, boarding the coach with haste.

'Bye,' she said in a small voice, turning back to the castle.

Jimmy stayed behind to watch Seth slump into his seat, visibly deflating in relief.

'Romance of the century,' he said wryly.

He turned to face two men loitering nearby. 'Can I help you gentlemen?'

The older one spun around, revealing a lined, weathered face and close-cropped grey hair.

'Morning,' he called as Jimmy approached. 'Me and my friend are looking for work. You haven't need of a night guard or two here, have you?'

'We could do with a lot of them, actually,' he said. His eyes darted across Elliot's broad shoulders. 'Or maybe just two of him would do.'

'Oh, thank you,' Elliot trilled, flexing his shoulders.

'Where are you from?'

'Stoneguard,' Marbrand replied. 'We were laid off by Prince Vladimir due to being surplus to requirements.'

'Sounds like something he'd say,' Jimmy commented. 'Follow me, the king will want to meet you, I expect.'

'May I ask what for?' Marbrand said carefully.

'Oh, he's a bad habit of lobbing employees' heads off in a random fit of rage,' he said like an accountant explaining payroll. 'He likes to get to know them first. Just through here.'

Elliot and Marbrand followed him into the keep with rising levels of anxiety.

King Theo reviewed them moments later from the top of the

throne room.

'Elliot Maynard,' he said thoughtfully. 'That sounds familiar. Have you a relative in these parts?'

'Yes, a Richard Maynard,' Jimmy piped up from the king's side. 'Bit of a thicky, but his heart's in the right place.'

'Ah, yes, Richard,' King Theo said in realisation. 'Has a penchant for squeezing people's heads in during combat. Good man, excellent. And this one?'

'Sir Russell Marbrand,' Marbrand said. 'Night captain of the Stonekeep, or, well, I used to be, anyway.'

'Now that's a name I haven't heard in a while!' exclaimed King Theo. 'I knew your father in the War for the Orchard, you know — briefly, when I was a boy. You must have an older brother, is that right? Named him Sadie if I recall rightly, the poor sod. How's he?'

'Er… we don't speak of him,' said Marbrand.

'Ah, backfired, eh? Never mind, just as well they didn't make the same mistake twice,' said King Theo. 'Mind you, your name isn't much better. Comes across as a fine name, but two times out of three he'll turn out a weed. Well, Jimmy will show you to your barracks. They're a bit snug, but they'll do. Hold back a moment, Marbrand, I'd like a word with you about young Vladimir.'

'Yes, your majesty?'

Jimmy led Elliot outside.

'You haven't word of him attending the tournaments, have you?'

'Not that I'm aware of, but I imagine he'll attend. Use the opportunity to announce his coronation, if I know him.'

'Ah, excellent.'

He rose from his throne to face Marbrand.

'I want you to keep an eye on him during the festivities,' he said, planting a hand on Marbrand's shoulder. 'Never liked him myself, the slimy creature. If he sat on the throne too fast, he'd slide off and zip down the great hall. But that wife of his is an Emmett, you see…'

Marbrand's face set. 'And if he were to die, the throne would go to them.'

'Ron first,' corrected King Theo. 'Or any issue of Vladimir and the Emmett girl… which is unlikely.'

Marbrand nodded. He recalled the girl well. The likeliest she would come to begetting an heir would be if they formally legitimised one of her rag dolls.

'It would be a nasty thing for him to be "drinking the wrong thing" or "eating something off" just before his coronation,' King

Theo went on, 'particularly if it happened under my roof of all places. Unpleasant as he may be, he's the lesser of two evils. The Emmetts are a sneaky lot, and, personally, if Vladimir's going to snuff it, Ronald ought to at least survive to claim his rights.'

'I'll ensure the princes remain unharmed,' said Marbrand. 'There won't be a mark on them… or on Ron, at the very least. Vladimir probably wouldn't appreciate it.'

'Just so. I'd much prefer a King Ronald, myself.' He lowered his voice. 'Currently unmarried, you see… and of an age with our Lilly, you understand…'

'Indeed, indeed. But king material, your majesty?'

'Doesn't matter,' he brushed it off. 'I've been grooming my daughter for rule ever since Seth had his little upset. She'll look after things in the north, and most likely he'll die childless also. Meaning the north will be, once again, *mine*.'

'What if Lilly interferes with this?' said Marbrand. 'I'm told she's difficult.'

'Lilly won't have a choice. Times aren't changing rapidly enough to let her run riot just yet. She'll do as she's told… or else.'

~

'Tell her we're leaving *now*.'

'She's busy,' Keith insisted. 'She'll be out in a minute.'

'But we're going *now*,' Howie snapped.

Stares became apparent from behind them as they stood around the entrance to the Crook.

'Says who?' said Keith, boldly standing inside the doorway with a bathrobe hanging loosely on his shoulders. 'Royalty shouldn't have to be ushered out by an inferior person. Particularly when said royalty is paying *my* royalties. Why do you have to go at the crack of dawn anyway?'

'Because I said so!'

Seth stood to Howie's right, his eyes glazed in horror and his mouth slightly open.

'Can't we just leave without her?' Ron asked in annoyance, leaning on the doorframe to Howie's left. 'She's a nuisance anyway.'

'That I can vouch for,' Seth concurred, still fixated in horror to Keith's lower torso.

Lilly elbowed past Keith to face the trio. She met Seth's gaze and jerked her shirt up under her chin.

'Morning, gents,' she said, bolting for the coach painted with writhing snakes behind them. 'Never said Seth was coming with you.'

'Last minute arrangement,' Howie said, following her. 'I thought you said you'd meet us at dawn?'

'Please do that up,' said Seth in a pained voice.

Keith glanced down, discovered his nether regions were indecently exposed and hastily hid himself.

'Well naturally, considering my radiance, I thought the sun rose when I did,' she joked in reply to Howie, settling down in the coach's luxurious interior. 'Did you bring anything to drink? I'm spitting feathers here.'

'We've only pear cider,' Ron said in distaste, sitting across from her. 'Seth's favourite.'

Lilly wrinkled her nose. 'Hardly any alcohol in them pears.'

'I like it,' Seth objected. 'What's the plan, then?'

'We're going straight to this Queen Wosserface and getting this talk over and done with,' Howie said. 'Then we can scout around for the king and ask a few questions.'

One of the accompanying guards, a Corporal Moat if Howie remembered rightly, snorted loudly.

'You'll be lucky to get an answer out of them.'

''Less you happen across a fellow human,' another piped up. 'And they might be dumbstruck for at least six hours.'

'We'd better take their word for it, Howie,' Adrienne said scathingly. 'If anyone knows "dumb", it's this lot.'

She pushed Howie into the coach in front of her.

Seth was close behind, enjoying the view of Adrienne's posterior as two guards assisted him by his elbows.

Howie watched, his upper lip raised. He struggled to picture the kind of kingdom Adem could become in future years with a king who couldn't climb up two steps without an escort.

The coach rattled west, followed by a smaller carriage containing their retinue of guards. The ride through Serpus's winding streets was slow and uneventful, the general dislike between them cutting all conversation to a halt. Howie soon wished he'd gone alone with Lyseria. At least she made an attempt to grunt along in reply.

Seth was sound asleep before they had even left Serpus, curled up at his sister's side like a little child. Lilly tickled him under his nose at momentary intervals, making him twitch and flinch.

Ron flicked dead insects from the windowsill with his head in his hand. And very little awareness of his surroundings, Howie noticed irately as half of them bounced off his forehead.

The rich food handed out during their first inn stop did little to help his mood. It stuck to his system like glue and gave him indigestion. He had yet to fully transition from a lower-class diet to rich people food; his stomach ached with the effort.

Adrienne seemed to be the only member of the group feeling entertained. She stared out the window, her hands folded demurely in her lap. It was probably a relief to travel with a group, he thought. He recalled her account of her trip to Serpus with a hot flash of guilt. He shouldn't have let her put herself into danger like that for him. He'd make it up to her, he decided – somehow.

With that thought in mind, he vanished into the woods that evening as they made camp and returned with some flowers he had found in the undergrowth.

Adrienne's face lit up at the sight.

'These are for you,' he announced.

He held them out to her and bowed with a flourish.

Her fingers crept softly over his, lifting them out of his grasp.

He straightened up to see her beaming at him, beatific.

'To say sorry for dragging you away from home,' he said in a small voice.

'That's okay,' she giggled. 'Oh, I love them, they're my favourites.'

She planted a firm kiss on his cheek, which reddened.

Seth's muttered voice could just be heard in the distance behind him, 'I asked you what your favourite flower was, and you told me it was bloody *leaves*—'

'I'll have to paint them before they go dry – oh, there's pansies here!'

'Pansies!' Seth exclaimed under his breath.

'They could come in handy, they're a relief for hives,' Adrienne said in earnest, her head bent over her little treasure hoard. 'And it's used to treat shaking sickness, at least that's what my teacher told me.'

'Oh,' said Howie. 'I just picked them because they were pretty.'

'*Dock leaves cure all sorts of things,*' Seth mimicked, his voice too low for Adrienne to hear, had she not been sufficiently engrossed in her pansy dissertation, '*they do this, and they do that, I don't really look at flowers much*—'

'We should put them in egg white and sugar, they'll keep for ages, you never know when you might need them…'

Howie watched her chatter away with a faint smile, his cheeks a pleasant shade of pink.

'You could have *said* pansies,' Seth mumbled relentlessly in low tones, 'I could have got you a bucketful of pansies, I'd have given you a *field* full of pansies if you wanted, but no, you had to make me look a berk, didn't you—'

'I know our family emblem is green and all,' Lilly said, 'but envy really is unbecoming on you, brother.'

'Oh, shut up,' Seth growled.

Adrienne trailed off for a moment and held the flowers out.

'Hold these, I must get my notebook. There's some I haven't seen before, I must do a sketch of them to show my teacher when I'm next in town…'

She piled them into Howie's cupped hands and rifled in her little satchel for her sketchbook.

A soft sensation floated through his ribs. Howie sat cross-legged in front of her at her command.

She knelt before him and bowed her head over the notebook, scribbling away with a small charcoal pencil. There was something pleasing in the way her hair flopped over her face in an auburn curtain, how she flicked it back and pinned it behind her ear with the end of the pencil, how her lips curled inward in concentration as her eyes darted up and down, drifting up to meet his on occasion with a warm, fond smile.

Howie returned it in earnest. A daft idea came into his head to kiss her. He indulged in it, planting a delicate peck on her temple.

Seth watched, his eyes flinty. A rather colder sensation was creeping into *his* ribs at the sight of them together, cold and stinging and angry. Seth exhaled through his nose and parked himself in front of the kindling campfire, his gaze fixed to the ground.

~

VI

Days passed like this, the tedium broken by dreams about Cienne, less entertaining dreams of finally finding King Samuel, and stops in the journey for the guards to have urine fights.

The latter came to a stop after Ron swallowed a stray mouthful – especially after he'd marginally been stopped from yelling Vladimir's lightning chant at them. Howie felt they were enough of a laughing stock without the Hornes' occult tendencies setting them off.

The Silver Lake came into view from the third day at momentary intervals, dappled in green and yellow. It waned in and out of view between the dense foliage. The Forest engulfed them, leaves shimmering in the fresh light of dawn after the showers of the night before.

Trees were never cut or trimmed in the Forest, according to

Corporal Moat, the infantry's leading expert on all things minus common etiquette.

'It's forbidden,' he said, one index finger rammed up his left nostril in a permanent addition to his face. 'Only three people have attempted to trim some of the trees, and the Queen fed them to her purple flames. She's a sorceress, you know. Got the head of a dragon.'

'Knowledgeable as you are, Corporal Moat, you must know the name of this queen, surely?' Seth drawled.

The corporal was silent, which clearly meant that 'Chapter Four: The Queen's Name' had not yet been included in the Encyclopaedia of Moat at this point in time.

And, as the Lake became a permanent fixture on their journey, Encyclopaedia of Moat neglected to mention that the Forest was, above all else, deserted. The trees and undergrowth lay undisturbed by houses or thoroughfare, the entire place showing no signs of inhabitancy.

This puzzled Howie. He had always assumed the Faeries were pretty much like humans, but very, very small. He expected to see little villages hidden between tree roots or a pillar of smoke from a chimney somewhere, but there was nothing but abandoned forest.

Also, he got the feeling there was something else about Faeries the guards weren't telling them about. Presumably, it was very funny and they were hiding it from him as a kind of joke. Howie mused hatefully about leaving a trail of honey around their coach while they slept and seeing how funny it would be when they were ravaged by a hungry bear.

They stopped in a meadow just under thirty miles down the river as their fifth evening approached. Howie got out of the stuffy coach to help set up camp. The night sentries emerged from the guard coach, rubbing the sleep from their eyes, and prepared food for their watch as the rest of the group emerged to stretch their legs.

Howie peered down at a panoramic view of the valley surrounding the river. He couldn't see a castle anywhere. He wondered if maybe the mapmakers had miscalculated the keep's position. He couldn't figure out why something on a map would have a dirty great 'X' scrawled over it.

Seth immediately made for the trees. He halted as a guard rose to accompany him.

'Do you mind if I take a piss by myself?' he asked with a frown. 'I don't need my hand holding, thank you.'

'I was instructed to guard you,' the guard said.

'Well, guard me from back there. And that's "your highness"

to you,' he sniped, striding haughtily into the woods.

'Yes, your highness,' the guard said to his retreating form.

He then mimed a royal assassination behind Seth's back.

Howie approached as Seth vanished into the trees.

'Glad to know I won't be the only suspect when someone strangles him to death,' he said.

'The whole world thinks he's a prat,' the guard spat, 'but who's doing anything about it?'

He held out a lined, scarred hand, which Howie shook.

'Sir Boris Necker, sir. Captain of the Royal Palace Guard – until the current king dies, by which time I hope to follow if it means not having to serve this twat.'

'Nice to meet—'

'AAAHH!!'

Howie winced. 'Can we just leave him there? Please?'

'Not if King Theo's axe has anything to do with it,' Necker said darkly. He drew his sword and headed for the woods. 'He'd have our heads on cocktail sticks if Seth so much as lost a hair.'

He gathered the prince's guard and led them between the trees.

Ten yards away, Seth was in a predicament. He'd quickly gone from answering a long call of nature in front of a thick elm to hanging upside down from said elm by one leg. With nothing but a short length of rope preventing him from landing in a pool of his own making, Seth dangled from a low branch. A rope, seemingly made of grass, cut into his left ankle as the rest of his limbs flailed helplessly around him.

To add insult to injury, this didn't stop him piddling endlessly into the air, sending yellow streams swirling around his spinning body like a hideously bizarre water feature, the rope twisting back and forth, clockwise to anti-clockwise.

Adrienne was the first to find this spectacle.

Seth reddened under her bemused stare.

The guards hovered behind her, waiting sheepishly for the water feature to stop.

'Well, help me, then!!' Seth shrieked.

He slowly rotated to a halt, hastily readjusting his trousers.

Loud guffaws from the back of the group announced Lilly-Anna's arrival.

Howie gawked, his jaw hanging open, as the guards circled Seth, craning for the rope around his ankle.

'Not to worry, your highness,' soothed Captain Necker, 'we'll have you down in a—*careful!!*'

One of the lance corporals had skidded on the newly soaked

soil.

Lilly cackled uncontrollably, bent double with her palms against her knees.

'How did he manage to…' Howie said, trailing off, '…h-why was he still *going*?'

'I don't know,' Lilly squealed, rubbing tears of mirth with her palms.

A grin burst across Howie's face. He cleared his throat and wiped it away with one hand as Captain Necker glowered at him.

Seth fumed, his face crimson. With a guard assisting from each shoulder, his feet finally touched the ground. He shrugged their hands from under his armpits with a scowl.

Necker squinted up at the foliage, searching for the attempted kidnapper between the densely set leaves.

A small blue head emerged for half a second before vanishing again.

'Halt!' Necker barked.

He unstrapped a crossbow from his back and aimed at a high branch.

'This is the captain of the king's guard speaking! In the name of King Theo Crey, I command you to show yourself!'

The figure leapt lithely from the tree to land before them.

It was a tiny woman, a mere five foot in height. Silvery-blue hair lay in a clumsily-knotted braid on her shoulder, while the rest of her – as seen beneath the scant clothing she wore – was a bright sky blue.

The entire group stood enamoured by the sight of her.

Except for Adrienne, who eyed her rags of grey cloth in distaste.

There was a pause.

'Why did you attempt to imprison the prince?' Adrienne said, when it looked like no one else would.

She turned to Necker in frustration.

'Aren't you going to say something to her?'

'Um,' he said thoughtfully, his gaze fixed to the youth.

There was silence.

Seth's head turned ponderously to one side.

A moment later, the Faerie vanished –

– as did the entire group, apart from Adrienne and Ron.

The two coughed in the wake of a large dust cloud and squinted blankly into the now empty space in front of them.

'What was all that about?' said Ron in bemusement.

Seth glimpsed a flicker of blue bolt up a tree in the distance and ran towards it.

He skidded to a halt at the foot of a huge oak, short of breath, and pulled himself up via a strong branch.

Only for a thinner branch to come into contact with his face.

'HA!!' exclaimed Howie from higher up.

Seth flipped face-down into the undergrowth.

'*You* need to review your marriage vows, your highness, before your wife lames the other half of your brain!'

He threw the branch joyfully into the air.

It bounced off Seth's back and landed beside him, each as lifeless as the other.

Smirking, Howie hauled himself upward to a secluded hollow in the branches.

A little lantern guided him to a door in the shadows, dappled in dim green light. Howie made his way from one branch to another, ensuring a firm grip on the trunk beside him. It parted in half ahead of him, one end sloping gently up to the doorway. He climbed onto it on all fours and crawled.

The door opened invitingly at his touch.

It was surprisingly spacious in the dark, windowless cabin. The floor sloped up from the front step, following the arch of the tree trunk underneath before levelling out enough to hold a small bed and cabinet.

The dark shadow of the Faerie lit a lantern and hung it from the ceiling, bathing the room in an amber glow.

Howie slowly lifted himself to his feet and closed the door behind him.

'Hi,' he said. 'I'm Howie.'

He frowned.

An odd sensation overcame him, like a fragrance in the air. It swirled around him and entered his pores, somehow endowing him with her name in return: Vhyn.

He hissed inward, his chest swelling. It felt... weird. *Good* weird.

Vhyn stood where she was, her hands clasped unassumingly at her waist.

Another sensation – a sort of pink sensation was the only way he could describe it – swept over him again, an invitation. This time closer to the nether regions.

Howie took a deep, shaky breath. With no further preamble, he strode across the cabin to meet her.

He became oblivious to the world after that. For a change, it left him well alone, travelling for cleaner pastures.

~

Twilight loomed overhead.

Ron extracted a tinderbox from his pocket and began to light a fire.

Adrienne slipped into the trees to relieve herself.

Ron fed the growing flames with kindling he had gathered in the forest and a dribble of alcohol from Lilly's abandoned flask. He had commandeered it a full five hours ago and managed to control himself enough to save the absinth within for fuel.

Still, the group hadn't returned.

Adrienne re-entered the camp with the same gloomy expression she had worn since their entourage had split up. Ron wondered if she was missing Howie. Or Seth, though the gods alone only knew what she saw in *him*.

'Do we have food left for tomorrow?' Adrienne asked, eyeing the large haunch of meat Ron was currently attaching to the spit.

'Plenty.' He gestured to the knapsack at his side, bulging with salted meat joints. 'Should be loads left for the others when they come back.'

Adrienne arched an eyebrow. '*If* they come back.'

She dropped into a sitting position and crossed her legs beneath her, holding her hands out to the flames.

Ron avoided her gaze, twisting the spit into the meat.

He didn't understand women. Granted, he didn't understand many things, but with women, he simply assumed they were like dogs and needed feeding and a pat on the head every now and again. Lately, he was discovering that not all women were like Felicity Emmett, contrary to his father's teachings, and the discovery was not welcome. Particularly after being lumbered with the worst kind: a teenager.

A rustling in the woods startled Ron from his musings.

Seth crawled over the undergrowth, his face bruised and bloodied.

'What on earth happened to you?' Ron asked in alarm.

He laid the meat aside and hastened to Seth's side.

'Your *buddy* is what happened to me,' he spat.

He leaned on Ron's shoulder as he hefted him upright.

'He hit me with a stick, and I fell from a tree.'

'Why on earth would Howie do that?'

'Because he was chasing that Faerie woman.'

Ron snorted. 'Don't see the attraction.'

'Oh, right, because you've never…'

Seth regarded him in sudden silence.

'No, you probably haven't,' he finished after a moment.

Adrienne reluctantly met Seth's gaze.

'Oh, what have you done to your face?' she snapped.

Seth recoiled at her vitriolic tone before scowling at her.

'Your boyfriend launched me out of a tree,' he barked. He spat a lob of blood into the fire, which hissed. 'Obviously couldn't handle the competition.'

Ron eyed him up and down and refrained from commenting.

Adrienne huffed, shuffled closer to Seth and jerked his face upwards by the chin.

Seth hissed through his teeth.

'What's your problem?' he asked sourly. 'I thought you enjoyed poking and prodding me?'

'It's like you get injured on purpose to annoy me,' she complained, examining his injuries.

'What of it?' said Seth with a wince. 'Maybe I enjoy your company.'

She shot him a warning glance. She poured rubbing alcohol into a cloth and gently but firmly cleaned the gashes on his face.

Seth squeezed his eyes shut, his face stinging.

'Ron,' said Adrienne, 'would you mind collecting more kindling, I think the fire's going out.'

Ron cast a cynical eye over the billowing flames.

'If you say so,' he said, rising.

Seth watched him leave the camp as Adrienne wiped the last of the blood away.

'Very good idea sending him into the woods,' he said. 'Any particular reason you wanted me to yourself this fine evening?'

Adrienne shot him a withering glance. 'Give me strength.'

She opened a glass jar and spread a liberal amount of some pungent cream into the scrapes.

'The cuts are superficial and you've split your lip. It looks worse than it is.'

'Thanks.'

He shivered.

'Chilly, isn't it?'

She pointedly ignored him.

He sidled closer, to no effect.

'This is cosy, isn't it?' he commented. 'Us two, camping together.'

She remained silent.

Seth licked his lips, wincing as the cut on his lip smarted.

'Just us two,' he went on, 'man and woman. Alone.'

Still, she said nothing.

Seth threw his eyes to the stars and gave the cut on his cheek a sharp prod.

'Oh, I'm still bleeding.'

Adrienne sighed, reaching for her medical kit.

There was a moment's pause as she pressed a small bandage to his cheek and fastened it into place with glued pieces of tape.

Seth glared at her. 'Wonderful bedside manner, I have to say.'

'Oh, what would you like me to say?' she asked wryly. '"Ooh, you poor wounded soul, let me just hop into your lap and administer some natural anaesthetic"?'

'That'd be nice,' he said pleasantly.

Adrienne made a disgusted noise and turned away.

'Keep pressure on the wound,' she said frostily.

'As you command.'

Another silence ensued, broken only by owls muttering in the distance.

'You could do whatever you'd like to me, you know,' he said. 'You only get hanged for banging royalty if you get them pregnant.'

She said nothing.

'What, more silence?' Seth snapped. 'You were talkative enough before your boyfriend decided to bequeath you a handful of weeds.'

'He's not my boyfriend,' she spat.

'Oh, is that space reserved for someone else, then?'

She said nothing.

'Don't you like me anymore?'

'What?' she snapped.

'Because plenty of women would snap at the chance—'

'Like your Cousin Elyse?' she sneered. 'Or perhaps the maid.'

'I only succumbed to *her* advances because she had nice hair, nothing else.'

Adrienne's eyes narrowed.

'That… sounded *less* nasty *before* I said it,' he conceded with a wince.

She rolled her eyes.

Seth watched her for a moment. 'Is it because you're frightened of it?'

'Oh, shut up.'

'You are. I could change that.' He shifted forward. 'I can be gentle…'

He traced her sleeve with the back of his knuckles.

She jerked away from him.

'So could Howie,' she said before she could stop herself.

'Who-ey? Oh, the one who hit me with half a tree so he could violate a member of another species? Yes, I suppose he could.'

She fell silent once again.

Seth heaved a sigh.

'What are you so bothered about him for? What's he got that I haven't, besides a stupid name and a total disinterest in you?'

She clenched her teeth. 'How about loyalty, dignity, youth—'

'What do you mean, youth?'

'You're old.'

'Old?' he exclaimed. 'I'll have you know, I'm in my prime! Thirty-three is only considered old if you're a peasant in the grips of the plague.'

'Compared to twenty? If you say so.'

Seth snorted. 'We haven't even gotten started and you're trading me in for a younger model.'

'I've known Howie a lot longer than I've known you,' she snarled. 'I suppose I just wanted Howie and… decided to accept you as a replacement.'

His face blanked.

'I see,' he said flatly. 'I suppose this is how my wife feels.'

'Your wife is right where you left her, you know.'

Seth glowered at her and hefted himself to his feet.

'It isn't my wife I think of every night I go to sleep and every morning I awake!' he spat at her before circling the fire.

Adrienne peered over her shoulder at him.

He dropped himself onto a log and put his head between his knees, rubbing his temples.

A hot flush crept up her spine, shameful tendrils. She tried to form some kind of apology in her head, but the words fluttered away from her before she could string them together. So she stayed silent.

~

VII

Laden with heavy logs and sticks, Ron halted with a deep sigh.

He was lost.

Deciding that finding camp again wasn't likely, he discarded some of the logs and, still holding an armful for a campfire later, headed north according to the moss growing on the trees around him.

Dew soaked the ground beneath his feet. The rocky path felt slick beneath his soles, the cool air pleasant on his face compared to the heat of the afternoon. Ron wondered idly whether their former entourage had gotten heatstroke running about under that heat. It then occurred to him that he didn't really care. Lilly-Anna and her palace guard were too patronising for his liking, and Howie was getting to be as irritable as Adrienne – probably for the same reason, only they were too stupid to notice.

After four miles or so, Ron was surprised to discover the silhouette of a keep in the distance, the first he'd seen in the Forest. He made straight for it, winding between trees and shrubbery. He pictured a nice bed in a warm room, bathed in candlelight, and sighed wistfully. He liked being one with nature, but he felt he'd much prefer it to be a bit neater and more symmetrical.

When the edifice came into clearer view under the gaze of the moon, his face fell.

The keep was a ruin. Rubble tripped him up, distracting him from the collection of half-towers and broken walls. Hints of foundations along the edges of a huge crater in the centre of the keep marked the placement of walls long since annihilated. He felt like an intruder walking through the building's ghost.

Tiptoeing through the wreckage, Ron found a corner of what appeared to be a dining hall and climbed into it, beneath a fraction of ceiling for shelter. He folded his legs beneath him, setting the kindling out delicately.

Once the fire was crackling contentedly thanks to some scraps of rubbish from his pocket, Ron examined his surroundings in the faint light. It looked the same: jagged rocks and dead, upturned earth, shadowed by cracked and crooked towers and shattered castle walls.

It was a moment before he realised that the lump digging into his knee was the ring handle for a trapdoor.

~

Seth tucked his knees under his chin and sulked. Adrienne glanced at him guiltily. He looked like a three-year-old that had been scolded for throwing his dinner at the wall.

'I'm cold,' he complained.

She threw her cloak at him.

It draped itself over his head like a shroud. He grabbed a fistful from within and shook it out sharply, draping it around his shoulders.

Adrienne gazed at him.

He tucked a fold under his nose, as if taking in her scent. He cocooned himself in it, swinging back and forth like a rocking chair. He seemed too vulnerable for a man in his thirties, hunched under the trees like a lost child, his face dark with bruising and red marks.

She realised she was shivering and suddenly regretted giving away her cloak.

Seth noticed. He held out a corner. 'Do you want this back?'

'No,' she said, still shivering.

He paused. 'Do you want to… share it?'

She shot him a hideous scowl.

'For warmth,' he said in an injured tone. 'I'm not a complete pervert.'

She froze stubbornly for a moment, before a spiteful wind drove her sheepishly across the camp to join him.

A short distance away, Howie toppled from the Faerie tree house and landed heavily on the ground, jarring his shoulder.

Rising to his feet with a wince, he scowled up at the foliage.

'You're *very welcome*!!' he shouted up at her.

The leaves simply swung serenely in the wind.

Howie cupped his shoulder and stalked back to the camp.

Upon entering the enclosed meadow, he spied two figures huddling by the fire. He was about to join them until the flames reared, illuminating their faces.

He skidded to a halt, leaves crunching underfoot. His blood boiled.

Adrienne's head lifted. 'Did you hear something?'

'No,' said Seth, the top of his head tucked into her shoulder.

'I heard someone enter the camp,' Adrienne said, starting to rise.

'Don't,' Seth murmured, holding her elbow gently. 'It was a rabbit or something, probably. Don't worry about it.'

She peered around for a moment before settling her head against Seth's.

Howie's nails bit the sleeve around his injured shoulder. The bruises smarted within his fist, but he was too furious to care. The smug little expression on Seth's stupid face was all he could think about. He knew damn well it was Howie entering the camp.

Howie inhaled a shuddering breath and pivoted.

I'm not sitting there looking at that, he fumed in silence.

He vanished into the woods, the image of the two printed on the back of his eyelids.

~

Fifty-seven, fifty-eight, fifty-nine, Ron counted relentlessly, descending, *sixty, sixty-one, sixty-two...*

Beneath the trapdoor had been a steep drop leading into oblivion. Ron had quickly found the ladder and, a minute later, was still climbing down, one rung at a time with a hastily made torch held very carefully between his teeth.

He estimated that the rungs were half a foot apart, so Ron counted every second step until he'd come to eighty feet and finally touched down on steady ground.

Feeling relieved and looking forward to a lie-down, he shone the torch around him. And, loudly, swore.

He could hardly lie down here. If he had, he would have been impaled.

Huge barbs of crystal stuck out of the rocky cavern. The torchlight bounced off each shard onto another, and another, and another, until the whole cave was illuminated in yellow-orange light.

The ground sparkled under his feet, gravelly in texture. A pleasant warmth flowed through the soles of his feet, echoed by the heat of the cavern itself. It was almost like a furnace.

He eyed the ceiling warily.

A hundred crystal spikes pointed down in his direction.

Each translucent shard was the same material as Howie's new sword. Ron could recall the blade from memory, the amount of times Howie had rubbed it under Seth Crey's nose – an act that made Ron's hair stand on end. Seth was bred from insanity, despite his wimpy appearance. King Samuel had once told Ron that cannibals occurred in the Crey line every fourth generation. He didn't dare calculate the chances of Seth turning out to be the next King Rubeous Crey.

He thought of his father again with a pang of sorrow before something clicked in his head.

He suddenly knew what this was.

The Battle in the Orchard had been regaled to Ron and Vladimir a million times. The war as a whole had spawned an entire childhood's worth of fascinating stories: King Samuel's deep, full voice was practically made for storytelling.

But one story that had always stuck out was the catacombs.

Ron's Uncle Leroy had given he and Vladimir the full tour one childhood afternoon, on a visit to his manor house. A huge castle had once stood there – Thintower, the estate's namesake – until a battle with the Queen of the Forest had resulted in an explosion a few feet underground, directly beneath the keep.

'A taste of what was to come,' King Samuel had often said.

The demon flames she employed were so powerful they went on burning long after the keep had disintegrated. Seeing the flames eat a growing crater in his estates and knowing there was no guarantee that they would even taper off, Ron's uncle's grandfather quarried a hundred tonnes of stone from the mountains nearby and buried the fire, hoping to snuff it completely. It did not.

Instead, a few years later, work on the basement of what was now Lord Tetzel's manor house had revealed a cave, every wall, ceiling and surface covered with sharp crystal. The demon flames had burned on beneath the quarried rock, melting and changing it to create a crystal cave.

Just like this one, Ron thought, gazing around.

Attempts to mine the crystal had been fruitless: like Howie's sword, it was unbreakable and impossible to move. So the Tetzels had built a family crypt within the crystal cavern, and so it had been ever since.

King Sam had believed that on the Night of Raining Thorns, the battle between the Queen and King Theo had created a similar cavern right here, beneath the rock dumped into the remains of her castle. Ron now had proof that he was right.

Ron's chest panged.

For the first time, he began to doubt the assumption that his father was still alive. Recalling the stories of the Battle of the Orchard made his heart hurt. He might never hear his father tell those stories again.

Ron wished he were with him now, to see the cavern he always believed was real. For a moment, he was seven years old again, gazing up at the sparkling silver cave face, his small hand held tightly in his father's. That just made him feel worse.

He heaved a sigh and shook off his pain. Curiosity had brought him down here, but there was nothing compelling him to wander over those shards.

He turned back to the ladder before noticing the torchlight rebounding on a large, flat piece of crystal. Upon further examination, Ron found more in the shape of some steps leading around a mass of shards in the centre of the cavern.

It was then that he realised what made this cave different from his uncle's. Many of the crystals had been cut away, shaped into stairs. It was being mined.

A sorcerer, he realised. *It's being mined by sorcerers for weapons.* He supposed there had to be some explanation for how Howie's sword came into existence.

Curiosity reared its head again, leading Ron onto the smooth steps. He paced gingerly onto each step, convinced they would shatter beneath him, but they didn't. They led him in an arch to the other end of the cave.

There was another door.

~

Howie hacked foliage out of his way impatiently.

The crystal sword sheared through as if it were butter, sending branches toppling everywhere.

It's a fucking disgrace! Cuddling up to a teenager? What is wrong with him? What is wrong with her?

Howie wondered what King Theo would think of his son being a de-facto paedophile. His smug face would be a smug decoration over the front gate.

Cradling that image close to mind, he hacked on until he reached the ruined keep. Howie gazed around at the blackened and broken walls, jutting out from a mountain of rubble. So this happened at the same time he was born. He wondered if there was a coincidence.

He slid the blade back into its sheath at his hip and explored the keep, his thoughts straying back and forth from the keep to Adrienne. He loved the girl to bits, which accounted for the desire to smash Seth Crey's head open like a walnut. But there was something more, something he couldn't quite recognise…

A dog's bark interrupted his thoughts for a moment.

He froze in his tracks and turned his head slowly. A large hound lay in one corner of the keep, supposedly keeping out of the chilly breeze. A low growl sounded until abruptly, it stopped.

'Oh fuck,' Howie said under his breath.

The dog was as big as he was. Its shoulder-blades lifted, the fur standing on end.

Howie backed away.

Snatches of old legends came to the forefront of his mind, about the vile creatures lurking in the Forest Queen's ruined keep. *I once knew an extraordinary woman…* Was this woman the Queen? Was this some kind of demon hound from the depths of hell? He squinted at it. The dog looked fairly normal from what he could see. It didn't appear to have three heads or a forked tail, to his best guess.

The dog lifted itself upright.

'Nice doggy,' Howie said weakly.

The dog's left ear twitched. Then it launched itself at him.

An animal wail escaped from the back of Howie's throat. His hands fumbled at the blade hanging from his belt, slipping from the hilt and sending the sheath swinging from side to side.

The hound landed on his chest, knocking him to the ground.

Whereupon a large, slimy tongue ran happily across his face.

Howie tried to blink. The tongue was as wide as his head. Struggling to breath, he slid out from beneath the hound and wiped a film of drool from over his mouth.

Did this dog know him?

The hound lapped his hairline again and promptly lifted its rear leg to urinate on him, quickly identifying himself as a male.

Howie scratched behind the hound's ears.

The dog dropped his chin across his knees. His head was enormous.

This could have been worse, he thought.

As Howie's heart rate slowed back to normal, he noticed the black collar around the dog's throat, half-hidden beneath a layer of thick black fur. It read, 'Theo. If found, return to Qattren's keep.'

He frowned at it.

Then his eyes widened.

Qattren (however that was pronounced) was the Forest Queen. Theo was named after the king, meaning that whoever this Qattren was, she liked King Theo enough to dedicate it to him.

Howie knew enough about the Crey family dynamic to see King Theo and Queen Eleanor had great contempt for one another. Maybe there was someone else once, someone he's broken away from after a certain event...

... and wanted to be reacquainted with.

Howie shuddered. Picturing King Theo with a woman was somehow more horrifying than picturing him eating someone's intestines. He was the kind of king you could only see eating, slaughtering or threatening.

Then it occurred to him. The ruins. The battles over the borders. The stories about how he arrived at the orphanage, his hair covered with thorns...

King Theo didn't explode her palace over some border dispute! He exploded her palace to get rid of the evidence... him.

He hoped King Theo had had a change of heart since then.

Before he could muse further on the matter, a thud startled him.

The dog jolted to his feet.

Howie rose with it to investigate.

The dog led him to the woods surrounding the keep. A tree had fallen a short distance away. Except, judging by the roots left behind it, it had apparently been torn from the ground.

Howie spied the tree in question laying across the undergrowth.

It slowly slid to the east.

The dog bounding ahead of him, Howie followed the tree, stepping into a deep groove left in its wake.

The broken roots of the tree ahead tilted upward. The trunk upturned itself into a wide pit a couple yards ahead and slid down into it.

Frowning, Howie edged after it.

The tree vanished with a sucking noise.

Seeing a lot of darkness and little else, Howie stumbled to a halt. Then he heard a faint sound, like a series of harps being softly strummed.

Thrrum… thrum…

Curiosity of the deadliest kind drew him closer.

Thruum…

His eyes widened.

~

His eyes widened.

Ron stood in an enormous entrance hall, decorated similarly to the Creys'. Instead of the serpent theme, tapestries and sculptures of a phoenix littered the hall, and threading between them purposefully were Faeries.

Hundreds of the beings hastened up and down the halls: palace servants, he realised. Many carried sheets and clothes to be cleaned, paperwork to an antechamber to be signed, food to a dining hall behind an arched entrance on the back wall. Complete silence greeted him, despite the throngs of people. The only sounds that came to Ron's ears were the soft shuffling of felt slippers on the crystal floor.

Ron stared at the vaulted ceiling in awe as the Faeries continued in their silent efficiency. The silvery crystal spikes converged to form a high arch at least fifty feet above his head. Candelabras hung from hooks fastened to barbs of glass, dozens of them swirling down the ceiling and around the marble walls to circle a huge chandelier directly overhead. Tiny *blue* flames illuminated the room from them, the glow rebounding from the sparkling ceiling and shining walls to gently illuminate the hall.

A Fae woman skidded to a halt directly in his line of sight, staring wide-eyed at him.

Ron stared back, as astonished as she was.

Because she was *exuding* pure astonishment: as tangible as the torch in his hand, the flame tapering out, forgotten. It spilled out of her, like water from a pot boiling over.

Ron stood stock still as the feeling swirled around him. A trace of something barbed and cool underlined it: fear.

More heads turned at this exchange.

At once the fear and astonishment pummelled him, knocking him back a step. Panic drew Ron's heart to a thunderous tattoo. He was terrified, shocked, bewildered. *What am I doing here? I shouldn't be here. I shouldn't be here at* all.

Ron turned to flee.

Footsteps skittered closer from behind him and a young girl appeared in front of him, gazing imploringly up at him.

A warm blanket covered the fear and bewilderment in an instant. Ron looked into the girl's eyes. A friend, he sensed.

She smiled, tentative, as though the action were unfamiliar.

He could trust her, he felt. He was safe with her.

She gave him a nod and strode around the throng.

Ron followed her. He felt she had requested it, despite the silence of the entire exchange.

She led him to an arch at the opposite end of the hall, tracing the wall with her hand. Entering what was evidently a throne room, Ron was surprised.

Not by the imposing mural of a giant phoenix staring down at him from behind the amber throne, beady-eyed, like a bird of prey surveying its quarry. Nor by the surprising smallness of the room in comparison to the entrance, making it seem snug and cosy.

It was the Queen herself.

For a start, she was human – or at least human by appearances. A mane of orange-red hair cascaded down her shoulders in loose curls, the front cut to frame her eyes. Striking green eyes gazed down at him from the dais. Her slim form was emphasised by the bemusing flowery, glittery, lacy, silky, shiny slim-fitting gown she wore, which splayed out at the waist in a mass of petticoats hiding both her legs and the bottom half of the throne.

'Prince Ronald,' she greeted in a clear Truphorian accent.

Her face held no identifiable expression. She sat back against the cushioned upholstery of the throne, her elbows resting on the light wood of the armrests, her delicate fingers toying with the end of a long ivory sleeve.

Ron hurriedly remembered himself and bent himself at the waist. 'Your majesty.'

'Have a seat, your highness,' she suggested.

A small chair sat between him and the queen, nondescript apart from the cushioning, a blood-orange colour trimmed in gold.

Ron gratefully made a beeline for it.

'Forgive me for the lack of ceremony,' said the Queen. 'I wasn't expecting to meet you and your entourage for another day or so. How did you find us?'

'By accident,' he said truthfully with a shrug. 'Our group was separated and I sort of stumbled on the trapdoor.' He hesitated. 'Er, your majesty.'

'Oh, never mind all that, call me Qattren,' she said offhandedly.

Ron relaxed slightly.

'It's a happy coincidence you arrived, actually,' Qattren continued. 'I've been looking forward to meeting you for some time.'

Ron tensed. 'Me? What for?'

'I wish to propose a marriage alliance with you.'

His eyes bulged. 'ME?'

'You.'

Ron gulped. He didn't like the sound of that. His father told him what 'making love' entailed. For an act that supposedly gave one pleasure, Ron didn't see anything remotely pleasant about it.

'I don't know about that,' he said in a pained voice. 'You probably don't know, but—'

'I know everything about you,' she said kindly. 'I know you've been dreading marriage, courting and indeed the act of lovemaking itself due to the fact that you're asexual and aromantic. I understand that the majority of your peers see this as an issue. My opinion is of the contrary.'

Ron was taken aback. He never knew there were terms for people like him.

'You mean you don't want—'

'—any of it,' finished Qattren. 'Except for a contract of alliance with Stoneguard, which is most easily acquired by marriage. Merely a matter of signing papers, exchanging rings and lying about a consummation. After that we'll be little different than any other noble match.'

Ron licked his lips. 'But you're sure you don't want—'

'Nope,' she said. 'I have more pressing matters to attend to without a rampaging husband tugging off my petticoats. And alas I'm infertile, so childbirth isn't within my many talents in any case. Fortunately, it makes our ruse all the more plausible. Your thoughts on the arrangement are more than welcome, of course.'

Ron thought about it.

'Well,' he said, 'it sounds alright, but I have to voice the condition that we include three rounds of the traditional game of snake and ladders every Tuesday.'

Qattren paused. 'That's... fine.'

'The board game, mind,' Ron clarified. 'Not some strange innuendo or anything.'

'Agreed,' Qattren said.

'Then that makes us housemates, then,' Ron said with a big grin.

Qattren smiled faintly.

A faint sense of alarm spiralled around the room, presumably from the Faeries.

Ron didn't see what was so frightening about her smiling. He thought it made her look younger.

Just as Ron was starting to relax, the smile slid from her face.

He turned.

Another Fae girl – the one from the Forest earlier today, Ron realised with a start – skittered across the flagstones, the end of her shirt wrung in both hands.

A helpless energy rippled through the air.

'I need you to come with me,' Qattren said to Ron, rising from her throne. 'One of your friends is in danger.'

~

The only light in the pit came from the moon, but the Hole was unmistakable. It was darker than the darkness around him, so dark Howie couldn't just see it, but smell and taste it as well – thick and all-consuming, a blackness that crawled over his skin.

It was a Hole that wanted to be filled.

Howie approached it slowly, baby steps, the huge hound in tow.

He couldn't say why he wanted to approach the Hole. It wasn't mere curiosity anymore – it had gone beyond that and out the other side.

The Hole hung in front of him in mid-air like a bad smell,

drawing him further and further into its presence. It was like a pothole in the air, no, in existence, and it needed filling – and Howie wanted to fill it. He wanted to leap into it, let it take him and dissolve him, dissolve every bad thought inside him, make the image of Seth Crey and Adrienne disappear for ever…

The dog barked in alarm and receded, whimpering.

Howie's gaze wandered momentarily to him and caught sight of something to the left of the void.

To where the Stonecrown sat on its side, a grey gleaming circlet.

Howie's eyes widened in horror and realisation.

It was King Sam's crown. It had to be: it was too well-shaped and polished to be a coincidence. He'd seen King Sam travel through the city on occasion: the man never left the keep without it. King Sam had been here…

Howie stumbled backwards.

But the Hole still clung to his mind, drawing him in, gripping him tightly…

Guiding him to his death.

He tore himself from the apparition and ran, scrambling over the lip of the pit on his hands and knees. The dog snatched his sleeve in his teeth, tugging him over the edge and nosing him out of the pit from behind.

Behind them, the Hole grew louder.

Thrum… THRRUM… THRRUUUUM…

As the trees in their wake swallowed the pit from view, Howie began to slow down, heart thudding. Fatigue claimed him and his surroundings wavered. He tripped and stumbled over rocks and mounds of dry earth – the ruins – and leaned his shoulder on a broken shard of wall to his right.

Energy seeped from his body, as if returning to the Hole.

Howie's eyes rolled inward. He tilted forward onto his face.

~

VIII

Morning arrived in green specks through the foliage above them.

After a breakfast consisting of more sulking than anything else, Seth wandered into the woods in silence.

His mind on Adrienne, he sank onto a fallen tree trunk between two patches of moss, his arms crossed onto his knees.

He honestly didn't know why he was bothering. She practically swooned over him back at the palace, but as soon as she caught wind of Howard Rose-Shitter copping off with someone that wasn't her, it was suddenly all Seth's fault. What made her more interested in him anyway?

Probably the upside-down pissing incident, he thought sourly.

He'd almost had a chance to change her mind last night, until Old Faithful *jerked* up ahead of time and frightened her so badly she practically jumped head-first into the campfire. It didn't seem to understand *timing*, Seth thought, glowering at his trousers in accusation.

He bowed his head with a heavy sigh to the thoughts raging around his head, letting the gentle sounds of the foliage wash them out.

Until a high-pitched squeal pierced his eardrums.

'Heeeeeeere, chick-chick-chick-chick-chick!'

Seth's head jerked up.

The irritating mantra seemed to be echoing from the north, beyond a crop of foliage too tidy to belong to the Forest.

Seth heaved himself to his feet, peering over it.

Sure enough, the corner of a thatched roof peered back out from behind a huge tree, and—

'Heeeeeeere, chick-chick-chick!'

The chant was coming directly from it.

Seth set his jaw and strode forward.

In a large pen behind the cottage, a man stood in the centre of a ring of poultry, scattering grain. A couple hens loitered by the coop. There were always a few stragglers.

'Heeeeeeere, chick-chick—EEK!!'

His collar abruptly cut him off. It was being jerked backwards by a firm, angry hand.

The chicken-farmer tugged it forward a few millimetres. He was dragged through the open gate of the chicken pen, his heels scoring lines in the dirt.

'Oi!' he croaked, squirming. 'Get off me! Who d'you think you are?'

'A man with a migraine,' Seth said, tugging him along. 'The least you deserve for your contribution is one in return.'

'What's the idea?'

'Oh, you'll see.'

~

Some yards away and six feet underground, a shovelful of earth hit Lilly square in the face.

She blinked into the light of the late morning sun.

A lump of dirt bounced off her left breast. She clutched it with a curse.

She lifted a lethargic hand over her brow, rubbing dirt from her forehead. Her left temple let out a yelp of protest, and her fingers came away bloody. *Oh brilliant.*

Another shovelful to the face informed her that she was situated in an open grave. A steadily-filling one.

She bolted into a sitting position, spitting dust.

'What the hell are you playing at?!'

A silhouette of a man peered in.

'Burying you?' he said, his tone lifting in uncertainty. 'I was hunting and I found you lying here with your head bleeding. I thought I'd shot you by accident or something.'

'Oh yeah?'

She rifled in the satchel at her hip.

'So where's my purse?'

The man shrugged unconvincingly.

'You took it, didn't you?'

'Maybe,' he said.

'And thought you'd bury me for good measure?'

'Maybe.'

Lilly sighed. 'Help me out and I promise I won't kill you *immediately.*'

'Okay,' he said in a small voice.

Once she returned to the surface, Lilly faced her burier – who she recognised immediately.

'It's Stan Large, innit?'

'Carrot,' Stan said resentfully.

'What are you doing out here?'

'I ran away,' Stan said moodily. 'I hate it there! Men should have no business putting their... pee-pees into peoples... people. I don't like it at all. It's unsightly. It's all too much there, even the food there is shaped like—'

'And it doesn't even taste nice,' Lilly agreed.

'Right. Well, I decided to live somewhere else and I had no money, so I had to hunt for food with my last crossbow bolt, which I was saving for Uncle Keith but that's another matter, and I saw you unconscious on the ground and I thought sod it, she won't need it where she's going, and I took your money.'

He shifted his feet.

'Do I have to give it back? You *are* rich, after all.'

Lilly gazed at him piteously.

'Nah, you can keep it,' she allowed. 'Although asking would have been more polite.'

'Well, thanks. 'Cause I ain't going back,' he said defensively.

'You know, any normal bloke would trade his mum for an uncle with a knocking shop.'

'Not many normal blokes get to meet him,' he said bitterly. 'Anyway, I never warmed to that kind of thing.'

'Not with a crossbow under your bed, you won't,' she said.

High-pitched squealing echoed from the distance.

Picturing Seth being accosted at knifepoint, Lilly bid Stan goodbye with a roll of her eyes.

A ten-minute stroll revealed Seth standing at the back of a garden shed, wielding a long stick. He swung it back and forth in a half-pendulum motion, aiming at a hen tied up on the ground with string.

The hen's apparent owner was a small man with black curly hair, hanging from the shed gutter via a rope tied around his bare foot.

Lilly stared at this spectacle with her mouth hanging ajar.

'Bleed helb me,' the man pleaded through a mouthful of woollen sock.

Lilly gaped. 'Seth? What are you doing?'

Seth glanced up and gave his little sister a smile.

'I'm playing a game with my little friend here! It's called, "Let's See How Many Dead Chickens It Takes For Mister Noisy-Face To Learn His Lesson".'

'Helb me,' wept the chicken farmer. 'He's going to gill me!'

Seth swung the stick to a halt behind his ear and brought it down, hard.

The hen soared into the sky.

The prisoner sobbed wretchedly

'What on earth,' said Lilly.

Seth dropped the stick and lifted a loaded crossbow.

'… did he do to deserve this?'

'Nuffing!' cried the gagged prisoner, wriggling. 'I was dust feeding my dickens!'

Seth loosed a crossbow bolt.

'He was giving me an earache. Ah.'

The quarrel sailed over the trajectory of the descending hen in a wide arc.

Seth tutted.

'Missed. D'you want a go?'

He offered Lilly the stick.

Lilly's jaw dropped.

'This is the most evil,' she said, her gaze fixed to the crossbow, 'petty, spiteful thing I have ever see—can I shoot them?'

~

Howie's eyes opened blearily to meet Ron's.

Ron stared down at him with a fretful frown. 'Are you alright?'

Howie sat up slowly. 'I think so,' he said. 'I think I fainted or something… am I ill?'

'Vhyn says you're perfectly healthy,' a woman with red hair said from behind Ron. 'We were hoping you could tell us what happened.'

Howie examined his surroundings, trying to think.

He was back in the Faerie dwelling, lying on a bed so short his shins dangled over the end. He crossed his legs beneath him, wondering how he hadn't noticed how small it was earlier. He supposed he'd been preoccupied.

Vhyn, the Faerie that had started all this, stood in the corner looking shifty. Howie was perfectly aware that his lapse of consciousness could have been caused by her unceremoniously shoving him out of the tree. He made this awareness clear to her by way of a nasty glower.

Ron perched on the back corner of the bed, wringing his hands. The red-haired woman stood just behind, wearing a white dress that seemed to be made of everything a dress could possibly be made of.

Howie swallowed under her expression. She looked distinctly displeased to see him.

'Um…' he said, '… I don't really remember what happened… um…'

A memory of something jumping on him came into focus.

'A dog. I found a dog, a big one…'

'Oh, yes, he wanders about as he pleases,' she said. Her voice was cold. 'He doesn't attack Creys. Unless you fainted upon seeing him.'

Howie frowned. 'No, it wasn't that. We saw something… a tree falling, I think. And we went over to see what happened and… found something…'

'This?'

She held up the Stonecrown.

His eyes widened. 'Where was that?'

'With you,' she said. 'Vhyn found you outside a pit near the ruins of my palace, unconscious. The crown was in the pit, so she picked it up and took it with her. She brought you here. Do you remember any of this?'

Howie shook his head, stunned. He figured he would have remembered being hauled to the top of a tree by a tiny blue person.

A pit?

There was a memory of falling against a wall. That would have put him *in* the ruins, wouldn't it?

Or would it?

'You had better let me know once you recall anything else,' said the red-haired lady. 'Because by the looks of it, King Samuel is dead.'

'He's dead? Was his body there?' Howie asked in alarm.

'No, but that pit didn't appear out of nowhere,' she said. 'He may have been swallowed by a sinkhole, but your sudden collapse hints towards something more… deliberate.'

Howie blinked. 'Meaning?'

'Collapses out of the blue usually means someone wants you to forget something. Someone powerful.'

He gulped.

'Like a sorcerer?' Ron asked in astonishment.

'Most likely.'

Howie shook his head in bewilderment. 'Who are you?'

'This is the Forest Queen,' Ron said cheerfully. 'Found her by chance last night. A lot nicer than people think. Not even remotely insane.'

Qattren remained silent at this remark.

'Oh!' Howie exclaimed. 'You're… Quah… Quot…'

'Qattren,' she said curtly.

'Catherine,' he echoed. 'Nice to meet you.'

She snorted in a way that told Howie it wasn't that nice to meet *him.*

She turned her gaze to Howie's sword. It lay on the ground beside her, the blade slightly out of the sheath, as if it were hastily dropped there.

'A gift?' she asked, gesturing to the blade. 'I doubt you would have gotten very far if you had attempted to steal it.'

'Er, King Theo gave it to me,' he said. He cleared his throat. 'He sent me to request a truce and that you attend the celebrations in a few weeks. If you want to,' he added.

Qattren glared at him.

'He doesn't order it or anything,' he went on miserably. 'It's completely voluntary.'

She paused.

'I propose a bargain,' she announced. 'I accept your invitation and your truce and will investigate King Samuel's demise in the meantime. But all of this is on condition that you never, ever, re-enter this Forest. Not for your safety, but for everyone else, because something is afoot here and I deeply suspect that it is inadvertently connected to you. Do you understand?'

Howie nodded immediately. 'Yep. I mean yes, I understand.'

'Good. I suggest you re-assemble your entourage and head back to the palace. People will need to be informed of the tragic news about King Samuel as soon as possible.'

'Yes, your majesty.'

Qattren nodded briskly and left the cabin, closely followed by Vhyn. Presumably to assist with the petticoats, Howie thought, picturing the haphazard path of branches leading up to the cabin door.

Howie met Ron's gaze with an apologetic grimace.

'Ron, I'm so sorry about your dad.'

'What on earth for? One to go and I'm king!'

He noted Howie's alarmed expression.

'Sorry,' he said hastily. 'Too soon for dead dad jokes.' He wrung the end of his jerkin in both hands, toying with a button. 'Just think if I don't laugh about it, I'll cry.'

Howie reached out and gripped Ron's shoulder.

'Can you talk to your mum about it?'

Ron snorted. 'She hates me. The doctors said it was something called post-natal depression, but my father said it was just her being a lousy mother.'

'Well, I'm here if you need anything,' he said firmly. 'Your brother might be a bit of a prick and your mum isn't much better, but you'll always have your best mate, eh?'

Ron pinched his mouth closed and, reluctantly, started to cry.

Howie flung an arm around his shoulders.

~

Lilly aimed a longbow at the back of the shed.

Seth stood behind her, shaking his head.

'The target, Lilly,' he said, his arms folded. He leaned the small of his back against the ditch. 'You're supposed to hit the *target*. You'll kill something in that tree if you keep hitting it!'

'Really?' Lilly said, her nose wrinkled. 'You're worried about little animals in the tree, but hurting an actual human being is perfectly fine?'

'We aren't hurting him,' Seth corrected. 'We're just trying to frighten the little sod so that next time the Prince of Adem comes to visit, he won't be interrupted in his thoughts by peasants in the woods going "*eeeeeah chick-chick-chick-chick-CHICK!*!*!*" he mimicked in a squeaky voice.

'He won't now you nearly took out his left eye.'

'That was an accident. Go on, aim then!'

'I *am* aiming!'

She frowned as Seth snatched her wrists from behind to aim for her.

A few feet away, Howie hopped from a low branch and landed in the undergrowth.

Qattren stood shortly ahead of him, frowning into the near distance with her mouth slightly ajar.

'Is there anything I can help you… with…' He followed her gaze. 'Oh God.'

Seth and Lilly cackled hysterically by the shed, longbow drawn in hand.

Lilly spotted Howie and Qattren with a start and yelped, releasing the arrow.

It quivered to a halt an inch above the victim's groin.

Qattren stared at them, her expression blank except for a slight narrowing of the eyes.

The Creys scrambled around the yard, feverishly hiding darts, crossbows and other instruments of torture – which only served to make them more obvious to Howie and Qattren.

Howie heaved a sigh and gestured at them.

'Behold,' he said, 'the heirs to the kingdom of Adem, Seth and Lilly Crey…'

'My new allies,' she said flatly.

Seth glanced at the man and gave his bonds a hasty tug.

The rope unravelled, leaving him crumple into the grass.

~

PART FOUR: THE TOURNAMENT

I

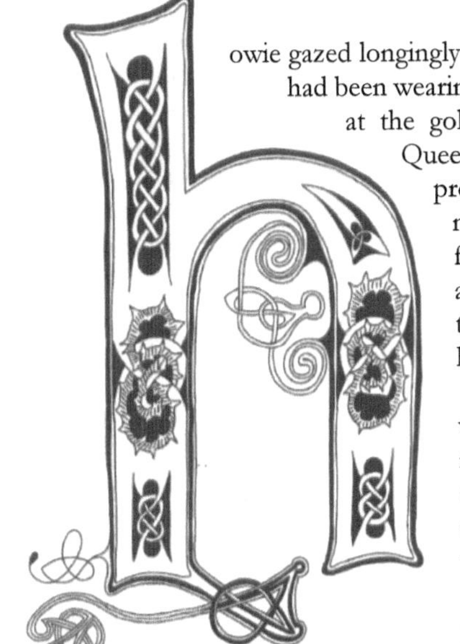

owie gazed longingly at the grimy riding clothes he had been wearing for the past few weeks, then at the gold-trimmed ceremonial outfit Queen Eleanor had lovingly presented to him earlier that morning. It fit perfectly. Apart from a tightness under the arms – apparently it belonged to Seth, which explained why it had no shoulders.

He put it on anyway, wincing as he jolted every muscle he had pulled in his arm practising for the melee and jousting competitions. It was King Theo's wish that he take part in the melee in particular, which didn't bode well. It meant he was up to something.

Howie glowered at the embroidery snaking around the emerald-coloured velvet. He didn't have the heart to tell Queen Eleanor how terrible her embroidery skills were. Whatever King Theo was up to, he hoped it had something to do with this outfit and a bonfire.

Upstairs, Seth reclined in his bath, thinking.

His father wanted him to play in the tournaments against the likes of the recently dubbed Sir Howard Rose-Prick, but he wasn't bothered about that. A generous tip in the right hands would sort the Knight of Thorns out.

Another thought occurred to him regarding the festivities – Adrienne would no doubt be attending. He smiled faintly. His mother had created a new outfit for him, he was told – black with emerald detailing. He was going to look *handsome.*

In the throne room, King Theo grinned to himself. A blacksmith had just left after presenting him with Seth's weapons for his approval. They were perfect for what he had in mind – as were Howie's. His plans were coming to fruition, and fast.

It was going to be a big week.

~

Pandemonium greeted the guests of the Creys as they flocked into the palace.

It was universally agreed among the noble classes that gold was an essential part of grand ball etiquette. To not wear gold to a party was like loudly passing wind in the middle of a wedding ceremony.

With that thought in mind, Lyseria had been placed inside the front entrance, where she would swiftly and eloquently eat anyone attempting to sneak entry without the standard requirement of a twenty-four-carat gold chain as stated in the official invitation as, a dragon being a dragon, Lyseria would know with accurate precision if anyone wore one less carat than required.

She had already eaten sixty-eight courses of opportunists and lounged next to the turrets as the Hornes entered.

Aaliyaa jumped slightly at the sight of the dragon.

'Dragons are a bad omen,' she said. 'They're an abomination. The prophecy states it.'

'Yes, mother,' Vladimir drawled.

He wished he had left her at home. Everyone in Adem thought the Seven were devils in disguise: she'd end up burned at the stake for being a heathen. Or maybe for just badmouthing the dragon. They hardly needed an excuse.

'Your highness, I assure you, the bodyguards are well armed should the beast attack,' Uncle Leroy said from behind Vladimir. 'You are perfectly safe.'

Aaliyaa eyeballed the beast regardless.

Lyseria peeled one eye open as they passed and did a mental tally of the small army accompanying them.

What had begun as a small trickle of visitors had grown to a flood of people. Influential characters from all over the world poured in.

Marbrand watched from the gate house. He was amazed at the capacity of the keep's ground floor. He wondered how many animals had to be skinned to make all the invitations – and realised he already knew, because he was the one who had had to skin them.

He yawned widely and scanned the sea of gold and silk for a glimpse of Ronald Horne.

In the entrance hall, Howie loitered by the courtyard doors, far apart from the guests and drinking heavily.

Adrienne and Archie had arrived wearing imperial-issue gold

chains and the standard second-hand ballroom attire. This didn't stop Seth Crey dribbling at her as she entered, to Howie's annoyance. The way he dressed her down with his eyes made Howie's skin crawl. By Adrienne's earlier expression, it had the same effect on her. *About bloody time.*

Having said that, Howie had been looking forward to seeing Cienne's attire and was disappointed to see her looking the same as always. Even Adrienne's mould-trimmed navy dress was more glamourous than Cienne's usual fifty-five petticoats.

One person whose attire did not disappoint was Prince Seth, leaning sulkily with his back against one of the gaping courtyard doors. Queen Eleanor had evidently aspired for a pattern featuring serpents.

What she got was a glittering mess of snot-green tangles with threads hanging out of it. It was hilariously hideous.

Howie laughed in Seth's face as he passed to get some air.

'You're supposed to use a handkerchief, not blow it down your clothes.'

'Piss off,' Seth spat, his arms folded.

In the dining hall, Jimmy collapsed against the table and nursed his left foot.

'I'm getting blisters out here,' he complained. 'Are you sure the beds don't need changing? I could make a good evening's work out of that. I have books to get through.'

'I was already ordered to do that,' a maid said, ushering him from the table to wipe it. 'In case the royal couple decide to have an early night.'

By the doubtful tone of her voice, Jimmy took that to mean Seth and Cienne.

It was common knowledge among everyone in the servants' floors that Seth Crey and the chambermaid had a sudden… understanding. Jimmy wasn't a bit surprised. Anna Beult was notorious for riding the gentry. Rumour had it she'd tried it on with the king once, just to see if it could be done. Which was probably the reason why she couldn't have children anymore. He dreaded to think what her poor husband must think.

It was a wonder Cienne hadn't sussed her out. Anna was making their rivalry as obvious as a shovel to the head, which would be her punishment if anyone important ever found out. Rich people had rubberneckers more deadly than any other establishment. Theirs had an executioner.

Jimmy lifted a tray of wine goblets and made his rounds around the steadily-filling hall. He paused a moment at the courtyard doors, sucked in a deep breath and entered the densely filled courtyard.

Contrary to all logic, he emerged with all six cups of wine intact.

Releasing a deep sigh, he made a beeline for the royal family.

Standing at the front entrance, Seth struggled with the guest list, which trailed from Queen Eleanor's hands down to a coiled roll on the floor.

'How on earth are you supposed to pronounce this?' Seth pointed at the scroll. 'You'd need three tongues to get this right! And what's this one? Some kind of skin disease? And where was this person when the vowels were being handed out?'

'Oh, they have vowels, they just don't write them down,' Jimmy said from behind him. 'The phonetics are obvious to everyone who speaks the language. You'll just have to guess, your highness.'

'HOW?? Look at how it's spelled! What am I supposed to say when *he* comes in? "Good evening, Mister Chronic Bowel Explosions, enjoy the festivities!"!'

'Thank you, Prince Seth,' boomed an accented voice. 'I certainly will!'

Seth spun around.

'Who was that? Was that his name?'

King Theo roared with laughter.

'Of course not! Nobody can get his name right, he doesn't care what you call him at this point! Chronic Bowel Explosions!' he repeated, laughing.

His face scrunched in bemusement, Seth searched the room for the mysterious Mister Chronic Bowel Explosions.

Just outside the inner portcullis, four men stood in the shadows.

'Has Vladimir arrived yet?' the youngest asked in a lilting accent.

'Yes, ages ago,' his cousin said in a flat voice.

'Oh.' He glanced at Cienne a yard away from them, greeting the visitors. 'Can we go say hello to Cienne?'

The cousin gave him a withering glance.

'Zephyr,' he said in a withering tone, 'is there a reason you brought the noisiest bastard with you?'

The youth flushed.

'Enough, Gomez,' the eldest of the four said. 'She's coming.'

Cienne recognised them immediately. Leaving a young woman in her stead, she rushed over, a grin spreading across her face.

'Uncle!' she exclaimed, kissing the older man on both cheeks.

'I'm so glad you made it!'

'Of course I made it!' Gomez Emmett Sr said cheerfully. His thick Mellian accent wrapped around the Truphorian words with ease. 'You look more like your mother with every passing day. A bit more sun on your skin and you'd be her image.'

Cienne smiled, though her eyes dimmed at the mention of her late mother.

'Cousin, you're looking pale. Do you eat at all these days?'

She shot Gomez Jr a half-smile. 'Little more than you, by the looks of it.'

Emmett twitched his mouth in an attempt at a smile. It was as much as his face seemed to be capable of.

Despite the name, he looked nothing like his father. Emmett Sr's olive skin and deep brown hair was replaced by slick black waves and an ivory complexion, and where his father was thick-set and weather-beaten, Emmett Jr was slender in every way. His bone structure put half the ladyship of Portabella to shame.

He also spoke in an immaculate Truphorian accent. He seemed to despise the Mellier lilt almost as much as Cienne had grown to despise her Portabellan one. Cienne enjoyed his company. He could be quite witty beneath the deadpan expression.

Cienne turned her gaze to the final two men with a wide smile. 'This must be one of your sons, Zephyr.'

The boy smiled shyly. He was his father in miniature.

Zephyr was a cross between the two Gomez Emmetts. Tall, slim, tanned and windswept, he was devastating to look at. It was a pity Cienne was related to him. She would have liked to marry someone like Zephyr.

Unfortunately, he was also quiet. He never got a word in edgeways.

'He doesn't count,' Emmett Jr said over whatever it was poor Zephyr had been about to say. 'Bastard born.'

'But born nonetheless,' Cienne added.

She smiled at the boy. 'It's nice to finally meet you.'

'Likewise, your highness,' he said politely, bowing his head.

Zephyr squeezed his shoulder fondly.

Cienne tore her gaze back to Emmett Sr. 'How fares my father, do you know?'

'Could not care less,' he said. 'He should have looked after my sister better. How fares your husband?'

'Could not care less,' she echoed. 'He should have looked after me better.'

He smiled sympathetically. 'Do not fret. I will have words.'

'So long as they are merely verbal. I still like his face, if anything.'

He laughed softly. 'If you insist.'

Cienne started at a scream by the drawbridge. She made a hasty farewell and hurried to investigate, leaving her maternal family by the door.

In the centre of a large group of shocked visitors, two figures materialised out of the dirt path with a purple flash. As the crowd parted, Cienne recognised one of them as Ron.

He waved at her ecstatically, a red-haired lady on his arm.

Stanley Carrot stood shortly behind them, trembling.

'Evening, your highness!' he called as Cienne tiptoed over. 'This is Qattren. We're married now!'

Cienne blinked. 'Really?'

Qattren was a beautiful woman. Her hair was knotted in a sleek bun that shone like copper and her silvery dress caught the torchlight in amber stripes. Ron... just looked like Ron, mud-stained clothes and all. Both wore gold chains like the other guests, and a deep crimson jewel hung on the end of Qattren's.

Cienne remembered herself with a start.

'That's fantastic news, I'm so pleased for you both,' she said with a smile. 'But do come in. It's awfully dusty out here all of a sudden.'

Qattren smiled, as though at a secret joke.

'Thank you, your highness,' she said sweetly.

They swept past elegantly – until Stan toppled to the ground and Ron had to return to pick him up.

'Where'd all this dust come from?' Elliot said on the battlements.

He stood beside Marbrand, who spat at the pavement below, narrowly missing a priest.

'I think I can guess,' he grunted, pointing.

Elliot followed his gaze to a red-haired beauty entering the inner gate, led by—

'That's Ronald Horne!'

'Looks like they've sold him to the Forest witch,' Marbrand grunted.

'He looks jolly happy about it,' said Elliot.

'I wonder why,' he said dryly.

Qattren took a small bag from Stanley Carrot and extracted a large sweet from within, to Ronald's glee.

'She's playing him like a fiddle,' Marbrand said in disgust.

'Least he's getting fed, eh?' Elliot said.

Sir Necker hollered up at him from behind the gate.

Elliot left Marbrand to squint at the Horne couple alone.

The tide of guests quickly became a trickle after that. Before long, all the guests had been accounted for and the drawbridge closed behind them.

In the dining room, Seth began to relax as the guest list grew shorter.

Until Qattren arrived in a sleeveless creation that trailed in her wake.

Seth spotted a number of guests trip over the hem.

'Hello,' he said, glancing down at the name the king was pointing at, 'um… Quat-Ren—'

'Qattren,' she said icily.

'Catherine,' he echoed.

'You're looking well,' said King Theo.

Qattren met his gaze, her chin raised.

'As are you,' she said courteously. 'I was pleased to receive your invitation.'

She eyeballed Seth.

'Almost as pleased as I was to make your son's acquaintance.'

'Lovely dress,' Seth commented. 'Where's the rest of it?'

King Theo opened his mouth to rebuke.

'Around each of the limbs of the Forest's sole human inhabitant,' said Qattren without missing a heartbeat, 'plus one eyebrow. He only moved out there for a bit of peace and quiet. He was very upset.'

'So was I, my ears were bleeding.'

'We'll speak of *that* later,' King Theo spat into Seth's ear.

As Qattren took her leave, a mousy-blond woman sidled up to them, wearing a plain grey gown with her mane of curls lying haphazard over one shoulder.

'Right, that's everyone,' she announced with a yawn.

Seth squinted. He found her oddly familiar.

'I know you,' he said. 'Have I slept with you at some point?'

She took a step back. 'No, but don't get your hopes up. You're not my type.'

Shock jolted his abdomen. Seth recoiled.

'Lilly?!' he said in astonishment. 'My God, you've *bathed*.'

'I know, I hardly recognise myself. Please can I change into some trousers?' she begged King Theo. 'There's a draft going right up my undercarriage.'

'Nonsense. Now hurry along and find yourself a rich husband. It appears your intended has given up on you.'

'Good. He's a weirdo anyway.' She made a face and stalked off.

'God forbid she might have to *pretend* to be female once in a while,' King Theo muttered.

'She doesn't look so bad with the shit washed out of her hair,' said Seth.

With that, the double doors behind them were slammed shut and the festivities began.

~

II

It was the first day since Howie had entered the keep that the dining table had been filled. King Theo sat at the head of it, in a throne facing all the food. Howie had been placed to his left and going down the table on Howie's left were Ron, who had ditched the wine for a change, Qattren, neither eating or talking to anyone, Stan, looking ill, Vladimir, giving Ron and Qattren the evils, the rest of the Hornes and nearly fifty others on that side of the table *alone*.

Vladimir seemed to have forgotten about his escaped captives – or perhaps Howie's seat at King Theo's side made him wary.

Queen Eleanor sat on Theo's right, next to Cienne, who tried to talk to Seth as he sat with his back turned to her, laughing hysterically at Lilly, who crouched to his right to show him the trousers she had put on under her skirt to combat the draft in her undercarriage.

Mister Chronic Bowel Explosions was next, eyeing Lilly in interest, and the Emmett family were beside him, chatting animatedly with a delighted Felicity sitting with Vladimir across from them.

For the first time that evening, Gomez Emmett Jr was genuinely smiling as his younger sister prattled on about her utterly tasteless dress. He hadn't smiled for anyone ever since he was fostered at the Hornes, or so Howie had heard. King Samuel had taken him in from early childhood to adolescence, along with a friend of his who had died during their time there, allegedly because of Vladimir. They hadn't said a civil word to each other since.

The author of a popular book from Nayport approached King Theo, looking very pleased with himself as he handed him several volumes. His joy quickly turned to horror as King Theo started hurling the thick volumes at the court jester with great amusement.

Vladimir turned to Ron and Qattren as cries of pain erupted.

'I hear you've been wed,' he said with interest. 'So sorry I couldn't attend. I'm afraid my invitation seems to have been lost during delivery.'

'It was an informal affair, merely the two of us and some servants at the ceremony,' Qattren said, picking apart her food with a fork.

'Last minute, was it?'

'Yes. It was a logical decision to bind our countries now that we share a truce with Adem, and what better way to do it?'

'Of course! Tell me, Ronald, how was the consummation?'

Ron snorted orange juice down his front.

Vladimir met Ron's stricken gaze with a patient smile.

Qattren patted her hair. More to divert attention to herself rather than tidy her already immaculate hair.

'Oh, wonderful,' she said in earnest. 'Simply wonderful. Not at all like I was expecting…'

She released a deep sigh, her eyelids fluttering.

Howie had to stop himself from applauding.

'… just wonderful. A fitting beginning for a truce, if ever there was one.'

Vladimir gawked wide-eyed at her, then at Ron in utter astonishment.

Seth's head also snapped up.

'Really?' he mouthed to Ron.

Ron gave him a hasty nod.

'Wow,' he murmured, casting a cursory glance over Qattren in approval.

Cutlery and conversation lifted the volume of the hall to a crescendo.

King Theo nudged Howie's elbow and leaned towards him.

'Up for a little task, my boy?'

Howie nodded, his mouth full.

'Keep eating, but listen closely,' he said in a low voice. 'Have you been practising for the tournaments?'

He nodded.

'Good lad. You see my boy there?'

He pointed at Seth.

'He hasn't, and it's about time he learned a little lesson in priorities. I want you to fight him in the melee, understand? And he must lose. Horribly. Understand? Good. I have a little reward for you should you succeed.' He pointed down the table. 'See my daughter-in-law over there?'

Very clearly, thought Howie wistfully.

'Wasted on him,' said King Theo, shaking his head. 'Bloody waste. You wouldn't neglect her like this if you were him, would you?'

'Nn-uh,' said Howie through a mouthful of lamb, shaking his head.

'No, of course you wouldn't. Which is precisely why I reckon *you* would make a much better Seth.'

Howie's brow furrowed. 'Hmm?'

'Look at him,' he said, pointing again. 'He's a weed. Never done anything useful in his life. And look at you. You solved the mystery of King Sam's disappearance, trained a dragon to rescue Prince Ronald Horne from a sinking ship, acquired a truce with the most dangerous woman in the world. All circumstantial, of course, but who cares! Everyone likes a good hero.

'I want you to fight in the melee with rigged weaponry. I'll have the squires sort you out: you need not worry about getting the wrong sword or anything like that. And when Seth is "accidentally" lamed in the fight by my younger – and very sorry – *son* – that's you, you understand – Seth will be given no choice but to abdicate his claim to the throne in favour of his little brother.'

King Theo gestured to Howie in triumph.

Howie swallowed, with difficulty.

'You want me to cripple Prince Seth?' he asked. 'And take his place in the royal family?'

'It will be a triumph!' King Theo continued. 'We will reveal to the world that the famous Sir Rosethorn is the heir presumptive to the throne. In disguise, protected against Seth's assassin in order to keep the Crey line secure should he ever return to finish Seth off. Wouldn't it be better for the people to have a competent man in charge after me?'

'I… I suppose,' Howie said in a squeak.

'Look at it this way,' King Theo coaxed. 'You will have a new wife to look forward to. A beautiful one.' He leaned closer. 'A *rich* one. All that country she owns as the only heir to the Fleurelles. All of that, and all you have to do is get rid of Seth.'

'But… they're married,' Howie said. 'Won't they still be married if he isn't king?'

King Theo grinned. 'Not necessarily. Princess Cienne's marriage certificate states that she is wed to the heir presumptive to the throne of Adem. The name "Seth Crey" does not feature in the document at all.' He smirked. 'Cienne's child *must* inherit both Adem and Portabella: that was the arrangement. I doubt King Fleurelle will object to a quick annulment and remarriage in the interests of his sole heir. After all, Seth's had twenty years to cement the marriage with a child and he's failed. Horribly.'

Howie gulped.

'You'll get all the help you need. And besides, it's *Seth*. You'll hardly find him much of a threat.'

Howie licked his lips.

'Am I your son?' he asked carefully.

King Theo eyed him up and down. 'No, absolutely not. You may be my brother's get, you have the Crey look around the eyes. Or perhaps an offshoot of Eleanor's, I've had my doubts about her virtue since we met. But mine? Certainly not.'

Howie's face fell. 'Oh.'

'But ignore all that. That's need-to-know information. You leave the lying to me. I've had practise.'

King Theo turned back to his dinner.

'We'll keep this between ourselves, yes? We don't want anyone patriotic hearing about this, do we?'

Howie shook his head anxiously.

King Theo glared at his son, who picked idly at his dinner with his chin in his hand.

'Aren't you eating, boy?'

Seth's head jerked up. 'Oh, no, I'm not hungry.'

'Nonsense! You can manage a wing, can't you?'

Seth pictured a turkey wing and nodded.

His face fell as a trolley came around. Lilly and Cienne moved aside.

Two male servants hoisted a griffin wing over Seth's head and onto the table in front of him.

Seth grimaced at it. It was over three feet long.

'Go on! It's only a small one!' King Theo jeered.

Seth groaned and pulled a small strip off.

The feast rose to a dull roar. King Theo continued to eat, winking at Howie every now and then. Lilly worked her way through the discarded wing happily.

Howie found he suddenly lost his appetite. He glanced at Seth, who leaned on the back of his chair, gazing at the guests milling around the hall. His personal dislike aside, did Seth really deserve to have his life taken from him?

Well. Yes.

But more importantly, was Howie the right person to take

over? Howie didn't think so. He could barely manage carpentry, let alone rule a kingdom.

Howie sat dejectedly in front of his half-eaten dinner, staring into space.

~

As the plates and meals were cleared away, music began to play. A harpist with voluminous red hair plucked a pleasant melody and sang in a lilting soprano.

Most of the guests rose to dance now, leaving their food unattended.

Seth and Cienne vanished in different directions as Zephyr dragged her for a dance.

She glimpsed Seth by the staircase, engaged in conversation with the chambermaid. He pulled her towards him, his back turned to Cienne, and kissed her gently on the mouth.

Cienne jolted at the sight, her eyes welling with tears.

Zephyr spotted this reaction and swung her around, scowling at Seth's back.

Stan and Ron conversed casually with Lilly as Qattren wandered onto the dance floor. Much of the crowd slid out of their carefully choreographed dance circle as she spun and flung her head to the music, letting it dictate her every move. The guests stood on the side-lines, enraptured, and the strong, dramatic drum beat played almost on default, the musicians mesmerised.

Howie rose in silence and made for the courtyard, tapping Ron's shoulder as he went.

They entered the torchlit courtyard together. Guiding Ron to the other side of the fountain, Howie placed his head close to Ron's.

'There's something I want to ask you about your wife. She owns that big dog in the Forest, right?'

'Oh, him, he's harmless,' Ron brushed it off. 'He wouldn't have bitten you if that's what you're worried about.'

'No, that's not what I meant.' He cast a cursory glance at a group lingering nearby, scanning for a familiar face. 'It's named after King Theo. I think she had an affair with him around the time I was born.'

Ron's eyes widened. 'Really?' He glanced back at the swirling silver silk in the dining hall. 'She's aged well.'

Something about this comment logged a trace of doubt in his mind, but he dismissed it.

Seth stumbled out of the kitchens, tying his trousers closed.

Howie's back was turned to him, but Seth spotted him immediately and wandered into the group of guests to eavesdrop.

'You don't think,' said Howie, 'you know, that I might be their... son?'

He swallowed.

'The dates seem right,' he went on, 'and the whole thing with the castle exploding... maybe he was trying to get rid of me, and Qattren gave me up after, save the trouble of...'

Ron made a face.

So, behind the group, did Seth.

'Well...' said Ron, 'first thing she said when I first met her was that she wasn't able to have children.'

Howie deflated. 'Oh.'

Ron smiled thinly. 'I'm sorry.' He shrugged. 'Maybe he had another mistress.'

Seth scowled. *The old man pulled her?*

'Lucky git,' he muttered to himself.

'Maybe your mother died in childbirth or something,' Ron said. 'Why else would anyone abandon someone so pretty?'

He patted Howie's face playfully, making him smile.

Adrienne danced out from the dining hall, past Seth, who gawked at her, dumbstruck.

She halted by Howie's side and proceeded to pull him inside for a dance.

Cienne passed them in the other direction.

'Everything alright?' Adrienne asked him.

'I suppose,' he said, crestfallen. 'I just... had an inkling I had found my mother.'

Cienne froze.

'It turned out to be a mistake.'

Adrienne gazed at him piteously. She linked arms with him.

'Don't worry. We don't need mothers.'

Cienne watched them go without a word, her gaze locked on Howie sadly.

~

After a fistfight between the city mayor and the Duke of Osney, a lost bet with Zephyr Emmett led Howie upstairs to his rooms for coin. He took a wrong turn, eight flagons of beer sloshing up and down his system, and somehow ended up in a familiar room decorated in peach curtains.

'I'm very sorry,' Howie slurred, 'I'm in the wrong bloody—'

Princess Cienne sat on a small settee, alone.

Howie blinked his eyes into focus, to make sure.

It was still Cienne, as he suspected. Her eyes were red-rimmed.

Seth, he thought with venom.

'Hey,' he said, approaching. 'Don't cry. At least you still have your looks.'

Cienne looked up at him. 'You've had far too much to drink.'

'Yes.' He hesitated. 'But at least I'm still smiling.' He grinned at her.

Cienne coughed out a laugh. He was as surprised to hear it as she was.

'Come and sit with me,' she said, patting the seat beside her.

'With pleasure, my lady,' he said with a bow.

Cienne smiled at him as he collapsed beside her.

'So,' he said, dropping his chin into his hand. 'What's he done this time?'

Cienne's gaze fell to her elbow, resting against the back of the settee. 'Oh, nothing new.'

She swung her gaze to the window, where a sweeping view of the clustered lights of Serpus greeted her.

'It's a lovely view,' said Howie.

'Yes it is,' she agreed, facing him, but he wasn't looking at the window.

He was looking at her.

'I meant you, I mean,' he said to clarify.

Cienne nodded with a sad little smile. 'I'm glad someone thinks so.'

'Everyone thinks so,' Howie insisted.

He shifted forward.

His senses had fled him along with the bet he owed Zephyr Emmett, but that didn't matter. King Theo said she was to be his wife now. What was there to lose?

'You're th'most beautiful woman in the entire world. Men sing songs about you.'

'Do they?' Cienne asked, amused. 'Sing me one.'

'I can't. They're extremely filthy.'

Cienne laughed openly. It was like bells in his ears. Or something romantic like that.

'Now I'm intrigued!' she exclaimed. 'Sing me one. I'm sure at age thirty-three, there's very little left to surprise me.'

'Yes. Of course, my highness.'

He cleared his throat and straightened his back. He inhaled.

'Oh wait, I can't sing,' he said, deflating.

'That doesn't matter!'

'It does matter! We should stick to talking. You can't talk out of tune, it's a fact.'

Cienne giggled.

Howie grinned. 'I like it when you smile properly.'

She grinned back. 'Me too.'

Howie gazed at her with a long sigh.

Her hand floated over to his face and settled there, just under the jawline. It tickled.

A rush of heat ran through him.

'You're too sweet for your own good,' Cienne murmured.

She stroked his lower lip with the side of her thumb.

He raised his upper lip in disgust.

'You only like my face 'cause it looks like Seth's,' he said sulkily.

Cienne shook her head. 'You're better-looking. You don't scowl as much.'

Their eyes met.

'I love you,' Howie slurred. 'He never will, but I do.'

'Really?'

He nodded. He tried to make his expression look smoulderingly handsome.

The effect was ruined by a sudden burp.

'I extremely fancy you a lot, at the very least,' he said thickly.

Cienne trembled.

Howie took that as a signal and swept forward to meet her.

Her mouth was exactly as he imagined it. He shut his eyes tight as waves of heat swept up his back.

Cienne cupped the back of his neck, just for a moment, but it was enough.

Teenage idealism was doing backflips at this point.

You need to get drunk more often, it told him, *this is great!*

Cienne squeaked in alarm and tore herself away.

'Ew, no, I can't!' she shouted. 'I can't, it's horrible!'

She lifted her skirts in her arms and fled.

Howie frowned after her. The door slammed behind her. He thought he could hear a man's laugh outside, but it might have been his imagination.

Horrible, she said.

Howie huffed a breath into his cupped palms and sniffed.

'Charming,' he said aloud, deflating.

~

As the drummers and harpists' repertoire died out, the guests began to retire upstairs. Qattren brushed her hair from her face and took Ron's arm as all flocked to the stairs, to apartments in the east wing of the top floor.

The Emmetts and the Hornes made their goodbyes, to estates of their own in Serpus, and the Creys lingered by the door to bid them farewell – apart from Seth. He'd vanished after the chambermaid again, to Adrienne's disgust.

Archie was haranguing the king about carpentry when Howie entered the throne room.

Adrienne stood nearby, fiddling with her jewellery.

King Theo sat on his throne with Archie in Seth's seat beside him, both leaning on the armrests between them. The king listened to Archie, rapt.

'... glad to see the throne's solid oak, good wood that, lasts forever, very underrated next to mahogany. The other two thrones are good too, but there's plenty of room up here for all the family. I would suggest – just a thought, you understand – that the minor thrones could be copied out five or six times, just to make spares, but you could fold them for storage by way of a system of pegs...'

'How long has this soliloquy lasted?' said Howie in amusement.

'About fifteen minutes straight. You know Archie.' Adrienne's eyelids drooped with boredom and fatigue. 'I think the king's fallen asleep with his eyes open. He's only nodding by default.'

'... so you see, you've got ten, twelve pegs holding the pieces on and they'll be tough as nails when you sit on it, and they'll fold up neatly when you've no more use for them...'

King Theo's head dipped up and down sleepily.

Howie nudged Adrienne's arm. 'You look lovely.'

'Oh, shush, I do not.'

'You do,' he insisted. 'You trump Princess Tent-Dress any day.'

She favoured him with a small smile. 'You look alright yourself. Lace suits you.'

'Only because I'm too polite to rip it off.'

She giggled.

Howie shot her a fond glance. 'Are you alright, by the way? I saw Prince Shitface hanging around some maid earlier, like a dog on heat.'

'Yes, apparently they had stumbled into the kitchen in a state of undress and collapsed on top of the butler's dinner. I'm beginning to think charming princes are overrated.'

Howie nodded in earnest. 'You can do better.'

'To be honest, I never really liked him that much to begin with,' Adrienne said. She hesitated. 'He just reminded me of someone I've liked for a long time.'

Howie felt a jolt at that.

Me, he realised.

'Maybe he likes you too,' he said, half to himself. 'Maybe he just didn't know it yet.'

Their gazed met. Something blossomed in his stomach and, looking into her eyes, he knew his suspicions to be correct. She liked him.

Every Cienne-based daydream dissolved at that moment. Her beauty seemed to dissolve with it: the Cienne standing in the front entrance a few yards away was a different creature now, a cold figure with a pinched face, any kindness or warmth in her as fleeting as a breeze.

He turned his back on it – her, the crown, all of it. He didn't need her anymore.

He linked his fingers in Adrienne's and watched her face turn pink.

He had everything he needed all along.

~

Seth entered his bedroom, closing the door behind him.

'You'll never guess what I saw earlier, it was hilarious.'

Anna lifted an eyebrow, reclining back on his bed.

The room glowed a dim red thanks to a lit brazier in the corner of the room. Seth swept into the darker half of the room and sat at Anna's side, throwing his head back to gaze at the ceiling.

Anna pulled herself closer and started to rub his shoulder.

'So,' she said as he stretched his shoulder-blades, 'is your ploy working as you planned?'

'Oh certainly,' he said. 'Jimmy told the entire palace about what we did on top of his dinner – well, you know, *pretended* to do. The whole household is talking about us now.'

'Ooh, I'm honoured,' she said wryly. 'So what was this hilarious thing you saw?'

'Oh,' Seth said with a laugh. 'Howard Rose-Prick tried to kiss my wife. I have my faults, but at least I never made a woman run from the room screaming.' He paused mid-chuckle. 'Apparently he has it into his tiny little head that my father and that red-haired woman from the Forest are his parents. She isn't even my age.'

Anna frowned with him. 'I thought it was your mother-in-law he had it off with.'

'My mother-in-law?' Seth grimaced. 'She had a face like a bulldog.'

'Not before she married the King of Portabella,' she said. 'She was quite beautiful once, apparently.'

Seth was intrigued. 'I never thought my father had the time for that type of thing.'

'There's an old rumour they had an argument on the Night of Raining Thorns and he killed her over it that night. If anyone, she's his mother. Howard was probably the thing they were arguing about.'

Seth raised his eyebrows. 'The plot thickens. Pity she didn't have an arrangement like ours. All of the attention with none of the groping.'

'The groping is equally welcome,' she said in his ear.

Seth looked her up and down. 'I'll bet it is.'

He slid away from her a touch.

'She'll come to me soon enough. Then I won't need you.'

Anna stopped in the act of massaging him and leaned towards his ear.

'I think you'll find that you will,' she told him, gently kissing his cheek on her way out.

Seth watched her go with a smirk. He admired himself in the mirror by the bed.

I could say I don't know what these women see in me, he thought. *But that would be a lie.*

He thought back to what Anna said.

Persephone Fleurelle and the King of Adem.

Meaning Howie had just passionately kissed his big sister.

Seth snorted and laughed with his own reflection.

~

III

The next day marked the beginning of the jousting tournament – which would have lasted a year if everybody from the feast had participated.

Instead the crowds had been narrowed down to sixteen contestants, among whom were Marbrand and Elliot (both suffering from acute fatigue from working the night shift and having to practise in the daytime) Sir Boris Necker, a mysterious rider nicknamed the Quarrel, Gomez Emmett Jr, Howie, King Theo and, to Cienne's dismay, Seth.

There would have been much more dismay had Seth gotten his way and ridden Lyseria into the lists, but King Theo put his foot down.

He just wanted her for himself, Seth mused moodily.

A week later, in the jousting pitch a mile south of the castle, the last two matches were about to begin. Marbrand and Elliot had been knocked out early in the tournament due to falling asleep at the reins and missing their respective cues. Necker had hilariously lost to a knight they later discovered had died moments before the tournament and won two passes by lieu of rigour mortis setting in at the opportune moment.

Howie lost narrowly in the previous day's session to Emmett Jr, who didn't show any emotion to this because, according to speculation, he didn't have any.

At the moment, Seth was assisted onto his horse at the end of the tilt, his helmet open to reveal a scowl. His performance so far, from Howie's perspective, was positively disgusting. He'd simply thrown money at his opponents until they threw in the towel – no doubt waiting for their bribes to first outweigh the prize itself before yielding.

Seth accepted his lance and braced himself.

The only jouster who ignored his imploring offers of coin was the Quarrel, who waited on the other side, astride a black destrier matching their armour. They aimed their lance right between Seth's eyes as King Theo himself announced them.

'On my left,' he bellowed, gesturing, 'bearing the blood of a very great jouster,' he thumped his own chest with a grin, 'my own son and heir, the future king, Prince Seth Crey!'

The crowd patted a rather limp applause.

Seth tilted his head to one side and twirled an arm in a very pretentious flourish.

'And he'd better win, too. His reign's going to be ugly enough as it is.'

King Theo circled his own face with one finger as he spoke, earning laughter from the crowd and a scowl from Seth.

'And on my right, a *mysterious* rider...'

The crowd jeered.

'... who's apparently doing a bloody good clean-up of the lists so far: the Quarrel!'

The crowd rose in uproar.

The Quarrel sent them a sharp salute.

Seth scowled at this and shifted slightly on his horse, which snorted hatefully.

Upon the call of a brief fanfare, the pass began.

Seth launched his mount forward, the lance unsteady in his right arm. He would have used his stronger left arm, but King Theo put his foot down about *that* as well. It was cheating, apparently.

The Quarrel had no such encumbrance and flew in his direction, barely a streak in the wind.

The Quarrel's lance smashed into Seth's helm, knocking him sideways in a shower of splintered wood.

Cienne gasped, her hand on her heart.

Queen Eleanor gave her other hand a squeeze.

'The lances are easily breakable, dear. The helm is pure steel.'

'For now,' King Theo muttered from his wife's left.

Just as Seth had regained his balance, the horse reared. Seth's arms flailed about in windmill motions until he tilted off and thudded to the ground. He waved a gauntleted hand across his throat, yielding.

The Quarrel slammed the remains of their lance to the ground and flung a hand into the air.

The crowd roared its approval.

A row in front of King Theo, Ron scrutinised the Quarrel as Qattren watched.

Stan glanced at Ron. 'What are you looking at, your highness?'

'Lilly,' he said in realisation.

'Lilly?' Stan asked, bemused.

Sure enough, the Quarrel pulled off her helm to reveal a mass of mousy curls and a triumphant grin.

'Yes! I win!'

'Lilly!' roared King Theo, bolting to his feet.

'What?'

She backed her destrier away as two guards approached.

'Wait a minute, what the hell, I—OI!'

They dragged her from the horse by her armpits.

She shrieked. 'But I won! I'm in the final! I'm the *winner!*'

She squealed as they lifted her away.

'Disqualified!' called King Theo as Lilly vanished. 'Disqualified for false pretences! Seth wins!'

Only half a dozen people applauded this time, including Cienne, as Seth jogged after Lilly in interest.

Next to face each other were Emmett Jr and King Theo, a

match quickly ceased when Emmett pulled out, declaring King Theo the winner.

This left two kings, present and future, to face each other.

Seth gulped.

Theo smiled.

They launched towards each other.

A dust cloud and a mass of splinters marked Seth's fall.

Cienne's heart was in her mouth.

Seth writhed on the pitch, clutching at a large dent in his breastplate. He tugged it and the helm off, sucking air into his battered lungs.

Theo laughed loudly with his fists in the air.

Seth yielded angrily and sprawled himself on the ground. He lay there as the prizes were handed out, his second-place token placed sheepishly beside him.

The crowds dissipated to join the feast back at the castle.

Cienne remained, making her way down from the gallery the Creys had been seated in. She helped Seth to his feet, tugging the rest of his armour off.

'How are you feeling?' she asked.

'Fine,' Seth said curtly, throwing a shoulder-plate to the ground.

She pressed her mouth to his ear and whispered.

He paled. 'What?'

She whispered frantically in response.

King Theo walked past from a distance of three yards, casting them a sideways glance.

Seth listened avidly for a moment and nodded, ushering her ahead of him.

The grounds emptied quickly, voices raised in anticipation for the upcoming melee contest.

~

The next day, however, Archie was not so anticipating.

'Howie, I don't want you doing this fight tomorrow.'

Howie looked up from his inspection of an expensive crossbow.

'Why not? I've practised, I'm really good.'

'That's what I'm worried about.'

They stood in the centre of Arthur Stibbons' Head, the city square. A huge market sale took place around them, the square brimming with gentry from all over the world. The weaponry dealers bore particularly heavy pockets as Howie quickly filled a wheelbarrow. His knighthood had earned him a small estate near Serpus, nicknamed Squirm until the council could conjure up a better name for it. He was the landlord for a small crop of farms, a position he never envisioned himself acquiring at the tender age of twenty. He was frigging loaded.

Archie shifted on his feet.

'What are you worried about?' Howie asked in exasperation. 'Nobody's gonna *die*. It's all play really.'

Mostly, his mind added.

'I know that,' said Archie. 'I just don't like the idea of you being a nob.'

Howie shot him a glare. 'That was uncalled for.'

'No, not that, you know, a noble. Like these people,' he said, gesturing around them. 'I don't want you to end up like them and start eating fruit with a knife and fork.'

'Archie, they don't eat *everything* with a knife and fork—'

'What kind of eatery are you running here, sir?'

Howie dropped his head into his hand.

'I'm not eating that,' Seth pointed at an innocent apple sitting on the counter, 'without cutlery. What do you think I am, a barbarian? After you *touched* it?'

'I wash my hands regular, your highness,' the stall keeper said in a hurt voice.

Seth snorted. 'And that's a tan, is it?'

'Well, yes, it is!'

Archie threw Howie a cynical glance.

Howie averted his eyes.

'Well… he does. But he was spoon-fed for twenty years! You can't judge everyone based on him!'

'I'm not. I'm judging *them* based on him.'

Archie glanced over at his niece, who inspected an ointment stall in interest.

'And what about Adrienne?'

Howie shot her a wistful glance. 'What about her?'

'She doesn't want to hang around with a snobby *melee* contestant,' he said, putting a haughty inflection on the word 'melee'. 'She's mates with a slightly useless carpentry apprentice, not the lordly bastard son of a king that uses severed heads as party decorations. With bite marks in,' he added as an afterthought.

'He hardly eats them as such,' said Howie, without much conviction.

Archie read his expression and gave him a look that said,

'Exactly.'

'You're a good kid,' he said firmly. 'People like you need to stay that way. Because nobles aren't people, kid. They'll trick you into doing what they want you to do, and if you don't...'

He ran his index finger across his throat.

'Better get out while you still can.'

Howie glowered at him. The weight of his purse felt far more comforting than Archie's warnings pertained.

He pointed at Archie's face.

'*You're* just jealous is all that is. He's looking after me, alright? I'm not gonna just give up and go home because you're scared of everyone.'

Archie's mouth hung ajar. 'I'm just saying—'

'I have some drilling to get in before tomorrow.' He eyed Archie's hurt expression and sighed. He handed him the purse. 'Here, go mad. And stop freaking out. It'll be fine.'

He spotted Corporal Moat nodding him towards the castle. Despite Archie's warnings, he followed him.

He clapped a hand of greeting on Ron's shoulder as he passed.

Ron shot him a passing grin, lingering by a baked goods stall.

His gaze fell on a disembodied hand groping the top of it.

So, some twenty yards away, did Qattren's.

Ron gave the hand a curious poke.

'Oi!' it squealed, vanishing under the stall.

Ron knelt, peering underneath the stall.

'What are you doing under there—'

'Ron!' Qattren called, beckoning. 'The cake merchant is from Stoneguard, he would love to meet the prince of his country...'

She trailed off as the dust cloud dissipated. The word 'cake' had probably done it.

Adjusting her skirts, she knelt in his place, the fine silk gathered in her elbows.

'And you're hiding beneath the bread stall because...?'

'You told me to be inconspicuous,' the bread stall replied. 'And also, I was hungry.'

Qattren lifted her eyes to the heavens. 'What is it?'

'I saw something,' he said. 'Shit's about to go down at the feast, and I don't mean the dodgy roast chicken.'

'What kind?'

'The "end of the world" kind.'

Qattren frowned, shifting her feet on the cobbles. 'You saw this in a vision?'

'While I was on the bog. Knocked my outhouse down when I keeled over and mooned half the countryside. It's just as well I've no neighbours.'

She gave him a sympathetic half-smile. 'It's a hard life, being a prophet.'

'It is,' said the Prophet.

Qattren ruffled his close-cropped black hair, being careful to avoid the wound on his left eyebrow. He hadn't changed much since they first met twenty years ago, Qattren noted fondly. *He'll forever look the age of eight.*

'Tell me about your vision.'

From the cake stall, Ron watched his wife caress the stranger's hair with an odd expression.

'So that's why she doesn't want relations,' he mused with a shrug.

~

The Crey household scattered from the throne room *extremely* quickly on the morning of the melee competition as King Theo's voice shook dust out of the walls.

'GET THAT HARLOT OUT OF MY CHAIR NOW!!'

Anna rose.

Seth pushed her back down by one shoulder.

'No,' he said simply.

King Theo clenched his teeth with an audible *snap*.

'Move her or there will be trouble,' he said in a low voice.

'Bugger off if you don't like her sitting there,' said Seth in an airy tone, leaning the small of his back against the arm of the chair.

Theo flexed his fingers in front of him, livid.

'I'd better leave, I don't want to miss the melee,' Anna said, rising. 'Farewell, your highness.'

'I'll see you later,' said Seth. 'Somewhere more… private?'

King Theo growled loudly.

Anna swept from the dais.

Seth flicked her long ponytail into the air behind her as she passed.

King Theo stepped forward slowly, with a face like thunder.

'You're treading thin ice, boy,' he warned.

Seth blinked, his arms crossed.

'Am I? It's not a crime, having a bit on the side. Kin-slaying, on the other hand, that's a different story. If you get caught. Is that right?'

Theo blinked. 'What are you saying, Seth?'

Hmm. He didn't call me 'boy'. That must mean I have his attention.

'Oh, nothing,' he said, looking smug. 'Just speaking hypothetically.' He stood up straight. 'Fair enough, having it off with a "harlot" is bad enough, and I may have gone a little too far sitting her in your chair, but when you compare that to, say, plotting to eradicate a senior member of the royal family to put someone in charge that's going to be taking your orders, well, that's a different story.'

Theo stared at him impassively.

'I mean, there aren't a lot of people affected by my bedroom habits, but we don't want anyone *disappearing*, do we? That would upset people.'

King Theo narrowed his eyes. 'Speak plainly. Are you insinuating something?'

'No, no,' he said, his facial expression saying, 'Yes, yes.'

He smirked.

'If I were going to insinuate anything, I would refer to that little spat you apparently had with my dearly departed mother-in-law.' He lifted an eyebrow. 'You recall her? I gather you know one or two of her children quite well.'

King Theo's upper lip twitched.

Seth shot him an arrogant smirk.

Then King Theo's face cleared and he smiled back.

'Son,' he said, placing a hand on Seth's shoulder. 'Let's take a walk around the grounds, shall we?'

He ushered his dubious son to the door behind him.

'We'll have ourselves a little *chat.*'

~

Jimmy hovered sheepishly inside the basement door, arms full of folded sheets.

Lilly approached from the vaults in a full suit of armour.

He eyed her with an uneasy expression. Mainly on account of the smoke filling the corridor in her wake.

'Dare I ask,' he said, 'but what's all that smoke about?'

Lilly opened the door. 'Burning some unwanted junk in the vault. And retrieving my armour. What's with the sheets?'

'Taking them back to the keep. Everywhere's too filthy in here for me to put them down long enough to open the door.' He grimaced at her breastplate again. 'Are you sure you want to risk annoying him again? He only ever says your name in tones of wrath as it is.'

'Pfft,' she said in contempt. 'You worry too much. It'll be fine, erm… what's your name again?'

'James,' he said.

'Oh, can I call you Jimmy?'

He pulled a pained expression and heaved a sigh. 'You might as well, everyone else does.'

'Oh, okay. Thanks Jimmy!' she said on her way out.

'Oh, could you hold the door a minute while I—'

She slammed the door shut.

Jimmy swore and, carefully, tried to turn the doorknob with his foot.

The knob hit the floor with a clank.

He swore again much more loudly.

~

Lilly fastened her helm as she walked past the Tower.

Seth entered it with unease, King Theo ushering him from behind.

Lilly made a U-turn at the sight of her father and jogged around the corner of the keep.

She squealed, skidding to a halt.

Stan leaned against the wall, his arms folded.

'I thought women weren't allowed to compete?'

'I ain't that obedient, as you can tell,' she said drily. She hesitated. 'You won't tell my ole man, will you?'

'None of my business,' he said, his hands in the air. 'Just remind me not to be around when he flays you.'

'He won't find out, me and ole Ron have an arrangement.'

She paused as a scream erupted from the Tower.

'And it sounds like Seth has an arrangement too.'

'What makes you say that?'

'He only screams like that when he has to get out of something. Come on, we'd better drag him back into his bedroom to recover.'

As Lilly, her helm fastened shut, and Stan jogged to the Tower, King Theo exited, looking rather satisfied with himself.

'Ah, you two wouldn't remove my son from the Wet Room, would you? I think he's learned his lesson now. Don't be late for the melee, we're holding it in the courtyard,' he said cheerfully, sweeping past.

Lilly and Stan exchanged glances and bolted for the Tower.

'Remind me,' Stan gasped, 'what's the Wet Room?'

'Cellar full of water used for torture and quiet executions.'

'Oh, how apt,' Stan moaned.

They burst into the ground floor, a small room with a low ceiling.

Lilly knelt on the slick tiles to wrench open a trapdoor in the floor.

Water rushed around Stan's ankles and Lilly's knees.

She stuck her arm into the trapdoor up to the shoulder, reaching. After several tries, she finally dragged him to the surface.

Seth choked and spluttered in a panicked frenzy.

'He's trying to kill me,' he gasped.

Stan helped Lilly pull him from the depths of the water chamber.

'He's going to have me killed! He's going to kill me!'

'Yeah, we didn't think he shoved you into a chamber full of water for a laugh,' Stan said wryly.

Lilly shot him a look and wrapped her arms around Seth's shoulders to steady him.

'Oh, what have you said?'

Seth shook his head, coughing hysterically.

'He's going to get it this time,' he vowed in a strangled voice. 'Both of them.'

Lilly glanced at Stan and dropped her chin on Seth's shoulder in dread.

~

IV

Two armoured opponents circled each other slowly, each armed with a great-sword and a shield. Emmett Jr was one of them, or so the spider emblem on his shield declared, and the sheer size of the other marked him to be Elliot Maynard.

'Your cousin is the ugliest person I have ever seen,' Seth commented from the front row, as far away from his father as possible without causing a scene. 'He's like a horse wearing a man's skin.'

'Horses are more sociable,' Cienne said from his left.

Stan glanced at him from the stands.

An hour ago, he'd had to drag Seth to his room for a bath and a change of clothes after the sheer amount of vomit and bodily fluid he'd come into contact with in the notorious Wet Room. He'd calmed down considerably now, albeit with a dark cast to his eyes that Stan misliked. He was even conversing with his wife, which Stan misliked even more. He'd already had one shock today without risking her wrath.

At the moment, Seth watched in disinterest as he waited for his first match of the day – against Howard Rosethorn of all people. He sat back, his arms folded behind his head, as Elliot launched himself on top of Emmett, knocking him to the ground and pinning him there.

Seth sniggered slightly as some guards carried the unconscious Emmett away.

Qattren sat beside Ron at the back row, three rows up from Seth and Cienne.

Vladimir sat at Ron's right with their mother and uncle, all looking relieved that Princess Felicity had parked herself with her father in the lavish rear gardens.

Marbrand hovered behind Vladimir, on King Theo's orders to watch him like a hawk.

A man in violet skittered to Vladimir's side and held out a silver goblet brimming with dark wine.

'Compliments of Lord Emmett, your majesty.'

Vladimir frowned at it for a moment. 'Oh.' He accepted it in his left hand, his right already cradling a cup of clear wine. 'Send him my thanks.'

The man bowed and skittered away again.

Vladimir exchanged a glance with his uncle and shrugged, taking a swig from his half-empty cup.

Two new contestants entered the courtyard from the throne room and were loudly introduced.

'From the Great Sands of, erm…'

The Creys' herald squinted at the parchment in his hand, trying to decipher a pronunciation. He settled for an indistinguishable mumbling.

'… the undefeated melee champion, er… um, Mister, um, Chronic Bowel Explosions?'

The crowds laughed.

Mister Chronic Bowel Explosions gave them a stiff bow.

'And his opponent,' said the herald, red-faced, 'from our neighbouring country of Stoneguard, Prince Ronald Horne!'

Qattren and Vladimir blinked and glanced beside them.

Ron jumped with a start. 'Oh, right, Lilly.'

King Theo rose in silence from the row below them. He descended to the middle of the courtyard, lifted the charlatan onto one shoulder and dumped the squealing Lilly into a manure pile in the corner of the grounds.

'I'll kill you, Ronald Horne!' she screamed through a face covered in horse excrement.

The courtyard rang with hysterics as King Theo strolled back to his seat.

Stan watched Seth rise to his feet to prepare for his match, his eyebrows knitted together.

A magpie landed on a flagpole directly above Marbrand's head and left a blessing down the neck of his back plate.

Marbrand squealed and pitched forward, knocking the wine goblet from Lord Tetzel's hand.

'Bloody oaf!' Vladimir snapped, seemingly unaware that it was Marbrand.

He handed his uncle a handkerchief, then offered his own cup.

'Here, uncle, take this one, I've not yet drank from it.'

'My thanks, your majesty,' he said, accepting the drink and taking a long swig.

As Seth took his leave, the crowd nattered as they waited for the next match.

Elyse, Queen Eleanor's infamous niece, leaned towards her aunt and King Theo.

'My father once said the Horne brothers were illegitimate,' she said in a low voice, staring at them. 'I heard their mother was in an incestuous relationship with her half-brother. What if those two weren't Sam's at all?'

King Theo's eyes widened and a brow lifted up. He glanced from Prince Vladimir to Lord Tetzel, who seemed to have drunk his wine too fast and was now coughing hysterically. He could see it.

'No, no, young Ronald is the image of Samuel,' Queen Eleanor disagreed.

'But Vladimir isn't,' King Theo said, more to himself than to his wife.

King Theo's musing was interrupted by a splutter and a crash.

Lord Tetzel writhed on the ground, blue-faced and clutching his throat. His wine goblet poured onto the gravel in red ribbons, like streams of blood.

'What the hell is wrong with you—' Vladimir exclaimed.

Two more red ribbons dribbled out of his nostrils. This time it really was blood.

'Leroy,' Aaliyaa squeaked.

She hoisted him upright and leaned him forward, thumping his back.

It was no use. Tetzel's eyes clouded over and his arms fell limp.

Marbrand burst forward, gripping Tetzel's chin in one hand and forcing his mouth open.

'His throat has swollen,' he announced. 'I can't get an airway.'

Tetzel's jerking abruptly stopped.

The entire courtyard froze.

'No,' Aaliyaa whined, falling to her knees beside her brother.

Vladimir dropped to her side, pressing a fingertip under his jaw.

'He's gone,' he said in astonishment.

King Theo clicked his fingers.

Two palace guards swiftly ascended to the top row. They quickly extracted the dead lord from Aaliyaa's grasp.

Vladimir held her in his arms, more to restrain her than to comfort her.

Marbrand turned to Vladimir and Aaliyaa. 'Perhaps I should escort you and Queen Aaliyaa to your chambers, your highness.'

'Yes, yes, whatever,' he said, looking up.

He trailed off as his eyes met Marbrand's. His gaze swung down to the snake-adorned crest soldered onto Marbrand's breastplate.

'A cover, your highness,' Marbrand lied in a low voice. The pay was too good to return to Stoneguard now, but Vladimir didn't need to know that.

He smiled reassuringly at him, but Vladimir's attention had wandered back to the goblet. It wobbled on its side as one of the guards jostled it with his foot. A tiny rattle sounded from within.

Vladimir lifted the cup and emptied it into his palm.

A miniscule, half-dissolved lump of what looked like sugar sat in his hand.

'Poison,' he said.

Aaliyaa shuddered, wiping tears from her eyes.

'He was murdered,' she said loudly.

'This was an accident, mother,' Vladimir corrected, rising, 'the drink was meant for me. Take him to our quarters in the palace. We'll have our own men prepare his body for state.'

He faced Marbrand and handed him the rock.

'We'll escort ourselves to our quarters,' he said coldly.

He scooped his mother in his arms and half-carried her after Lord Tetzel.

Marbrand frowned down at the lump in his palm. He lifted his gaze to meet King Theo's.

King Theo ran a hand through his beard with a frown, one arm flung across the back of his chair. He finally mouthed 'we'll speak later' with a wink.

Some moments later, the silence was broken by the soft clunk of armour.

The next two melee contestants had arrived, flanked by a pair of squires carrying a broadsword and shield. Both contestants wore identical armour and a shield bearing a red rose.

The audience applauded stoically, still in a state of shock from Lord Tetzel's demise.

King Theo squinted at them.

'Who gave Seth that shield?' he asked his family at large.

'Seth requested a shield bearing my family emblem,' Cienne said. 'In my honour.' She turned a little pink as she spoke.

'That's not like him,' King Theo muttered.

'Isn't the Fleurelle family emblem magenta?' Elyse asked.

Cienne paused. 'It's a tricky colour to render onto steel. Or so we were told.'

King Theo cast a beady eye across Cienne's face. 'Is that so?'

Cienne refused to meet his gaze.

~

Oblivious to the events of the past twenty minutes and dreading the next ten, Howie faced his enemy as a squire not much younger than him handed him his weapon.

Seth stood facing him, sword and shield in hand.

'... from the neighbouring kingdom of Stoneguard, having recently been knighted for services to the crown, Sir Howard Rosethorn!'

Howie ignored the thunderous applause and stared his adversary in the helm slit.

'And our very own prince of Adem, the heir to the throne, Prince Seth Crey!'

Seth ignored the crowd, which largely ignored him back.

'Let the melee… begin!'

A trumpet rang.

The two circled each other, short sword in hand. Howie watched Seth's left hand like a hawk, his grip tightening on the blade in his own left hand.

The two launched themselves at each other on impulse, sword slamming into each other with a deafening clap.

~

King Theo sat back in his seat, throwing a glance at Cienne. She flinched rather theatrically, her gaze locked on who was presumably Seth.

The crowd watched with overlapping commentaries.

'Which one's which?'

'They're identical!'

'The taller one's Rosethorn, everyone knows Seth's the runt of the litter.'

'They look the same height to me!'

One of the fighters swung his sword in a horizontal arc.

The other crouched, his shield above his head.

The sword smashed into pieces.

Cienne yelped, clutching her jaw in horror.

The attacker stared in bemusement at his virtually empty hand.

'That's Seth,' Cienne said, grabbing King Theo's elbow. 'Call it off, his sword has been tampered with! Call it off!'

'Don't baby the boy,' he growled. 'He won't be harmed, he'll just have to be creative about it.'

Cienne's jaw dropped in disbelief.

'Don't you see what he's done? He's swapped Seth's sword! He's trying to take your son's life! Call him off!'

King Theo ignored her, his attention fixed to the match.

The attacker stood stock still. He'd picked the snapped blade off the ground and was trying ineffectively to put it back on the hilt.

His opponent scrambled to his feet, his own blade lifted.

The crowd leaned forward as one.

King Theo suppressed a smile.

The armed opponent rushed into the other and slammed his blade into the other's helm.

Seth – presumably – was knocked sideways, clutching his head.

His opponent rushed into him, slamming his shield into the breastplate.

Seth toppled to the ground in a cloud of dust.

The crowd jeered and applauded. The sole remaining sword in the match clanged against Seth's armour again and again. He feebly lifted his shield to block the blows, half of which simply glanced from the shield to hit him anyway.

A gauntleted foot kicked the shield from the fallen opponent's grasp.

Seth lay exposed under Howie's shadow.

Cienne watched, wide-eyed – a little too wide-eyed.

King Theo half-smiled.

Adrienne bit her lip from the stands.

The crowd waited, enraptured.

Howie stood over him, his feet on either side of him to prevent escape.

The stands could almost hear Seth trembling, his armour shifting with the motion.

Howie snatched the collar of Seth's dented breastplate, lifting him a couple of feet from the ground.

He held his sword to Seth's throat.

'Remove your helmet.'

King Theo frowned.

'That wasn't part of the plan,' he said to himself.

He eyed Cienne, expecting hysterics.

A suppressed smile greeted him instead.

Seth reached up to his helm and hesitantly pulled it off.

The crowd gasped.

King Theo bolted from his seat.

It was Howie.

The real Seth dropped his sword and tugged his own helm off, revealing a smirk.

'Well, then,' he said with a grin. 'I believe that means I've won. Unless anyone wants his head as a souvenir?' he asked the crowd loudly.

'No,' Howie whimpered, hastily shaking his head. 'I yield.'

Seth tossed Howie and his helm on the ground and threw his hands into the air.

There was a pregnant pause.

Seth pivoted to face his father.

King Theo's teeth ground audibly. His expression remained clear.

Slowly, he began to clap.

The spectators burst into uproar, a cacophony of cheers, cat calls and applause ringing around the courtyard.

King Theo clapped steadily, fixated to his son.

Seth dropped his arms and stared him in the eye.

Cienne applauded the loudest, grinning from ear to ear.

Seth caught her eye and winked, bowing theatrically in her direction.

Cienne inclined her head with a smug grin.

Her gaze shortly met with that of King Theo and saw pure fury within. He caught on to her theatrics quicker than she thought.

As the last contestants of the day entered the courtyard, Seth scooped up his helm and wandered off to remove his armour. Cienne quickly followed him. Social etiquette demanded King Theo to stay in the gallery with his wife, to Cienne's relief.

Adrienne had to be called down to help the squires remove Howie from the courtyard. He nursed his ribs with a bitter scowl as he was half led, half dragged back into the main hall.

'It was a fix,' he said, frowning. 'I should have won.'

'I know, I know,' Adrienne said, removing his armour and his shirt to check the bruising. She handed him a leaf. 'Chew this, it will help with the pain.'

He put it in his mouth and chewed. It was watery and tough and made his head spin slightly.

'Thanks,' he said.

He watched her hands as they crept over his ribs and stomach. They left a pleasant tingling sensation behind. He doubted it was because of the leaf.

Their eyes met for a brief moment before quickly darting away.

'I should have won,' he said.

He hissed as Adrienne prodded a rib.

'I know,' she said absently. 'You're a bit bruised, but you'll live. Come on, let's take this lot back to the armoury and get you a drink. You could do with it.'

Howie nodded, sulking.

When they entered, Howie spied Seth in the next room, with Cienne. Seth lifted Cienne into the air via a joyful bear hug. Howie gritted his teeth at this.

'I knew it was a fix!' she exclaimed joyfully.

Rage boiled over in Howie's stomach.

'Aren't you glad I swapped the weapons now?'

Seth grinned at her. 'It appears I owe you a debt.'

They exchanged a look that told Howie exactly how he expected to pay that debt.

A hand on his shoulder startled Howie.

He swung to face Adrienne.

'Everything alright?' she asked gently.

He nodded with a smile.

She beamed at him.

The anger blossoming in his stomach swiftly dissipated. He deflated slightly, the tension sloughing from his shoulders. She had a knack for it, he thought, making his worries just melt away with one look…

His hands crept about her waist.

Adrienne's eyes darted down, then traced his arms back up again. Her face flushed deeply. 'Uh…'

With a mischievous glint in his eye, Howie snatched her up and swung her back and around in a dramatic display of affection—

—only for his ribs to give out, causing him to drop her on the floor.

Adrienne screamed a curse as her hip hit the flagstones.

'What were you trying to *do*?' she snapped, rubbing her side.

'Wanted to be… romantic… but my ribs… oh God,' said Howie, doubled over in agony.

Seth and Cienne craned their necks around the door curiously.

Adrienne pulled him to his knees via his waistband. Tentatively, she pressed her lips to his.

His pulse quickened. She'd been eating something sweet, he discovered – she tasted like grapes or something. She tilted her head slightly, her hands cupping the back of his neck. His palms traced around her shoulders and curled around her ribs. She slid closer to him, without breaking away. The pain was a distant echo at this point.

Cienne eyed Seth.

Whose eyes bored into the back of Howie's head as though trying to explode it.

They broke apart.

'How are your ribs now?'

Howie smiled. 'I think they're alright.'

~

V

Guests filed nervously to random beholders of very strong alcohol.

Marbrand caught up to Elliot inside the dining hall.

'Any news on his lordship?'

'Dead as a dodo,' said Marbrand. 'They're carting him off home tomorrow. Any sign of Ronald?'

'Round somewhere, I expect. His missus is over there.'

He pointed at Qattren, who conversed with Felicity Emmett in varying degrees of tedium.

Marbrand glared at her distrustfully. 'Any word of her?'

'Seems to be treating him well, by all accounts,' said Elliot. 'Are we still going to—'

'Yes, but not so loud,' said Marbrand. 'Someone's already bunked off Tetzel, we don't want Ron or, more importantly, us to be next, do we?'

His eyes flitted to the courtyard. He could just about spot Ron in the stands, chatting animatedly with his manservant Stan.

'I reckon once this shindig's over, we hand King Crey our notice and head off after them, see what she's really doing,' he said to Elliot, who nodded. 'And while we're heading there, we can leave the two yellow-haired bastards to wipe each other out. Adem's monarchy isn't my concern at present.'

'Even though the prince has it in for the fourth Christ?'

Marbrand made a face at Elliot.

'Frigging fourth Christ,' he scoffed. 'If he's that, then I'm King of Portabella.'

'Marbrand!'

They pivoted.

King Theo's silhouette loomed in the doorframe, huge against the beaming sun.

'Buggery,' Marbrand muttered. 'Time for a bollocking over Lord Tit-zel. Meet me back here at the feast. If I'm not here, I'll be in the woods by the back gate, getting some air.'

'Right-o,' Elliot said.

Marbrand met King Theo at the door and halted with a low bow.

Theo jerked him upright by his breastplate.

'What in hell,' King Theo hissed, 'was all that about with the prince?'

'He thinks I killed him,' he said upfront.

Theo gave him a little shake. 'Why?'

'Because I was standing there, that's why,' he snapped back. 'Prince Vladimir needs little excuse to fling death threats about.'

He remembered with a start that it was the king he was speaking to.

'Apologies for my tone, your majest—'

'Yes, enough pandering,' he snapped. 'If you're going to be blunt, don't apologise for it.'

He released Marbrand.

Marbrand stumbled a bit before straightening.

'Get to the bottom of this,' he hissed. 'And make sure you let Vladimir see you do it. I don't need my creatures accused of villainy – enough of them get up to that on their own.'

He punched Marbrand's breastplate in passing.

Marbrand gave his back a withering glance and rolled his shoulders.

'I'd better get a bloody good pension for this,' he grumbled under his breath.

He strode to the courtyard to make some enquiries.

~

If he'd taken his enquiries to the back gate of the keep, he might have found two men huddled there, whispering. Though it was better that he hadn't. The Mellien archer on the battlements above them had extraordinarily good aim.

One of the huddlers, a grizzled little man in violet uniform, extended to the other a vial of what looked like lumps of sugar.

'Pity he handed his drink to his lordship,' said the man in uniform, his tone laced with an accent. 'It would have made for a nice, clean exit. Now we'll have to be a little less… tidy.'

'I dare say we won't need to do a thing,' said the second in a lazy Truphorian drawl. 'He has his eye on Cienne Fleurelle. It doesn't bode well to covet another man's property, even if said man is an imbecile.'

'Agreed. An imbecile he may be, but his father is quite competent in the art of murder. However, *he* has plans for Ronald's succession – and that is not such a good idea.'

'His alcoholism would be ruinous,' his boss agreed.

'His childishness would destroy the realm.'

'His wife…'

The two shuddered.

'It would be best,' said the Truphorian accent, 'if the two made a disappearing act altogether.'

'Indeed. Stoneguard needs an intellectual in charge. The Hornes' reign is coming to an end, early as surmised.'

Gomez Emmett Jr smiled. 'And the Emmetts' reign is just beginning.'

~

Cienne was interrupted on her way to the stairs by King Theo's voice.

'In the courtyard, your highness.'

Fear shot through her windpipe.

'Of course, your majesty.'

They met at the door. He gave her his elbow and she took it. The servants were busy dismantling the seating arrangements ringing the courtyard; they gave them no notice as they strode into the depths of the bustle. He led her in a stroll to the fountain and around it, circling it from the left.

'Cienne,' he said. He gave her hand a comforting squeeze. 'Try not to be frightened, dear. I'm not here to accuse you of treason.'

Cienne simply nodded, her heart hammering.

'You've been married twenty years now, is that right?'

She nodded again.

'You do regard us as family, don't you, my dear?'

'Of course, your majesty,' she quavered.

'Good!' he exclaimed. 'You're practically a daughter to me, you know. I've always admired how you deal with the boy, you have far more patience with Seth than I do. Which brings me to my question. What exactly brought you to the conclusion that I wished to murder our Seth?'

The abrupt bluntness of the remark stunned her for a moment. She decided to return the favour.

'You had his sword and shield tampered with, your majesty.'

'Yes, that's correct,' he said.

Her mouth dried. 'You don't deny it?'

'No!' he said. 'I had his weapons rigged to break. Would you like to know why?'

Cienne swallowed a moment before settling for a nod.

'To teach him and Howard Rosethorn a lesson.'

Cienne frowned. 'Sorry?'

'I need Seth to do as he's told,' King Theo said. 'I can't have my realm put into the hands of someone who will lead it to ruin, can I? He needs to see what happens when you nurse a personal grudge in public and make enemies. We've all seen the way he treats Howard, it's un-regal! And as for his comments today about young Mister Emmett…'

'The horse comments,' Cienne said in a faint whisper.

'This behaviour worries me,' he said in a whisper. A rare occurrence. 'The Emmetts are a touchy sort, they mislike every authority figure in power today. Seth will lead the country to war on a whim. There's only so much an advisor can do with someone like that. We've all heard the legends about my grandfather, haven't we?'

The cannibal, she thought, though she dare not say it aloud.

'The cannibal,' he echoed, as if hearing her thoughts.

'Yes, your majesty,' she said in a small voice. 'But Seth isn't like that.'

'No, of course not. But he has got a spiteful streak. And he brings it out far too often.'

'So what was supposed to be the outcome here?' she asked. 'Maim Seth to make him unfit for rule and place Howard on the throne in his place?'

King Theo bellowed a laugh.

'Absolutely not!' he roared. He dropped his voice to a murmur again. 'That's what I told Howard we were doing, but I have no intention of honouring that promise. As I told him, I'm a practised liar.'

Realisation dawned. 'You were going to call it off at the last second.'

'Actually, I was going to let him maim Seth first,' Theo admitted, 'you know, to teach the lesson – but let him kill my boy? Of course not! I instructed him to injure Seth's leg – that way, he could be easily mended following the arrest and subsequent execution of the conniving little bastard that injured him. Do you see?'

'But you knighted him,' Cienne said, stunned. 'You gave him a knighthood yourself. And lands. And titles.'

'All to lull him into a false sense of security,' Theo said. 'Honestly! I'd sooner put Lilly on the throne than Howard Rosethorn, though she has as little interest in it as she has in doing what she's told. I have yet to hear back on my enquiries about his origins. I imagine he's one of Osney's gets, he has his temperament, you know.'

Cienne swallowed repeatedly, trying to muster enough moisture to ease the scratching in her throat.

'Not to worry,' he said finally, giving her hand another pat. 'We'll find another way to get rid of the little sod. I have another idea to drill some sense into Seth – something less drastic, I assure you,' he added to her concerned expression. 'I have a quick announcement to make at the feast tonight. Make sure you're both there, there's someone I want both of you to meet.'

'Who?' she asked.

King Theo planted a finger over his lips.

'Soon,' he said. He tapped her nose. 'Prepare for the feast. We will speak more tonight.'

'Yes, your majesty.'

He released his grip on her hand and she slid away, walking back to the throne room.

Seth stood inside, watching her.

She turned to the stairs, giving him a meaningful glance.

He swooped over and touched her wrist. 'Are you alright?'

She stared at him, touched. This was the first time he'd ever enquired about her well-being.

'Yes. Seth, come upstairs, I need to speak with you about the fight…'

Seth waved this off.

'Let me deal with this,' he said. 'I can take it from here.'

He gazed at her for a moment before sweeping in.

Before she knew it, his lips brushed against her cheekbone. It burned in his wake.

'Thank you for today,' he said in her ear.

Cienne trembled. 'Any time.'

Seth half-smiled, kissed her again more firmly and strode outside.

Cienne stood for a moment, wobbling, before making her way to the stairs.

~

As servants bustled to and fro, Seth poked his head into the door.

King Theo stood beside the fountain, earning a wide berth from the cleaners.

'Everything alright, Father?' Seth asked sweetly.

Theo glared at him.

'Good win today,' he commented.

'Thank you,' he said with a little bow. 'I owe it to my loving wife for her support.'

A vein bulged in Theo's forehead.

Seth circled his father slowly, swinging each leg forward with the utmost carelessness.

'Pity you opted out of the melee,' Seth said. 'Would have been interesting to see you in action – or, rather, see you knocked to the ground and watch you struggle to get off your ass again.'

Theo didn't deign to grace this with a reply.

'You know, I've never seen you fight,' Seth said. 'I've heard so much about your prowess. It's been a long time since you used a sword. Being so used to the ole execution axe and all.'

'I'm partial to the odd sword fight now and again,' Theo said, facing his son. 'Fancy a bit of sparring, boy? I can show you how difficult it is to knock me to the ground and watch me struggle to get off my backside again.'

He nodded to a discarded pile of melee swords in the corner.

'Fetch me one, boy.'

Seth lifted two broadswords and hoisted one in the king's direction.

It was an awkward throw. Theo lunged to one side and caught it in one hand.

Seth held his in both hands, struggling with the weight.

'Bit too heavy for you, boy?' Theo jeered, circling him. 'Should have taken Howard's sword. It was much lighter than yours.'

'Because it was made of tin, yes,' said Seth wryly. 'Had my name on it, isn't that right?'

Theo responded with a swing to Seth's throat.

He caught it with a *clank!* and delivered blows of his own, once, twice, thrice – all deflected by his father with ease.

King Theo laughed. 'You'll have to try better than that, boy!'

Seth gritted his teeth and threw himself at King Theo.

The blade wavered dangerously in his hands. He gripped the hilt as best he could, but his palms slithered on the surface, the hilt too short for him to hold comfortably with both hands.

King Theo deflected his blow and made a few of his own, hitting Seth on the hips and shoulders.

Seth's jaw clenched so hard he could feel the tendons pounding in his neck. The blows connected with bruise after emerging bruise, not hard enough to deliver serious harm but enough to bloody hurt, particularly without armour.

His blood boiling, Seth threw his sword at King Theo.

It sailed off about a foot away from him.

King Theo grinned and pelted him some more, the blunt blade rebounding from shoulder to tailbone.

Seth cowered, his arms over his head.

'I see old age has left your swordsmanship intact.'

King Theo halted his blade.

Qattren stood inside the door, her arms folded.

'Old age? Hah!' King Theo roared. 'You'd know all about old age, wouldn't you?'

Qattren smiled faintly. 'Do leave the poor boy alone. I think he's learned his lesson now.'

Theo smiled, throwing aside his sword. 'If you say so.'

Seth fell to his knees, nursing his wounds.

'I think he could do with another thrashing, myself,' King Theo went on. 'He has a mean streak that needs beating out of him.'

'Like father, like son, then,' Qattren said mildly. She nodded him to the door. 'Come, show me this new pet of yours. I thought they were untameable?'

'Generally, yes, but this one was bred specially by the Ambassador of the Dead Cities,' he informed her.

He ignored his injured son behind him and offered Qattren his elbow.

'I finally got my hands on it after that fiasco at Seth's wedding, he was loath to give it up…'

Seth groaned and slowly rose to his feet.

'You'd know all about old age, wouldn't you?'

What did that mean?

~

VI

Later that evening, another feast ended the day.

As the Creys' guests rose to dance, Qattren gestured for Ron to follow her outside.

'Everything alright?' he asked.

She swept into the courtyard.

'Yes, everything's fine. I think I've had enough festivities for one week.'

Ron nodded sympathetically. 'Not your cup of tea, is it?'

'No,' she said.

They crossed the courtyard and passed through the throne room.

'I'm more of a lone wolf these days. I'd quite forgotten how grating these events can get after a while.'

They left the keep arm in arm and exited the castle grounds. They reached a small stretch of woods surrounding the keep. Once there, Qattren visibly relaxed, stretching her arms out and arching her back.

'What now, then?' asked Ron.

She reached upward for the stars, flexing her fingers.

'Home, I think.'

Her hands snapped together.

They both exploded into dust.

Ron sucked sparse amounts of air into his lungs. The atmosphere began to melt away around them and the dull blue sky lightened to a pale lilac, the forest's features dulling as light and shade became distorted. A bitter taste permeated the air and their surroundings became more… fluid.

'Remind me,' gasped Ron, 'what did you say this was called?'

'Sal'plae,' she said, standing in a relaxed position among the purple-tinted trees. 'It's an Aspect of the realm, allowing people with certain abilities to temporarily shed their bodies and traverse large distances in seconds. You don't need to suck in air like a fish out of water, by the way,' she added. 'We left your lungs behind.'

'Sorry,' said Ron, trying to adapt to the lack of oxygen. 'Force of habit.'

He began to walk in the vague direction of his new home.

'You're doing that the long way,' Qattren said in amusement. 'One step usually takes me wherever I need to go.'

'Ah.'

He hesitated before squeezing his eyes shut and taking a step.

Once his foot left the ground, he vanished.

Qattren smiled faintly and followed suit, stepping forward to meet the entrance to her castle – or what was left of it.

She hasn't passed through here since it happened. The ground rose and fell in craters and dunes beneath her feet. She remembered when it was just flame here, a stronger kind of flame than the kind people were used to seeing – the kind that burns for years on end, decades sometimes, until it's either buried under a mountain of rock or tapers off on its own. The kind that burns through human flesh in an instant. The kind Qattren released on occasion, many years ago, when the anger fed it until it burst from her like yolk from a dropped egg.

It would have taken the walls too if she hadn't come to her senses in time to bury it. The charred walls enclosed the mound of stone, half-buried and casting odd shadows everywhere.

Qattren swung her attention back to the present.

Ron loitered around the rubble outside in disorientation.

She led him into the wreck gently by one hand.

'I don't like this,' he said, clutching his brow. 'It gives me a headache, worrying about all my fibres.'

'You'll get used to it,' she said, leading the way to the trapdoor. 'The fibres of a physical body get replaced all the time. When cells die, new cells replace them. Traversing merely speeds up the process to a greater degree.'

'It's sorcery. I don't trust sorcery.'

'That's only because you can't see it,' she said with a smile. 'I can. It's as natural and safe as air.'

'Not all air is safe, you know,' he said darkly.

'Nothing is ever *completely* safe.'

She stood over the trapdoor and walked downwards through it, as thought it was a staircase. Ron watched her head slide diagonally through the floor with increasing degrees of distaste.

'Sod this. I'm going down the normal way,' he called through the trapdoor.

'I know, you don't need to yell,' she said calmly. 'This place operates telepathically. I can hear you anywhere here.'

'How come I can't hear your thoughts, then?'

'You can. I don't think constant streams of nonsense like most people do. Worries about needing the loo when outside my physical form don't apply to me.'

If Ron had his blood about his person, it would have risen to his face in embarrassment.

'Of course not. But what if you do?' he added. 'How do you pee without your body?'

'You wouldn't need the loo here, love. It would wait until you returned to your physical form. Unless you thought about it too hard and mentally wet yourself, which would be unfortunate and much more embarrassing.'

'I'm off,' he said abruptly, trying not to think. 'I'll see you in the real world.'

'Alright.'

He could hear the grin in her voice and scowled.

Ron sighed heavily and shut his eyes, recalling Qattren's instructions. Picturing the dust he had shed when entering Sal'plae – picturing it on a tiled floor, to be tidier – he swept it up with both hands.

He felt himself being pulled together, slotted back into place. He shuddered as everything solidified and the purple tinge faded, the Aspect's comfortable temperature growing chilly in the forest air.

He sucked in a huge gulp of air and exhaled in relief. He was back.

After patting himself to make sure everything was in order, he pinched an iron ring from the floor and pulled open the trapdoor. A putrid smell drifted past him and his head snapped up.

His eyes widened as the odour made itself apparent. He backed away slowly.

The corpse swung back and forth on its noose, its armour clinking gently in the breeze.

~

Two Finger Si exited the Hornes' quarters, clapped eyes on Anna and shot back in again.

She strode down the hall without giving him a second glance.

Watching her round the corner, Si exhaled in relief.

It was times like these he was glad for the stupid rock helmet.

Adjusting his breastplate, he made for the stairs.

Today's feast was in full swing as he sidled between the dancing nobility. Si scanned the throngs for Vladimir and found him sitting by the canapes with his mother. Si craned his neck.

There were no bodyguards to be seen anywhere.

His brow furrowed, Si made a beeline for the table –

Only to smash into Elliot and knock a steel platter of hot chicken flying.

'Oi, mind out!' Elliot barked.

The chicken landed on the flagstones with a wet *plap*.

'Sorry, my fault,' said Si, kneeling to pick it up.

'That was for Marbrand,' Elliot said in dismay, glancing back at the table from whence it came. 'I'll have to squeeze past all those toffs to get another one. That'll take me at least another hour.'

'You're too polite, is all that is,' Si commented, cradling the platter in one elbow. 'You'll find my way is much more effective.' He inhaled. 'OI! MOVE!'

A small group of people fluttered out of the way.

'Cheers,' Elliot grinned, striding through the gap.

Si accompanied him, relinquishing the platter to a grateful server.

Who promptly brushed it off and returned it to the table.

'I take it you work for the Hornes,' Elliot said evenly.

'Judging by the stupid rock helmet, you mean?' He jerked a thumb up at the steel half-helm, gilded with thin slivers of granite, to his immense disgust. *It's pieces of junk like this that give Stoneguard a bad name*, he seethed, envying Elliot's no-nonsense leathers and simple iron half-helm.

'Take it the job's a last resort, is it?' Elliot commented.

'Yeah, for my sins. As if anyone's going to attack creepy old Aaliyaa Horne.' He shot her a passing grimace with a shudder. 'Me, I was made for the sea.'

'What's stopping you?'

Before Si could reply, Vladimir caught sight of him and clicked his fingers.

'Looks like you've been summoned,' Elliot said with a rueful grin. 'Give us a shout later on if you're free, we clock off at first turn. I'm Elliot Maynard.'

'Pleased to meet—'

'BEULT!!'

Si performed a strangulation mime, making Elliot laugh.

'Yes, your highness?'

'That would be "your majesty" now,' Vladimir said in reply as Si halted at his side. 'My father is dead, that makes me the next king of the realm.'

'Yeah, that's usually how it works,' Si marginally stopped

himself from saying.

He also marginally stopped himself from correcting Vladimir on the fact that he wouldn't be king of the realm until he was coronated – which wouldn't take place until they'd shaved enough of the Stonecrown off for Prince Vladdy's weedy little neck to bear its weight. They'd been at it for the past week and it was still too heavy.

'Where are the bodyguards?' asked Vladimir before Si could produce an appropriate reply.

'I wasn't aware they were missing, your majesty,' he said. 'I'll look for them immediately.'

'See that you make it quick. My uncle died earlier this afternoon. Let us make sure the rest of his kin don't follow in the same fashion.'

Vladimir waved dismissively.

Si rolled his eyes on his way to the courtyard, almost wishing he'd died on the ship after all.

Meanwhile, at the other end of the table, King Theo watched his son converse with Cienne. She giggled and leaned on the arm of Seth's chair as he made silly impressions of random guests to amuse her.

On King Theo's other side sat Howie and Adrienne, who had locked lips again and weren't unlocking except to giggle at each other and, very occasionally, eat.

Archie tried half-heartedly to spark a conversation, to little effect.

'Duck's lovely, isn't it?'

Adrienne stuck her hand up the back of Howie's shirt.

Archie eyed this with acute discomfort, placing his fork back on the plate.

He wondered if he should have been angry when they told him an hour ago that they were seeing each other now. He found he couldn't quite bring himself to. Though he wished they would keep their affection child friendly.

King Theo regarded Howie in silence, deep in thought.

Cienne meanwhile had flung a wistful glance at the group playing music in the gallery above. Seth followed her gaze and offered her his hand.

Cienne frowned in amusement. 'You've never danced a day in your life!'

'I've been known to make an exception,' he said mildly.

Cienne grinned, accepted it and giggled as he pulled her after him.

They joined two rows forming in the front half of the dining hall. Facing each other, Seth and Cienne joined hands, bowed and began to twirl.

King Theo eyed this with a scowl.

A moment into the dance, Seth was lost.

Cienne grinned at this and gently led him, counting the paces aloud.

Seth eyed her carefully, his own movements tentative.

They quickly traded partners. Seth found himself suddenly facing his cousin Elyse.

Elyse winked.

Seth swallowed in discomfort. He quickly pawned her back to his Uncle Fred, interrupting the careful arrangement.

Cienne's laugh tinkled from behind him, the sound melting into the music.

He pivoted and swept her up in one fluid motion, with a grace he seldom applied. He then promptly tripped over his other foot, spoiling the effect.

Cienne staggered with him, giggling helplessly, holding Seth's forearms around herself.

The bard's tempo sped up, lifting into a jig.

Seth regained posture and skipped directly between the others, Cienne stumbling along, still encased in his arms. Everyone abandoned the arrangement and followed suit, skipping in time with the musicians' drumbeats and chanting.

A flute ended the tune in a soft melody.

Seth and Cienne twirled gently to a halt together.

King Theo rose and strode to them.

'Fancy a little stroll, boy?'

Seth glowered at him through his lashes, his chin tucked into the crook of Cienne's neck.

'No, not really,' he drawled. He gestured down the length of Cienne with a flourish.

Cienne gripped his hand in warning, her smile falling away.

'Allow me to rephrase,' King Theo said coldly. 'Fancy doing what I say and living a long and relatively painless life? Boy?'

Seth exchanged a glance with Cienne.

'I suppose I could spare a *minute*,' he said with reproach.

He whispered something into Cienne's ear and kissed it.

Her face turned a deep crimson.

'I'll see you later,' she managed.

Seth winked, his arms slipping from her grasp.

He and King Theo entered the deserted courtyard in silence. A chilly breeze had sent the guests flocking indoors, but King Theo paid no attention to it, strolling for the throne room with utter nonchalance.

Seth followed him, piqued.

'Where are we going?'

King Theo ignored him.

As they passed through the south wing of the palace and entered the forest surrounding the castle, King Theo finally spoke.

'Good win today,' he said, repeating his earlier statement.

'Yes, it was,' said Seth. 'Especially considering my weapons were rigged to break.'

He glanced at Theo at that note.

'Can't take the credit for figuring that one out. I have my lovely wife to thank for that.' He kicked a weed in the gravel path. 'It was you who made the order, I assume?'

Theo's eyes widened.

'Me?' he asked theatrically. 'Why would I do that? I had you released from the Wet Room after you accidentally fell in and locked yourself in from the outside. That's not something a murderer would do, is it?'

Seth shrugged. 'Since you haven't yet arrested the little prick, I'm safe to assume that you know he had nothing to do with it.'

Theo laughed mockingly.

'Son,' he said, almost kindly. 'What reason do I have to kill my only son? Apart from simply disliking you, which isn't really an excuse, is it?'

'Neither was throwing Jimmy's predecessor out of the bedroom window because the wind was blowing the wrong way.'

'It ruined the royal portrait and he was being gobby about it!'

King Theo paused after this outburst to take a breath.

'As I was saying,' he said more calmly, 'I could hardly justify it if I tried. It's not my business if you insist on acting like an idiot.'

'An idiot?' Seth said innocently. 'Do elaborate.'

'The chambermaid,' Theo sneered. 'The snide comments about members of court. Your treatment of your wife—'

'I can't be treating her that badly,' Seth commented. 'She all but swooned a moment ago.'

'You know full well what I mean. Twenty years you've been married and you only took her virginity a mere few weeks ago. And it doesn't look like you've made up for time yet: her ladies-in-waiting tell me she bled less than a week ago.'

'I can't work miracles,' Seth drawled. 'As you well know. It took ten years after the birth of yours truly for you to muster the ability to beget another child. Incidentally, you may wish to recheck the virginity part. I have it on good authority that your court favourite was caught alone with dear Cienne on a number of occasions.'

King Theo frowned. 'What?'

'Oh yes,' Seth said with a vicious grin. 'I caught them myself, sucking face in the middle of my drawing room a couple of days ago.'

Inspiration struck and he smiled slyly.

'In fact,' he added, 'I'm certain I wasn't the first man to enter that cave, if you'll forgive the euphemism.'

Theo snorted derisively.

'I'd know if that was the case,' he said. 'She's an open book, that one. And whenever you bluff, your bad eye twitches up a storm.'

'It does not!' Seth lied hotly.

'Oh, yes it does!' Theo exclaimed, with a vicious grin of his own. 'I've seen you lie your way through existence your entire life. I know when my son is lying.'

'You'll recall I was mentally ill for the last twenty years of it,' Seth snarled. 'If anything's twitching, it'll be down to the assassin *you* let into our home!'

The two regarded each other.

'Assassin,' Theo said with a laugh. 'That Archie really did a number on you, didn't he?'

Seth's brow furrowed. 'What?'

'You were never ill!' Theo sneered, stepping forward. 'You faked it to get out of your duties as prince of the realm! While I was interrogating the entire guest list, finding out who tried to kill my son, you were tucked up in bed, too traumatised to eat – only for you to sneak off in the early hours and eat half the kitchen when you thought no one was looking! I applaud you for your persistence, boy. I never thought you'd keep up the pretence for twenty years, but then adulthood always was a terrifying prospect for you.'

Seth bristled. 'I did not fake a moment of it.'

'Ask your sister. She helped with the charade as she got older. Ask her how often she brought you food on your request. And don't forget your Cousin Elyse – you were far from dead during one incident when she came to visit. Your poor wife was a witness to that.'

Seth released a deep shudder and jerked his head to one side, dismissing the image of his Cousin Elyse.

'If I faked my illness for the past twenty years, why can't I remember any of it? Why can't I remember any of my adolescence but an intruder pushing a wet cloth into my mouth? Why can't I remember how I got this?'

He shoved the palm of his hand in Theo's face, where the thick scar marked his flesh.

'I can't answer for that,' King Theo said. His voice was soft, but his expression had nothing in common with that softness. 'Unless this convenient amnesia is a lie as well.'

'It isn't!' Seth spat. 'I would have thought you of all people would be able to tell the truth from a lie. You've been lying to all of us for long enough.'

King Theo's eyes narrowed to slits. 'Go on.'

'I don't think I need to. I can see the truth written all over your face.'

Seth stepped forward, his arms crossed.

'No one did tell me why Howard and I look so alike. Anything to explain?'

King Theo's expression turned impassive.

'I've heard the name Persephone Fleurelle dropped a few times,' said Seth with a half-smirk. 'I wondered why you were so keen to have me married to Cienne so quickly. Cienne was so young at the time, her mother would have no choice but to stay here with her. With you.'

Theo stared at him.

And roared with laughter.

Seth frowned. 'What?'

'You think I played away with her?' he asked in amusement, bellowing with mirth. 'That dumpling? She looked like a bull! And if she didn't, I'd hardly have been able to tell behind all the silk petticoats. Her and her lady-in-waiting had difficulty getting through the double doors in single file!'

'Well…' Seth faltered, his convictions fading.

King Theo craned his neck backwards, laughing at the stars.

'   well, what about Queen   Thingamajig? The one that seems to know so much about old age. I've heard Howard Rosethorn has been making some enquiries about her. Didn't think redheads were your type.'

Theo stopped laughing abruptly.

Seth smiled faintly. 'Shall I go in and ask her why you've been staring at her since she arrived?'

King Theo frowned.

'You mean the fire witch? What do you think I am, mad? She'd burn me alive at the drop of a hat! Have you not seen the west side of the country lately?'

Seth paused. 'What do you mean, witch?'

~

VII

'Where is Silas Beult?' Vladimir barked.

'He went to search for Sir Eric, your highness,' one of the guards replied. 'He and a small number of men vanished at the beginning of the feast. We haven't heard from him since.'

Vladimir flicked his tongue from the roof of his mouth. 'Who are you guarding, me or Sir Eric?'

His scolding was cut off by his mother, who elbowed him.

'The princess is unattended.'

Vladimir squinted down the length of the table.

He spotted Cienne with a start, leaning on the back of a chair, her chin in her hand. Seth had done another vanishing act, he observed.

'This is your moment,' Aaliyaa whispered.

Vladimir's eyes rolled into their sockets.

'Mother,' he drawled, 'I don't have time to go off chasing skirt. I have a kingdom to rule, alliances to forge, stupid guards to find—'

She grabbed his elbow.

'It's your destiny!' she hissed at him. 'The prophecy demands it!'

'Not interested,' he said airily, lifting his glass to his lips.

Aaliyaa snatched it out of his hand and smashed it into the tiles behind them.

Vladimir flinched.

No one else seemed to notice. Apart from the customary group in every gathering that vocalises at the sound of shattering glass.

'Woaaaay!' came the distant bellow.

'Your uncle died today,' she said thickly. 'Protecting *you*. You *will* seal your destiny with the princess, or you will face my wrath. Do you understand?'

Vladimir flung her a withering glance.

'Go!'

Vladimir heaved a sigh, rose, swiped a goblet of wine from a random woman's hand and approached Cienne.

The woman flexed her empty hand and glared at him. He paid no notice.

'A drink, my lady?'

Cienne glanced at him in disinterest. 'Oh, no thank you.'

Vladimir shrugged and drained it, sitting in Seth's place.

She met his gaze uneasily.

He gave her a pleasant smile. The expression was unfamiliar. 'So,' he said.

He glanced around the hall.

'Having a good time?'

Cienne frowned slightly. 'Yes?'

'Good.'

A pause ensued.

Vladimir wracked his brains for small talk. His stores had run empty.

Cienne flung him another uneasy glance. 'Is there anything I can help you with, Vladimir?'

He frowned at her. Vladimir? No 'your majesty' or 'your highness'? Who did she think she was?

Thinking of his mother's wrath, he decided to keep a civil tongue.

'I've been looking forward to meeting you for many years,' he said. 'I'd like to get to know you, that's all.'

She scrutinised him with a guarded expression.

Vladimir swirled his wine.

'I've always admired you, Cienne.'

Cienne closed her eyes for a moment.

Vladimir gave a quick laugh. 'This may sound silly for a man of my position, but I often harboured fantasies of marrying you one day.'

Cienne's eyes snapped open. 'I'm already married.'

Vladimir shot her a glare, annoyed. 'Hardly very happily married, though?'

'I don't think that's any of your business,' she said, bristling.

Vladimir lifted his hands into the air. 'Only a comment. We've all heard the rumours.'

Cienne sat up straight. 'For your information, we've been getting along spectacularly the past couple of days. I have high hopes for our marriage now that he's recovered from his Great Illness.'

'For now,' he cut in. 'What if he has a relapse?'

She didn't respond to this.

Vladimir lifted an eyebrow. 'You deserve better.'

'And how am I supposed to get out of this marriage, pray tell?' she said mockingly. 'Kill my husband and elope? The king's favourite knight already harbours such ideas, sir. I will not betray my husband.'

Vladimir shrugged. 'Please yourself. It's your kingdom.'

'What do you mean?'

'Think of your country,' he said idly. 'You're the sole heir to Portabella, what will happen when your father dies? I sincerely doubt Seth Crey has it in him to give you an heir, and do you really think King Theo will let you rule alongside your child if he does?'

Her eyes glazed over, the idea intruding into her head.

Vladimir gave her a piteous glance.

'I have the misfortune to be married to a woman dead behind the eyes,' he said. 'All because my father wanted an important friend. I will never have children by her, and you won't by Seth either.'

Cienne's expression stiffened.

'Whatever it is you're about to say,' she seethed, 'I would advise you to reconsider.'

'Why? He's a twat anyway.'

Vladimir met Cienne's affronted gaze and lifted both eyebrows.

'What? He's an imbecile – even worse than my pitiful excuse for a wife. We could bung them both off the battlements and elope, no one would think anything of it. They would assume it was self-inflicted.'

Cienne glowered at him. 'I ask you not to speak of my husband like that. Or my cousin Felicity, come to that.'

Vladimir frowned. 'You're related to Felicity?'

Cienne lifted an eyebrow, her expression icy.

'Oh,' he said. 'No offence.'

Cienne rose, her mouth ajar.

'I will not murder Seth,' she hissed. 'And I would never marry a man who would dare contemplate it.'

She swept across the hall.

Vladimir frowned after her.

'I was joking!' he exclaimed, rolling his eyes. 'Honestly!'

He drained his cup, discarding it on the ground beside him.

A short distance behind them, Gomez Emmett Jr leaned back in his chair with an expression of mild interest, his cousin's words echoing in his ears.

~

Qattren prodded the hanged man, making him swing back and forth slightly.

'Throat slit,' she said, 'post-death mutilation in the vicinity of the groin… could be a lover, with some imagination.'

'That doesn't seem romantic,' Ron said uneasily.

'A scorned lover, rather,' she corrected herself.

The wind picked up. Ron wrinkled his nose at the rotting smell drifting his way. He felt increasingly panicky. In no small part thanks to Qattren's utter nonchalance about the matter. She was more concerned about the wind, by the sour glances she was giving it.

'He looks to be one of your brother's guards,' she said, turning the body.

'How did he get all the way to the Forest?' Ron asked in bewilderment.

'I'll need to investigate that one,' Qattren said, flinging a glare at the sky. 'He looks to have had his throat cut open before being hanged from this tree, all moments before being eaten by a wild animal.'

'In a convenient place,' he added, feeling ill.

'Animals never pass on soft meat when it's available.'

'I didn't need to be reminded of that, Qat. It worries me how easily you can advocate a wild animal.'

Qat smiled.

Ron looked about for signs of the killer. He realised he didn't know what to look for. Entrails? Did homicidal killers leave blood trails?

'They might in a forest if you looked close enough. Blood trails can be passed off as the work of animals in the woods.'

'Don't do that,' he said with a grimace.

'Sorry, the telepathy tends to linger,' she apologised with a smile.

'That had to be a passion killer,' he muttered.

'What did you say?'

He snapped his eyes up at her.

She stared at him in alarm.

'When you were…' he said, 'with the king…'

'How did you know about that?' she demanded, stepping closer. 'I never told you anything about that! Who told you?'

'Howie,' he said. 'He found the dog and saw it was named after him. Put two and two together.'

She blinked. 'Which king are you referring to?'

'King Theo?'

She breathed a sigh of relief.

'No, it wasn't him, that was his—someone else, from… somewhere else. He was mistaken.'

'But the collar—'

'We're just very good friends!' she barked.

'I see.'

He hesitated.

Qattren swallowed. She deflated in defeat. 'That was a lie.'

Ron blinked.

'There's something you should probably know, now that we're wed… about what happened in the Wastelands all those years ago. Ron… I'm what you might call…'

~

'… not human,' King Theo said.

Seth blinked.

'She's a witch,' he said simply with a shrug. 'No better word for it.'

'And that's why you're sleeping with her?'

King Theo made a face. 'What?'

'Well, it makes sense,' Seth said. 'You didn't want her here initially because you had a domestic, but now you've resolved it you had a change of heart and decided to let her in as a bit of backside to look at. Nothing wrong with that, you just won't admit your little secret because it will contradict all the flack you've been giving me lately.'

Seth raised an eyebrow.

King Theo raised one as well. 'You are a right royal twit, aren't you?'

Seth made a face at him.

'You are right, however. She was sleeping with the King of Adem.'

'With you?'

'With my father.'

Seth pulled his head back with a frown.

'With your…'

He wrinkled his nose.

'*Your* father? Granddad? King Seb?'

His jaw dropped in bemusement.

'When, when she was two? She's only what, twenty-five? He died when Lilly was three!'

King Theo strode to his side and hissed in his ear, 'I told you she wasn't human.'

His mouth still open, Seth pivoted as his father walked past.

'How old *is* she, then? My age? No, older than that. *Way* older. Or maybe it was recent. Did she kill him by exhausting him?'

'No,' Theo said. 'He died of old age, the man was decrepit. All of that happened a very long time ago, back when I was a boy.' Theo shook his head in disgust. 'As if I would look twice at that thing! She's been around longer than I have! She's like a second mother to me!'

Seth gawped at him.

'She was here when Granddad was *young*? I didn't think the man was *ever* young.' Seth shook his head. 'Witches still age. If she's not at least thirty-five, I want to know where she gets her wrinkle cream.'

King Theo rolled his eyes. 'She doesn't *age*. She's immortal.'

~

'Before I was Queen of the Forest, Seb Crey and I were in a romantic relationship,' Qattren began.

'Aw,' Ron said with a smile. 'He sounds lovely.'

'You haven't the slightest idea who Seb Crey is, have you?'

Ron inhaled. 'Nope.'

Qattren grinned, despite herself.

'He was King Theo's father,' she said. 'When the Hornes took over the province of Stoneguard, he hired me to help him destroy them. After a rebel army stormed Serpus and killed some close friends of mine, I...'

She exhaled.

'... took things too far,' she finished. 'And thus the Wastelands was created. Seb understood the situation completely, but I'd just annihilated half of his kingdom... and things were never the same.'

She fell silent.

Ron hesitated. 'And that's why King Theo brought down your castle?'

'No,' she said. 'We've had border disputes ever since he took the throne, but it was nothing that warranted an attack. Perhaps, in my fury, I used the disputes as an excuse to blame him that night, but I know now he would never have launched an attack without warning. I'm no threat to him. We know each other too well for that.'

Ron made a face.

'But... but King Theo's nearly sixty,' he said in bewilderment. 'And his father must have been about a thousand years old!'

She shot him a lopsided grin.

'Actually, I'm not as young as you think,' she said. 'In fact, I'm a great deal older than both of them.'

Before Ron had time to register this, a gust of wind slapped him in the face.

He retched.

Qattren placed a hand on his back as he doubled over.

'The smell,' he said weakly.

'I know.' Qattren paused. 'But the wind is coming from the other direction. It should be blowing the smell *away* from us.'

She squinted into the wind, Ron following suit.

Another set of armour became apparent in the gloom.

~

'Here,' said Si outside the main portcullis. 'You haven't seen a group of morons wearing funny rock helmets, have you?'

'I'm looking at one.'

'No, I meant others, obviously,' he said, rolling his eyes.

'Hang on, I'll ask Elliot,' he said, turning to the trees. 'Oi! Have you finished offloading yet?'

'Nearly!' said Elliot in a strangled voice.

The man sighed.

'Well, I'm Marbrand,' he said, shaking Si's hand. 'If I see them, I'll let them know Vladdy's on the rampage. Check the woods around the castle. They're probably in a similar predicament to Maynard. I told Jimmy that chicken looked dodgy.'

'Will do,' said Si, vanishing into the trees.

~

Seth watched his father stare at the moonlit sky pensively. Nothing more had been said of Qattren. Seth didn't want to press the matter. King Theo had spilled enough family secrets for one evening. He didn't want to give him a real reason to silence him. Not now he was just getting to know Cienne…

Instead Seth stood with his arms crossed, frowning against the wind.

'Is Howard Rosethorn my brother?'

'No.'

Seth's eyes narrowed. 'Sure about that?'

'Quite sure. The only woman I've ever known was your mother.' His upper lip turned. 'Unfortunately.'

Seth eyed him. He seemed to be telling the truth.

Inspiration suddenly hit.

'Is he this Cousin Mortimer you're always banging on about?'

Theo rolled his eyes. 'No. Cousin Mortimer isn't as gullible.'

'What's so special about him, then? That he should be king and not me?'

Theo faced him irately. 'Why don't you ask your wife? I told her the entire plan, once I realised she had sussed it. I'll warrant *you* had nothing to do with it. I've said it before, you're nothing but—'

'... a worm,' Seth finished. 'So I've heard.'

'And a gobby one at that,' Theo added sourly. 'It's no wonder the crowds hated you. They couldn't wait to see you get thrashed in the field. You're too soft. Little boys like you aren't fit to rule a sock drawer.'

Seth reddened.

'I am not a boy,' he hissed, looming towards him. 'I am a grown man and I will not let a stupid old fart tell me what I am.'

King Theo regarded him for a moment.

And punched him in the face.

Seth toppled to the ground, his nose shattered from the blow.

In a show of poetic justice, King Theo leaned over him – as Seth had earlier leaned over Howie – and lifted him by the front of his shirt until they were nose to nose.

'Remember your place, boy,' he leered. 'Nobody backchats the king, not without exiting a third story window.' He dropped him on his back in disgust. 'Wipe your nose.'

Seth held a trembling hand to his bloody face, rolling to one side.

Around him, the groundskeeper had been landscaping all afternoon. His gardening tools were strewn around them, abandoned.

'You've been around your mother for far too long,' King Theo jeered, stepping back. 'She molly-coddles you. Your real successor is worth ten of you. You're not fit to lick his boots, never mind run a kingdom.'

Seth wasn't listening.

He was shuffling forward. Towards the shovel.

'You'll meet him soon enough – along with Cienne. She'll soon change her allegiance once she sees *him*. She wouldn't have had anything to do with you if she had a choice, and neither would your little servant friend if your chamber pot wasn't fully hallmarked silver.'

Seth paid him no attention. The handle in front of him became the world.

'And as for that girl, what's her name? Ah yes, Adrienne.'

Seth froze in the act of dragging himself to his feet.

'Handy to have around the place, I think,' pondered King Theo. 'Puts you in your place, doesn't it? Knowing she doesn't want anything to do with you.'

Seth's teeth clenched.

'She at least has some taste,' he said. 'Perhaps I'll let the medic keep her as a little ornament. Her type aren't worth much else.'

'Shut up,' Seth gritted, '*shut up*, SHUT UUUP!!'

Seth shoved himself to his feet, the polished wood in both hands.

'I'VE HAD IT WITH YOU!!' he howled.

He swung in a horizontal arc.

~

VIII

Qattren gasped loudly.

'There are more bodies,' said Ron, pointing. 'It's like a trail. Are you alright?'

Qattren choked violently, clutching the side of her neck as though in pain.

'Qat?'

~

Si slumped against a tree, eyes bulging. His jaw hung open.

'No,' he whimpered.

His hand gripped his left tendon, his nails boring marks into the skin.

~

Breathing heavily, Seth released the handle.

King Theo stood stoical for a moment, a wood-cutting axe buried in the crook of his neck at an odd angle. Blood poured from the wound, soaking his doublet, turning it from emerald to black.

With one last gurgle, he toppled forward in a bloody heap.

Limbs trembling, Seth stared at the corpse, then slowly turned around.

A shovel lay just behind where Seth had lain a moment ago.

'Shit,' he squeaked.

He had grabbed the wrong handle.

~

Qattren dropped to her knees, coughing and gasping.

'Qat!' Ron barked, shaking her shoulders. 'Qat! What's the matter?'

The coughing subsided.

Ron rubbed her back as she wheezed heavily. Then she exploded, covering Ron in a coat of dust.

Sal'plae opened around her, enveloping her. She quickly relaxed, rising from her knees.

Someone had been murdered. Someone close to her.

She moved quickly.

The Creys' Keep rose above her head, casting her completely in shadow. She spun on one heel to face the victim.

King Theo prodded the left side of his neck with a frown.

'Theo?' whispered Qattren.

His lingering spirit looked at her in bemusement.

'Qattren? I thought you'd gone.' He gazed upwards. 'Sky's gone a funny colour, hasn't it? Have they served the dessert yet?'

Qattren gulped. 'Who did this?'

'The gardening? The groundskeeper, of course.'

He frowned at her, then at the woods, where was currently staring.

A familiar man, disguised by the muted shades of Sal'plae, shuffled backwards into the depths of the woods. He dragged a dark bundle with him, leaving a trail… blood.

'That's me on the ground, isn't it?' he asked, nonchalant.

She nodded, still in shock.

'Ah. Never mind. Could have waited until after dessert, I was looking forward to that.'

He squinted at his murderer.

'And the gent with the yellow hair?'

Qattren's mouth hung open for a moment, reluctant to relay her reply.

'I believe that's your son.'

King Theo froze.

In the distance, Seth jumped with a shriek at an owl taking wing. He slipped, falling half on top of his dead father.

The late King Theo bared his teeth and roared, making Qattren jump.

'STUPID BLOODY BOY!!' he howled. 'YOU'VE DOOMED US ALL!!!'

His final shriek faded with the rest of him.

He vanished upwards in a bluish trail.

Qattren stared in his wake, trembling.

Then she glared at Seth as he regained his footing.

The words of the Prophet rang in her ears.

King's gonna die, he said in his nonchalant way. *Tried to stop it, but there's no point. Go easy on the new one, alright? He's got issues.*

She realised in horror which king he had actually meant.

Qattren fell to her knees and wept.

'What have you done?'

~

Ron dusted the remains of Qattren from his front, gagging.

Why didn't I just marry Lilly-Anna Crey like my father wanted me to? Poor personal hygiene is a small price to pay for a life outside of the occult.

He knew it wasn't the occult really, but to his mind anything that caused human beings to spontaneously explode couldn't be any better.

He turned back to the row of corpses in front of him, hanging like meat in a slaughterhouse. After a moment, he followed the trail.

~

Qattren sat in the undergrowth where King Theo had just died, feeling empty.

Seth had vanished beyond sight hours ago – or at least it felt like hours in Sal'plae. Time was optional here. As if time's passing had any effect on her anyway.

She spotted a figure wandering aimlessly through the woods, presumably to mark his territory. His steel helmet was adorned with slices of grey stone – a Horne family guard, she realised.

Her thoughts drifted to King Samuel and his crown, lying abandoned in a crevice in the—

Qattren's thoughts abruptly halted.

In the Forest. Ron was unattended in the Forest.

She threw herself to her feet.

She rematerialized at the spot they had been standing before, during their conversation. Her eyes scoured the Forest, trying desperately to readjust her night vision. She spotted him at the end of the trail of bodies and broke into a run, her white skirts billowing behind her.

Ron halted as the corpse trail ended.

A large hollow lay open before him. His eyes caught movement below and he began to descend.

Qattren caught him by the shoulders and swung him around. 'Ron! Come away!'

'What is it?' he asked, peering in.

'Don't go down there, it isn't safe,' she said, clinging to his elbow.

He edged closer to the pit. 'It's alright, it's just your dog…'

He trailed off, staring into the abyss.

'Ron?'

He slid carefully down the edge.

'Ron!'

Qattren ran after him and stumbled into the pit. She skidded down the slope, the ends of her white gown in muddy tatters.

Ron caught her at the bottom, her gaze still locked on the Hole.

Qattren followed his stare with wide eyes.

'Ron,' she said, turning away from it, 'Ron, we have to go, this thing is dangerous… Ron, stop staring at it, we have to go… RON!'

She slapped him across the face.

Ron blinked, snapping out of it.

'This thing killed your father.'

Ron gawked at her.

Qattren laid a hand on his cheek piteously. He looked so helpless, like a child.

'We need to leave,' she said firmly, taking him by the hand.

The Hole *thrummed*.

'Come!'

She snatched his hand and pulled the two of them into Sal'plae.

Their underground fortress materialised and solidified.

Snatching a quill and parchment from a random Faerie's hand, she swung her around, leaned the sheet on her back and began to write.

Ron materialised behind her, wavering.

'Qat, I feel odd…'

The feeling was mutual. Spots filled Qattren's vision, but she blinked them away, impatient.

Ron's eyes rolled inwards. He collapsed into a heap.

Faeries swarmed around the two as Qattren wobbled on the spot. Her vision fading, Qattren faltered on the last word. Before she could get it out, everything went dark.

~

Howie and Adrienne cackled as they rushed upstairs, leaving the festivities behind.

Cienne heard their laughter pass her quarters as she sat in the drawing room with some embroidery, throwing a wistful glance at the door every now and then.

In the woods outside, Seth stood over the body of his murder victim.

King Theo's body was now cold, his face grey like concrete. Seth had knitted the dead man's fingers over his stomach. It still didn't look like his father. He lay on a bed of sticks and branches, hastily torn from the trees around them.

He took a discarded rucksack he had found among the groundskeeper's things and rifled through it for a tinderbox.

In Qattren's fortress, Vhyn delicately laid a damp cloth on Qattren's forehead. She prised the parchment from Qattren's lifeless hands and pinned it to the bedside table with a paper weight.

King Theo is dead.

Seth lit a small fire by his father's side. The flame caught the foliage immediately, leaving a blue echo.

The Hole killed Samuel Horne.

He let the flint slip from his fingers and watched the flames lick his father's clothes and grow.

The Prophet warned us.

The flames were now a bonfire, wrapping itself around the king.

It made Seth – in particular, his face – extremely visible in the gloom.

Apocaly

Tears ran down Si Beult's face as he watched King Theo's body dissolve before his eyes. King Theo had been kind to him. Kinder than he felt he deserved.

Si sucked in a shaky breath, his gaze locked on Seth Crey.

He would pay him back for his kindness.

Qattren dreamed of dragons and steel, and of flame. A terror gripped her, the like of which she had never felt before.

Seth Crey watched impassively as his crime slowly burned away.

~

Aaliyaa looked intently at Father Toffer.

He gazed at her uneasily and gave a little wave.

She nodded at the door.

He shook his head.

She picked up a spoon and held it between her thumb and forefinger.

It drooped.

Father Toffer got the hint and made a miserable beeline for the door. Following a few sightings from a couple of willing interrogatees, the priest strode to the forestry surrounding the castle, his cloak wrapped tightly around him, and lost himself in the trees.

It was here he stumbled across a small forest fire.

With his target lying in the centre of it.

Father Toffer squinted to double check.

King Theo's build was unmistakable, even as it dwindled within the flames.

Toffer tugged a tinderbox from a pocket of his cloak and squinted inside in case his heavy drinking had provoked a bout of amnesia. The contents were complete. Just as he thought.

Someone had beaten him to it.

His thoughts wandered to the dragon, his next target. And quickly sprinted away again.

The contract seems to have changed hands, he decided. *He can bloody well kill the dragon.*

~

Si ran into the castle grounds, wildly searching for Marbrand. He finally found him standing with his back to the east keep wall and swung him around by both shoulders.

Marbrand frowned at him. The tears in particular.

'Got the runs as well, is it?' he said in sympathy.

'No!' Si choked, wiping his eyes. 'It's the king! He's killed him, he's killed the king!'

Marbrand bolted to his full height. 'When was this?'

Si gulped and cleared his throat. 'Only a moment ago. I couldn't stop him, I was too late.'

'Who? Who killed him?'

And then they saw him, creeping along the inside of the castle wall opposite, among the shadows.

'*He* did it?' Marbrand asked in alarm.

Si nodded once.

Elliot rounded the corner, giggling.

'Look over there,' he said, pointing at the figure. 'Prince Twatface only went and fell in my—'

'That is the least of his problems,' Marbrand said darkly.

'You would say that, you weren't the one who had to push—'

'Enough about your leavings, Maynard!' snapped Marbrand. 'He's just killed King Theo Crey!'

Elliot froze. 'What, the prince did?'

Marbrand nodded briskly.

'Oh. Bugger.' He glanced at Si. 'You alright?'

He most certainly was not alright, Marbrand realised. His eyes relinquished fresh tears as they spoke. They rolled off a cheekbone, the torchlight shimmering from each one.

278

'You work for the Hornes,' he said. 'What could King Theo possibly be to you?'

Si choked again. 'Nobody. I have to go.'

'Hang on—' Marbrand said.

Si vanished into the shadows.

Marbrand stared after him, wracking his brains. He looked familiar. Who is he?

Elliot waited. 'Shouldn't we arrest the prince?'

Marbrand stood very still.

Elliot lifted his eyebrows. 'Well?'

Marbrand frowned at him. 'Are you mad? Of course not, he's the prince! Why would we?'

'Because he went and killed someone?' Elliot exclaimed.

'Yes, and because of that, he's now the country's highest-ranking person!' he barked. 'Higher than me, and certainly higher than you! And if he's somehow capable of killing King Theo bloody Crey, then we're goners, so you keep your mouth shut about this, do you understand?'

Elliot hesitated before snapping a reluctant salute.

Marbrand glanced around. 'Any word on Ronald?'

'Think someone mentioned he'd left. Presumably with the wife.'

Marbrand paused. 'Best place for him.'

'But I thought you wanted—'

'Never mind what I wanted,' he said in a firm tone. 'This is above our pay grade. If he can kill his own father, there's nothing stopping this prick from popping off a couple—'

A tap on his shoulder interrupted him.

A cloaked man stood before him, holding a letter.

'Dispose of this, would you?' he said, nonchalant.

'I'm not a bin,' Marbrand spat.

'It's very important,' the cloaked stranger insisted.

He shoved it into his hand.

'Burn it. There's a bonfire going in the forest, come to think of it, but I didn't think of putting it in at the time on account of the body...'

He froze.

Marbrand shot him a severe glare. 'What body?'

The stranger stood still a moment. Then bolted for the gate at a sprint.

'Oi, wait!' Elliot snapped at the figure.

Marbrand tore open the letter and scanned the contents. His

eyes bulged.

'This is King Samuel's handwriting,' he muttered. 'I'd recognise it anywhere. There were only three other people in the Stonekeep who weren't illiterate.'

'Which?' Elliot asked, craning his neck.

Marbrand crumpled the letter in half.

'Prince Ronald's business,' he said. 'I'll pass this to him at some point. He'll be safe with his wife. I overheard she's infertile – if she wants anything to do with Stoneguard, she'll leave him well alone. It's his family I'm worried about – particularly if they piss off our murder suspect.'

Elliot's brow crumpled. 'What do we do now, then?'

Marbrand exhaled. 'Nothing.'

~

Seth snuck across the castle grounds, the blood-stained axe behind his back. He chastised himself as he kept to the shadows, avoiding the torchlight illuminating the keep.

What have you done? You bloody idiot, why did you pick that up, why did you want to pick up anything at all, why did you have to hit him in the first place?

Because he badmouthed Adrienne.

He sighed heavily. Adrienne. An image of her plastered to the little kiss-ass rose to the forefront of his mind, not for the first time that evening. He quickly put it back out. It wasn't worth getting upset about. There were others, he reminded himself. Perhaps seeing someone his own age might be better for his health.

He placed his guilt firmly aside. He deserved it anyway, he thought with venom. He tried to kill me. That's reason enough in itself.

He halted at the basement door and turned the knob – only for it to come off in his hand.

He swore and shoved the door irately. Then he realised he was holding an axe.

The lock smashed, sending the door swinging open.

Seth entered at a jog, made a beeline for his father's vault at the end of the corridor and dumped the axe inside, slamming the door.

He hurried back to the stairs until a sound made him jump.

'Is that Seth?'

Jimmy appeared, still holding the folded washing he'd been locked in with earlier that afternoon.

'Yes,' he replied.

'Oh good, you've opened the door,' said Jimmy. 'I've been stuck in here all day. I've had nothing to eat but the lemons we stick in with the washing.' He grimaced. 'Not pleasant. Got all the washing done, though,' he added brightly.

Seth gave him an odd glance.

'I'm gonna re-promote you to butler, Jimmy,' he said. 'For your health, at least.'

'Oh, good,' he said with feeling. 'I was starting to hallucinate from the fumes off Lilly's drawers. Thanks.'

Seth grimaced at the mental image.

Jimmy ascended the stairs.

Making sure the vault was closed, Seth followed him back to the keep.

Seth's clothes bore a fine coating of pungent yellow shit from the forest. As such, everyone tactfully decided to ignore him as he passed them. Seth was thankful as he swept up the staircase, a hand over his bloody nose.

Once at the top of the stairs, he jogged into his quarters, crossed the darkened bedroom to the privy and cleaned his face in a basin of water by the window. Just bruised, he observed with relief. Double-checking for bloodstains by touch, he peered out at the castle grounds below as he undressed. All was calm, for now.

A faint rustling sounded from the next room.

'Seth? Is that you?'

Cienne.

Seth felt something stir in his chest. They'd been quite close since she helped him with the melee charade. He rolled his eyes. *She'd probably want another performance*, he thought, thinking back on their last intimate encounter with a shiver.

His eyes widened. That was an idea. It would get him off the hook, wouldn't it?

He poked his head around the door.

'You're not too tired, are you?'

~

Howie frowned in concentration.

Adrienne smiled in amusement, sitting upright in his lap.

'What are you making faces at me for?'

'I'm thinking of all the love-making advice I ever received and working out the best way of going about this,' he said. 'It's really hard. A lot of it contradicts each other.'

She shifted forward a bit.

He let out a low hum.

'… I think we'll be fine on our own,' she said with a grin.

He pushed himself upright to kiss her. She melted against him, sending another jolt through his abdomen.

'This is going significantly better than my last conquest,' he commented, collapsing back onto the pillows.

'What did she do, run from the room screaming?' she teased, settling her weight onto him.

She started rifling, to his immense enjoyment.

'Pretty much,' he said. 'Princesses are overrated.'

Adrienne halted in her tracks.

'Princess? Princess Cienne?'

Howie lifted his head blearily.

'I… may have… kissed her a bit,' he confessed.

'Why?' she said loudly.

'… because I fancied her?' he squeaked.

Adrienne licked the front of her teeth and lifted herself up.

'Where are you—wait, don't go,' Howie whimpered.

He crawled to the end of the bed as she stalked out.

'I don't fancy her anymore, I fancy you now, please don't go, come back, I didn't mean—'

The door slammed behind her.

Howie whined, dropping his forehead against the bedpost.

You had it! Teenage Idolism scolded. *You nearly had it and you blew it!*

He head-butted the post several times.

~

Cienne felt around the top of the bedside table for a candle and took it to the fireplace to light it.

'That was spirited.'

Seth made no comment, lying with his arms behind his head.

Cienne stood the candle on the table and climbed back in beside him, ruffling his hair.

'What's the matter? You seem very… taut.'

He dropped his head to one side to gaze at her.

'It's nothing, I'm alright,' he murmured.

'It's your father, isn't it?'

Seth felt a chill run down his back.

'He means nothing by it,' she soothed. 'He explained to me about the melee. It was a trick to get Rosethorn out of the way, he never had any intention of killing you.'

Seth blinked at her. 'Sorry, say that again?'

'He wasn't trying to kill you. He was going to have Rosethorn executed for injuring you in the fight. He thinks he's a bastard son of the Duke of Osney getting high ideas.'

Another chill ran up his spine, running deeper.

'Oh,' he said in a hollow tone.

Cienne ran her hand down the back of his neck and down one shoulder.

'Did he do this?'

She touched his nose, which she had accidentally bumped against in their intimacy earlier, alerting her to his injury.

'Yes,' he said. 'We argued.'

'Whatever he's said, it's meaningless,' she said. 'He won't hurt you, I won't allow it.' She smirked. 'I'm more dangerous than I look, you know.'

He raised an eyebrow. 'Oh, I know.'

She grinned. Hesitantly, she brought her lips to his.

Seth lifted an arm in alarm, but it froze in mid-air. It was good, he realised. Apart from another twinge from his bruised nose, it felt good. She slid a hand along his arm and threaded her fingers between his. That felt good too.

By the time she'd pulled away, he was trembling.

She licked her lips, evidently pleased with herself.

'Goodnight,' she said softly, turning her back on him.

Seth stared at the ceiling, his mouth ajar and his hand still aloft.

'Goodnight,' he said about five minutes too late.

~

IX

Qattren stirred.

Stan watched her in concern.

'Are you alright, your highness?'

She sat up. Her head spun. 'How did you get here?'

'Uncle Keith knows a sorcerer. It may have escaped yours and Prince Ron's attention that you forgot about me last night,' he said sourly.

'My apologies, Stanley. Consider your salary doubled.' She rubbed her eyes. 'How long have we been unconscious?'

'Ten hours, according to the little blue servant. The sorcerer translated.'

Qattren sat up and glanced at Ron, still unconscious beside her in the bed.

'Rosethorn,' she murmured.

Ron gave a low moan. 'Gods, how much did I have to drink?'

Qattren glanced at the bedside table, at a scruffy note pinned to the centre in particular. She grabbed it. Her eyes widened at the word 'apocaly'.

'Nothing,' she replied to Ron's question.

~

Midday passed before anyone realised King Theo was missing.

Tournaments and parades came to an abrupt halt. Search parties scoured the countryside, noblemen and common folk alike, led by his most fervent searcher: his daughter, Lilly.

A returning party poured into the throne room to greet Queen Eleanor.

Seth, typically, was nowhere to be seen.

Until Jimmy entered Seth's drawing room and was inadvertently mooned.

'Ugh, God,' Jimmy spluttered.

He lifted a hand to shield his eyes from the bedroom door, which gaped open.

'Queen Eleanor requires your presence in the throne room,' he said over the rattling headboard.

'Piss off, Jimmy, I'm busy,' Seth grated, panting.

'It's about your father, it's pretty import—is that the princess?' he asked in astonishment, craning his neck.

'What about King Theo?' Cienne squeaked, peering around Seth's armpit.

Jimmy laughed aloud. 'It is in all! Carry on, I'll come back.'

'Stay!'

Cienne shoved Seth to one side and swiftly adjusted her nightgown.

'What's wrong with King Theo?'

'He went missing last night. Search parties have been out all morning.'

'What? Why didn't anyone tell us?' Cienne said irately, throwing herself out of bed.

'We sent a runner this morning. He must have just kept running,' Jimmy said. 'Can't say I blame him. One of the search parties came back, Queen Eleanor wants you there for the report.'

'We'll be there in a moment. Seth—'

Her glance lingered on him.

284

Seth paled, his face slack.

'Seth,' Cienne said, perching at his side. 'He's fine. No harm could possibly come to Theo Crey of all people.'

'Then why are they bringing a report and not him?' Seth asked, his voice tremulous.

'We won't know unless we speak to them,' Cienne said softly.

A shuddering breath escaped Seth's lips. 'I can't go down there. They'll want me to look at him, I can't, not again—'

'Nobody said he was dead,' Jimmy said mildly. 'They just said they had news.'

They turned to the sound of pounding on the flagstones.

Marbrand skidded to a halt just behind Jimmy.

'Queen Eleanor sent me as a matter of urgency,' he wheezed.

'Yeah, I'm getting them, Christ,' Jimmy said, rolling his eyes. 'Tell her to keep her hair on. The search party doesn't seem that urgent.'

'It's not them,' he said, leaning his hands on his knees. 'Corporal Moat reported a small forest fire just outside the castle. Apparently that area of woods was overlooked this morning.'

He met Seth's gaze.

'He said human remains were found there.'

Seth swallowed, his throat bobbing.

Cienne observed Seth's expression and straightened her back. 'I will see these remains in a moment.'

'My lady,' he said in astonishment. 'Allow us to see to the matter—'

'Because I'm too feeble to possible cope?' she said coldly. 'The day I arrived here, I watched my mother carried into this keep on a stretcher, her body split open from chin to waist. She was but the first body to be carried through those doors that year. I may not be as acquainted as your hardened soldiers, but I am no stranger to death, Sir Marbrand. Give me a moment to dress. I will see this body shortly.'

She case a critical eye over Seth.

He sat upright in bed, his shirt hanging open and his knuckles tightening around the edge of the blanket.

'I'll tell Queen Eleanor you've been taken ill,' she decided.

Seth nodded. He stared at Marbrand, who stared back.

Cienne pecked Seth's lips and ushered the two men out.

As she emerged later in a simple black dress, she led them to the stairs.

'What Seth said earlier,' she said. 'About seeing him dead. What did he mean by "not again"?'

Jimmy lifted a shoulder. 'I presume he meant his grandfather. He was the one who found him after he'd passed.' Jimmy grimaced. 'He'd been there a while. It was about a year or two before you'd arrived. Seth was only twelve.'

Cienne's expression crumpled in sympathy. 'He must be devastated.'

Marbrand's expression behind her was significantly less sympathetic.

I doubt it, my lady, he thought privately.

~

As Cienne and Marbrand arrived at the scene of the fire, the smell of charred flesh assaulted them in a rancid wave. The body lay in the centre of a circle of ash, burned beyond recognition. Patches of red flesh glistened within the black, the only indication that the lump was once a person.

Cienne pressed a handkerchief to her mouth and nose.

'Is it him?'

Marbrand knelt beside the remains. With one leather-gloved finger, he plucked a heavy gold chain from the remains.

She choked. Whether it was grief or nausea was yet to be seen.

Marbrand picked at the chain with his free hand.

'There's a gouge taken out of one of the links,' he said, peering. 'There's a large wound too, right alongside. An axe wound.'

'They must have attacked from behind,' she said. 'He never fell in open combat.'

'I don't think this was combat, your highness,' Marbrand said, rising to his feet. 'Moat spotted a trail of blood crossing the castle grounds. It led from here to the chambers beneath the keep, where he found a bloodied woodcutting axe. It looks as though someone followed him, found the groundskeeper's tools lying around and took their chance.'

Cienne choked again. This time, it *was* tears.

'Seth was with him,' she said. 'They could have killed him too. How did he get away?'

Marbrand paused. 'I don't know, your highness.'

Cienne wiped her tears with one palm. 'So Seth's going to be king.'

An involuntary shiver ran down the back of Marbrand's neck.

Cienne sported a look of utter despair.

'He isn't ready,' she said in a whisper. 'He'll never be ready.'

'There's always the council to help him,' Marbrand said,

feigning optimism.

Cienne scoffed. 'The council.' She snorted mirthlessly. 'The place will be run into the ground. It will be Eleanor and I left to help him. As always.'

'Then the realm is in safe hands,' he said.

Cienne gave him a watery smile.

'Let's hope so,' she said. 'Our first task will be to tell Seth and Lilly their father is dead. That will be an ordeal in itself.'

Marbrand bowed his head in agreement.

~

Howie dropped a fist on Lilly's door three times. She opened it mid-knock.

'I'm so sorry for your loss,' he said. He held out his arms. 'Do you want a hug?'

Lilly looked him up and down. 'Give me strength.'

She stood aside, letting him and Adrienne inside.

The three rooms marking Lilly's domain were remarkably hygienic – Howie made a note to commend Anna on her efforts. The drawing room bore little in the way of decoration: a jade rug with matching curtains caught the torchlight surrounding an elliptical dining table, and a yellowing tapestry bearing the Battle in the Orchard hung above an antique writing desk Archie would only die for.

A few empty bottles littering the dining table bore the only sign of Lilly's troubles. Howie hoped for her sake that she'd shared the contents around – liver failure was the last thing she needed.

'You doing alright?' he asked gently.

'Let her alone, will you?' Adrienne hissed at him. 'Her father's just died, what do you think?'

'No, it's alright,' said Lilly with a weak smile. 'Have a seat.'

Howie threw a timid glance at Adrienne out of the corner of his eye. She had visited Seth this afternoon, Anna had informed him in her dulcet if gossip-mongering tones. Howie wondered how his life expectancy would fare if he mentioned the meeting in casual conversation. Probably not very well.

'Jim's on his way up with dinner,' said Lilly in a dull voice.

She dropped herself at the dining table and began shaking a few of the bottles.

'This can't be real, you know.'

She flicked a bottle down the table in disgust.

'I know,' said Howie as it rolled past him. 'He was practically invincible. It's hard to believe he's actually—'

'Oh, he's dead, I knew that was coming,' she said.

A tinkle sounded from within a rotund little green flask. She quickly drained it.

'It's what's coming after I'm worried about.'

'Seth's ascension to the throne?' said Adrienne.

'Yuh-huh.'

Lilly upturned the newly emptied flask and threw it on the rug behind her.

'The old man was grooming me for rule, you know,' she said.

Howie lifted an eyebrow. 'You're supposed to be queen?'

'Seth was "ill",' she said, jiggling quotation marks in the air. 'He wasn't getting better. Dad gave him until he hit twenty to get better, and he didn't: he just got worse at faking it. So he started bringing me to council meetings.' She shrugged apathetically. 'That went out the window when you "reincarnated" him, mind.'

Howie pulled a wince. 'Sorry.'

'No, it's not like that, I wasn't interested,' she said, sitting up straight. 'Bores my head off, sitting there watching them lick my father's arse clean. Just a funny thought, that's all.'

A dampened thud landed on the door.

'Can you let me in?' Jimmy called from outside. 'My arms are full.'

Adrienne answered the door and quickly relieved Jimmy of two of the plates.

'Cheers,' he said, offloading onto the table.

Four plates of heavily garnished roast boar greeted Howie, along with a jug of wine and four ornate cups almost too pretty to drink from. Much of the flank had been scorched to a thick black crust.

His appetite quickly evaporated.

'Chuck that away,' Lilly said in disgust, shoving hers to the centre of the table.

Jimmy huffed.

'I know it's in extremely poor taste, but I'm bloody starving,' he said, tugging his plate forward.

Lilly gazed at the ceiling as Jimmy ate.

'How's Seth?'

Jimmy glanced at her, pulling his fork from his mouth.

'He's been sick a few times. Probably shock.'

Howie felt a pang of sympathy for him. Just a pang.

Adrienne poured herself a drink. 'He did look very pale a few moments ago.'

'You've been to see him *again?*'

Adrienne jerked to Howie, eyes ablaze.

'When I need approval for my *conquests*,' she snarled, 'I'll be sure to let you know.'

Howie averted his gaze, his tongue locked behind his left cheek.

Lilly and Jimmy exchanged glances, brows raised.

'Alright, then,' Lilly said lightly.

They sat in silence, Lilly watching Jimmy eat and the other two scowling at opposite ends of the room.

'You really ought to eat,' Jimmy told Lilly. 'Do you want me to get you something else?'

'Nah,' she said, sliding her chair across the flagstones. 'I don't really feel like eating anyway.' She rose and tugged her shirt down, smoothed it. 'My dad's things haven't been shunted down to the basement yet, have they?'

'Not that I'm aware.'

'Good. I'm gonna have a root through it. There's something he told me I should take if he ever, if he...'

She trailed off.

Howie looked at her.

She stood frozen to the spot, her shirt stretching in her hands, her gaze locked to the tapestry above the desk. Her face lost all the cheerfulness and fierce pride that was quintessential to Lilly Crey. What was left seemed vulnerable, childlike. Water gathered in her eyes, and lines appeared around her mouth, signifying her grief.

'Lilly,' he said, rising.

'No, no, it's alright, I'm okay,' she said, her voice thick. She pulled a breath into her nose and exhaled tremulously. And just like that, the vulnerability was gone.

'I'm just trying to remember where he stashed that huge great-sword he was saving for me,' she said with a grin. 'Want to lay claim to it before my dear brother gets ideas. Be a waste letting him take it, wouldn't it?'

Howie forced himself to smile, albeit thinly. The tremor in her voice ruined the delivery of her remark.

Lilly swallowed the lump in her throat and shot Howie another grin, ruffling his hair as she passed. 'Be back in a minute. Don't go anywhere.'

Jimmy watched her leave, shaking his head.

'I've never seen her like this,' he said.

'She seems to be doing okay,' said Howie.

'For now. She doesn't cry. Ever,' said Jimmy. 'She won't let herself. It's unhealthy.' He examined the heavy oak door Lilly had shut behind her. 'I dread to think what will happen to the murderer when she finds out who did it.'

'You think we ever will find out who did it?'

'Probably not,' he conceded. 'It could have been anyone. The Creys aren't exactly revered the world over.'

Howie paused. 'You don't reckon Seth did it, do you?'

Adrienne glowered at him with a disgusted expression. 'If you saw him earlier, you wouldn't ask such a stupid question.'

Howie shot her a sidelong glance.

'I doubt it,' said Jimmy, pulling a face. 'He couldn't fight his way through clotted cream. He'd be annihilated. What makes you ask that?'

Howie shook his head, his lower lip jutting out. 'No reason. Just popped into my head.'

~

X

'We can't parade Seth around the country now! It's too dangerous!'

'We have to show the culprit that the Creys will not be beaten,' Queen Eleanor said stubbornly.

A fortnight had passed since King Theo had been found. The guests had been shipped out of the palace as soon as King Theo's remains arrived at the castle morgue: though not before Marbrand had meticulously collected and recorded all of their movements from that fateful night. He was nothing if not resourceful.

Unlike her children, Eleanor was showing very little emotion in the wake of her husband's demise.

Probably looking forward to having rooms to herself again, mused Jimmy, as opposed to one pillow and most likely the inside of the wardrobe.

'The murderer will kill him,' Cienne said angrily.

'Not in broad daylight,' she insisted. 'The killer likes striking in the dark. Seth will be guarded day and night in any case. He's going to be king, Cienne!' she added with joy. Actual *joy*, Jimmy noted with amusement. 'Imagine, our little Seth, king of the realm! I want to celebrate this, we *need* to celebrate this!'

Cienne sighed. 'Fine, if you insist. But I want Adrienne to go with him and look after him.'

Jimmy snorted. 'She'll do that alright.'

Cienne glared at him. 'Your cynicism knows no bounds, James. She's not some silly girl, she's a strong, independent young woman. She wouldn't look twice at Seth even if he wanted her to. And besides, she's besotted with Howard in any case.'

Jimmy thought back to that fraught evening two weeks past with a raised eyebrow. 'Of course, your highness.'

'There you are, then,' Eleanor said in satisfaction. 'A trained medic at his side and a full guard at his back. And a priest will be waiting at the Duke of Osney's manor as well. He'll be protected from all angles.'

'A priest,' spat Cienne. 'What bloody use is he going to be?'

'Now you're starting to sound like Theo,' Eleanor said sharply.

'He had a point. Anyway, he's *dead*, I thought people were supposed to be unfailingly nice about dead people?'

'Why?' asked Jimmy. 'He's not here to execute us anymore.'

~

Seth bounced uncomfortably down Ablyminded Street. He pondered nauseously on the float's inapt name. It was a hideous thing consisting of a raised throne made of stuffed, intertwined snakes, hauled down the thoroughfare by half a dozen horses. It was built for Theo. The seat was much too large for him.

Seth grimaced at the hordes of people squashed into the side-lines on either side. Each squinted up with an air of scrutiny – only to promptly cease their applause and wander to the pub in disgust.

He must have seemed a silly wisp of a man compared to the great King Theo Crey and the savages that came before him. Seth almost wanted to scream out his crime to the world, just to show them what he was capable of – almost.

The float took a sharp turn, sending Seth sliding to the right.

The parade continued to the south side of the city, past the abandoned keep King Seb had discarded fifty years ago in favour for the current Creys' Keep.

To be closer to his mistress, Seth thought with a shudder. As if a witch wasn't bad enough, it had to be a perpetually youthful one. Seth didn't think he could cope with an ageless lover. Being twenty-one forever wasn't fair. It was downright deceptive.

He gawked at the old fortress, all soaring towers and spiked gates. The new keep was sissy by comparison. It housed Seth's grandmother now: Dowager Queen Gertrude Crey, King Theo's mother and female equivalent, a woman so terrifying in her own right that her birth family had placed aside all reservations regarding Seb

Crey and took her to Serpus as fast as her horse could carry her.

Even though his father had been a *cannibal.*

Seth flung the castle a concerned glance. He liked his grandmother, despite her fiery temperament – she always treated him with doting kindness. A messenger had been dispatched to her to deliver the bad news, but Seth hadn't had word of her at all. The death of her eldest son must be…

He quickly diverted his mind away from his grieving grandmother.

A skeleton dangled over the front gate. *Some thief,* he mused, his gaze lingering on it. It seemed a thematically appropriate placement for one, considering the history of the castle's contents.

King Theo told stories of the walls holding the framed skeletons of his dead aunts, the fabled sisters of King Seb. King Rubeous was best known for eating *his own children* for being born female instead of male. Each had a different mother, King Theo used to tell with zeal: the first two wives of King Rubeous Crey had ended their own lives, but King Seb's mother had beaten the savage king to death upon giving birth to Seb's younger sister, Lilith.

We have her to thank for Lilly's genes, he had joked, ruffling Lilly's often bedraggled hair.

He had taken immense pleasure in regaling the tales of his father's horrific childhood. Perhaps unhealthy father-son relationships ran in the family.

Seth's pulse quickened, the image of his father's burning remains papered to the back of his eyelids. He dismissed them with a shiver, feeling like his thoughts were being watched.

Many long and bumpy hours later, dusk slowly broke over the Duke of Osney's estate. It was incredible, Seth thought – at least it had been, before it had evidently been beaten about with a giant rock until every wall looked prone to collapse. The pitfalls of being the spare, Seth thought, glad for once that this wasn't the case for him.

A ring of bodyguards surrounded Seth as he left the ridiculous barge, blocking his view of the entrance to the house. His views of the corridors, ornaments and even his bedroom were also obstructed until Seth threatened to aim his own urine at them if they didn't leave him pass water in peace.

As the door shut behind them, Seth stood in blessed solitude. He glowered at the torchlight lancing into the door to the veranda and moved to close it.

The guards' footsteps faded outside, but a close rustling disturbed the silence.

Seth frowned at the bed.

Leaning next to it and bracing himself for an attack, he reached underneath and pulled the man out by his collar.

'Lost, are you?' he asked sweetly.

The priest coughed nervously, proffering a sheepish smile.

His weapon slipped from his hands and clattered into the rushes.

Seth eyed it with interest.

'That's a big sword, isn't it?' he said. 'What's a nice man like you doing with a big sword like that?'

'You see, your highness, it wasn't my idea,' the priest said swiftly.

'Really? Who sent you?'

'I was implored not to say—'

'Who sent you?'

'I'm under oath not to—'

'Who sent you?'

'Your highness, I can't—'

'Who sent you?' Seth repeated a final time.

He snatched the broadsword and held it to the man's throat.

The priest squeaked. 'She said if I told, she'd—'

'Don't make me ask again,' Seth snarled, the blade moving closer.

'Alright! It was a woman, I've no idea what her name is!'

As he suspected.

Seth dropped the man to the floor unceremoniously and examined the sword in interest.

'I told her no!' he continued despairingly, holding his throat. 'I said I didn't want to kill you, I'm a firm patriot, I told her, I come from Serpus originally, I said, but she wouldn't listen, she kept harping on about the prophecy and the dragon—'

'What prophecy?'

'The prophecy about the Knight of Raining Thorns,' he said. 'It states that you are the Antichrist.'

'The what?'

'The opposite of a Christ, which is the son of a god come down upon earth to get everyone drunk or something,' he said flippantly. 'It's all in the Testament. The Antichrist brings the end of days.'

'So you thought you'd hide under my bed and put a sword through me because the red-haired witch told you I was an evil religious figure?' asked Seth in outrage.

'Well, I can't vouch for the hair colour, she had a hood up, but yes, that's the general gist of it.'

'Right. Get out.'

'But I'm unauthorised, how am I supposed to get past the—'

'Do you want to see yourself out or shall I start removing limbs?'

'I'll, I'll see myself out, thank you,' the man stuttered, leaving quickly.

Seth's eyes narrowed on the back of his burgundy robe.

His thoughts wandered to Queen Qattren. Of course she'd want him assassinated. The bitch had never liked him, he thought sourly. Clearly she thought she would resolve her border dispute with Adem by exterminating the Crey line.

Unless she saw him kill King Theo?

Seth decided not to entertain that notion and prepared for bed.

Then he remembered the prophecy.

The Knight of Raining Thorns.

He'd have words with him, he decided grimly. Perhaps he'd give him a flying lesson, ala King Theo's late butler.

But not before showing Rose-Prick what he was *really* capable of.

~

Elias read the missive given to him by a Crey messenger and bolted to his feet.

Qattren Meriangue had been asking questions. Lots of questions.

He fell to his knees and scrambled under his bed for the vial and the stained fragment of cloak. Then he fled from his cabin.

Colour was just beginning to return to the forest skirting Creys' Keep. Elias moved with a hand across his thick brow, squinting against the dawn. He dropped the items on the ground and crouched beside them, trowel in hand.

'Ah, Elias.'

The trowel spun into the air.

Qattren materialised in front of him.

Elias leapt to his feet.

'Your majesty, a pleasure,' he said breathlessly, doubling over in a hasty bow. 'To what do I owe—?'

'What are those?' Qattren asked, craning her neck with an air of faint curiosity.

'Those? Nothing. Some old scraps of clothing, you know how my word tends to stain—'

'And the vial?'

'Vial?' he asked vaguely.

Qattren lifted an eyebrow.

Elias deflated. 'You got it out of her, then.'

'Actually, no. I just guessed. Only you were stupid enough to attempt such a thing as this.'

'Oh, what harm could it have done?' said Elias, dusting himself off. 'She wanted the boy, and I wanted the experiment. And what a success he was! It isn't my fault she decided against him after all.'

'Oh, what a success he was,' Qattren echoed in a dull monotone.

'What?' Elias said. 'You've seen him, spoken with him. He's magnificent.'

'He's a silly little boy, like all men his age. Nothing more. All this trouble seems for naught to me: a tavern girl could have produced better fare.'

'What trouble? The procedure was a doddle.'

Qattren growled and grabbed him by the forehead.

The forest lost its shape entirely, melting and shifting. Within the blink of an eye, the ever-looming Creys' Keep had vanished, to be replaced by a lump of misshapen rock.

Elias felt a stab of horror before realising she had taken them to her domain and not, in fact, razed the surrounding area in one of her fits.

'Why have you taken me here?'

Qattren pointed.

Within the border between the ashen ruins of Qattren's palace and the rest of the Forest, a crater lay open a few yards ahead. Elias examined the edges, nonplussed, before his gaze was drawn to the Hole.

'Oh dear God,' he whispered. 'Is there nothing we can do?'

Qattren folded her arms. 'I was hoping you would be able to tell me that.'

~

Vladimir trembled.

Felicity looked at him with a blank expression. 'What's the matter?'

A scattering of candles illuminated their faces to each other in a vague amber light. Felicity's delicate profile stood out sharply against the shadows of their bedroom.

They sat side by side in their bed, backs straight, legs crossed beneath them.

Vladimir looked at her, his brows furrowing upward in a seldom-used show of distress.

'Nothing,' he said, swinging his head away.

They lingered in a pregnant pause, the heavy silence engulfing them.

Vladimir's fingers laced themselves together, kneading his knuckles until they strained with the movement.

'Why am I sleeping in here?' Felicity said.

Vladimir closed his eyes.

'Because Queen Aaliyaa says so,' he said in a whisper.

'But why? I always sleep on my own.'

'I know, but…'

Vladimir heaved a breath and released it, a shuddering exhale.

'I.. I have to… see, I, I… I have to go.'

He threw the blanket from his lap and swung himself off the bed in one fluid motion.

Felicity watched him, nonplussed.

He swept from his quarters, past candelabras on a long dining table and through the pitch-black drawing room to the corridor.

'Must I hold your hand, Vladimir Horne, and direct you step by step?' a voice drawled from the corridor.

Vladimir flinched violently backwards.

Queen Aaliyaa leaned on the doorframe, her arms folded.

'You have your instructions,' she said coldly. 'Now do your duty.'

'Mother, I can't, she isn't all there!' Vladimir said despairingly, throwing a hand in his wake. 'She doesn't know why she's even there, I thought you were going to speak to her?'

'I did. She has taken the tonic of her own volition, as planned. She'll soon grasp the idea.'

'No, it. It isn't right. I'm supposed to be the Knight of Raining Thorns, heroes don't do things like that. What happened to marrying Cienne Fleurelle?'

Aaliyaa snorted a laugh. 'She's been despoiled by the Antichrist. Discard her. The Emmett girl has better connections. We will be more likely to defeat the Antichrist with her family at our back. But we need to cement them to our cause. With blood.'

Vladimir's blood ran cold. 'I can't.'

Aaliyaa bared her teeth. A thin hand crept around Vladimir's chin, long nails pinching grooves into the skin.

'You will do as the Seven command,' she snarled into his face.

'Or I will discard you like I did your wretched brother. Don't think I lack the heart.'

He didn't.

She released him, thrusting his head back.

'Go,' she told him. 'If I enter your rooms in half an hour to find her intact, you will rue defying me a second time.'

Vladimir trembled, ice sliding down his veins.

When he returned to the bed, Felicity sported the upturned eyebrows in concern.

'Are you sure you're alright?' she asked again.

Vladimir thought he heard a somewhat more mature timbre to this question. Before he could dismiss it as his imagination, he replied to it in a similar tone.

'I'm going to have to do something to you and it's going to hurt.'

Felicity froze. 'What?'

Vladimir swallowed a lump in his throat and, gently, pressed her back against the pillows by one shoulder.

'I'll be as gentle as I can,' he said thickly before tucking his hands beneath the sheets.

∼

A tinkle sounded from the bell over Adrienne's bedside table.

She sighed, wiping her eyes.

A delicate peach light poured into her small room in Seth's quarters. It gave the austere room a quaint glow, but Adrienne's eyes were too sore to enjoy it. She closed them firmly, easing the red ache momentarily.

It had been too perfect. The little touches, the shy glances, all of it had been too close to her own imaginings. She should have known the real thing wouldn't have been executed as smoothly as the daydreams. She tried to conjure up those glances of his again and only came up with glowers.

The tinkle noised again.

Adrienne deflated.

Seth wanted her. Rather too desperately, she thought with a cringe. He had been hinting for her to discard her bare servant's room for his bed since they arrived. It was disgusting.

And yet…

She tugged the sleeves and hem of her shirt down in exasperation.

She couldn't help thinking of him in the courtyard. It was the same quality, the shy, tentative glance, head tilted down… they were the same really, just misguided. One more misguided than the other, she thought in distaste, thinking of what Cienne must think of her husband trailing after a younger woman like a dog on heat.

Then her thoughts went to Cienne with her mouth wrapped around *her* boyfriend's.

A petty red haze crept over her own guilt.

It wasn't as if Seth and his wife were *seeing* each other, she rationalised. It was more of a transaction, really. There was no emotional bond there. She wasn't hurting anyone, really.

Except for Howie.

Who hadn't had any of these reservations during his own *conquest*.

The red haze intensified and rushed over her head.

The bell chimed again, a delicate tinkle on the edge of hearing.

Images began to bleed into her consciousness. Particularly of Seth's arms, which, unremarkable in most circumstances, seemed to have a potent significance in certain positions, most notably around her torso. They muffled the red haze with an alarming competency, and a thread within her began to tense.

Adrienne squeezed her eyes shut.

By the time the next chime had sounded, she was gone.

~

PART FIVE: THE HOLE

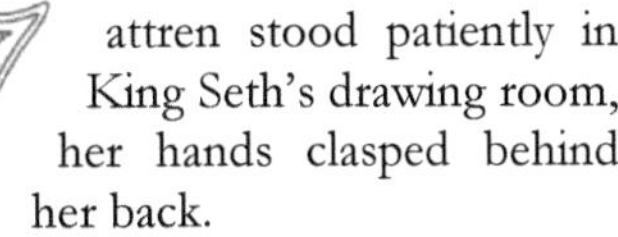

attren stood patiently in King Seth's drawing room, her hands clasped behind her back.

Ron was just behind, remaining as ever one of the least interesting people in the room next to Qattren's feathery accoutrements, which in a previous life had been a peacock… or ten.

Footfalls on the corridor flagstones marked Jimmy's arrival.

'Highness, I need your signature for a letter to the undertakers *again*—'

He blinked at Ron and Qattren.

'Who let you in?'

'Oh, we let ourselves in,' said Qattren airily. 'Is Prince Seth back from the parades?'

'Couldn't tell you, I've been too busy trying to get hold of those undertakers,' he said, shaking his head. 'King Theo's stinking up a storm in the morgue, the ignorant bastards don't seem to be the least bit concerned about it. Why?'

'We're here to discuss preventative action against the impending apocalypse,' said Qattren, as though suggesting they stay for tea this evening.

Jimmy blinked again.

'Alright then. I'll have a look downstairs for him.'

He left rather quickly, muttering to himself.

Qattren smoothed down her dress and folded her hands behind her back again.

Ron shifted on his feet uncertainly.

'So,' he said. 'You never did tell me your friend's name?'

'Elias,' Elias said from behind Ron, with a friendly smile.

'And,' Ron said, 'why have we brought a hermit called Elias into the Creys' palace with us?'

'Because this particular hermit,' said Qattren, 'is largely

responsible for Howard Rosethorn.'

'Ah.' Ron frowned. 'How, exactly?'

Seth's entrance interrupted her reply.

He stormed in between them and swung his desk chair to face them, throwing himself into it.

'Can I help you?' he asked Qattren, coldly.

She smiled.

'Yes,' she said airily. 'I have an issue to discuss with you as regards to King Samuel Horne's death. But I would prefer to discuss it with a few more persons present. Ron, would you be a dear and hunt them down? You can give Elias a quick tour while you're at it,' she said as an afterthought. 'It's rare for him to see such opulence first hand.'

Ron noted her unceasing stare at Seth, who was staring right back.

'Right you are,' he said, pivoting.

Elias shuffled close behind him.

This left Qattren and Seth to glare at each other in silence, narrowed eye to narrowed eye.

'Have you no shame?' Qattren said in a low monotone.

Seth shrugged with a quick shake of the head. 'Which, sorry?'

Qattren stepped forward, her feathered skirts shimmering.

'I don't think you need reminding,' she said. 'A few weeks of gallivanting across the countryside shouldn't have made you forget so easily. You only get to kill your father once, after all.'

Seth licked his lips.

'Who told you?' he whispered, almost silently.

'No one,' she said. 'I saw you. I was with your father just after the fact.' She leaned forward. 'He wasn't happy.'

He arched an eyebrow. 'Ooh, that's *terrifying*. What's he going to do, haunt me to death?'

'Don't underestimate the dead, Seth,' said Qattren, looming closer until they were nearly nose to nose. 'Some don't quite stay dead.'

She pivoted back around.

Her long ringlets whipped Seth in the face, making him flinch.

'You yourself are a prime example of such.'

Seth's upper lip twitched. 'I was a traumatised little boy!'

'Of course,' she said, returning to the centre of the room.

'And I was ill. Ask anyone.'

'As you say. I'm sure they wouldn't lie.'

'What are you saying, that I faked it?' said Seth, rising to his feet. 'You want to know what happened to the last person who insinuated that? Made a right mess of his clothes. I'd hate to splatter that pretty dress of yours, it looks very expensive.'

She tilted her head to one side, her hair tumbling over one shoulder.

'I'm terrified,' she said in a dull tone. 'Yet here I am, my hand as steady as a rock, while you stand trembling like a maid on her wedding night.'

Seth licked his teeth and sat, crossing his arms and legs, as if to stem the tremor.

She smiled again, almost kindly.

'You will never frighten me, Seth Crey. Your threats mean nothing to me, so if I believe that you faked your Great Illness, I'll announce it. Deny it all you like: you may have forgotten those years, but we both know what you are.'

'Speaking of denying what you are,' he said.

Qattren lifted an eyebrow.

Now it was Seth's turn to rise from his seat and approach Qattren.

'You've aged remarkably well for someone of your years,' he said, the words idle. 'Tell me, how old are you exactly?'

Qattren's eyes became slits. 'You had a chat with your father before trying to lob his head off, then.'

'That I did. A secret, is it? Personally, I think secrets are childish.' He regarded her a moment before adding, 'Although I may be inclined to keep this one. We don't want your private business getting in the wrong ears, do we? That massive fire in the Orchard hasn't quite faded from memory yet, has it?'

A pause. Then she said, 'You make a fair point. And we can't have your situation tarnish your brand-new reign.'

He smiled sweetly and turned back to his throne.

'It's been tarnished enough already as it is.'

He froze in his tracks.

The front door opened with a clang, shattering the tension.

Ron strode in, flanked by Howie, Elias and a rather green-looking Adrienne.

Qattren whirled to face them amiably.

'Ah, you're all here,' she said as though their exchange hadn't happened, 'except for Princess Cienne. Any idea where she might be?'

The door clanged again.

'Are my ears burning?' said Cienne in icy tones.

She sauntered to Seth's side in a whirl of ivory silk. The sheer mass of her gown almost put Qattren's outfit to shame.

Jimmy skittered at her heels – or rather, the hem of her dress, which trailed about two feet behind her. Despite the looks Qattren was giving him, he had no intention of leaving a good show go to waste.

'What is it you wanted?' Cienne asked, a hand on Seth's shoulder.

'I have news on the untimely demise of King Samuel Horne.'

'And the apocalypse,' Ron added.

'And the apocalypse,' Qattren agreed.

Seth snorted. 'My father's dead now, love, I don't think we have anything to worry about.'

'Destruction comes in many more forms than King Theo,' Elias cut in.

He spotted Seth's irritated expression and quickly bowed.

'Elias Dale, your majesty, from the Forest. Princess Cienne, I believe we have had the pleasure.'

Cienne's breath caught in her throat. Her eyes darted around the room, meeting the curious gazes within.

'Yes, I believe we have,' she managed.

Seth half-frowned, giving the hermit a side glance.

Elias had a thick brow shadowing two watery eyes, with a nose and mouth to match both. His face and crown were clean-shaven: an unusual occurrence in a hermit, along with the ermine cloak he was wearing.

What does she have to do with him? Seth wondered.

Elias continued unheeded.

'Queen Qattren met me a few days ago for knowledge of King Samuel's final resting place.'

'You found him?' Howie asked from behind him.

'Not exactly,' Qattren said. 'Elias has lived between this palace and my Forest's border for forty years. He's a bit of an experimentalist in biological sorcery, so I sought him out to quiz him on an anomaly I found near the ruins of my old home.'

'It's a Hole, in mid-air,' Ron supplied. 'Looks as if it swallowed him whole. The Stonecrown was lying a short distance away from it.'

Cienne frowned. 'A hole in mid-air?'

'In the very atmosphere, yes,' Elias said. 'And it's growing.'

Seth raised his eyebrows. 'He must have tasted horrible. Maybe it's about to spit him back up.'

Ron looked stricken.

'Maybe so,' Qattren said coldly.

She gave Ron's hand a brief squeeze before continuing.

'In any case,' she continued, 'it wasn't after King Samuel in the first place. He was merely in the vicinity when he was drawn inside. That Hole is waiting for something in particular – someone, namely. If it doesn't get it, it will take everything.'

'It's been drawing in wildlife and surrounding earth and trees since it opened,' said Elias, 'but the woods around it are getting sparse. If it doesn't get what it wants, it will consume more and more… and who knows how big it will grow. We must give it what it wants – the person whose very existence resulted in its opening in the first place.'

There was a pause.

'Who is…' Seth trailed off, hoping against hope.

'Howard Rosethorn,' said Qattren and Jimmy in unison.

They glared at Jimmy.

'What? It was obvious,' he said with a defensive shrug.

Howie's eyes glazed over.

'You want me to die.'

Elias sucked in a breath and nodded.

Howie glanced from face to face, mostly finding pity in return – except in the case of Seth, who gazed at Qattren and Elias, rapt.

'Why me?' he asked hoarsely.

Qattren faced Howie, her expression piteous for a change.

'You were created unnaturally,' she said gently. 'You grew up in an orphanage and under the tutelage of Archie Hart because you don't have parents, correct?'

He nodded, his expression blank.

'That's because you never had parents,' she said. 'Not biologically, anyway.'

Only Qattren noticed, out of the corner of her eye, Cienne biting the edge of her thumbnail.

Qattren swung around to face the Creys, making Cienne jump.

'The Night of Raining Thorns was the day of the assassination, correct?'

'Yes,' said Seth.

'And the killer caused you no physical harm apart from doping you into unconsciousness and making an incision on your palm?'

'Yes.'

'And all was seen by none but a raven peering into your window, thus leaving you with an acute fear of the species?'

Seth shuddered. 'Correct.'

'That was no assassination attempt,' said Qattren. 'That was someone collecting a sample of your blood to create a clone of you. To what purpose? We don't know. We only know that it resulted in the creation of a child, and that child is…'

She pointed at Howie.

'You.'

Howie gaped at her, wide-eyed.

Seth's eyes ran up and down the length of him. He snorted, starting to laugh.

'Hah! Him? A clone of *me*? He looks nothing like me! He's a foot shorter, for a start.'

'Indeed,' Qattren said. She then added, purely out of spite, 'His posture is also better, his face more pleasant on the eye and his hair is thicker and sits much more attractively than yours.'

Howie ran a hand through his fringe with a stricken expression.

So did Seth, self-conscious.

'In *your* opinion,' he said finally, frowning.

'But let's not split hairs, as it were. He's the you that you never were – albeit with a better upbringing and some improvements, possibly brought on by the sorcery.'

Seth slouched back in his seat, his face turned upwards.

'My father did this, didn't he?' he said, scowling at the ceiling. 'He was ashamed of me, so he made a replacement.'

'Actually,' Elias said, holding a hand up, 'it was me.'

He eyed Seth's astonished expression.

'At the request of an anonymous young lady – not King Theo by any stretch of the imagination.' He wrung his hands and rattled on unheeded, 'I attempted to stop the whole event at the last minute. The raven you saw, that was me in disguise. That's what awoke you a moment too late on that night, it was me, trying to wake you.'

'You made me ill,' said Seth, his voice hollow. 'You made me think I had died.'

Elias winced in distress. 'I'm sorry for making you afraid. I wanted to end this chain of events before it grew to this extent—'

'So why did you make him in the first place?' Seth demanded.

'She had on her person an outrageous amount of money,' Qattren said dully.

'Irrelevant,' he snapped. 'She was upset, that was my reason. I'm a soft touch, that's my only confession. She wanted your clone so badly I thought, how bad could it be to give the world a copy of a person so evidently easy to love?'

'Incompetence,' said Jimmy. 'You should have met him to clarify first.'

Seth pointedly ignored him.

'And the hoard of birds chasing me through the forest? After the end of my illness? Any particular reason why I had to get sunstroke at the exact moment that Adri…'

His eyes flitted to Cienne.

'That I was to meet Lilly on the practise field?' he finished lamely.

Elias paused. 'That I can't explain.'

'Probably just didn't like you,' muttered Howie.

Seth shot him a loathsome glance. 'You speak to the king like that after all this?'

'Seth, please,' Cienne said.

'No,' he said, leaning towards Howie, 'you come here, try to *kill* me, *ridicule* me and you're not even human?'

'I didn't know this—' began Howie.

'Didn't you? Oh, that's alright then, since you didn't know… so I suppose you didn't know about the priest you and the red-haired bitch over there sent to butcher me in my sleep either?'

'He doesn't,' Qattren said, 'and neither do I.'

'*Bullshit*,' Seth announced loudly.

'Aaliyaa Horne has been proclaiming her eldest son Vladimir as the Knight of Raining Thorns for the last twenty years,' Qattren continued, as though uninterrupted. 'I would imagine it was they who sent him, if anyone. If your priest did name-drop Howard Rosethorn – a fact you appear to have omitted, I note – then it was likely a lapse of communication on their end.'

'And I'm to take your word for that, am I?'

'I would,' Ron said from behind her. 'I've first-hand experience of my mother, and besides, Qattren isn't a liar.'

'A pity I'm not,' Qattren said. 'If I were, I could have had you *both* pushed into the Hole and done something productive with my afternoon, like knitting.'

Seth squinted his eyes with a sarcastic smile and turned away.

'So who's his mother, so to speak?' Jimmy asked curiously.

'I have no idea,' Elias said. 'She begged to remain nameless, only that the boy be named Howard, after a grandfather, I think. When he arrived as a new-born rather than a young man as she expected, she panicked and fled. So I gave him the first surname to come to mind and left him at Madam Teuilliary's orphanage and nursery.'

Cienne swallowed.

Qattren lifted her gaze to meet hers.

'Your highness,' she said. 'What was your grandfather's first name?'

Everyone frowned. Then turned to face Cienne.

Who twiddled her thumbs and produced a shaky smile. 'Which one? Most people have two.'

'It was you.'

Seth sat erect in his seat, his face impassive.

Cienne dropped to her knees.

'Seth… I didn't know… I didn't think any of this would…'

He froze, his gaze locked straight ahead.

'I never meant to hurt you, Seth!' she said desperately.

His silence cut her like a knife. It was like his catatonics come again.

Cienne's eyes filled with helpless tears.

Howie stared at her in disbelief.

'*You're* my mother?'

Cienne deflated. 'It was silly.'

Her voice dropped to just above a whisper.

'My whole life revolved around Seth. I'm my father's sole heir: marriage was my only lot in life. My father admired King Theo a great deal, so he jumped at the chance to marry us, thinking Seth would be a copy of his father. I didn't like the thought of marrying a miniature Theo Crey, but when I saw Seth, he was so different…'

'Thank God,' Seth muttered.

'… he seemed so regal, so beautiful… then I got to know him.'

'Happens to the best of us,' Jimmy said in empathy.

'He thought I was just the stupid foreign girl because I didn't know a few of his words. The years I had spent imagining our first meeting, planning this day. My life revolved around him, and he treated me like an imbecile. So I ran to Elias.

'We'd brought him along with us on the way to the palace after he had healed a favourite of my father's. He had been mauled by, I don't know, a boar or a bear or something, and our healer was about to remove his leg when Elias barged past and saved it. I thought if he could do that with his powers, he could make a copy of Seth, one that would reciprocate my feelings for him.'

She cast a helpless glance at Howie before turning her eyes to the floor.

'We didn't expect you to arrive as a new-born. I couldn't take you with me, I didn't know what to do, so… I just left you there and ran. I thought I could put you out of my mind and while I was caring for Seth, I did, but… you arrived here. I should have avoided you, I shouldn't have even spoken to you, but I was curious. I wanted to see what kind of man you were, and you're perfect, you really are. It just…

felt all wrong.'

Howie swallowed, breaking the stiffness growing in his face.

'… that explains a lot,' he managed in a croak.

A long silence ensued. Cienne threw a glance at Seth, who propped his chin on his thumb, two fingers massaging his temple.

Anna entered with a tray of wine cups and skittered to Jimmy's side.

'What did I miss?'

'*Everything*,' he whispered back in earnest. 'I'll fill you in later.'

The silence resumed.

Seth cleared his throat. 'You're going to sacrifice him to this Hole, then?'

'Yes,' Qattren said quietly. 'The Hole will grow in a matter of years, slowly swallowing surrounding materials. In less than a decade, it will expand wide enough to consume the continent and everything on it. The sooner we deal with it, the better.'

Howie pressed his knuckles into the back of his neck. 'How do you know that'll fix it?'

'It's a rip in the world,' Elias said gently. 'The atmosphere stretched and ripped when you entered it as an unnatural life. It cannot withstand your presence along with the set number of lives in it, so it needs you to seal the tear.'

'What if it doesn't work? The king would have fixed it if that's what—'

'We don't know if King Samuel was even alive when he was taken inside,' Qattren said softly. 'He could have had an accident beforehand for all we know.' She placed a hand on his shoulder blades. 'We aren't making this decision lightly. It brings me no pleasure to ask a young person to die. It's the only solution we can think of. Your death is our only hope.'

'I don't want to die.' His voice broke mid-sentence.

Her anger of the past weeks forgotten, Adrienne burst forward and pulled him into her arms.

'There has to be something else,' she said over his shoulder. 'Maybe he doesn't need to jump into it, maybe a bit of his blood will seal it, maybe he just needs to—'

'Perhaps if the rift was a few inches wide,' Qattren said, 'but we're far beyond that point now.'

'You can't just kill him!' Adrienne exploded, tears pouring down her face. 'You can't have him, you can't just throw him away, he's too good, you don't kill good people, you can't, you can't, you can't…'

She buried her head under his chin and rocked him, another 'you can't' sounding every other moment in a childlike whimper.

Howie cradled her neck in the crooks of his elbows, paling.

Adrienne disentangled herself in a frenzy.

'He's got Seth's blood! Doesn't that mean anything? He's a copy of *him*, can't Seth just—'

'Die in his place?' Seth finished in a soft voice.

'Charming,' Anna said a tad too loudly. 'And after all that in the Duke's mansion. That's gratitude for you.'

'After all what,' Cienne said, 'in the Duke's mansion?'

'She slept in his bed that whole week, didn't you know?' Anna said airily.

'Blabber mouth!' exclaimed Seth in a shrill timbre.

Adrienne's pulse quickened. 'How did you know that?'

'She was probably waiting for her turn,' said Jimmy.

Anna scowled at him.

Howie stepped back to look at her, his arms falling limp at his sides.

'What?'

'I was upset with you,' she mumbled. 'I'm sorry.'

'You slept with him,' he said in a hollow voice. 'You yelled at me for kissing *her* before we even *got* together and then you slept with that *old man*?'

'*Thirty-three years of age is not old!!*' Seth screeched at him, his face beet red.

Qattren heaved a sigh and examined her nails.

'It is compared to her!' Howie shouted. 'You've been *married* for longer than she's been alive! Where I come from, you're practically a pensioner!'

'Unlike the residents of the *slum* you come from,' Seth sniped, 'I have breeding. And I was plenty young enough to please her.' He gestured to Adrienne, who flushed with humiliation, and leaned forward with a sneer. 'Age is nothing to her when the candles go out. I didn't get a single complaint all week.'

Howie bared his teeth. He slid his crystal sword from his belt, swung it over his head and threw it at Seth's face with a shriek.

Adrienne screamed.

Seth ducked.

The blade plunged into the back wall to the hilt, the pommel trembling.

Seth craned his neck around the back of the chair.

'Did it just go *through* the granite block wall?' he asked in astonishment.

Jimmy's mouth hung open.

'I've never been a sword man, but I *want* one of those,' he said, pointing.

Adrienne tried to contain Howie via a bear hug.

'You dirty BASTARD!!' Howie howled at the top of his voice.

'You're the bastard!' Seth bellowed, thrusting himself to his feet. 'Your mother doesn't want you, and now neither does she!'

'And I really thought beginning with the word "apocalypse" might inspire an adult conversation,' Qattren said to herself, shaking her head.

Howie launched himself at Seth.

Adrienne shouldered him back.

'Stop it!' she shouted at him, planting herself between them. 'Stop it, he isn't worth it!'

'That's not what you were saying at the Duke's mansion,' Seth said with glee.

'Oh *please*,' she drawled, flinging her gaze in Seth's direction, 'you were *hardly* worth the walk to your rooms.'

Jimmy released an explosive laugh.

Seth flung him a glower. 'What are you laughing at?'

'This is the most entertainment I've had in this job,' he said, sipping a cup of wine. 'I haven't had this much fun in ages.'

Seth mimed a strangulation. 'Put the kettle on and make some tea. Now!'

Jimmy rolled his eyes and shoved his cup in Anna's hands.

'I'll put the kettle on alright,' he muttered, 'right on your frghin—'

'What are you saying?'

'Nothing!'

Howie stretched his shoulders, breathing heavily.

'Don't forget the rat poison,' he told Jimmy in passing.

Jimmy lifted a contemplative eyebrow.

Seth hissed in annoyance, swinging on his heel.

Qattren waited a moment.

'Finished, are we? Oh, good. When you're quite finished screaming at each other, I suggest we sleep on the matter. We can spare a few days before organising how we'll be going about this.'

'Oh, I know what my plan is,' Seth said, striding to the veranda to look out onto the courtyard. 'Howard Rose-Prick can go to the Tower until I'm fit and ready to push him into the Hole. You can follow him,' he pointed at Qattren, 'for being rude. And you.'

He faced Cienne, who trembled.

'You can stay here where I can see you,' he said, his voice low. 'Only because it isn't *technically* a crime to reproduce me.'

Cienne remained silent.

Seth clicked his fingers.

Anna bolted to the corridor, calling the guards at the end of the hall.

Qattren flicked Elias a quick signal.

He touched Ron's arm and the two dematerialised.

'Just as well it isn't a crime to reproduce you,' said Qattren.

'Why?' Seth asked, his eyes half-lidded.

Four guards flocked around Howie and Qattren.

Qattren nodded at Adrienne.

'Why don't you ask your mistress?'

Adrienne stared at her, her eyes feverish.

Seth frowned at them both.

The guards seized Howie and Qattren, only for the latter to burst into dust.

'When,' Seth said quietly, 'were you going to let me know?'

'I didn't know myself,' Adrienne stammered, cowering.

Jimmy re-entered at that moment, laden with a teapot and some cups. His eyes passed from guard to guard before noting the dust cloud where three guests had once stood.

'What did I miss?'

Seth glanced sharply in his direction.

'*Everything,*' he said, scowling.

~

II

Morning arrived awkwardly through the black clouds over Adem, as though sensing the atmosphere and striving to sneak around it.

Howie watched it slide past the Tower's narrow fourth floor window. His bones ached after three nights crouched in captivity. The plain brick box of a room measured at three feet every way, the ceiling deliberately made too low for him to straighten out in any direction.

In the keep, Adrienne woke with a guilty flush. She had been ushered into a deluxe suite of rooms on the third floor – the rooms next to Seth's, in fact, which was odd considering he wasn't speaking to her. She felt it might be a nice gesture, as father-to-be to child – or else he was subtly pressing her to agree to Howie's death sentence. An odd turn of events since subtlety was to Seth what social skills were to… well, Seth.

She rose grudgingly from the silk wrapped around her and dressed slowly, taking note of the faint curve of her stomach. There was no way she could possibly go through childbirth if Howie died. The distress of it all would kill her, if the child didn't on its own. She knew very well it could: she had killed her own mother in childbirth, after all.

Though her mother didn't have a prince fussing over her at the time.

Adrienne smoothed the plain servant's dress she had put on, deliberately rejecting the silks and finery Seth's servants had left out for her.

He's as thick as two short planks, she thought sourly. Peasant girls weren't supposed to be treated like this. If she were a duke's daughter or something, that would be one thing, but here she was just the king's whore. She imagined the entire palace scorning her, already condemning the unborn child within her – that was no way for a child to start a life.

Adrienne swallowed on the lump in her throat, dropping herself back onto the edge of the bed and reaching under for her shoes.

How did Qattren even know? Adrienne hadn't known for certain until she'd said it. She had suspected, of course, but she was still in the blissful persuasion that she merely had a severe case of indigestion.

She halted in her tracks, one shoe still in hand.

If Qattren could tell that by glancing at her, maybe she could sort it for her just as easily.

She thought about it for a long moment, and ran.

~

Cienne sat across from Seth, forlornly moving her breakfast in figures of eight.

Seth stared at his own nauseously from the other side of the table, taking no notice of her.

Jimmy stood between the two on one leg, nursing a blister on his heel.

'Why don't you just sit at the same end of the table?' he exploded with exasperation. 'I can't keep running from one end of the room to the other, not when this one's a mile long.'

'Nope,' Seth said abruptly.

Jimmy sighed. 'Can I at least grab another milk jug?'

'No, that would be a waste. She can pass it across the table like everyone else.'

'But nobody passes the milk, do they? They just get the butler to do it. My feet have more blisters than toes.'

Seth ignored this lament. He just glared hatefully in Cienne's direction.

'Pass the butter,' he said.

Jimmy threw his arms into the air and pivoted, limping down the length of the table.

'Torturing the butler doesn't cross me as a good way to resolve conflict.'

'Who said I wanted it resolved? I'd have to speak to her then.'

Cienne's chair skidded across the flagstones as she rose.

'And I like seeing you suffer,' Seth went on, paying her no notice. 'It compensates for all the backchat I've been receiving lately.'

Jimmy eyed Cienne's retreating form in concern.

Seth whistled impatiently, making spreading motions with his knife.

Jimmy glared at the ceiling, snatching the butter dish.

'Unbelievable,' he said. 'The axe-wielding maniac dies and *then* the torture starts. Un*believable*.'

He slammed the dish in front of Seth.

Whose hand revolved in the air.

'Does his majesty require a diagram on the art of buttering bread, or would that be too baffling for him?' Jimmy sneered.

Seth shot him a look. 'Do you fancy her or something?'

Jimmy made a face. 'No. I *value* my life.'

Seth snorted. 'So you're scared of her?'

'No. I just think that despite her keen interest in the welfare of others, the shovel overshadows her good points, literally and figuratively.'

'Shovel?'

Jimmy blinked at him. 'You... don't remember the shovel episode?'

Seth shook his head slowly.

'Surely that's one of the highlights of your life up to this point?'

'I wouldn't know,' Seth drawled. 'I've lost all memory of the last twenty years before I was apparently struck by lightning.'

He gave Jimmy a sideways glance.

'What's she been doing to me?'

Jimmy opened his mouth to reply and shut it again.

'Um...'

Seth raised his eyebrows.

Jimmy hesitated. 'I'm not going to be done for excusing attempted rape, am I?'

Seth frowned.

Jimmy gulped. 'See… with you being uncooperative in the… in… you know, the bedroom…'

Seth's eyes narrowed.

'… she resorted to measures, you see, that… did not work. Whereupon the urge to wield a heavy iron object began to manifest itself.'

He wrung his hands.

'And then she hit you with it. On the head. Not hard or anything, but hard enough to possibly warrant your recent memory loss… alongside the dirty great dent on the side of your head.'

Seth stared at him, making sense of this development.

'What… measures did she resort to, exactly?'

Jimmy halted. 'Well, the usual.'

Seth lifted a hand into the air, which revolved.

Jimmy made a pained noise in the back of his throat.

'You know… suggestive clothing. Performative masturbation. Diagrams of, of odd… positions. Something to do with oil? We were forbidden from the third floor during these episodes, so I can't be very specific.'

Seth stared into space, an eyebrow arched.

'Oil, is it?' he said vaguely.

Jimmy gave him an uneasy glance. 'Yes.'

Seth's eyes glazed over. 'Interesting.'

Jimmy blinked repeatedly.

'There was a lot of domestic violence, though,' he pointed out.

'Indeed,' said Seth, with an air of absence. His eyes flicked up to Jimmy's. 'You wouldn't know where she happens to keep this… oil?'

'Literally just detailed,' Jimmy said in a pained voice, 'an episode of attempted murder—'

'In the shrine, maybe?' Seth wondered aloud, scrutinising the ceiling.

'Probably,' Jimmy relented, 'but I wouldn't recommend rooting through her things, her anger management skills aren't quite—'

Seth lifted his chair up by the seat and, delicately, lifted it back a bit to rise.

'I… will be upstairs for the day. If you need me.'

Seth licked his lips and practically ran for the stairs – not before snatching Anna on the way as she descended, sending her basket of washing flying across the flagstones.

Jimmy stared in his wake from the corner of his eyes.

'He's going to shag himself into an early grave,' he muttered to himself, shaking his head.

~

Cienne sat stiffly in the throne room, atop what was now her throne as the king's consort.

The hall was resplendent as always. She gazed at the alternating pattern of royal statues and deep green curtains. Late morning beamed in shades of violet through the stained-glass windows high above the marble kings of Truphoria, but Cienne was far from beaming.

She leaned over her thighs to stare at the flagstones, her arms wrapped around her ribs, waiting for the pain within them to ebb. This was worse than before. Before, she could have convinced herself his behaviour was mainly because he was a pillock. This time, it was *all* her fault.

He had a good reason. He may have faked it for many years, but for the first year he was a genuine catatonic. And that was her doing. Her actions were a crime deserving of death. It was only fair he should keep her alive to meet his illegitimate child instead.

She wouldn't let herself cry over it. Not now, anyway. That nonsense could wait until under the cover of darkness, when Seth would most likely be dreaming of his other woman. Cienne didn't know which was worse, him hating her or him loving someone else.

A hand on her shoulder startled her from her thoughts.

It was her cousin, holding a cup.

'You look utterly bereft,' Emmett Jr said. 'Here, have some alcohol.'

Cienne smiled thinly. 'Thank you.'

'May I sit?' He gestured to a small chair lingering nearby.

'Of course, please.'

Emmett made a beeline for it and hoisted onto the dais beside her.

Cienne took a sip. Whiskey. She smiled. He knew her so well.

'What made you decide to stay?' she asked. 'I notice the rest of your family left very quickly after the tournaments.'

'They aren't far,' said Emmett. 'My father and uncle are staying in a new manor I acquired in a district just beyond Serpus. We've decided to stay and support Felicity during her uncle-in-law's funeral.

She was quite close to him.'

'How is Felicity?' Cienne asked.

Emmett arched an eyebrow. 'Your guess is as good as mine,' he said bluntly. 'Vladimir Horne has been keeping her under lock and key. I stopped by on a number of occasions to his estate in the city and was abruptly dismissed. I find it quite concerning.'

Cienne furrowed her brow. 'I can imagine. Would you like me to send a letter?'

'No, no, it's nothing we can't handle. My thanks for the offer.' She inclined her head.

'You must visit the new manor sometime,' Emmett said. 'My father suggested the idea at the tournaments, but with the events concerning the king, it completely slipped my mind.'

He then, to Cienne's great surprise, proceeded to give an aural tour of the house and grounds, with great detail. It was the longest speech he had ever given unprompted.

'I would like that,' she said with a faint smile. 'It definitely sounds preferable to lingering here with a husband who despises me.'

Emmett tilted his head to one side. 'Would you like me to send a letter?'

Cienne grinned at him. 'No. Thanks for the offer.'

He stuck out his lower lip and turned his head, examining the hall.

'Let me know about a visit to the manor,' he said, rising.

'I will,' she said. 'Thank you.'

He gave her a faint smile, another irregularity. Then he left.

Cienne gazed after him in open curiosity. *How strange.*

~

The Prince Death hid behind a wall of scaffolding. Men scrambled up and down the metal bars, hastily removing all evidence of the satirical name lest its namesake call for a sudden visit. Or perhaps to upgrade the 'Prince' to 'King', Adrienne wasn't sure.

Adrienne glanced up and down Arthur Stibbons' Street. No sign of anyone watching her. Which was good because what she needed was a stiff drink.

She pivoted to enter the pub and flinched violently.

'You wanted to see me?' Qattren said.

Adrienne cleared her throat. 'How did you know?'

'I have a penchant for guessing these things. Plus I've been keeping an eye on you. You look decidedly unhappy.'

Adrienne trembled. 'I don't know what to do.'

Qattren placed a hand on her elbow and guided her inside.

'I don't think I can do this,' she continued in a whisper as Qattren guided her between the close-set tables. 'It's all too much. I can't, I, this, the sacrifice, everything, I can't do it, I can't even tell my uncle what's going on, he'll be so disappointed in me.'

Her eyes welled up.

Qattren led her to a table in the corner and rubbed her back.

'I'll help you,' she soothed. 'You won't need to worry about a thing. I'll make sure you come to term with no complications. We can organise something for the child when the time comes.'

Adrienne gazed at her through watery eyes.

'Is there…'

Her eyes dropped to her lap.

Qattren tilted her head. 'Is there…?'

'Is there a way of using it to seal the Hole?' Adrienne murmured into her lap.

Qattren froze. 'What?'

Adrienne swallowed. 'It would make things easier, wouldn't it? It would have a terrible life otherwise. I won't be able to manage on my own—'

'It will not work,' Qattren said, stunned. 'The rift will only close with its intended subject in it. That's just how it is.'

'But I want to try—'

'Do you?'

She trembled. 'I just want it to go away.'

Qattren sighed, her eyes on Adrienne's stomach.

'I wish I could help with that. But you're too far to term to abort without him being in great pain. He's not just a dot in the womb anymore, he's a developing person now.'

Adrienne stared at the floor.

Qattren reached forward and took her hand.

'You're having a hard time,' she said gently. 'Please don't make any rash decisions. I can help you bring the child to term and give him a home, away from you and your uncle, if you wish. You won't need to worry about his wellbeing, or yours. But I can't assist with the death of a child. And I know your conscience can't take that either.'

Adrienne swallowed a lump in her throat. 'Okay.'

Qattren hesitated.

'If there's a slim chance,' she said, 'of King Samuel's death being unrelated to the Hole before he was drawn in, another sacrifice to test beforehand might work. Perhaps an already-convicted criminal?'

Adrienne met her gaze.

'Seth might agree to try,' Qattren said. 'If you were the one to suggest it.'

Adrienne nodded. 'I'll ask.'

Qattren smiled.

It was only after Adrienne had walked a mile uphill that she thought to wonder, *How does she know it's a boy?*

~

Seth listened to her plea with rapt attention.

'Nope.'

Adrienne stared at him, agape. 'Why not?'

They stood in the slim corridor leading to Seth's quarters. Seth stood in front of a tall window, elbows leaning on the mahogany lining either side. Adrienne hovered behind him, hands twisting the hem of her shirt.

'Seth!' she pleaded.

'I refuse to release that freak of nature. He tried to kill me on numerous occasions. He's a danger to my family.'

'But I need him,' she said through tears.

'Can I say something?' Jimmy asked from the stairs. 'Since you're clearly intending to obstruct the corridor forever?'

They gave him a sheepish glance and slid to one side.

'Thank you,' said Jimmy, sidling past.

Seth watched him go before leaning close to Adrienne.

'It can't be anyone else,' he said. 'You heard her yesterday. It has to be him.'

'So you're going to leave me raise this child alone? You're just doing this because you hate him, can't you find another way?'

'Like what?' he snapped. 'Throw myself in like you suggested? I'm sure you wouldn't find any complaints here, murder appears to be the perfect solution so long as everyone hates the victim.'

Adrienne flinched back. 'I'm not saying that.'

They stood in hostile silence for a moment.

'There might be war if he dies,' she said. 'Have you thought of that? People think he's some kind of saviour.'

'I don't care what they think. Look.'

He tucked her hair behind her ear.

'You're a beautiful, intelligent person. There's going to be another human in the world with the chance to inherit that. Don't you think I want them to be happy? You don't need him. *I'll* look after you, both of you. Let me look after you.'

Adrienne's eyes glazed over. She already had a rough estimate of how long that intention would last.

She curtsied, which she felt had offended him somehow. She'd never curtsied to him before.

Seth's face took on a steely cast.

She took that as her cue to leave.

The walk back to her quarters in the medic turret was a lonely one: she couldn't bring herself to return to her lavish rooms next to Seth's. She climbed the steep stairs circling the turret, ignored Erik glowering at her from the bookshelves upon entry and made a beeline for the inner stairs, beginning the climb to the top of the tower.

A brisk knock interrupted five steps up.

'It's Adrienne, isn't it?' a kindly voice said by the door.

She turned to face a man, late sixties, with a black robe and an amiable smile.

'Father Giery,' he introduced himself with a short bow. 'I gather you're courting poor Howard. Would you join me in the north greens? I may have a solution to save your boy.'

Adrienne hesitated a moment.

'I work for the Creys, you can trust me on this,' he said, sensing her discomfort. 'I kept the king's own cousin in my keeping over at the chapel when he was a child. I'm practically a family friend. My ideas are purely above board and legal, I assure you.'

She searched his eyes and found a comforting Archie aura within. That convinced her.

She descended to the main room and followed him out.

~

III

In a turret he'd made his own at the north end of the castle, Archie set his chisel onto the top corner of a lavishly decorated chest of drawers he was just finishing off and carved a capital 'A'. He set the blade to one end of a pencilled 'H' as Seth threw the door open with a bang.

Archie jumped violently.

His arm jolted across the chest, scoring a deep line into the top carvings.

'Oh, bloody hell!' Archie shouted, pivoting. 'What d'you do that for? Now look what I've—'

'I'm not interested,' Seth said. 'Where's your niece?'

'Oh, I don't know, buggered off with Howard I imagine,' said

Archie. 'Which brings me to another point, where's he? I haven't seen him for three days, has he been murdered or is he just slacking off?'

Seth left the door dangling open behind him without deigning to leave behind a reply.

'Charming,' muttered Archie.

He faced the chest of drawers, perfectly carved with intertwining grapevines but for an angry line running diagonally through it. On further inspection, a couple leaves had come free also.

He heaved a groan and took a hammer to it with gusto.

It was midway through this irate destruction that the door burst open again, this time thanks to the younger prince of Stoneguard.

'Did you know Howie's been locked up?' Ron demanded.

~

'Where's Adrienne?' Seth asked Lilly in the courtyard.

Lilly swung their father's great-sword in figures-of-eight. 'Who-ey?'

Seth wrestled the sword from her grasp.

'*Adrienne,*' he said. 'Tall? Pale? Auburn hair down to her exquisitely rounded arse?'

Lilly snatched the sword back, giving the blade a loving stroke.

'Oh, your girlfriend. Yeah, left this morning on her little horse. No idea where, though.'

'She came back since then, I spoke to her. You haven't seen her since then?'

Lilly's attacks at the mayflies fluttering around the fountain presumably indicated a 'no'.

Seth exhaled through his teeth.

He had hoped to keep Adrienne in her rooms. He didn't want her appearing outside the front of the castle out of nowhere. He was bringing Howie to the Hole today.

Moat and a couple of lackeys hovered at the throne room entrance, awaiting orders.

Seth gazed at them a moment before giving them a nod. Might as well do it quick before she found out.

He led them to the Tower.

~

The Duke of Osney planted a wide hand over Adrienne's.

'I am extremely sorry for your situation. Howard is a wonderful lad, my brother the king was most besotted with him. Be assured that my counsel to King Seth does not go unheard.'

Adrienne nodded with a smile, wondering why he had decided to join them.

Father Giery had whisked Adrienne to the lavish gardens behind the castle chapel, an approximate acre of spiralling patterns alternating in gravel paths and verdant flowers. It was the most colourful part of Creys' Keep, and even better, it had a distinct lack of princesses.

Cienne and her mother-in-law Queen Eleanor had shot their filthiest looks at her on their walk of the southern green, and Lilly-Anna had been spotted roaming the grounds with a sword. Adrienne could do without them trying to bore holes in her head, literal or figurative.

Seated at a dainty white garden table within the northernmost spiral, Adrienne found herself surrounded by the priest himself, a handful of his acolytes, the Duke and the master of coin, a Mister Philip Manderly. The table felt incredibly overfilled.

'Have you spoken to Howard since his imprisonment?' the Duke asked.

'No, I didn't think I would be allowed to see him,' she said. 'I hope he's alright.'

'Of course, you were courting, weren't you?' the Duke said, dripping with sympathy.

Acid reflux threatened to overcome Adrienne. Whether it was morning sickness or the Duke's syrupy tones, she couldn't be sure.

'Has the king divulged when he might go ahead with this execution?' Father Giery asked keenly.

'Not to me, he hasn't. But then he wouldn't, would he? In case I tried to stop him.'

'I dare say even your tender love for the boy couldn't stop him,' the Duke said. 'Once a Crey gets an idea into his head, he'll follow through.'

'Not to worry,' Giery said easily, rubbing his hands together. 'We can have this sorted in a matter of hours. I'm sure there's no hurry just yet.'

'What do we have to do?' asked Adrienne, leaning forward in anticipation.

'Practically nothing,' he said, giving her hand a reassuring pat.

These people seem to have a penchant for patting hands. It made her skin crawl.

'Our faith, as you may know, is with the god, Salator Crey: the first king of Truphoria. Howard is a product of an immaculate conception: an *extremely* immaculate one, in fact, being that in this case, there isn't a human father or in fact a *mother* either. That makes him the son of Salator Crey.'

Adrienne was more convinced by Qattren's explanations, but that wasn't going to get Howie freed. Instead she turned to a slightly different subject.

'How did you know Howie wasn't born naturally?'

The Duke of Osney's eyes widened. 'Oh, on the grapevine, you know…'

The court eavesdropper, Adrienne realised. 'I see.'

'Now, deity sacrifices are nothing new to any religion,' the priest went on, as though uninterrupted, 'but immaculate children generally do something of *use* before snuffing it, don't they? He was placed here for a reason, but it was not simply to die. We must find out why he was put here to save him. We must contact Salator Crey Himself directly.'

Adrienne stared at him, agape. 'How? I thought it was only the Seven Gods that responded to their following?'

'The Seven Gods are nothing but charlatans, my dear,' Giery said, as though speaking to a small child. 'A pack of meddling sorcerers, nothing more.'

'Some sorcerers are powerful enough to halt their own aging completely,' the Duke supplied. 'That faith was a relatively obscure one until a few decades ago when, for no apparent reason, the Seven – whatever they *actually* are – decided to perform little miracles in their chapels. A total hoax, if you ask me.'

'Of course it is,' the priest said easily. 'Salator Crey would not waste His energy making little objects fly about the place. He only comes in the direst of circumstances: and what more dire than the impending death of His own son?'

'You think He can save him?' Adrienne said, her hopes fading with every word.

'I know He can save him,' Father Giery said. 'I have a theory. This Hole in the Forest business is just a test. The true intention here isn't to throw anybody into oblivion, like Queen Qattren would have you believe. It's a mere test of your character. I believe you are intended to be Howard's wife, Miss Hart.'

Her heart fluttered at the idea.

'All we need to do,' he went on, 'is call upon Him, bring you to the altar to beg His audience, and you simply need to prove your love for Howard. That's all.'

A faint frown tarnished her brow. 'That's all?'

'That's all,' he said with a smile. 'Matters of religion really aren't all that complicated when you get down to it.'

The frown deepened. 'How will He want me to prove my love?'

'A simple offering will suffice. Perhaps you might have a treasured belonging? A gift from your beloved, maybe?'

'Howie did give me a little trinket box,' she said. 'He made it himself. I keep it with me all the time.'

'Excellent!' he exclaimed. 'Made with his own two hands. What more could a god ask for?'

She hesitated. 'And what if Salator Crey doesn't show up?'

'Then we'll be standing around like a group of fools, won't we?' he said with a giggle. 'No harm can come of trying. If it happens to fail, the church will appeal to King Seth for Howard's release. He would be a fool to ignore the influence of the church at this early stage in his reign.'

'I'll keep an eye on him,' the Duke offered, 'try to find out when this death warrant is to be carried out. We will be the first to know if Howard goes anywhere, and it will take him at least a week to get to this Hole in any case.'

'Plenty of time to get ourselves ready,' Father Giery added with another smile.

Adrienne threaded her knuckles together, her grip tightening.

'I suppose I have nothing to lose,' she said finally.

Father Giery clapped his hands. 'Excellent. I will prepare the chapel – the place needs an incredibly deep clean if Our Lord's coming a-calling,' he said jovially. 'You know how it is.'

She smiled tremulously.

The Duke patted her hand again with a sympathetic smile, and the men began to disperse.

'My lord, I don't suppose it would be possible for you to acquire a gold box for this event?' Father Giery asked one of the accompanying lords. 'Preferably solid gold?'

'Why would you need that?' Adrienne wondered aloud.

'To place your offering in. A bit of gold never goes amiss in an offering.'

He winked. It made Adrienne's stomach turn. A voice in her head, a loud one, told her something was amiss with Father Giery. But a smaller voice told her Howie needed her to trust him. She needed to try.

She smiled at him and they dispersed in silence.

~

Howie heard a clang in the darkness.

He bolted upright and banged his head on the ceiling.

'Hello?' he called through the steel door.

The Creys' Tower clearly had something against bars: all that separated one brick-and-mortar wall from the other was a small door about three inches thick, with a peephole at the top to let air in. And noise, from the sounds of it.

Prisoners probably escaped through the bars, Howie thought. He gave his ribs a poke. The stale bread they threw in to him once a day went nowhere. He was weak with hunger.

Another clang echoed into the spyhole, followed by a thunk and an indignant, 'Ah, my bloody head! Who's idea was it to make this ceiling so frigging low?'

A grin crept across Howie's face, despite the cold cell and his aching stomach.

'You should see the ceilings in here,' he called out.

'Howie!' exclaimed another voice.

Ron's beaming face appeared at the peephole.

Archie's grumbling informed Howie that he was loitering somewhere behind him.

'Thank God we finally found you,' Archie said, edging past Ron to see him. 'I've been spat on by about half of my old Serpus neighbours, God know what diseases I've caught.'

'How'd they let you in?' Howie asked in wonder.

'They didn't,' Ron said. 'I, ah, commandeered the keys to the cells.'

He produced a ring of keys with a jolly rattle.

'Along with the bribes the other prisoners have been throwing out at us,' Archie added. 'It pays well, hanging around with a prince of the realm.'

'How did they manage to hang on to money?' Howie said in disgust. 'They took everything off me but the clothes from my back.'

'Well, a purse is slightly less dangerous in the hands of a prisoner than, say, a magic sword,' Archie pointed out.

Howie deflated, thinking mournfully of the blade glinting in the sunlight.

'I s'pose,' he said glumly.

Muffled conversation from the grounds below sent a shiver down Howie's spine.

'They're gonna kill you when they find you in here!'

'So?' said Archie with a grin. 'You didn't think we were gonna leave you in there, did you?'

Howie beamed at him.

Ron unlocked and unbolted the door.

Howie threw himself into Archie's arms, only half because his knees had given up two inches out of the cell.

They descended the stairs, Howie propped between them.

At the bottom, Ron stuck a leg out and swung the front door inward, which had been hanging ajar.

'Going somewhere, are we?' Seth asked lightly.

The three froze.

Half a dozen men surrounded Seth in an arc at his back. All were armed.

Howie groaned.

'If you want me back in my cell, you're gonna have to carry me. Those stairs have buggered my knees as it is.'

'You're starting to sound like me,' Archie said.

'Actually, you saved us a lot of bother,' Seth said with a grin. He gestured to the keep. 'There's a coach outside with your name on it. Won't hurt your knees too much, I shouldn't think.'

'Where are you taking me?'

'To the Hole, of course,' Seth said with glee.

~

A clergy underling burst into the turret.

'Miss Hart, you're needed urgently in the palace chapel,' he gasped.

Adrienne dropped the bandages she was cutting and fled to the grounds.

The slow wait since her chat with Father Giery had apparently come to an abrupt end. The acolyte jogged up the path running along the east side of the keep and crossed the spiralled gardens to the chapel door, kicking gravel into the grass rings with his sandals.

Adrienne followed, her breath shortening with every sprint. She slipped between the doors as he held one open, beckoning her inside.

A long red carpet yawned down the length of the chapel, lined on either side with elaborately carved stone pillars. Father Giery stood at the top of the altar, flanked by the Duke and Philip Manderly.

'The king left with Howard a week ago,' the Duke said, his voice urgent. 'He's scheduled to arrive at the Hole sometime today. We need to call Salator Crey immediately if we want to stop the execution.'

Adrienne's chest pounded. Her belly lurched: the first movement the child within had ever made.

'What do I have to do?'

'Do you have the box?' asked Giery.

Adrienne held it up, glad she had the presence of mind to keep it in her pocket.

'Good.' He paced down the aisle and thrust in front of her a solid gold box, three times the size of her tiny trinket.

She placed the gift inside, already mourning the loss of it.

'Follow me to the altar.'

They strode together up the crimson carpet. Philip Manderly offered her a weak smile as she halted between them, and the Duke gave her an encouraging nod.

'Just kneel right here on this middle step,' Giery directed.

Adrienne obeyed, her hands folded behind her back.

Giery nodded in approval. A table sat in the centre of the altar, one foot wide and three feet long. Giery placed the stacked boxes in the centre, smoothing the white tablecloth beneath it.

'If you'll just close your eyes for me while I light these candles,' he said to Adrienne.

She complied, unsure of the purpose but unwilling to ruin the ritual.

'Mister Manderly, if you wouldn't mind swinging the censer?'

She heard him swinging it in a pendulum motion. The smell wafted over her.

The baby jolted slightly again, as though objecting to the odour.

A wave of affection swept over her. The thought of trading him for Howie seemed alien to her now, as fleeting as it was to begin with. *This is my child*, she realised with a start.

'It's okay, baby,' she whispered, with no idea why. It wasn't as if he could hear her yet.

Father Giery began to mutter in a voice too low for Adrienne to make out. Presumably, it was some ancient language the holy texts had been written in.

The incense smoke climbed up her nose, stinging her eyes.

Giery's prayer appeared to be at an end. His robe rustled closer to her, and an object landed on the step in front of her knees with a gentle thud.

Against Father Giery's wishes and her own self-restraint, Adrienne peeked through her lashes.

The gold box sat open against her knees, Howie's lopsided creation sitting within. A ripple of black velvet hanging behind it alerted to Father Giery's close proximity.

Why is he—

'Drink this, dear,' he said, handing her a goblet.

She accepted the drink and swallowed hard. She coughed and spluttered.

'What is it?'

'Give you a bit of courage, that's all.'

Adrienne disliked the idea of alcohol being in her system while she was carrying a child, but she withheld her feelings on the matter.

There was an expectant silence. Moments of it passed.

Adrienne kept her eyes firmly closed. Her waist and lower back began to cramp, presumably from the awkward position.

'Do I have to say a prayer or—'

Her abdomen clenched. Violently.

Adrienne sucked in a breath.

'What…'

Fear bit into her lungs.

She peered into the discarded cup.

Violet leaves clung to the bottom of the gold chalice. White dust had been sprinkled over it: a smattering still lingered on the edge across from where she had placed her lips. An accelerant.

'No…'

Water ran between her thighs, a warm heavy flow. She couldn't bear to look at it. Looking at it would mean that it wasn't water and it had to be water somehow, it *had* to, it *couldn't* be blood, not from there, she just passed water, that was all…

She stared at Father Giery, helpless with terror.

He closed his eyes to her pleading gaze. There would be no help there.

She turned to the Duke of Osney.

'I'm sorry,' he said. He almost sounded like he meant it. 'It's for the realm.'

The poison twisted her insides. And then there was pain.

~

IV

'Right,' Seth said brightly.

Moat dragged Howie to the edge of the pit.

'Just here will be lovely.'

Howie landed on his knees, aching anew.

The sun was splitting the stones, Howie observed with a flash of anger. Somehow everything terrible seemed to happen to him when it was sunny. The Hole sat in front of him like a lurking beast, the black void pulsing rhythmically. Howie tried not to look at it.

Beams of heat and light poured over the Forest, through every leaf and blade of grass. It landed pleasantly over the prisoners, who kneeled in chains in a row running from prince to peasant.

'You realise there will be war if I'm thrown in there, don't you?' Ron said pleasantly.

Seth paused. 'You're quite right.' He clicked his fingers. 'Better stick him back in the coach. Oh, and make sure he doesn't "commandeer" any more sets of keys, eh?'

Moat grumbled something unpleasant, hauling Ron back to the coach two feet away.

Seth circled the pit, calculating. He formed his thumbs and index fingers into a square and held it against the Hole, as though lining up the composition for a painting.

'Should get a nice view over here,' he said, his teeth bared in concentration. 'Yeah, here should do it. Where's my throne?'

And to Howie's tangible disgust, large heavy pieces of wood coated in gold leaf were hauled over and assembled.

'Aw, look, he had my design made!' Archie said, delighted. 'Knew it would come in useful.'

Howie shot him a disgustful look. '*Cheers*, Archie. Now he has a lovely chair to sit on while he watches me *die*. How *very* useful.'

'It is lovely, isn't it?' Seth said thoughtfully. 'Maybe I won't kill *him*, then. Maybe I'll keep him as a woodworking slave.'

'Would that mean I get a workshop rent-free?'

'Archie!' Howie shrilled, hurt.

'What?' Archie scoffed. 'The world doesn't end when you do, you know.'

'We can only hope,' Seth said.

Seth's ego lent Howie another half an hour of life as the guard struggled to put together Seth's fold-up throne. With Archie's usual loud, unhelpful comments about the pegs, it was eventually stable. Just in the nick of time, too: Howie had been about to give up and roll down the pit by himself.

'Now,' Seth said, reclining with one leg crossed over the other. 'Everybody ready?'

'All except you,' Howie said. 'I thought you were throwing me in?'

'What d'you think they're here for?' Seth scoffed, gesturing at the guards. 'You don't buy a dog and bark yourself, do you? Mister Moat?'

Moat stepped forward, to Howie's relief. He'd gotten on well with Moat. Hopefully well enough to warrant a daring last-minute rescue…?

'You can have the honours, Moat, whenever you're ready,' Seth said, lounging.

'Right,' Moat said uneasily. He placed a hand on each of Howie's shoulders. Seth probably hadn't noticed Moat giving Howie a comforting squeeze while he was at it.

He definitely hadn't noticed the shackle key falling onto Howie's leg.

Howie strived to keep it that way as his fingertips crawled over the shackles towards it.

Luckily Qattren diverted everyone's attention in her quintessential style. She appeared out of nowhere to Seth's right, her voice startling Seth into a violent leap.

'Ah, the theatrical approach, is it? You really are quite insufferable, Seth Crey.'

He pivoted in his seat, facing her. 'Some women find my boyish charm endearing.'

Howie whimpered.

The key had slipped into the grass.

Archie reached over to pat his knee – and snatched up the key while he was at it.

'Attractive, even,' Seth went on. 'Almost as attractive as my attention to detail. Which can be put to horrific uses if Uncle Archie doesn't *hand over that key.*'

Archie winced, surrendering the key to a more loyal member of Seth's entourage.

Howie drew a shuddering breath, his hopes evaporating. He resorted to the last thing he could think of, which was to stall Seth and hope the Hole closed itself out of boredom. *You never know.*

'How's the conception of your next heir coming along, Seth?' he called in the most patronising tones he could muster.

Seth grimaced. 'Mind your own business, Prickface.'

'Not great, then,' Howie said with a smirk. 'Too old for you, is she? Poor Cienne, shunned for a teenager.'

'Oh, why don't you send her a sympathy card?'

Qattren rolled her eyes.

'Oh, no, wait, that would be embarrassing, wouldn't it? Didn't you fancy her at one stage? Imagine, coveting your own mother. Even I never resorted to that.'

'She isn't related to me, it isn't weird!' Howie shouted, his face reddening. 'And what do you care? You never wanted her anyway!'

'How do you know? I could have been saving her for a special occasion.'

'Like the day your old man died?'

The colour drained from Seth's face.

'Nice little celebration once you realised he was gone, is it?'

Seth thrust himself to his feet.

'Right. I was thinking of letting you go free,' he lied, 'you know, find some humane way of sealing the thing, but no, you had to be cruel, didn't you?'

He rolled his sleeves to the elbows methodically, one arm at a time.

The Hole *thrummed* almost gleefully.

Howie began to regret his ingenious plan.

'Stand up,' Seth said, finishing his other sleeve.

Howie struggled to his feet, trembling. His gaze sought out Qattren's. Hers was locked on the Hole in patient expectation.

Archie gawked up at his apprentice with glassy eyes. His earlier thoughts of rent-free workshops evaporated. Howie saw panic in their place, just behind the eyes.

Seth strode to Howie's side, planting a hand on the small of Howie's back.

'I won't forget you, Howard,' Seth sneered into his ear. 'I owe you my child's existence. Perhaps we'll name him after you. No, actually, scratch that, Howie's a dog's name. Maybe we'll give him a dog named after you, then.'

Seth half-grinned at his own wit before licking his lips, eyes locked on the Hole.

'Don't worry about your not-mother, I'll look after her. At least she's still got her looks. I'll have you replaced soon enough, don't you worry about that.'

Howie trembled with silent fury.

'I hope you catch every disease Anna got from the Duke of Osney,' he seethed in reply.

Seth's grin slipped.

'She's diseased?'

His eyes widened.

'She's lain with the *Duke of Osney*?!'

Howie shot him a savage grin, all teeth.

'They don't call her the palace jockey for nothing.'
Seth's face twisted.
He snatched a fistful of Howie's waistband.
Howie's spine went cold.
He sailed into the pit.
'YOU BASTARD!' Archie bellowed.
He threw himself palms-first at Seth, who staggered.
The dry soil around the edge of the pit crumbled.
Archie scrambled backwards.
Seth and Howie soared for the Hole.
'HOWIE!!' Archie shrieked.
With a *fop*, everything stopped.
Archie fell backwards.

A gust of wind slapped him. Literally *slapped* him in the face: it was like being whipped with a towel.

The air surrounding the pit rippled, as if it were a linen sheet being shaken out.

Qattren's head snapped back.

Moat soared backwards into the rest of the guards.

The coach lifted onto two wheels, halted for a moment and fell back into position again.

Archie's craftsmanship had proven itself: the fold-up throne was seemingly unaffected.

Seth and Howie landed on the bottom of the pit in a heap.

All this happened in a second: one second of Howie's life he didn't think he would live to see.

Howie shoved Seth off his arm and sat bolt upright.

The Hole was gone. The pit it had resided in remained, but the circle of pure darkness had vanished into thin air.

Howie patted his chest and stomach, ran both hands through his hair.

'Why am I still here?' he called up.

Archie faced Qattren in bemusement, and his face slackened

The girl was white as a sheet.

Seth twisted around, jerking his gaze around him for the Hole.

'Where'd it go?' he shrilled. 'It was here a minute ago!'

'It's gone,' Archie said, distant. 'It fopped out of existence just before you hit the ground.'

'Why didn't this *git* fop out of existence with it?!' Seth shrieked, shoving Howie's arm.

Seth threw himself to his feet, hauling Howie up with him.

'Get off me, you lunatic! It's gone!' Howie snapped at him.

Seth dragged Howie just over halfway up the high slope.

'We'll try this again, shall we?' he said viciously.

'For Christs' sake, it's gone!' Howie wailed.

Seth threw him into the pit again via his jerkin.

Howie tumbled across the width of it, sliding to a halt up the opposite slope.

Qattren stared into space, her face a picture of abject horror.

Seth stormed across the pit, to throw Howie again into the Hole that was no longer there.

'No,' she said.

Howie squealed, soaring into the pit again.

'She can't have,' Qattren said, her voice hollow, 'no, no, no, she wouldn't, she…'

Howie cried out in pain.

Seth picked him up by the armpits and shook him.

'TAKE HIM!!' he howled into the heavens.

Archie watched the two in avid interest.

Qattren barged past him.

She skidded into the pit, her skirts gathered around her knees, and dropped to a halt against Seth's arm.

He released Howie to steady her.

'I know what happened,' she gasped, close to tears. 'I should have told you earlier, but I didn't think she would actually…'

Seth frowned. 'What are you on about?'

She met his gaze, her eyes filling with tears.

This alarmed him, and Howie too. Qattren had never cracked her steely exterior before.

She snatched Seth's hand in her own. Before he could wriggle away, she grabbed Howie's in her free hand and the three exploded into dust.

Howie tumbled again, this time through purple landscape. The Forest sped past him in a blur of disembodied trees until a road opened up, leading them soaring uphill to the familiar walls of Creys' Keep.

To his alarm, they soared through those as well, making a supernatural beeline to the palace chapel. The north green surrounded them and gradually returned to the colour green as they landed on their knees, still clutching each of Qattren's hands.

Howie gulped down an intense feeling of nausea. He'd just felt himself *slot* back together. How does Ron do this on a regular basis? He shivered. The feeling was hideous.

Vomit burst onto the gravel path before them.

Seth clearly felt very much the same way.

Qattren wrenched her hand from Howie's grip. Her other hand, Howie noticed, still encased Seth's on her right. She jerked Seth to his feet and led him down the path to the chapel, paying no notice to Howie.

Well, I know where I'm not wanted.

He got up and followed them anyway.

He wished he hadn't.

Blood dripped all over the altar inside, presumably from a large pool dribbling down the steps. Three figures bolted for the back door as Howie entered, and he could see why. It was like a heathen sacrifice had taken place.

A fourth figure knelt in the blood.

They walked the length of the chapel, Howie a couple steps behind.

'What happened in here?' Seth asked softly. 'Who is that?'

Howie's eyesight was clearly superior to Seth's. He knew who it was immediately.

'Shit, shit, shit, fuck!' he hissed, barging between Qattren and Seth.

Adrienne knelt on the middle step of the altar, her head hanging down, the ends of her hair soaking up blood from her lap.

Howie burst forward and scooped her up.

'What happened?' he gasped, settling her into his lap. 'Tell me, tell me what happened…'

His gaze wandered downwards. 'Oh Christ.'

Blood seeped through her skirts, climbing the hem of the blouse she wore. He didn't know a girl so slight could hold so much blood.

'They took the baby,' Adrienne whispered, ever so faintly, '…so it wouldn't take you…'

Howie's eyes locked onto the chalice, wide-eyed.

'What did you do?' he breathed, horrified.

Adrienne swayed backward.

Howie caught her around her back, cradling the back of her head to settle it onto his shoulder.

Qattren folded both hands around Seth's left.

'I told her *not to*.' Tears flowed freely down Qattren's cheeks now. 'She asked me to help her, I thought I had talked her out of this. I told her it was too late for that…'

'Worked, though,' Seth said, his voice deadpan.

Qattren choked. 'What?'

'She saved her beloved little Howard.' His face fell slack. 'Just like she planned all along.'

Adrienne whimpered something.

Howie ducked his head closer to hers.

'I didn't know,' she said, breathless. 'He just wanted… the box… I didn't know he wanted the…'

Seth pushed Qattren's hands away. He strode up the altar, heedless of the blood soaking his shoes and splashing against the end of his trouser legs. He climbed the dais and peered over the table, into the solid gold box.

He turned, his gaze locked on Howie.

'What's in there?' Howie asked hoarsely.

Seth didn't answer. He just glared at Howie as if he had forced the poison into her mouth himself.

Howie decided he'd had enough of Seth's hatred for one day.

He slid both arms under Adrienne and lifted her upright as carefully as he could. He ignored Seth and Qattren and hurried out of the chapel.

Seth and Qattren ignored him right back.

Their attention was fully absorbed by the blood, a trail leading from the congealing pool on the steps to the table. Their eyes refused to acknowledge the horror of the previously pristine white tablecloth and the gold box, now splattered in dark red droplets like everything else.

Seth's stomach roiled. The sight of the unborn sacrifice lingered behind his eyelids, even though the gold box had been completely empty when he peered inside it.

The interior of the gold box glittered, unlike the blood-coated exterior. It had been cleaned out.

The sacrifice, and the trinket box it had lain in, had vanished into thin air, just like the Hole.

~

Howie paced across the gardens in a daze, Adrienne limp against his shoulder. They must have looked a sight in the pristine palace gardens: he felt eyes on him from all directions, aghast. He found he didn't much care. Passers-by parted in his path. He paid them no notice. Blood dribbled from his hands and from Adrienne, leaving a trail in the cultivated lawn. *I'm ruining their grass. Oh well.*

Someone had run to fetch the medic. Erik met him halfway across the sound greens and scooped Adrienne into his own arms.

Howie collapsed a moment after. One of Erik's assistants

helped him back upright.

'She's carrying a baby,' he said.

The assistant half-carried Howie to the turret in Erik's wake.

He was deposited into a chair as Adrienne lay flat on her back on a trolley to one side. Erik sniffed her breath and lifted an eyebrow, as if confirming something to himself. Blood still dripped onto the flagstones beneath her.

'She's carrying a baby,' Howie said again, in case nobody heard.

Erik glanced up and met his gaze.

'She isn't anymore.'

His words met a stricken silence.

Erik turned back to Adrienne. 'She's bleeding too fast, she must have taken an accelerant. I have a fix for that.'

Howie stared into space. 'The baby, though.'

The assistant caught the pallor of his face and passed him a sick basin just in time.

~

Cienne sprinted into the main hall to find Seth in his throne, leaning his forearms on his knees and looking desolate.

'Oh Seth.'

He didn't reply.

Cienne approached hesitantly.

She had just seen Howie crossing the gardens. She and Queen Eleanor had waited a full half hour for word on what happened. Eleanor was still in tears when she left her in the gazebo with Lilly.

'Poor Seth,' she wept.

Cienne thought 'poor unborn child' was the more appropriate lament.

She sat on her throne beside him.

A lone tear rolled down his right cheek.

Cienne planted a hand on his shoulder blades and rubbed in a circle, trying to ease the grief out.

She gave him a moment to compose himself. All thoughts of his attitude to her for the past couple of weeks were gone at this point.

'She must have been tricked,' she said. 'That priest you mentioned, who tried to kill you. He must have come here and tricked her into sacrificing it.'

Seth struggled to clear the lump in his throat. 'She did it on purpose. Qattren told me.'

Cienne's windpipe grew cold. 'She…'

He nodded once. 'She wanted Qattren to help her with it.

Qattren refused. The child was too far along, it would have caused him physical harm…' His voice broke. He cleared his throat to steady it. 'So she got our priest to do it instead.' He drew a shuddering breath. 'The Hole's gone now, it's gone for ever.'

Cienne sat in stunned silence.

'Why?' she whispered. 'It needed him, how… how did she even do that? *Why* would she even do that?'

'Because she didn't want *him* to go in there instead,' he said fiercely, his voice wavering again.

'We could have tested this with a criminal,' Cienne said, aghast. 'She could have appealed you and asked us to take someone from the jails first. Why didn't she just do that?'

'She did appeal to me,' Seth whimpered, fighting through tears, 'I refused her, I wanted him dead and I refused her, I'm stupid, I'm so *bloody stupid…*'

He buried his head in his elbows.

Cienne stared at him.

'This isn't your doing,' she said sharply. 'Hang her.'

'I can't,' he said hoarsely, his voice muffled. 'If it were anyone else I would, but it's her…'

Cienne's chest stung.

Seth sobbed and spluttered incessantly, his narrow shoulders shaking.

Cienne heaved a sigh and placed her internal injury aside.

'You need to grieve,' she said finally. 'Have them both dismissed from the palace. It will be easier to heal without them lingering on the premises.'

Seth's head lifted. His eyes sunk into hers. 'You never wanted him dead, did you?'

She considered lying. Then she sighed. 'No, not really. I still feel… responsible for him, in a way. It wouldn't have sat right with me if he had died.'

'Of course it wouldn't,' Seth said softly. 'I can't imagine wanting to feel something like this.' Pain crossed his features again. 'I'm so sorry.'

'Why?' she asked gently.

'For putting you through all this.' He swallowed hard. 'I put you through all this hurt, I didn't understand… I've been such a child…'

She took his hand, threaded her fingers between his. 'It doesn't matter anymore.'

He sniffed. They sat in silence for a bit.

'Thank you for staying with me,' he said through a clogged nose.

She squeezed his hand.

'I didn't leave ten years ago when you broke a dinner plate over my head,' she said with a smile. 'I'm not leaving now.'

Seth kissed the back of her hand. 'Good.'

~

V

Howie entered the chapel three weeks later and bowed at the casket before him. Not at the king inside it, or what was left of him, that is, but at the figure of who was apparently Salator Crey hanging from a noose on the wall at the top of the altar.

He supposed it was probably best to bow now that there was tangible proof he existed. Even if he did hate the bastard with every ounce of his strength.

It was beyond Howie why any respectable religion would have a monument of their god hanging by his throat as their main motif. The three Christs were there, holding sick children and so forth, and then there was their dad next to them, choking to death. By a narrative point of view, the layout of the church was flawed. Surely cutting him free would be higher in their priorities than wiping a runny nose.

Howie sighed heavily. It was the first of three days in which King Theo Crey would be on exhibition in the chapel of Serpus before being paraded around the kingdom for nine weeks. They had wrapped King Theo in elegant silver cloth. It only served to accentuate just how much of his body was missing, burned away in the makeshift pyre. No small wonder the Creys were nowhere to be seen. Howie had only been allowed access due to an assumption that he was Seth.

His blood boiled. Father Giery had had the nerve to shake his hand after he'd heard about the rift – *shake his hand*, as if he'd saved the world. As if it mattered to Howie that the child-murdering monster was impressed with him. Adrienne's recovery was slow, but not slow enough to hinder her ability to talk. She'd told him all about Father Giery's trick. And the Duke of Osney had stood up in front of Seth Crey and his council and told them it was all her idea, the bastard. Howie wished King Theo were here. King Theo would have given them what for.

Howie gulped down a lump in his throat and stared at the king's remains.

He had liked him. He was alright for a raving lunatic. He might have been a bit suss for wanting to maim his own son to make a point, but it wasn't as if Seth didn't deserve it.

He wondered who had killed King Theo. There were hardly a remote number of suspects: the Hornes had always had it in for him, except for Ron of course, and the Emmetts hated everyone that drew breath. Just about everyone had it in for him, except for Howie. Only who said it was someone who knew him? Perhaps it was some priest, thinking he was the Antichrist?

A warm flush crawled up the back of Howie's neck. Another death on his conscience. It was as if he'd as good as killed him himself. He could scarcely imagine being driven to such an act, coming up behind a man with a vicious weapon and—

And the image came into startling focus.

Hang on.

Did he actually—?

He wouldn't, would he?

Howie's eyes bulged.

The doors burst open.

He quickly composed himself as heels thumped gently on the blue carpet. He eyed the figure from the corner of one eye as they knelt briefly at Salator Crey's macabre monument before rising to stand at his side.

He tried to catch Qattren's eye.

She didn't give him a second glance – or even a first one, come to that. Nothing new there.

'Good morning, your highness,' he said politely.

She paid him no notice. She just gazed at King Theo's corpse, her mind a million leagues away.

'How are you?'

She didn't respond.

Howie heaved a sigh. His innate politeness was beginning to exhaust him.

'Who d'you think did it, then?' he asked suddenly.

Qattren glanced at him sharply.

'Killed the king, I mean.' He discarded any form of consideration altogether, purely out of spite.

She looked him up and down in distaste. 'I know exactly who did it.'

He froze. She said it calmly, as though King Theo meant nothing to her. Wasn't she supposed to be his mistress once? Or had he gotten that part wrong?

'Well, I reckon Seth did him in,' he said idly, his gaze returning to the corpse. 'Gets to shag his way round the castle all he wants now, doesn't he?'

She stared impassively ahead. 'If you divulge this half-baked hypothesis to anyone, I will kill you myself.'

Howie stepped back in alarm. 'What? Why?'

She glowered at him. 'Who physically attacked King Theo makes no matter. You are the cause of this mess. And it isn't over yet, not by a long shot. One of you will end up killing the other, and as you can tell, I want Seth to live a very long life ahead of you.'

With that she swept out.

Howie's eyes followed her as the doors were closed behind her.

'I didn't do anything,' he said, but as usual, nobody but King Theo bothered to listen.

~

Cienne sat on the edge of the fountain, losing herself in blissful peace. Now that the summer was drawing to a close, the bright flowers were disappearing, leaving nothing but browning leaves and verdant greenery. She soaked up the dim sunlight and the sound of running water behind her, her mind on Seth's mental state.

He hadn't left their quarters since that day. With the funeral arrangements, Cienne only saw him at night, and the few times she checked in on him during the day, he was in the same place: tucked up in bed, eyes clenched tightly away from the world.

Except for when she entered the room. He was opening up to her, she thought with a warm flutter. He had even begun holding her at night, though she felt it was more for his own comfort rather than her gratification.

She heaved a sigh and wracked her brains for a way to ease his suffering.

A shadow fell over her.

'You know, this is the second time I've stumbled upon you looking terribly depressed,' Emmett Jr said.

Cienne favoured him with a half-smile. 'Sorry. It's my default expression, I'm afraid.'

'No need to apologise.' He held out a hand. 'I come at the behest of a higher power. My father's coach waits at the inner portcullis. We were wondering if you would like that visit to the new manor?'

Cienne paused. 'You know, I would love the distraction,' she said thoughtfully. 'Is it very far from here?'

'An hour by coach. The weather is ideal for it, actually.' He hesitated momentarily. 'We were hoping to be able to have Felicity along with us, but alas the Hornes have not deigned to respond to any of our messages.'

'No?' Cienne said, frowning. 'She hasn't responded in the last three weeks at all?'

'No. It's... concerning, to be frank.'

Cienne eyed him. 'Accompany me to the coach. We'll speak with Lord Emmett together. If there's any way I can help, I will. It isn't like Felicity not to reach out to her family.'

She accepted a hand up.

Moments later, the Emmett family's coach trundled down the main road to Serpus.

~

Half an hour later it trundled back up again at high speed.

Emmett Jr leapt from it and sprinted into the keep.

Seth's peaceful sleep was soon interrupted by crashing doors.

'Oh, piss off, will you?' he shouted out of the bedroom door.

Emmett skidded to a halt at the doorframe. 'Your highness, Princess Cienne has been abducted.'

Seth bolted upright. 'What?'

'She was accompanying my family to my manor, we were accosted at knifepoint in Serpus,' he rattled off rapidly. 'She was dragged into a coach. I came back as fast as I could to alert you, your highness.'

Seth stared into space.

Emmett waved a hand in the air irately. 'Your highness?'

Seth blinked rapidly. 'Yes, fine, I'll round up some men. Any idea where they went?'

'None, your highness. Their accomplices warded us back until the coach disappeared.' Emmett fought to catch his breath. 'The coach bore the colour grey, your majesty. We suspect the Hornes may be behind it. My father is dispatching men as we speak. Shall I send word to other districts?'

Seth frowned at the doorframe. 'Yes. Do that. Yes.'

Emmett bolted out.

Seth sat between twisted sheets, stricken. *No. No. Not her too.*

He quickly shook himself off.

'GUARDS!!'

~

Howie watched Archie re-organise his brand-new workbench for the fifteenth time that afternoon.

'Surely it's perfect now?' he asked tiredly.

'Not… quite. Hold these.'

Archie shoved several tools into Howie's arms.

Howie exhaled, his gaze drifting in Adrienne's direction. She was stretched out sideways in her favourite armchair, dozing under a quilted blanket she had made herself a few years ago. Some colour had returned to her face now that she was eating properly again, but not much. At least it was an improvement.

He had been expecting tears. *Many* tears. But there was nothing. To be judged by her lack of reaction, she was feeling nothing. And he couldn't ask Archie for advice because Archie had no idea the baby had even *existed*. She was mugged, he was told. That was all Adrienne wanted him to know.

Not that Archie found anything suspicious about the story – he had his own problems after trying to shove Seth Crey into oblivion. After being forgotten about outside the Hole, Ron had to guide Archie into Qattren's fortress and give him ten cups of tea before he would calm down. Then he had to flee on an abandoned horse after a hoard of Faeries tried to ravage him during a call of nature. It was the most traumatic afternoon of Archie's life – even if he was a bit pleased by the Faerie women's reaction to him.

Archie was still so terrified of Seth's wrath, he had tucked himself away in a recently disused premises of Keith's in the darkest back alley of Arthur Stibbons' Street and gone so far as to change his workshop name to 'Arnold Hort's Carpentry Museum'.

He needn't have worried. Seth hadn't given him a second thought. It was Adrienne that Howie was worried about.

He dropped the tools onto the floor, much to Archie's annoyance, and perched on the arm of her chair.

'You alright?' he asked, stroking her forearm.

'Mm-hmm,' she said with a thin smile.

'Alright then.' He paused. 'But if you want to talk about it, you know where I am. Or not talk about it, either's fine. We can just cuddle if that's better. Cuddling's easier. Not that I want you to feel like you can't talk to me, that wouldn't be ideal, your health is more important than me having a difficult conversation or anything—'

'I know,' she whispered. 'I know.'

She sat upright and wrapped her arms around his waist, her face pressed to his side.

He wrapped both hands around her head helplessly.

'Oi, Loverboy,' Archie snapped.

Howie and Adrienne flinched away from each other.

'Last I heard, you still worked for *me*, remember?'

'Sorry,' he said hastily, stroking Adrienne's hair as he left.

'Leave him alone, Archie,' Adrienne scolded. 'He's just being sweet.'

'Not on my time,' Archie retorted. 'Now clean the tools you so unceremoniously dumped on the dusty ground or I'll be forced to actually kill you for deflowering my niece.'

Howie rolled his eyes. 'I haven't even touched her yet.'

'And you won't with that tone,' Archie said, cuffing his ear.

Adrienne beamed at them both and curled back up in her seat.

A cacophony outside diverted them from the workbench.

Howie wandered to the door to peer out, ignoring Archie's eyerolling.

A small army of royal guards marched down Arthur Stibbons' Arm in formation, fully armed to the teeth and searching the alleys.

'Get away from the door!' Archie barked at him.

A man Howie recognised from the palace guard waved from the main street.

Howie waved back.

'Don't wave at him!!' Archie shrieked.

'Archie, calm down, you're causing a scene,' Adrienne said sleepily, hiding in her elbows.

'Of course I'm making a scene! He's gonna get us killed!'

Marbrand met Howie at the door.

Archie dropped himself behind the desk, throwing a length of floor covering over himself.

Marbrand frowned in at him.

'He's agoraphobic,' Adrienne explained.

'*Severely* agoraphobic,' Howie added.

'Ah.'

'So what's going on out there?' Howie asked as guards jogged past them.

'New queen was abducted. Bit silly of her leaving the castle unattended after a king's murder, but that's princesses for you. You haven't seen a suspicious-looking coach pass by in the last two, three hours?'

Howie shook his head. 'I'll come with you if you think I can help.'

'If you can really saddle the hell beast of the Creys, that would be a great help.'

'Can do.'

Marbrand paused. 'I was joking.'

'No yeah, I actually can,' said Howie.

Marbrand narrowed his eyes. 'You can actually steer that thing around without being seriously injured?'

'Yeah, it's like riding a horse.'

Marbrand shot Adrienne an imploring glance.

Adrienne shrugged apathetically.

'Some handsome knights slay dragons,' she said blithely. 'Mine tames them.'

Howie smirked at her.

Marbrand lifted an eyebrow. 'Handy out. Shall we head?'

Howie side-shuffled a couple paces to kiss Adrienne goodbye before jogging out.

'Who took her, then?' Howie said, squinting into the blinding sunlight.

'Dunno,' Marbrand said. 'But if you ask me, this whole affair stinks of Aaliyaa Horne.'

~

Once the guards had been dispatched across the city, Seth quickly returned to his previous post: curled in the foetal position in the centre of his bed.

He had been crying again, Anna noticed, standing over his bed with her arms folded in irate irritability. She didn't hold with men who cried. Her husband never cried, and he was a sailor who had been abandoned by his parents at birth. Why should a rich king be any exception?

She kicked the side of his bed.

'Not going after them, then?'

Seth peeked up at her through his lashes – and two folds of silk sheets.

'No.'

Anna lifted her eyes heavenward. 'So you're just going to sit there and blub all day?'

Seth jerked his head upright to scowl at her.

'What use would I be?' he demanded, through tears. 'I couldn't even stop a girl from killing my child.'

Anna exhaled deeply and swung her head back to stare at the ceiling. Then she grasped a handful of his duvet and yanked it away from him.

He recoiled, tugging his nightshirt over his knees.

'Give me that back!' he shrieked.

'It was scarcely a quickening of the womb,' she snarled. 'Not even human. Get over it.'

Seth eyeballed her stormily.

'You have more pressing matters to attend to than your self-centred depression. Queen Cienne has been snatched by the Hornes. What to know why?'

'Enlighten me,' he sneered, cradling his shins.

'I spotted him coming out of the courtyard, a couple hours before it happened. Vladimir. The good-looking one with the Far Isles look?'

The phrasing caught his attention. He met her gaze sharply.

'Cienne had been in the courtyard all morning, alone,' she said. 'Probably waiting for him.'

Seth paused. 'He abducted her in the courtyard?'

Anna rolled her eyes. '*No.* She met him there before the "abduction". She ran off with him.'

Seth sat completely still. 'And I should believe her *biggest* fanatic because…'

'Because she's got it in for you. For taking a mistress.' She shrugged. 'I heard her talking with him before the king died. They were planning to kill you and elope.'

She doubled over, her breath tickling his ear.

'You see, I keep an ear out for these things,' she whispered. 'I'm loyal to you that way. I seem to be the only woman with your best interests at heart.'

She straightened up, sweeping her long hair onto one shoulder.

'Get rid of the traitor you're married to and I'll show you what interests I have in mind.'

Seth's eyes narrowed.

'Keep talking,' he drawled, in a lilting, interested tone.

Anna smiled faintly.

~

A carriage pulled by two horses screeched to a halt.

Howie saw Ron emerge, looking anxious.

'Howie!' he called, jogging over. 'What happened that day the Hole closed? Qattren finally came home in tears. The woman *never* sheds tears. What went on at Creys' Keep?'

Howie glanced around.

The last of the summer heat acquainted itself intimately with the armour-clad party on the outskirts of Serpus, in a close-set smattering of cottages known as the village of Teal. The sun shone hard and hot on the thatched roofs as the knights congregated around them – specifically around Lyseria, who had grown overtired and was making unpleasant noises to passing villagers.

Howie made sure none of the sweaty soldiers were listening before leaning to Ron.

'Adrienne was carrying Seth's child,' he said. 'Seth's uncle caught wind of it and hired a priest to… sacrifice the child in my place.' Another wave of fury consumed him briefly. 'They tricked Adrienne into going along with it. We found her bleeding on the chapel floor when we got back.'

Ron paled. 'No wonder she was upset. How is Adrienne bearing up?'

Howie sighed.

'She doesn't hate me,' he said finally. 'It's my fault, she ought to despise me. I consider that bad, to be honest.'

Ron wrapped a hand around his shoulder. 'She must really love you.'

Howie half-smiled. 'The feeling's mutual.'

Ron gave a small, sad smile.

Marbrand sidled to them with a casual salute.

'His majesty has sent word for us to return to the palace. Will you be joining us?'

Howie hesitated for a moment.

'I suppose so,' he relented.

Ron blinked, bewildered.

Howie gave him a brief rundown of recent events.

'Marbrand thinks your mum might have something to do with it, for some reason,' he finished with a shrug.

'Wouldn't surprise me,' Ron said darkly. 'She's a loon.'

Marbrand's eyes widened. He wagged a finger.

'Your highness, I have a letter to give to you,' he said, rummaging in his breastplate.

'Oh, lovely,' Ron said brightly.

Similarly, something occurred to Howie.

'You said to Vladimir before,' he said, 'back in Stoneguard, that I looked like "the bloke that nicked his girly-girlfriend"? Does this have anything to do with Cienne and your brother—?'

'Being a couple?' Ron chortled. 'Nah, he wishes. He's been in love with her portrait since he was six. My mother was trying to get them married. I wouldn't be surprised if she's trying to force it still.'

Marbrand rifled for his shirt pocket. 'Hang on, I nearly have it.'

'Take your time,' Ron said absently.

A coach rolled up.

'Need a lift, gents?' Moat asked from the reins. 'Lyseria's getting narky, I wouldn't chance riding her back to the castle.'

Marbrand struggled with the breastplate. His hand was stuck.

Ron and Howie climbed aboard the coach with thanks, the letter forgotten.

Marbrand brandished the letter into the air in triumph as the coach rattled off.

'Oh, you forgot your letter,' Howie said a moment later.

'Oh. Never mind, can't be that important,' Ron said with a shrug.

'So anyway, your mum?'

'She's a religious fanatic,' Ron said, rolling his eyes to the ceiling. 'She had a dream about him kissing a rose and figured the Seven were telling them to marry into the Fleurelles. Except my father thought King Fleurelle was a prat, so he refused.'

'Does Vladimir want this?'

'He used to,' Ron said. 'Until recently. He was mouthing off about her last time I saw him. Something about her being rude.'

There was a brief silence broken only by stamping hooves and rolling wheels.

Hesitantly, Ron said, 'You don't still fancy her, do you? Because she is technically your—'

'I know,' Howie said sharply. 'That's why I'm worried about her.' He fell silent for a second. 'But even if I did fancy her, she's not technically related to me. She just… made me. Out of Seth. *Only*,' he emphasised.

'Alright,' Ron said easily.

'Fact, biologically, I'm Seth's much younger,' Howie rambled, 'kind of *almost* identical twin.'

'Of course.'

Howie paused.

'Not that it matters, anyway. I like Adrienne much better. *She* never abandoned me in a forest with a strange bloke in a robe.'

'No,' Ron mused. 'She saved your life. As awful as it turned out, it's kind of special.'

Howie stared out at the countryside, his face drawn. He made no comment.

~

VI

'No,' they said as one.

'What?' snapped Seth. 'What do you mean, no?'

On Seth's orders, the entire male population of Serpus gathered in the palace green for a sit-down – or rather a stand-up, seeing as sitting on the ground in Adem was like eating a plague-ridden rat topped with laxative.

Seth stood in the front porch of the keep, overseeing his people with unease. When he had sent the runners out with the announcement that morning, he hadn't envisioned quite so many pitchforks to be in attendance.

Anna stood on his left and Jimmy on his right, both with their hands behind their backs.

Ready to bolt inside should any sharp objects come soaring his way, Seth sidled closer to Jimmy.

'We don't want any part of your disagreements!' called a resident of Serpus. 'We've children to feed! Businesses to run! We can't run around after your missus!'

'What else are you bloody here for?' Seth exclaimed.

'Might want to rephrase, sir,' Jimmy politely suggested, 'there's a man sharpening something towards the back of the crowd.'

Seth sighed. 'Look, we'll look after you! We'll give you food, wages, armour, weapons—'

'Not much good to us if that Horn-ee woman finds us,' objected a grizzled war veteran. 'She's a banshee, that one! She'd put a curse on us!'

'Oh, hardly,' said Jimmy, derisive.

'Think of our families!' a resident called. 'We can't leave them fret about us being killed by witches! What will happen if war breaks out? Only no money, no food, no home if people are fighting outside our door! I've been through all that the day you had your upset, with the mad Faerie woman's fire magic! We ain't doing it again!'

The crowd erupted into bellowing agreement.

Seth tried vainly to quiet them with a series of platitudes and finally managed it with a good old-fashioned, 'SHUT UP!'

The cacophony ceased.

'I shouldn't have to be begging you!' he shouted. 'I'm your king, I shouldn't even have to ask! If it were my father, you'd be charging over there as we speak!'

'He knew what he was doing!' someone pointed out. 'You've been in power for all of two minutes, mate, and you want us traipsing across continent to settle a bleeding marital dispute?'

Seth sucked in a breath.

'Contrary to popular belief,' he snarled, 'not all noblemen send for the troops for help with things like taking a tricky shit! She didn't run away! She was taken by the Hornes! The entire point of this is someone committed an act of war. Not just someone: a real *asshole*, and guess who his mother is?'

The silence said, 'The banshee.'

'This isn't me flexing my privilege,' Seth snarled. 'I am asking for your help. A hostile member of nobility has snatched my wife from her cousin's coach. I can't get her back on my own. I'm not asking you to launch yourselves into the path of a million flaming arrows. I am asking you to help me look for her.'

'Get your troops and shit to do it?' an impertinent voice piped up.

'I can't,' Seth said, waving his hands helplessly. 'I can't incite war this early in my reign. My councillors have refused me. They prefer to confirm the loyalty of Stoneguard's nobility over the safety of their queen. I have no wish to enable powerful lords to take what doesn't belong to them – because if they think they can get away with claiming the queen of Adem, they will not hesitate in hurting my people. *You.*

'They have allies with money and influence, but I don't have that. I never spent my adolescence with people like that: I spent it with real people like you, people who looked after me when I was ill instead of brushing it under the rug! My interests are with you, not myself. If you help me with this, we will go on with our lives as normal. I just need this one favour of you.' He met several gazes, imploring. 'Please?'

There was a ponderous silence.

'Nah,' one said unanimously.

'Oh, come on!' he shrieked in exasperation. 'What do I have to do for you people? I'll do it, whatever you want! I'll give you gold, I'll give you silver, I'll give you…'

He gestured about himself helplessly and glanced at Anna.

'Whores,' he said, pointing at her.

Another silence.

'How many?' a young voice asked.

'A whole one *each*,' Seth said eagerly.

'Ooh,' muttered some of the younger population.

'I'll do it!' the young man said. 'Let it not be said I'm unpatriotic.'

'Me in all!' piped up another.

'And me!'

'I'll have one too, if they're going!'

'Ah,' Jimmy sighed in relief, 'the younger generation.'

'Thank God, we're *saved*,' Anna spat at them.

Seth shot her a side-glance. 'What's with you?'

Anna glowered at him. 'What, the whore? Nothing.'

'Whore?' he said quickly. 'I never said "whore", I said "girls".'

He made an 'oops' face at Jimmy.

Jimmy craned his neck to meet Anna's gaze.

'He did,' he said loyally.

Anna scowled at the pair of them.

As the crowd dissipated, some heading for the armoury, most for home, dust began to swirl on the now virtually empty gardens.

'Wind's picking up,' Seth said.

Jimmy frowned. 'What wind?'

The dust began to take form…

… and Qattren stepped out of nowhere.

'A word, your highness?' she asked politely.

The three stared in utter disbelief.

'How did you…' Jimmy trailed off.

Anna flopped onto the ground.

'Your highness,' Qattren pressed.

Seth gaped at her.

'Uh, cuh, come inside,' he said, gesturing to the door.

Jimmy watched her follow Seth into the throne room. They had to step over Anna's unconscious body on the way.

As the door shut, he quietly contemplated what he'd just seen and neatly threw up in the corner of the porch.

~

Seth stalked to his throne, spun on one heel, and sat.

'Can I help you?' he asked, trying to gather his bearings.

'Actually, no,' Qattren said. 'I've come to help you.'

Seth blinked, nonplussed. 'Why? You despise me.'

'That as the case may be,' she said, 'I happen to despise the opposition more.'

Her steely exterior softened, ever so slightly.

'How have you been holding up?'

Seth frowned slightly. 'Fine, thank you.' He shifted slightly in discomfort.

Qattren licked her lips. 'You have my sincere condolences for the loss of your child.'

Seth tugged his sleeves over his hands.

Qattren hung her head. 'I wish I had properly prevented this.

It was a lapse of judgement on my part, to let her leave with those thoughts in her head when there could have been another way.'

Seth was engrossed in his sleeves, twisting them together at the ends.

'We were both responsible in that regard,' he said quietly.

He met her gaze through his lashes.

'Thank you for the kind words.'

Qattren smiled faintly.

Seth leaned an elbow on the arm of his throne, planting his chin on his palm to observe her.

She seemed to have a feather fetish, he noted, eyeing her dove-feathered gown.

'So you wish to fight for me, is it?' he said jovially. 'You'll ruin that dress.'

'This dress has seen more battles than you've had hot dinners. It will suffice. However, I'm not just offering myself. I have troops for you.'

He narrowed his eyes, picturing the stature of the average Faerie. He thought of his payment plan with the young men outside and felt a glint of optimism. *Kill two birds with one stone.*

'What kind of troops?' he asked opportunistically.

'Demons.'

His plans evaporated. He shot her a sideways glance. 'Why? What do *you* have against the Hornes?'

'It's Aaliyaa Horne in particular,' she said, calmly as ever. 'Their abduction of your wife, no doubt her half-baked plan, has put her sons in an impossible position. As the wife of one of those sons, it is my place to intervene. Vladimir relies too much on his frankly unhinged mother. The Hornes' reign has come to a swift end. I propose to bind Stoneguard and Adem once more under your power.'

'Oh? And what about Ron? Or have you even asked him?'

'We have discussed it. He has no interest in ruling a country whatsoever. His position in the Forest is adequate enough to satisfy him.'

'So I don't get the Forest?'

Her brow furrowed slightly. 'Um, no. That is still mine. Unless I've also abducted a member of your immediate family and simply let it slip my mind?'

Seth arched an eyebrow. 'I see.' He rose. 'So you wouldn't be planning to, I don't know, steal the lot from me once we win?'

'Of course not.'

He squinted at her. 'I hope you're sure because I intend to rule them.'

'Absolutely. I have great confidence in you.'

He snorted.

'I don't,' he said, frankly. 'Why should you?'

Qattren gazed at him, almost fondly.

'You love your family,' she said. 'You give off the air of a selfish man, but when it matters, you come through for them. That's why no usurper has ever overthrown the Creys. Anyone can offer peace, prosperity, protection – but loyalty is inherent, not offered. People will always turn to the Creys.

'You descend from an honest clan. Some will hate you, many will fear you, but all will follow you. When it counts.' She paused to inspect his bemused frown. 'You have merits, Seth, albeit heavily buried beneath petty spite and superiority. It takes some study to discover them, but they're deeply rooted.'

Seth's eyes thinned again. 'Are you trying to get me into bed?

Qattren blinked. 'I beg your pardon?'

'It sounds a bit like you are.'

'I'm sorry, you appear to have me mistaken for your *chambermaid*,' she said icily. 'As your father informed you before his murder, I have been around for a long time. Little boys do not interest me.'

Seth's upper lip twitched.

'If my intention was unclear,' she went on, the effects of Seth's 'merits' swiftly fading, 'the point I was making is that you will make an excellent king. I don't make this point because I believe it – bedding anyone who throws a compliment at you qualifies as a bad move,' she added with a cynical smirk. 'I tell you this to convince you, no one else. You are the one who needs to convince everyone else, and you will. Soon.'

He lifted a sceptical eyebrow and thrust himself to his feet.

Qattren eyed him in interest.

Seth strode to the wall behind his throne, to where King Theo's ornamental weaponry adorned the white bricks. He fingered the handle of Howie's sword, the latest addition, recalling the pleasure of claiming it upon his arrest.

'Quite good, isn't it?' Qattren said.

Seth took it from the wall mount and held it in his left hand. The only weight came from the hilt and a small piece of lead within the crystal for balance. It felt too dainty to be a broadsword. It was like wielding a dagger.

'I heard you made it,' he said.

'Yes.'

'Hmm.'

He hurled it around, the crystal swinging for Qattren's neck.

Before halting an inch from her copper ringlets.

Seth tried ineffectively to move the sword.

It was frozen in mid-air.

'I assumed you weren't *really* trying to kill me, but I had to take precautions,' said Qattren. 'I had my hair done not long ago and I'm quite partial to my length the way it is.'

Seth released the sword to rub hilt grooves from his palms.

The broadsword remained suspended in mid-air.

'I don't recall what I said to make you so afraid for your life, Seth, but I want you to realise that I am, to all intents and purposes, *invincible.*'

Seth gave the pommel a poke. It didn't so much as wobble.

'Your glorified knife does not frighten me. It will not even penetrate my skin.'

Something in the air gave way. The sword plummeted to the ground with a clang.

Seth snatched it from the flagstones and held it to her throat regardless.

'Ah, but you see, this isn't an ordinary sword,' he said.

'I know,' Qattren said patiently. 'I made it.'

'It's *unbreakable*. It will go through anything, *especially* a little slip of a thing like you. Would you like a demonstration?'

'Oh, I'll give you a demonstration,' she said.

She flicked the surface of the blade with one finger.

The crystal – the *unbreakable*, genetically *enhanced* crystal, created by an unquenchable flame that burned for two decades underground, a crystal with the ability to penetrate *anything* in the known *universe* – shattered under the impact. Cracks spread over the middle of the blade like spiders' legs, intersecting over and over. With one last *clink*, the blade disintegrated onto the floor.

Seth stared in horror at the foot-long remains of his 'unbreakable' sword.

'It's broken!'

He turned it this way and that.

Qattren smiled faintly.

'That,' Seth squealed, 'was the best sword in the whole world and now it's *broken!!*'

'Mmm, shame when that happens,' she said, examining her nails.

Unintelligible protests followed Seth's anguished wail. His eyes flitted to the remains of the sword. Without further thought, he slid it into her stomach.

It cut into the feathered dress and *sizzled* on contact. Six inches of the crystal dribbled onto the floor in a pool of molten slag, like a stick of butter being driven into a brazier.

Seth yanked it back with a yelp.

Qattren glanced down.

The hole Seth had cut into her gown blackened around the edges. Flecks of translucent red slag lingered on the fabric, still boiling – but the skin behind it remained pale and unbroken.

Qattren frowned slightly at the damage. 'I liked this dress.'

Seth gulped audibly. 'I'll… buy you a new one?'

Qattren arched an eyebrow, her eyes trained on his.

Seth recoiled.

'So, this, these troops of yours,' he stammered. 'Good, are they?'

'Exceptional,' she said.

She plucked at the cooling specks of crystal.

'Alright. When, when were you thinking of, of bringing them?'

'Is tomorrow good for you?'

'Great. Yes. Good. Good. See you then?'

'Oh, certainly.'

'Alright. Goodbye.'

'Goodbye, Seth.'

She gave him a warm smile, as though nothing had happened.

Brushing at the scorched edges of her gown to crumble away the damaged fabric, she threw Seth a wink, turned and left, her feathered skirts rustling behind her.

Seth watched her go in stunned silence. He swung his gaze to the sword.

Once a glorious three-and-a-half-foot shard of crystal, it now measured at under half a foot in length and dribbled to a halt, looking more like a candle than a blade. Its clear surface clouded over as though filled with a red fog.

As Seth held it up to the light, the last three inches began to curl.

It was ruined. All it had done was touch her skin.

Seth stared at it.

It dribbled.

He let it slip from his fingers to hit the ground.

Howie waited in line for weapons with the rest of Seth's coincidentally underage army as Qattren approached.

Ron smiled at her from behind him and noticed the hole in her dress. He indicated at it by circling his own belly button.

'What happened? It's your favourite dress.'

'A small mishap with Howard's sword,' she said, throwing him a cursory glance. 'I'm afraid Seth's accidentally broken it.'

Howie looked bemused. 'But it's unbreakable.'

Qattren didn't reply to this. Instead she told him, 'You can queue up for weapons later. I have a task to do that needs your assistance.'

Howie's mind was elsewhere. 'What did Seth do to my sword?'

'Do you want me to come?' Ron asked Qattren.

'How does someone break,' Howie exclaimed, 'an unbreakable sword?!'

'No,' she told Ron, ignoring the outburst. 'I'm afraid that if you came with me, I might not get you back. Howard is no loss to me.'

Evidently, he seethed internally, recalling her words in the mausoleum.

'Forget it,' he snapped. 'No one's sending me to my death, not without my magic sword.'

'Forget your magic sword,' Qattren barked back. 'No one's going to die. You just might not be allowed to come home. Come along.'

Ron gave him a meaningful glance.

Howie rolled his eyes and followed her out of the palace.

Once on the bridge, Qattren faced him and held out her right hand.

Hesitant, he slowly handed her his.

His breath suddenly became short, the air becoming thin and sparse. A lilac fog spread across his vision and their surroundings wavered, as though fluid.

'What's happening?' he gasped.

'We're entering Sal'plae,' she said calmly. 'I need to bring you somewhere far away in a hurry – this is the fastest way there is. I call it traversing.'

Recollection hit him in place of the now missing air.

'This is how we got to the castle the day—'

'Yes.' The assertion was short and harsh. 'Now I need you to concentrate. You see that, in the distance?'

He followed her finger into the sky.

'No,' he said with a squint.

Qattren's eyes fluttered upwards.

'Of course not, you aren't even looking,' she muttered with a sigh. 'The moon. Do you see it?'

His brow furrowed. 'Barely. It's daytime, in case you haven't noticed.'

'I need you to focus on it,' she said. 'We need to go there.'

His entire face furrowed now in bewilderment. 'Have you finally lost it? We're going to the moon? How? Why? Why do you want me on the moon?'

'You can ask your endless tedious questions when we're there,' said Qattren, her voice sharp. 'Just do as I ask.'

Howie's eyes rolled inwards and he glared upwards.

'What's up there?' he asked, unable to help himself.

Her reply was even more bizarre. 'A palace.'

~

VII

After many false starts, Howie finally landed on the Moon – the roof of it, that is, before Qattren had to fetch him down. Turns out the moon wasn't a lump of dry rock after all.

'That's just the roof,' Qattren had explained. 'It's a building, hanging just outside the edge of the sky. It shows up from Truphoria when the sun hits it a certain way. Only in Sal'plae can you enter it.'

Now, they stood at the front entrance of the palace – though a giant, squashed mushroom was how Howie would describe it. The roof sloped like an arc over the pillars surrounding the outside walls, its surface ridged like an orange with its peel off. Thick wooden walls bearing carvings of heroic figures rose between the pillars, and steep steps led the way to the arch they stood in. Beside the lavishly decorated doors, Howie saw with wonder, was a water font.

'It looks like a chapel,' he commented.

'Oh, it's meant to,' she said, approaching the doors. 'On the outside. Don't touch the water.'

Howie took a quick step away from the font.

Qattren knocked thrice.

A slit in the door opened and a gold eye peeped out.

'Who wishes to repent their sins to the Seven Gods?' a voice intoned.

'Oh, do shut up and let me in. It's Qattren.'

'Qat!' exclaimed the voice as the doors swung open. 'And you've brought me a present!'

Howie peered at her hands for the present before realising with a feeling of dread that *he* was the gift.

Now the interior had been revealed, Howie saw what Qattren meant. Inside, the purple tint of the rest of Sal'plae had vanished, the large hall vividly multi-coloured. A large round table bearing wine goblets and roast pork sat in the centre, with portraits of the Seven Gods littering the walls around it – only instead of the usual images of love and gentle kindness, they were pulling rude faces.

Howie had just gotten a good look at the portraits when a hatchet came whistling at him at a hundred miles an hour.

Howie screamed and threw himself to the floor.

It sailed over the top of his head and lodged itself into the half-open door – not for the first time, Howie saw, trembling.

Soon he saw why: several melee weapons followed the path of the hatchet, pouring their way from a seeming void at the back of the hall and into the direction of Howie's face.

Their host clicked his fingers, diverting the weapons to the right.

'Come in, come in!' exclaimed the gold-eyed man, closing the doors behind them, the hatchet still attached. 'Make yourselves at home, there's food for eating and fools for everything else. Fools!'

Several men and women in motley materialised from the edges of the circular hall, somersaulting and cartwheeling around the table. Howie glimpsed scars and bruises on their faces and arms.

'I am called Geldemar,' he said to Howie, grasping his hand and shaking it, uninvited. 'How are you? Please, don't look so alarmed, blonds aren't my type!'

He beamed at his own joke, though his eyes still searched hungrily down the length of his torso.

Howie folded his arms in discomfort and leaned his head back to examine Geldemar from a safe distance.

Slim and dressed in black trimmed with gold, Geldemar's hair was silver in spite of the man looking the age of thirty at most. He had a narrow face with penetrating eyes, which avidly examined Howie as though eyeing up something he could eat.

'Who are—'

Qattren pushed Howie's head to the ground as another hatchet sailed over it.

'Who are these people?' Howie said, squatting with a hand against the laminate flooring.

'Don't you recognise me?' Geldemar asked with a grin. 'Oh, of course not, I have changed my appearance significantly over the years. We…' he paused for effect, '… are the Seven Gods.'

Howie's back stiffened.

Qattren gripped his shoulder firmly. Whether it was to comfort or restrain him, Howie couldn't say.

'Come! Meet my comrades! This is Rubena, goddess of rebellion.'

He introduced a woman with striking red hair and a velvet suit to match.

'Gale, god of nature…'

A green-clad, emerald-haired man saluted.

'Meddles with the course of nature, you know, causes mishaps in the female reproductive system and generally causes a lot of mess. These are Fortune and Misfortune…'

A pair of conjoined twins, in a tunic parted in two sections coloured black and white, each gave a wave in symmetrical unison.

'… and this is Liana, goddess of desire… her real image is a fully clothed sewer rat, if that makes your mouth drier…'

Howie snapped his mouth shut, wiping his chin.

A cross between Cienne and Adrienne smiled at him, wearing a sheer nightrobe with a corset accentuating her—

Howie averted his gaze to the ceiling.

'… and the seventh is of course Theo, god of war.'

Theo rose to shake Howie's hand. The man was King Theo's visible opposite – clean-shaven and slim, his hair straight and slicked back against his skull, he bore a stronger resemblance to the frightening Gomez Emmett Jr than his royal namesake. He wore a burgundy velvet suit, the colour of blood. Even his dark hair had a reddish tinge in a certain light.

'A pleasure,' he greeted, his hand warm and soft. 'I've wanted to meet you for a long time.'

'I've been trying to get rid of you, to be honest,' Howie said bluntly.

The god of war smiled. 'I've never been the most popular.'

'Now tell me,' Geldemar said to Qattren. 'What can the Seven do for you this time?'

'Well…' said Qattren.

She pulled Howie out of the path of three darts.

'… there's a predicament in progress back home, and as you can imagine…'

She shoved him under the table.

An anvil landed where he had been standing.

'… many human lives are at stake, so I was wondering…'

She dragged him out by his ear.

A harpoon sailed past the other one.

'… if I could borrow some demons for the day.'

Howie staggered, his head spinning.

Geldemar tutted, his arms folded.

'Now, that's what you said last time, young lady, and we didn't get them back for a month. I may be the god of greed, but advocate, I am not.'

'I assure you, a day is all we will need,' she insisted.

Geldemar regarded her sceptically.

'Alright,' he said, 'BUT: you must play for it.'

'Poker? Too easy,' Qattren teased.

'Not when the stakes are high,' he pointed out. 'So I will propose this. We will play one round, and whoever wins gets what they want. You get your army… or we get your boy.'

Howie blinked. 'You knew this would happen, didn't you?'

'Oh yes,' she sighed. 'But I hoped our friendship would dissuade him.'

'You know we love you dearly, Qat,' Geldemar said fondly. 'Which is why we'll give you your army anyway. We don't want you getting into trouble over a little game, do we? But of course, you must play the game to get it.'

'You're an asshole,' said Howie.

'They call me one of the Seven Devils,' Geldemar said with a grin. '"Asshole" comes with the territory.'

'I know, I was talking to *her.*'

Theo shuffled a deck of cards.

Qattren and Howie sat at the table.

'Do switch off these weapons, Theo, they're most distracting,' Geldemar said.

Theo clicked his fingers.

All flying weaponry dropped to the floor.

More at ease without the flying weaponry, Howie reclined in his chair, the smooth wood pleasant through his shirt.

'What's it like being a god?'

'They aren't gods,' Qattren said, cutting across Geldemar before he had a chance to speak. 'They're more like meddlers. They're no more powerful than I am.'

'What kind of meddling? Big stuff, small stuff…'

'A bit of both,' Geldemar said. 'Small changes to bring about major events, big things to help a minor catalyst. Or sometimes we just meddle for the sake of it.'

'A bit of both,' Howie echoed.

Qattren eyed him warily – noting his odd tone of voice.

'Say, for example,' Howie went on, 'causing a cat to fly, making a certain person embark on a certain quest?'

Geldemar smiled. 'Maybe.'

'Or zapping a prince's memories out with lightning to help a certain person gain favour at court?'

'We only thought of that after,' Gale cut in, sheepish. 'That one was just for fun.'

'Or altering the migration patterns of a flock of ravens to scare a witless prince into getting sunstroke and meeting the future mother of his child?' said Howie sharply.

'Howard,' Qattren warned.

'OR,' Howie cut in loudly, 'OR, sending some nonsense sign to a priest of your opposing religion to kill said child and close the Hole. Stuff like that, is it? Little things like that?'

Geldemar leaned back in alarm.

The others sat in stunned silence.

'That was the Crey god,' he said, hurt. 'We don't do things like that.'

'The Crey god isn't known to make things vanish, is he?' Howie snarled. 'You lot are.'

'That's just it,' Geldemar said emphatically, 'we make *things* vanish. Pottery. Coins. Pieces of fruit. Not human *lives*. I'll be level with you, we did do the rest of the things you mentioned. But the child… no. We would never condone that kind of villainy.'

'But why do all this?' Howie demanded. 'What is the *point* of it? If you wanted me to throw myself in there so badly, why couldn't you just manipulate me into doing it of my own free will?'

'Because the Hole wasn't meant for you,' Theo replied.

Howie frowned. 'But I thought—'

'Right, let's get started,' he interrupted, dealing.

'Hang on,' Howie said, holding a hand up.

'Hang on,' Qattren cut across him. 'There are seven of you and two of us. That isn't fair.'

'Oh, alright then, spoilsport,' huffed Geldemar, sweeping the cards back up. 'The twins will play, then, making both sides quite even. And since you're so keen on fairness, all distractions and tampering with the deck and players by third parties is prohibited for this game.'

He eyed Liana and added, 'Perhaps you ought to leave the

room for this one, Li.'

Liana vanished up a staircase at the back of the hall.

Howie watched her leave with an air of wistfulness.

Geldemar dealt the cards anew.

They lifted their hands to their faces. Qattren remained as expressionless as ever. The twins each tried vainly to hide their cards from each other whilst peeking into the other's hand.

Howie examined his own hand, puzzled.

'These cards are odd.'

'They're from Cientra, in the Far Isles,' Qattren said.

'How am I supposed to know if I'm winning?'

'Best you don't,' Qattren advised. 'If you don't know what you have, any nosy mind readers present won't either.'

'I told you, we have different rules for this game,' Geldemar said.

He peeked into Howie's hand in blatant disregard for his 'rules'. He hissed through his teeth.

'Crap?' Howie said with dread.

'Utter crap, yeah,' Geldemar said with a wince. 'Put down these ones, we may be able to salvage this.'

They swapped two cards into the deck and received two more with a strange moon on them. Geldemar gave up at the sight of these and left, shrugging apologetically.

Howie glanced around.

Qattren was also wincing. Considering her dislike of Howie, he wasn't sure whether to be relieved or terrified.

The twins remained nonchalant, their cards folded neatly on the table.

Howie released a low whine.

~

Back at the Creys' Keep, Keith gaped at the new King of Adem as Seth explained his business proposal. Once Seth had finished talking, Keith opened and closed his mouth twice in disbelief, the proposition so obtuse it left him speechless.

Finally he spoke.

'You want all my girls to pay your armies with sex and my payment is *thin air?*'

'Yes, because if you don't give them to me, you won't be getting any air at *all,*' Seth added with a patient smile. 'You'll bring them, say, midnight?'

'I ain't bringing them at all, you skinflint!' Keith exclaimed.

'They can do 'em at the Crook like everyone else!'

'Ah, well, you see,' Seth said, putting a friendly arm around Keith's shoulders, 'that wouldn't be any good because they would have to pay *you* then. And the poor lads, they haven't a penny to their names. Whereas if they're on *my* premises, then *technically* they're *my* girls, and currently I have a sale on for militia recruits. Buy-none-get-one-free, this week only.'

'And what if I refuse?'

Lyseria's stomach growled loudly from the front gate.

'Er…' Keith trailed off.

Seth nodded with a smile.

'… midnight it is.'

'Great!' Seth grinned, shaking Keith's hand.

Keith mooched away sullenly, giving Lyseria a wide berth.

Marbrand sidled up to Seth. 'Has he agreed?'

'After some persuasion,' Seth said. 'Any word on my wife?'

'The Hornes have been in touch,' he said, producing a slip of parchment. 'They deny abducting her, but they're willing to lend men to your cause in exchange for a specific prisoner.'

'Please say Howard Rosethorn, please say Howard Rosethorn,' Seth chanted, his hands pressed together.

'Actually, Queen Aaliyaa requested you, your majesty.'

Seth lifted one side of his upper lip in distaste. 'Sod that. Tell her she can have Howard Rosethorn or burn in hell.'

'What's our next move?'

'I'll be leading a small group of household guards to Stoneguard, make it look like we're going to investigate. In the meantime, the boys will be sailing around to Maketon, and we'll… suss out the rest from there,' he finished speedily.

You mean I will, Marbrand thought resentfully.

'Good idea,' he said aloud, 'but can we wait that long to confront the Hornes? It will take up to six weeks to get to Maketon from…'

He caught Seth's smug grin.

'You don't mean to travel through the Wastelands?'

'Yes,' said Seth, as if this was obvious. 'It will take less time and besides, I hate sailing.'

Marbrand's jaw hung open. 'It's called the *Wastelands*.'

Seth frowned. 'Your point being?'

Marbrand bristled. 'There's nothing there. No food. No shelter. Nothing. How in hell do you expect me to get you across it in the manner with which you're accustomed?'

'What manner?' Seth asked in outrage.

'All due respect, but the tantrum about the grapes having pips in still lingers in servant memory.'

'I was tired,' Seth said hotly.

'It's far too dangerous. The men will never agree to it.'

Seth rolled his eyes. 'It was set on fire over fifty years ago, I *think* it's gone out by now. Anyway, the one who did it declared for us. We won't be in too much trouble with her around.'

Marbrand froze, wide-eyed.

'You hired the Forest Witch?'

Seth nodded impatiently.

'Have you any comprehension of the damage she could do if set loose in Stoneguard again?'

'Yes,' said Seth, 'which is why I'm pointing her *away* from us.'

'My liege,' Marbrand said curtly. 'Qattren Meriangue is a madwoman of the highest order. Her morals range in the minus scale, her origins are even more dubious than that of Howard Rosethorn and her most common war tactic lends a whole new definition to genocidal. Why on earth would a king risk his country's health knowing her responsibility for the climax of the War for the Orchard and the slaughter of millions of innocent people?'

'Because, as his majesty says,' a voice said behind him, 'he is pointing me in the opposite direction.'

Marbrand slowly pivoted.

Qattren 'Madwoman' Meriangue watched him impassively.

His spine stiffened.

'Your highness,' he said with a bow.

He turned to Seth, who smirked.

'I will begin the arrangements to cross the border immediately, my liege.'

'Jolly good,' Seth said brightly.

With that he returned to the palace guards at a light jog that, as soon as Qattren's eyes were averted, became a fast sprint.

'Why would he be doing that, Seth?'

Seth met her gaze and said slowly, 'Because I told him to?'

'The Wastelands isn't an option. Direct your troops elsewhere.'

Seth's nostrils flared.

'Why? It's hardly dangerous, nobody lives there thanks to you! Anyway, I thought you were bringing the demon army?'

'That isn't the point.' Her usual impassive façade took on a reluctant hardness. 'My army and I will not be crossing the Wastelands. We will meet you on the other side, unless you're joining us on our route?'

'You mean spend all summer sailing around the bloody continent because you're afraid of ghosts?'

'I mean traversing to Stoneguard through Sal'plae, thus missing the Wastelands and spending a little over five seconds travelling. You'll recall we traversed back here when the Hole closed?'

Seth gaped at her. 'The exploding thing.'

'Yes.'

'Forget it.'

'If you want to cross the Wastelands and risk waking three million dead souls,' Qattren said blithely, 'be my guest. But my army and I will be in Sal'plae.'

Seth huffed a short laugh. 'You will not.'

Qattren blinked rapidly. 'Excuse me?'

'Your army can do as they please, I'm not going to try to stop them,' he said wisely. 'You, however, broke my sword, which slightly pissed me off. So you're staying where I can see you.'

Qattren's voice lifted in volume. 'You do not have the jurisdiction to force me into the same route as you. I volunteered to help you of my own good will.'

'And you'll be *volunteering* to follow me across the Wastelands. Unless you want people to find out you're owed a substantial pension?'

Qattren blinked.

'Was that supposed to be blackmail? Because you seem to have forgotten your dear father's demise. Perhaps you and your kin require reminding?'

'Maybe you need reminding of your part in killing a child. No?' he added as the comment hit target.

Qattren fell silent, stunned.

'Well, then. Off you go find a coach.' He waved her off with both hands.

Qattren stood stock still, her expression irate.

Marbrand returned.

'My liege, if we're going to spend three weeks travelling to Stoneguard, should we send someone ahead with Lyseria to scout the countryside for the coach?'

'We could if she didn't keep eating the staff,' Seth said, rolling his eyes. 'The only person who can saddle that thing is Lilly, and there's no way I'm sending my baby sister into the path of that Far Isles loon.'

'What about Howard Rosethorn?'

'Oh wonderful idea, let him play hero again and steal my wife as well as my mistress,' said Seth sourly. A thought occurred. 'Unless I neutered him first. That would work.'

'Oh, you can't do that,' Qattren said lightly.

'Why not?'

'I traded him for the demon army.'

Marbrand's eyes widened. 'You did what?'

'Traded him to who?' Seth asked shrilly.

'The Seven Devils of Sal'plae,' she said, as if discussing the sale of a silver ring as opposed to a person. 'Is that a problem?'

Seth's face stated the contrary. It was practically euphoric.

'Problem?' Marbrand said, dripping with sarcasm. 'No, only that he was part of a major religious prophecy, nothing *big*.'

'Ah yes, but remind me,' said Qattren in a similar tone. 'What deities does this prophecy refer to?'

'The Seven… oh.' He sighed. 'Devils.'

Qattren smiled sweetly.

Seth tilted his head to one side. Then he offered her a hand.

She took it.

'Do this more often with people I don't like and we might just be friends.'

'I don't think so somehow,' she said with a half-smile. 'So we will meet on the west side of the accursed necropolis in a week?'

'Ah, no. Nice try, though,' Seth said in admiration. 'You *almost* had me bowing at your feet for a minute there. Now, there's a coach over there heading straight through the accursed necropolis. Why don't we share it?'

Qattren deflated, following him to the coach.

After a moment Seth spoke.

'You didn't really trade him, did you?'

Qattren shot him a knowing side-glance.

'How did you guess?'

'His hair is more attractive than mine, of course you didn't,' he said bitterly.

~

VIII

Five minutes after Seth had departed for the Wastelands, a whistle from behind the palace attracted Lyseria's attention. She vaulted the wall soundlessly.

One minute later, Howie took to the skies on her shoulder

blades.

Thinking back on earlier events, he wondered if Qattren's ploy had worked…

~

'You realise why I brought you here, don't you?' she said, leaning against the pillar outside.

Howie plonked himself on the step, his arms folded.

'To trade me for a magic army,' he said grumpily.

'No.'

Howie rolled his eyes. 'Why, then?'

'As you're aware,' she said, braiding some strands of her copper-coloured hair, 'Seth and I have agreed to join forces to eliminate the Hornes from power – except for Ron, of course. That will mean Seth will try to order me around. And I don't take to that sort of thing.'

Howie planted his chin in his palm.

'So I needed a reason for him to take my suggestions. Giving away his worst enemy for his gain should do the trick. Although,' she said as an afterthought, 'he's brighter than he looks, so he may see through my ploy.'

'You're going to lie and tell Seth you traded me?'

Qattren heaved a long-suffering sigh.

'No, I'm going to tie a bow around your neck and hand you back to Geldemar,' she said, with increasing levels of sarcasm.

He bristled.

'Oh, good,' he retorted loudly, 'let's do that then, shall we? I bet being his sex-slave-jester-thing or whatever those people are'll be a damn sight better than having Seth Crey try to fucking kill me again.'

Qattren cocked her head to one side. 'Do we need to talk?'

'What do you think?'

Howie threw himself to his feet.

'Within the past year, I've been expected to chase off after a drunk king, babysit the grandchildren of a cannibal, try to *kill* one of them, and lastly—and I *think* you'll agree that it's outside the job description of *even* a religious hero – jump into a *fucking black hole* and fucking die! And to top it all off, my pregnant girlfriend just got attacked by a creepy priest because of me. Do I need to talk about it?'

He slammed his back against a pillar.

'*Probably*,' he barked at her.

Qattren's impassive expression remained unfazed by the outburst.

'You do seem a bit upset,' she conceded.

Howie gripped the air in front of him in a strangulation motion.

Qattren held up her hands, placating.

'I apologise,' she said firmly. 'My part in this is significant. I am sorry for taking advantage of you.'

He tucked his hands under his armpits, his gaze to the ground.

'I'm aware that I haven't exactly been… friendly,' she went on. 'But this has never been about you. We're trying to gather as much force as we can to find Cienne Fleurelle—'

'Why does it have to be at my expense?'

He kicked a stone down the steps before realising that one of the Seven had probably put that stone there especially for that purpose.

'Why don't you trade Seth for them? He's the one she's so desperately in love with.'

Qattren gazed into his sulky, downcast eyes.

'Let me tell you a little secret,' she said softly. 'This prophecy you're supposed to prevent? It hasn't been prevented yet.'

'The Hole is closed,' he said, frowning at the ground.

'The Hole is only the beginning,' she said. 'This is to do with the Crey God. He ripped a hole in the world the day you entered it, to kill you. But instead of waiting an extra three seconds for us to throw you in, He took Adrienne's child.'

She snatched his chin and turned his face upward.

'Everyone knows He refrains from interfering with human affairs – you said as much yourself earlier. The last time He took a human life, it was when the dragons were created. When a person plays God, God tends to have something to say about it.

'You've seen what the Seven are capable of. Now imagine that power a thousand-fold: imagine a power that changes the laws of the earth as quickly as you could change a shirt, a power that makes Gale's "maternal meddling" seem like sleight-of-hand by comparison. A power with no comparison – you can imagine that He can get a bit jealous when people out-do that power.'

Howie's eyes locked to hers. 'He's pissed off because I was made with magic?'

'He's pissed off because it's misuse of holy blood. Crey blood runs in your veins. You're a descendent of Salator Crey, just like the entire Crey family, and you're a violation in His eyes.'

'So why doesn't He just strike me with lightning or something?'

'Because it would be construed as coincidence. He doesn't

want people playing God: that's His job. He wants people to know what happens when things aren't done His way.

'He's trying to manipulate you, Howie. Not like Geldemar and the others do for fun – this is much more subtle. He's pitting you and Seth against each other. And who do you think will win when it comes down to it? A lowly carpenter's apprentice or a man with a kingdom and an international alliance at his back? He wants you to do something stupid and start a war, and you're walking right into His plot.

'You need to forge some kind of truce with Seth, and to do that you need to bring Cienne home safely. I can deal with Vladimir and Aaliyaa – they're little liked among the nobles and only associate with each other, I have more difficulty brushing my hair than sorting the likes of them out. Once you deliver Cienne safely into Seth's arms, you and Adrienne will return to Stoneguard and forget you ever made the King of Adem's acquaintance.'

'And you don't think he's gonna find it suss when I show up with Cienne in my lap? What if decides she'd rather have the hero on the dragon after all instead of...'

He trailed off.

Qattren's expression could have withered grass.

'Honestly?' she drawled. 'She's your biological mother, to all intents and purposes. Do you really think she would sleep with someone whose infant bum she would have been wiping had events conspired differently?'

Howie flushed.

'She loves Seth completely.' She smiled. 'And as for him, I think he's smitten. I wouldn't raise an army for someone I was indifferent about. They'll only have eyes for each other by the end of this. Take my word on that.'

~

Adrienne awoke from her afternoon doze to the sound of the latch

'If it's money you're after, we haven't got any,' Archie said sharply.

Adrienne sat up, craning her neck.

An elderly couple stood at the door, cradling a basket.

'Oh for God's sake, Archie, do you have to be rude to everyone that comes to the door?'

She lifted herself to her feet. Her strength had returned, thankfully: at least physically. She elbowed Archie out of the way and smiled at the visitors warmly. 'What can we do for you?'

Archie heaved an audible sigh behind her and pottered back to his carpentry.

'We come from the church,' the woman said with a smile.

Adrienne's smile slid from her face.

'Father Giery mentioned you in his guest sermon yesterday, we all had a whip-round and…'

Blood.

She bristled, her spine tensing. Panic began to lift in her chest, like goosebumps. Her tongue began to tingle. The images flashed in and out of focus, blood, blood, the box, tablecloth, candles, *blood…*

The woman was still talking, she realised.

Adrienne shook herself off. 'I'm sorry, I was miles away. What was that?'

'We brought you a little something for the house,' the woman repeated. 'My name is Phyllis, and this is Ted.'

Ted smiled, a frail thin figure.

'Oh,' said Adrienne, stricken. 'There's no need, really—'

'We volunteer at the church on Ablyminded Street,' she said kindly. 'We won't keep you long, we just wanted to drop off a little something from us to keep you going, alright, my love?'

Adrienne accepted the basket. She had little choice. It was being pressed upon her with surprising strength for a little old lady.

'You have our sympathies for your loss, miss,' Ted said solemnly.

Adrienne threw a quick glance at Archie.

He was engrossed in an ornate table edge, pointedly ignoring the strangers.

'Thank you,' she said, turning back to the visitors.

Phyllis took one of Adrienne's hands from the arm of the basket and gripped it in both of her own.

'We will light a candle for you,' she said firmly. 'You know where we are if you need us. You younger people are so sceptical in the ways of the Lord, but the parish is *real*. We look after each other.'

She tucked an overflowing bunch of grapes back into the rim of the basket, amongst blocks of cheese and endless jars of chutney.

'If you need somewhere for comfort, the church is always open. Feel free to wander in if you need an ear to talk to.'

Adrienne opened her mouth to speak.

Fear clung to her chest at the thought of it, strangling her.

'… I will,' she managed.

Phyllis gripped her hand again tightly with a gentle smile.

'Keep safe,' Ted said, touching his forelock.

Adrienne nodded slightly.

The pair left, quietly.

Adrienne closed the door, the basket hanging from one hand.

'Pushy, weren't they?' Archie grunted. 'Bloody churchies.'

Adrienne said nothing. She merely returned to the sofa, setting the basket beside her. Her gaze fell on the corner of a letter peeking out from under the cheese. She tugged it free.

It was tied to a pouch full of coin.

Adrienne, the letter read. *Please accept this monetary token from us and King Seth. Our thanks for your help in our noble cause.*

It was signed Duke Richard Crey of Osney.

She crumpled it up and threw it into the fire.

Archie glanced at her. 'You alright?'

Her eyes met his, welling up.

Archie deflated, placing aside his equipment. He stepped forward, perched beside her and gathered her into his arms.

Adrienne sobbed audibly. She buried her face in his shoulder.

He rubbed her arm.

'I know, I know,' he murmured. 'I don't like chutney either.'

A giggle erupted between sobs.

Archie smiled weakly.

As quickly as it came, the laugh tapered off. Adrienne wiped her face as her thoughts spun in circles, images of the blood, the box, those placating words. What upset her most were Phyllis and Ted. They were so oblivious…

She wondered if they had any idea what actually happened.

Archie ruffled her hair.

'Promise me,' he said softly, 'if we bump into the bastard that did this, you'll point him out so I can brutalise him.'

Adrienne's eyes welled up again. The truth swelled in her chest, fighting to get out. Her common sense quickly stuffed it back down.

'I promise,' she said.

~

The people of Serpus gathered on the side-lines of the main thoroughfare, waiting.

A rumbling blur on the horizon told of approaching men.

The first to rattle down the cobbles was Seth's coach, with King Seth himself leaning out of the side, an arm raised in greeting.

A smattering of polite applause responded as always.

Appearing behind him in the overcast light of the afternoon was Marbrand, mounted and gleaming in fresh steel-plate armour and toting a large emerald banner.

Being a view more akin to expectations, he earned a more enthusiastic ovation.

And the young men of his retinue followed, haphazard in formation but all extremely happy to be there – which may or may not have been due to Keith's best staff, Keith himself thought sourly from the main door of the Crook.

The torrent of men poured down the thoroughfare, past queues of watching civilians, as Seth's coach rattled out of hearing. The entire city ground to a halt to watch them pass.

Except for one other coach, who rattled up the side street parallel.

As Seth's group vanished west in the direction of Osney, the solitary coach soldiered uphill, out of Serpus to the crop of forest beyond and over the barbican of Creys' Keep.

Eleanor lingered at her balcony window, eyeing the view of Serpus, as if seeing Seth and watching him go. The city sprawled below, beyond the more immediate woods and over the river beyond, a grey mass of miniscule roofs.

She eyed the rogue coach during its climb to the keep, letting her gaze follow it lazily.

The sun began to set now, casting the evening in a pink glow. Rosy clouds hung low over the city, an ominous streak of red.

After some time, a knock sounded.

'Enter,' she said.

A head poked in.

'Your highness, the Emmetts have arrived.'

Finally. Eleanor thanked the girl profusely and rose.

She froze at the bottom of the stairs.

'Eleanor!' Cienne exclaimed.

She rushed forward to embrace her.

Eleanor stood stock still in Cienne's arms.

'You're here!' Eleanor said in disbelief.

'Of course, I live here,' Cienne said with a laugh. 'You look as though I've returned from the dead!'

She stepped back and her face dropped.

'*Are* you alright?' she said in concern.

Eleanor's eyes grew very wide.

'Seth told us you were kidnapped,' she said in a monotone. 'On the way to the manor. Your cousin told him.'

'Did I?'

Emmett Jr glanced innocently from Eleanor to Cienne and

behind him to Zephyr, his uncle.

'That's what Seth told us,' Eleanor said. 'He said the Hornes took her.'

'The Hornes?' Emmett repeated, mystified. 'I mentioned we were having trouble contacting Felicity, but I definitely told him Cienne was coming with us. How puzzling.'

Cienne swung back to Eleanor. 'He must have been confused. Where is he now, upstairs? He isn't upset again, is he?' Her brow wrinkled in concern.

Eleanor's voice became hollow. 'He's gone to Stoneguard now, to confront the Hornes.'

Cienne's eyes grew very wide. 'What?'

Her voice dropped to a whisper. 'He has an *army*.'

~

IX

Seth and Qattren sat alone together in the large coach, watching the scenery of Adem drift past beneath the setting sun.

'Did you, out of interest,' Seth said, 'actually try to trade him?'

Qattren looked up.

It had been a silent two-week journey so far, spent on her part wondering how Howie was getting on. Seth's ragtag troops had departed down the river at Osney, leaving them and a small retinue to continue ahead by horse and coach. This was their first conversation since leaving the keep.

'Yes, I did,' she said in reply. 'His habit of overstating the obvious incredulously during conversation irritates me.'

'Makes you want to slap him, doesn't it?'

Qattren grinned into her lap.

'Indeed it does. I don't know what your father was thinking, raising him to a court favourite.'

Seth heaved a sigh. 'You know, there's no greater mystery in life than what King Theo Crey thought about anything. Reading his motives is like trying to straighten a meandering river.'

Her eyes bored into Seth's forehead, as if trying to read *his* thoughts.

'What do you suppose his last thoughts were of you?'

Seth tilted his face to the coach ceiling.

'Since you ask,' he said, 'I figured it was something along the lines of, "Get this axe out of my throat, boy, it's blocking the food tunnel".'

Qattren accepted this without comment.

'Unless I'm wrong?'

'Actually, that sounds about right,' she said in retrospect. 'At least initially.'

A small commotion interrupted Seth as he opened his mouth in enquiry.

Guards fled past the window, steel flashing.

Horses whinnied noisily.

The coach rocked back and forth.

Seth clung to the edge of his seat. 'What the—'

The litter pitched forward, thudding to a halt on its bottom front edge.

The floor sharply slanted beneath his feet.

Seth soared across it, his seat expelling him. He faceplanted into the wall beside Qattren.

'What is going on?' he exploded.

They steadied their footing on the now-diagonal floor, peering out.

All the horses had vanished, their bonds severed and strewn on the grass beside them, abandoned. Even the guards' horses had done a runner, their owners too preoccupied with the fighting to notice.

Qattren didn't even notice the fighting.

The scorched mountain range cut through the Wastelands, looming over their heads in black shards piercing the sky. Between them and the mountains lay grey and blackened moors, cut across with equally charred roads ending in a stark border mere yards from the vivid green countryside the party resided in.

The overcast sky seemed much brighter on their side of the border, as if smog still lingered over the dead earth. Qattren fancied she could even see the remains of the cottages in the near distance – cottages that had held living people on her last visit.

She blinked the memory of her last visit away and composed herself.

Seth peered over her shoulder.

'What a friendly welcome,' he said wryly.

Qattren scowled, interpreting this snide remark as being aimed at her.

Then the group of robbers approached.

~

Cienne pivoted, seating herself in Seth's throne.

'Fat lot of good the council are in a crisis,' she grumbled to herself. She commenced a whining impersonation, '"We didn't authorise a strike on anywhere"—so why is it happening then??' she demanded, cutting across herself in frustration. 'Honestly, it's been two weeks now, surely someone would have been able to get a bloody message to the man!'

Eleanor perched on her right, in the middle-sized throne.

'Cienne,' she said tremulously. 'Why have we brought a hermit into the throne room?'

'Because this hermit,' Cienne said grimly, 'will magic me to Stoneguard.'

'He will *what?*' Eleanor asked, incredulous. 'Cienne, I really think we ought to leave this to—'

'To who, Eleanor? The council who couldn't keep one man from raising an army for one bloody afternoon? It's not as though I was gone for weeks, I was gone for a single afternoon!' Cienne rolled her eyes, throwing her mane of blond hair over one shoulder in impatience. 'If you want something doing, trust anyone but the council.'

Elias stood in awe before the enormous rose window above the courtyard entrance behind them. He reached into his pocket, withdrew a rock and, very deliberately, hurled it at the window.

It *poinged* off the glass and rebounded.

Elias ducked to the left.

It bounced off his right shoulder.

'Sorcery!' he exclaimed. 'I knew it!'

'Elias,' Cienne said in withering tones.

'Sorry,' he said hastily.

He skittered around the dais to face them, rubbing his shoulder.

'We need to reach Stoneguard today and collect my husband, before he causes any more damage,' she said. 'Can you arrange that?'

'Certainly.'

He clapped twice.

Dust surrounded them in an explosion – which quickly imploded and became their physical forms once more as they solidified in the heart of Stoneguard's market square.

Cienne steadied herself, clinging to Eleanor's elbow.

'Elias?'

'Yes?'

'Do we really require the entire dais to come with us?'

He gave the circular platform and the thrones a cursory glance.

'… no, your highness.'

He waited sheepishly for them to remove themselves before sending it back with a wave.

'I should like to find an inn,' Eleanor quavered, paling.

'Straight away, your highness!'

Elias burst forward, ever eager to assist.

'Just be quick,' said Cienne. 'I need your help to find my husband immediately.'

'I will be as swift as a bird, your highness,' he vowed.

He guided Eleanor to his side by an elbow, very gently, and dissipated once more.

After appearing at the bar of a stricken-looking landlady, Elias deposited a shaking, vomiting Eleanor to a deluxe suite at the back of the house before returning to the square – not before cleaning out the dowager queen's sick bucket three times and tucking her in, at her behest.

By the time he had rematerialized, Cienne had already wandered away.

~

Howie circled the skies above Stoneguard on his second week of search before getting fed up. He set Lyseria down in a tiny village a mile south – Shepton, according to an engraved boulder nearby.

He entered an inn on the crossroads, bought a pork pie and sat outside on the side of the road to eat it, keeping an eye out for Qattren lest she materialise to scold him for slacking off. He honestly had no idea what he was supposed to achieve. Looking for a grey coach with Cienne in it was like spotting a thimble in a patch of grass. Bleeding *everything* in Stoneguard was grey.

Howie glared at the road opposite, chewing slowly.

Lyseria dropped onto her stomach with a *thud* and, with an idle flick of her tongue, lapped up a couple of pigeons loitering nearby. Howie watched the remaining pigeons waddle around her, completely anxiety-free. The most reaction Lyseria gave them seemed to be mild annoyance, in spite of the amount of their kind she was currently crunching down on. Howie wished he were a pigeon.

He heaved a sigh and rose, dusting pie crumbs from his lap. Ensuring that Lyseria was happy with the pigeons, he gave the dragon a friendly pat before strolling to the city.

The familiar streets opened out around him, the cobbles and wood panelled buildings clean and inviting. Howie glanced around, entranced. The place was actually quite pretty, he thought – at least compared to Serpus.

Shithole, he thought venomously. At Seth in particular.

He followed the old road to a side alley and counted to the middle house – Archie's. He extracted a key from his shirt, where it hung on a string. Force of habit had led him to keep it on him at all times, as if Adem was just a day visit.

The workshop held a chill and the faint smell of damp but was otherwise immaculate. Adrienne had tidied up before she left – he could tell it was her because the tools were actually *put away* as opposed to simply laid out in an aesthetic manner.

Howie opened the drawers and took them back out, arranging them neatly on the worktable in tidy rows. He observed his handiwork, adjusting a tool to ensure symmetry. Archie would be proud, he thought in satisfaction.

He wrinkled his nose at the smell clinging to the room and made a beeline for the door, opening it wide to let the light breeze in. Wandering listlessly, Howie finally settled himself into the armchair in the living half of the room.

He deflated, sighing deeply.

Despite the cloying stench of absence, for the first time since he entered the church outside the Stonekeep, Howie felt totally relaxed. He reclined into the buttoned back armchair, his gaze fixed to a rivet in the corner of the ceiling. He reached a hand backwards to grasp a fistful of crocheted wool – the blanket. Adrienne had made it.

He'd head back tomorrow, he decided, and take Archie and Adrienne home. To hell with Princess Cienne.

He was just envisioning a nice sleep in his own bed upstairs when thundering footsteps drove his attention to the door.

A priest stood before the waning sunlight, pointing at him.

'There he is, your highness,' he said shrilly. 'The pretender!'

Howie groaned.

Reaching behind him, he pinched a fold of the blanket from the back of the chair and simply threw it over his head.

~

The robbers circled the party, examining their weapons intently.

Marbrand clicked his fingers.

The guards surrounded Seth and Qattren's coach.

The two sat inside, waiting.

'Heading through the Wastelands, is it?' sneered one of the robbers.

Marbrand planted a hand on his sword's pommel, his eyes

narrowed at the group.

In fact, they seemed less of a group and more of a barbarian army. The ragtag gang were dressed in pelts and leather, as though they lived in the northern ice of the Far Isles rather than the mild climate of Truphoria. On closer inspection, Marbrand found the pelts to be dog-skin – these robbers must have ridden into the Wastelands and killed their animals for food and clothing. There was nowhere to buy or steal supplies in the Wastelands.

Their numbers amounted to one score, just short of Marbrand's, but most of them carried multiple weapons – mainly axes. Nevertheless, Marbrand stood up straighter and said with an air of authority, 'Be on your way, strangers. We're no concern of yours.'

'Oh, I believe you are,' another said, his scruffy beard and colossal sledge hammer concealing his facial features. 'Heading for Stoneguard? We come from there.'

He approached Marbrand slowly.

'Queen Aaliyaa says King Seth's after our King Vladdy. We can't have that, can we? We're in the back arse of nowhere. Who would deal with the riffraff if the Hornes were gone?'

'What riffraff are you referring to?'

The man grinned. 'Us.' He raised his hammer.

Marbrand launched himself at his attacker, his broadsword swinging.

The brute hurled his hammer forward. It snapped the blade in two.

'Oh,' he said, almost sorrowfully. 'Seems like I broke your sword.'

He dropped the hammer and grabbed the front of Marbrand's breastplate, a knife in hand.

The northerners launched themselves at the guards, blades raised.

Marbrand's attacker twirled him into a headlock to plunge the knife in his throat.

Marbrand deftly dodged to the left.

The barbarian buried it into his own jugular with a gurgled scream, eyes bulging.

Marbrand pulled the man's other hand from around his chin and grasped a narrow bicep to hurl him into the ground. Beneath the pelts, he felt soft flesh rather than the hard muscle he expected. *That explains the knife use. Surprised he managed to pick that hammer up, never mind use it.*

Shoving the bleeding man to the ground, Marbrand faced the

coach.

A small group of bandits hacked at the guards, throwing blood in all directions. One of them cut through to the door, threw it open —

– and was instantly hit in the chest by a tiny ball of blue flame.

He soared past Marbrand in a blanket of flames and tumbled into a ditch outside an old mill, setting the mossy wooden fence alight.

Taking the hammer from his dead attacker, Marbrand swung it at the nearest bandit. An alarming amount of cracking and crunching ensued as he fought his way to the coach. He ignored it. He focussed on the swings, the aims, building momentum. He was used to blocking out the screams.

In the coach, Seth cowered behind Qattren, his hands clinging to her back.

She thrust her palms out. The muscles under his hands clenched.

'What are you trying to do?' he squeaked.

'I'm not trying to do anything,' she said, 'I'm *succeeding*.'

The blaze consuming the fence turned from blue to white.

Qattren yanked her hands backwards.

Flames poured towards them, cutting a path through the grass and everyone in it.

Skin and flesh sloughed from the bandits' faces in an instant.

Seth retracted his hands from Qattren's ribs. He fell back, whey faced.

Screams filled the air. Seth couldn't tell how many of his own men were victims. He didn't dare ask Qattren if she knew.

Amidst this horror, Seth was pulled backwards.

The protection around the door at his back had been forsaken. A mugger now held Seth fast by the back of the jerkin.

A knife soared up to his face.

Seth caught the wielder's knuckles, holding the tip a bare inch from his jaw. He dug his nails into the soft flesh of his enemy's hand, driving the blade lower.

Marbrand circled the coach and saw Seth prise the knife from the man's grasp.

His face twisted in a grimace, Seth brought the dagger back behind his ribs, plunging it into the centre of his attacker's bowels.

A sharp exhale indicated the knife had hit his target.

Seth pivoted on one heel and pounded him with it, over and over, boring holes over his entire torso. Blood – an angry, bright red – sprayed into Seth's face, but he persisted, pounding and pounding until the man crumpled into a heap.

Seth thrust the knife into the ground, wiping his eyes with his sleeve.

By now, the score of bandits had been reduced to a handful of yielded men and a mountain of broken flesh. Marbrand dropped the hammer and leaned against his knees, panting.

His gaze flitted to Seth.

The new king stared at the late attacker, now lying in a spreading pool of dark redness.

'First kill?' Marbrand found himself saying.

Seth glanced at him, then at the burning ditch, his breathing heavy.

'What did you let that loose for?' he barked at Qattren.

Qattren threw the flames a passing glance. The bodies it had consumed were gone, along with a patch of grass a yard wide and counting. Not even ash remained: just a black stain in the earth.

She threw a gesture at the Wastelands.

'What's another yard beside this?'

Nevertheless, she held a hand over the flames.

A crack erupted from beyond the flames. The abandoned mill behind the fence came tilting down. It collapsed onto the blaze, covering it in stone and dust.

'This should hold it,' she said, straightening her skirts.

Seth scrutinised the ditch to make sure and nodded.

He had, Marbrand didn't fail to notice, ignored the comment about his first kill.

~

The priest grasped a handful of crochet and yanked it off.

'Rise to greet the queen, charlatan!'

Howie glowered at him. 'Or what?'

The priest – Toffer, Howie realised with a start – hauled him up by his collar and shook him.

'Stop shaking me,' Howie snapped at him, shoving him away. 'What happened to Our Lord and Saviour? Knight of Thingy? Holy trousers and all that?'

'This saviour has money,' Toffer said bluntly. 'A man has bills to pay, you know.'

Aaliyaa threw him a horrible glance. She looked very much like Vladimir, Howie thought – he had inherited the narrow scowl. Her face was rounder, more feminine, and still quite youthful. He wondered how old she was before realising that he didn't quite care.

'Where is the dragon, Antichrist?'

'Not in here, evidently,' Howie said wryly.

Toffer hit him over the head with the flat of his hand.

'Answer her most humble highness!'

Howie exploded with laughter. 'Humble? Look at the state of her!'

The woman wore half a wardrobe's worth of cloth-of-gold. She looked like a giant candelabra.

Toffer hit him again, silencing him.

Aaliyaa drifted to the workbench and ran a hand over the tools.

'These are very sharp, aren't they?' she commented. 'These should get you talking.'

She picked up a particularly rusty specimen, an old sentimental tool of Archie's he was loath to throw out.

Howie rolled his eyes. 'You're not doing your image any favours, are you? Aren't you queens supposed to be all serenity and light? I don't think it's in the job description to threaten civilians with a rusty chisel.'

Aaliyaa bared her teeth, grinding them together.

'The Seven forgive all violence in service to their will,' she spat. 'Now reveal the location of the hell-beast before I'm forced to ruin your arrogant face.'

'Ruin away,' Howie said blithely. 'See if I care.'

Aaliyaa's eyes thinned to slits.

Howie gave her a bright smile.

The comfortable calm they had interrupted still, strangely, appeared to linger. Now it took a cool edge as the rusty chisel came closer to his chin.

'Release him!'

Their gazes swung collectively to the door.

Cienne stood in the light of the sun.

'Princess Cienne,' Aaliyaa demurred. 'What are you to the Antichrist?'

'She's my mum,' said Howie.

Cienne grimaced. She pointedly avoided his gaze.

Toffer frowned. 'She's your *mum?*'

'Kind of,' said Howie.

He made a face at Cienne. 'What?'

Cienne glowered at him. 'What?'

'You just rolled your eyes at me.'

Cienne put her hands on her hips. 'I do not *roll my eyes*—'

'You just did!' Howie said hotly.

Aaliyaa watched this exchange with a blank expression.

'What's your problem?' he demanded. 'Why'd you bother coming here to help if you dislike me so much?'

'I didn't come to help *you*, I came to help—'

Cienne snapped her mouth shut mid-sentence.

Howie smirked wryly. 'Oh, I see. You came here because you thought I was Seth.'

'That's not—'

'That's *clearly* what you were about to say!'

'Alright, fine, I didn't know you were here!' Cienne exploded. 'Happy?'

'No!' Howie howled at her. 'Why would it, you stupid woman?'

Aaliyaa sighed loudly. 'I am bored of this conversation.'

She snatched the scruff of Cienne's collar, along with a handful of hair, and dragged her stumbling into a strangle-hold.

'Tell me,' Aaliyaa hissed at him, 'where your dragon is or I will be forced to kill your mother.'

Cienne's eyes widened, her breath becoming shallow.

Howie stared blankly at them.

And shrugged.

'Go ahead. I'm off to the pub.'

Shrugging out of Toffer's grasp, Howie straightened his jerkin and strode past them without a second glance.

'Um…' Aaliyaa hesitated.

They stood in stunned silence broken only by the fading pad of leather on cobblestone.

Aaliyaa's jaw hung open in confusion.

'That,' Toffer said, 'was unexpected.'

Cienne replied by kicking Aaliyaa in the shin.

Aaliyaa howled.

Cienne wrenched herself free and scrambled for the open wood chest in the corner.

'Toffer!' Aaliyaa barked, clutching her knee. 'Seize the boy! I'll—'

Clunk.

Aaliyaa tilted forward and face-planted into the flagstones.

Cienne dropped a piece of timber on her head and fled.

Toffer observed the situation in bemusement. And swiftly realised that this was above his paygrade.

He carefully stepped over Aaliyaa's lifeless form and hurried out.

~

Dusk dulled the landscape slowly as the only living creatures in the Wastelands strode northwest. Four squires towed the journey's supply cart, and the rest of the entourage walked with Seth and Qattren, the former in front and the latter taking the rear.

Seth glanced up at the darkening sky. Five shadows flashed back and forth overhead.

'What are those?'

'The demon army,' Qattren said.

Seth made a face. 'Half a dozen birds?'

'Demon soldiers,' she corrected. 'They fly. That makes them useful for catching things that run.'

'And you couldn't trade the son of God for an army of more than five?' Marbrand snapped from Seth's right.

'I did. Twenty of them are waiting for us at the Stonekeep. These five are escorts in case we run into trouble.'

'Nice of them to help out with the bandits,' Marbrand muttered, ignored as always.

'Who said he'll be keeping her at his castle?' said Seth. 'What if he's keeping her elsewhere?'

'I have someone working on that. Keep walking.'

Seth huffed. 'I'm starving. Who's for setting up camp for the night?'

The guards made agreeable noises.

The four squires dropped the supplies, not deigning to wait for further instruction.

Qattren's five escorts touched down and stood stock still around them, their hands clasped behind their backs. Naturally, Seth approached to wave a hand across their visors.

'Hello?' he pestered. 'Hungry? You want a cake?'

'They don't eat, Seth,' Qattren said, rubbing her eyes.

Seth ignored her and strode to the supplies cart, elbowing past one of the squires.

'Mind out, then, let me get the man some—*have you been in here the entire time?*'

Everyone stopped moving and rushed to surround him.

Lilly hopped out of the cart, rubbing her eyes.

'Mum wouldn't let me come, so I snuck in, yeah,' she said with a yawn. 'That a problem?'

'We're going to battle, my lady,' Marbrand said in annoyance.

'So? I wanna help!'

Seth looked her up and down. 'You're only a baby, Lilly. Get back in the cart.'

'I'm not three, Seth. I can be useful. Fight me and I'll show you,' she challenged, clenching her fists in front of her.

'We've already seen how useful you are,' he said. 'We had a fight only an hour ago while you were cowering in there.'

Lilly looked confused. Then her face crumpled in fury.

'Bollocks, I slept through it! You should have woken me up!'

'Nobody knew you were there!' Seth exclaimed.

Lilly spotted one of Qattren's soldiers and waved. 'Nice armour.'

The demon didn't respond.

'You a mute or something?' she called, approaching.

'Lilly, get away from that!' Seth shouted, pulling her arm. 'It'll eat you!'

'No it won't, it's more obedient than that,' Qattren said, frowning. 'It won't harm anyone that isn't attacking us.'

'Better get off me arm, then,' Lilly said, shrugging Seth off.

She strolled right up to the demon's face and lifted the visor.

'Ew, his nose is fluffy,' she said, a hand inside the visor to rub it.

'Lilly, get your hand out of there!' Seth hissed, pulling her away.

'Pity neither of you can restrain your childishness,' Qattren muttered. 'It would have been useful to have a competent Crey with us.'

Seth pulled a face. 'What's your problem?'

Qattren sweated profusely, her hands clenched into fists by her sides. Her gaze locked outwards and her jaw set stiffly, she shook her head.

Seth rolled his eyes away from her.

Marbrand nudged his shoulder.

'My liege, I'm not sure she should be here.'

'There's no stopping Lilly from being anywhere she wants to be. You do, however, have royal permission to *bash* her head in, though.'

Lilly stuck her tongue out.

'No, not her, Qattren,' Marbrand said.

'Why? What's she doing that's so bad?'

'Nothing yet—'

'Then leave her be. Maybe she is psychotic and antisocial, but so long as she's offering to fight my enemies for me while I watch from a safe distance, I don't really care.'

'Look at her!' Marbrand protested, pointing at her. 'She's on the verge of a meltdown! It's bad enough us being in this necropolis without bringing her out of spite!'

'She's not having a meltdown,' Seth said flippantly. 'She's just hot under all those feathers. Aren't you?' He turned to face her. 'Hello?'

~

X

Qattren paid Seth no attention. She was currently preoccupied with the ghosts.

Pale figures danced in circles around her. She felt that familiar heat behind her neck. Not the guilt – the anger.

And it all rushed back… the flames, the smoke, the ashes, all falling around her in pieces and spinning like a blizzard… the screams, the calls for mercy, all morphed into a furious drumming song, and she was dancing to it, not out of pleasure but as a catharsis, the motions trying desperately to throw out the anger—

But it wouldn't go away, it kept clinging, controlling her as if she were a string puppet, swinging her around and around, palms up, fire soaring upwards before falling like snow, engulfing everything in smoke and flames.

Not red flames, like dragon fire, or the timid yellow flames men used, nor purple, like everyone thought, but blue flames, flames the colour of death, painful death… everything black and blue…

Except for the blood.

Qattren screamed.

The ghosts screamed back, knocking the images into every pore.

Children were crying, men lay dead where she left them, their bodies concealed in the trees, at least for the moment. Qattren hadn't seen the families. She'd seen the rebels – at least, before the demon fire had taken them and left nothing but a shadow – but their families, their wives, their children… they had been hiding in the houses, where it was safe.

She won't get us in here, they thought. She won't get us here, they *believed* it…

She'd burned them anyway.

The song had drowned out the screams and, blood pumping, half-mad from the heat, Qattren ravaged the country.

And now, it ravaged her back.

Qattren screamed.

~

'NO!!'

Seth leapt backwards in alarm.

Qattren dropped to her knees, the burned soil staining her dress. She sobbed and cried out, her arms covering her ears in a childlike motion.

Seth stared at her, eyes narrowed.

'Alright, maybe she *is* having a meltdown,' he conceded.

Qattren hurled her head upwards and howled at the clouds.

~

'Murderer…'

'Slaughterer…'

'Barbaric…'

'Killer…'

The whispers cut into her brain, leaving holes.

The music was starting, but she could still hear them.

'DIE!' they screamed, circling her like a whirlwind. 'DIE, SLAUGHTERER!'

'I CAN'T!' she shrieked, throwing herself in all directions.

~

They watched her burst into dust, her screams echoing in their ears.

Seth took a breath. For a moment, he had the feeling she would burst into flames and burn the Wastelands up all over again.

'I CAN'T!' she had screamed.

Can't what?

'My liege,' Marbrand said in a low voice, 'may I offer you counsel?'

'By all means,' Seth drawled, 'if it's important enough for you to ask permission first.'

'I suggest we sack her forthwith, if that's alright with you. Women exploding into miniscule particles after yelling into the void tends to unsettle… pretty much everyone.'

Seth nodded. 'Agreed.'

~

Qattren tumbled and landed in a heap in a small paddock in Stoneguard, her usual grace shaken out of her by a thousand emotions. The furious song faded out, to her relief. Geldemar nicknamed it 'The Kill-Kill song' because once it began, she killed. Relentlessly.

She paused a moment in the grass and held her ribs, breathing steadily until the sobs subsided and her heart rate slowed. The urge to scream was replaced with fatigue, a rare occurrence.

Slowly, she rose to her feet.

The sky was black now, but the stars had not yet revealed themselves. The perpetual clouds of the Wastelands had gone.

She sighed heavily, the memories still clinging to her mind. All the regret, built up over fifty years, had been wearing her down – none so much as the memory of his face when he'd found out.

She shook the thought from her head. *Not now. Now isn't the time for that.*

She examined her surroundings, trying to place where she was.

A village could be seen over a fence ten yards west. An uphill road led to the Stonekeep some five miles away, peering over the roofs of the city, but Stoneguard wasn't what clinched Qattren's attention.

Flames – of the yellow variety – billowed out of a steeple to the left of the keep.

Qattren frowned and slipped into Sal'plae to investigate.

A figure stumbled on the flagstones outside the front door.

Qattren glimpsed Howie and relaxed. He would sort that. She had bigger fish to fry.

Qattren left directly after that.

~

Cienne turned into another side street and staggered to a halt with a sigh of exasperation.

She was lost. Stoneguard was tiny, according to every map she had ever studied – how could she possibly be lost?

Cienne heaved a sigh and glanced around.

Cobbles and wood panelling surrounded her through the navy tint of dusk. A lamentably minute amount of distinguishable landmarks separated one wall from another. She could be walking in circles for all she knew.

She leaned a shoulder on a nearby wall for a moment, lifting one foot into the air to ease the dull ache. A warm glow from the distance caught her eye as she shifted to the other foot.

A church spire was aflame.

There's a church by the Stonekeep, she recalled.

Cienne followed the source of the light.

~

In the Wastelands, the group waited.

Despite the lack of natural resources, the Wastelands was no more uncomfortable than any other terrain they had camped in on the way to the border. The black earth was dry enough for a campfire to catch, thanks to the logs and kindling a foresighted Marbrand had collected on the way through Adem. Half the group sat contented around the flames, turning a lump of meat on a spit.

The other half were twenty yards behind, shovelling at the ashen ground on the orders of Lilly.

'There's this crystal stuff, right,' she had said when Marbrand questioned her, 'really valuable unbreakable crystal. Apparently you find it wherever Qattren threw her demon flames about. This place burned for about two years solid, there's bound to be some here. I'm gonna dig it up and get Qattren or somebody to make me an *unbreakable scimitar*,' she finished, practically salivating at the thought.

'It's made when the blue flames are buried under rock,' he had corrected, 'the flames weren't buried here,' but she wasn't listening, as ever.

Marbrand cast a wary glance across the plain, his vision well-adjusted to the gloom. Nothing out of the ordinary jumped out at him – yet. He was sure more thieves lurked in the shadows. Now Qattren had vanished, it was the opportune moment for any more to appear.

Deciding to worry about the danger when it came, he flexed his shoulders and made a beeline for Seth.

Seth stared back at where Qattren had dematerialised.

Marbrand approached in concern. Pensive expressions were not something that often happened to a Crey.

'Everything alright?'

Seth met his gaze. 'Mmm, everything's fine.' He glanced back to the pile of dust that marked Qattren's departure, a light patch on the blackened ground. 'I'm just wondering if she's alright.'

Marbrand frowned. 'Now I'm *really* concerned. All due respect, but compassion was never known to be your strongpoint.'

Seth shot him a look before turning his gaze upward.

'You forget, don't you?' he said. 'I mean, you think constantly of what's happening to *you*, but it doesn't occur to stop and think about what's happening to *others* until something *big* happens to you where you realise that what *you're* thinking about is what *they* were thinking about and that instead of worrying about your silly problems, you should have been worrying more about them.'

He sighed and looked at Marbrand's blank expression.

'Just seems a bit unfair, that's all.'

Marbrand stared at him blankly. 'Yes.'

He wandered off, wondering what the hell he was talking about.

Seth gazed at the stars, his thoughts on Qattren's ghosts, and his own.

It was then that Qattren came up behind him and pulled him away.

~

The Church of the Seven wavered from side to side, along with the rest of the street. And also the sky.

Howie collapsed.

An owl hooted in the distance.

'Oh, what are you laughing at?' Howie slurred with malevolence, glowering at the cobbles beneath his hands.

He scrambled forward as his beer bottle rolled away.

A wave of heat consumed him from the nearby flames. Howie rose to his feet, cradling his bottle under his chin.

Dust consumed the street for a moment.

Seth disentangled himself from Qattren's grasp and swung to face her.

'What are you playing at? First you disappear into thin air, then you come back and *grab* me—'

He glanced around and frowned at the church.

'Where am I?'

'Stoneguard. Vladimir is on his way home from a social call, so I suggest you review your terms.' Qattren eyed his jerkin critically. 'You may want to do something about all the blood you're wearing.'

Seth ignored her. His gaze had diverted to the left.

A figure staggered in circles outside the flaming chapel, clutching a bottle.

'Ah,' Seth said, with a grin. 'The heroic Howard Rosethorn.'

Howie slammed sideways into a wall and bounced off it, blinking in confusion.

Qattren watched this, her mouth ajar.

'Howard?' she ventured.

Howie's head jerked up with a bleary, repetitive blink.

'What are you doing?'

Howie jerked his bottle in the direction of the church.

'Burning this piece of shit to the ground.'

Qattren's head shook twice. 'Why?'

'Because it *looked* at me funny,' he said with venom.

Seth flung him a withering glance.

'Of course it did. Right, shall we head to the keep—'

'What did you say?' Howie demanded in a high squeak.

'What?'

'You were *muttering.*'

Howie stumbled forward until they were nose to nose.

Seth's nose wrinkled. 'You should probably consider reviewing your bathing schedule.'

Howie slammed his bottle into the cobbles.

It shattered.

'Howard, back away,' Qattren warned. 'We have things to do.'

'No,' he grunted, his gaze locked to Seth's. 'I've backed away for long enough.'

He jabbed a finger at Seth's nose, opened his mouth to snarl and promptly forgot what he was going to snarl at him.

Seth lifted an eyebrow.

'If you're quite finished staring at me in malevolent silence, I have an appointment,' he said crisply.

Seth tried to step around him.

Howie stumbled back into his path.

'No, I'm not finished,' Howie slurred, glowering up at him. He frowned. 'Why are you taller than me all of a sudden?'

Seth made a face. 'I've always been this tall.'

'No you haven't! You've grewn! What's that about?' Howie demanded squeakily.

Seth heaved a sigh. 'I don't know. Now *please* move. I have a wife to retrieve.'

'Oh yeah,' Howie snarled, '*rub it in,* why don't you, you smug, suspiciously tall bastard.'

'Seth, just walk around him,' Qattren said wearily.

Howie shushed her, holding a finger up.

'You're *in* the *way,*' Seth said irately.

'Good!' Howie spat. 'How's it feel being the one being annoyed for a change? You think you're so great with your money and your tallness and your, your... shoes. You're like a big, ugly weasel. You don't deserve money, or a big castle, or nice shoes. You don't even deserve your name – why'd you get such a nice name anyway? What did I ever do to deserve the stupid shite name made up on the spot by a little girl and a drunk wizard—'

'I don't *care!*' Seth said, exasperated.

Qattren rolled her eyes and circled them.

'You think it's nice, having a first name that won't suit you until you're sixty?' Howie shouted at him.

He took a swig from his bottle before realising he had smashed it a moment earlier. He flexed his empty fingers in disappointment.

'You think it's nice being dumped in a forest by a rich teenager and having to race around on a dragon like a *berk* looking for her twenty years later? You think that's fair? How is that fair—'

Qattren grabbed the back of his hair.

Howie soared five miles through purple-tinged streets and houses before being tossed to a halt in the centre of a market square. He landed hard on one shoulder.

'Rude!' he roared into the empty market.

Something hard and flat whacked him on the back of the head.

He howled.

Toffer roughly turned him over, grabbed the purse dangling from his belt and pegged it.

'Rude,' he said again, weakly.

He flopped onto his back.

~

Qattren rematerialized a short moment later.

'Thank God for that,' Seth said, rolling his eyes.

The Stonekeep loomed over them from the top of the hill. If Seth ever thought his home was ugly and impractical, it was only because he'd never seen this one.

The Stonekeep stank of cliché malevolence. Rickety stone towers lurked over a pitiful two-story cylinder, all circled with a poorly filled wall that made the straw-topped mud cottages of Teal look sturdier.

While the Serpent's Knot – always nicknamed the Creys' Keep – had the advantages of a dizzying height and firm, thick walls, the Stonekeep looked as if it had been based on a child's pebble castle, stone for stone. And if the Creys' extravagant windows weren't dangerous enough, the Stonekeep had huge windows everywhere, many broken with missing panels due to the Hornes' financial deficits

The next point Seth noticed about the castle was that it was empty. As was the street, come to that.

'Where is everyone?' he said, climbing the hill to the main portcullis. 'The guards? The smallfolk? The clergymen, even? Doesn't anyone care that the church is aflame?'

'Considering that their most prominent representative is Queen Aaliyaa, probably not,' Qattren said bluntly. 'I imagine the clergymen currently reside in the palace now that their head of church is working for Aaliyaa.'

She met Seth's gaze.

'That would be your assassin at the Duke's mansion, in case you were wondering.'

'Ah.' He reddened. 'Thanks for investigating that.'

'You're most welcome.'

They strode up the gravel path to the main entrance. On the way, their gazes darted momentarily to an extremely vocal tree howling in the distance.

'Wind's picking up,' Seth said distantly.

Qattren frowned. 'What wind?'

He realised with a start that the tree was in fact a woman. She raised her hands in the air, screeched and clapped both hands to one side of her head with a distant, 'Ow.'

Seth gestured at her. 'Now what exactly is the story with that?'

'God knows,' Qattren muttered.

Seth shook his head, trudging upward.

'Weirdos!' he exclaimed. 'This entire city is full of weirdos!'

Qattren's eyes lingered on the figure with a suspicious squint before they abruptly arrived at the portcullis.

'Wait here a moment,' Qattren said. 'I will be back momentarily.'

'Why?' he asked dubiously. 'You're not going to hurt that old woman, are you? Because if you are, I want the first punch. She's extremely annoying.'

'Leave her alone, she's clearly mentally ill. I have a greater task at hand. Rest assured, I will not make the same mistake as the Battle in the Orchard and slaughter perfectly good employees. You will see shortly.'

She dissipated.

Five minutes later, the portcullis was hastily winched open. Dozens of men, women and children streamed out of the gates in varying states of confusion, panic and haste.

Within moments, the entire castle had been evacuated.

Seth blinked, bemused. Surely they hadn't just taken one look at Qattren and made a break for it? He had a mental image of her waving her hands with a 'shoo'. That would probably have done it.

Seth entered the empty forecourt as Qattren beckoned.

'So now we just have him to deal with?'

'Unfortunately not. His mother is the difficulty here. That would be why the castle lacks reinforcements. It didn't need protecting.'

Seth shot her a side-glance. 'You actually believe she will

incapacitate us by torturing us via a hand knitted caricature?'

'No, I'll believe she'll blow out our eardrums with her incessant screeching and remove our sense of balance. The dolls will be just for show.'

She shot him a side-glance and added in a serious tone, 'We might take the piss out of her idea of "sorcery", but she has got some skills – mainly terrifying the locals into doing her bidding. I'd rather not see a pitchfork into your eyes. Two dead Crey kings in one year might be a bit excessive.'

Her eyes glinted.

'Not to worry,' she added brightly. 'I have friends who will sort her out as soon as she arrives. Vladimir will be arriving back shortly.'

'Fantastic,' Seth said with forced enthusiasm.

There was a moment's silence.

'Tell me about Seb.'

Qattren threw Seth a look. 'Why?'

'Just wondering what he was like in his prime,' he said with a shrug. 'I only remember him being bedridden and senile.'

Qattren smiled faintly.

'He wasn't always like that,' she said softly, her eyes to the sky. 'We met in the Forest. He came to drive me out, the day I pitched a claim.'

'Didn't work, evidently.'

Qattren snorted. 'You could say that. Despite our intentions, we got on spectacularly. We had a good rapport, amongst other things.'

'Mmm, other things,' Seth said, amused.

'We engaged in a physical relationship that very night. And all in all, it was great.'

Seth averted his gaze, trying to forget he had raised the subject.

'He was caring,' she said. 'In his own little ways. He was a lot like you, he hid behind his ego and this mask of contempt for others, but I knew him. I knew him properly. Intimately he was warm, gentle, skilled—'

'I… *hate* to interrupt, but when I said, "tell me about Seb", I meant his personality, not his…'

Seth gesticulated in the direction of his trousers.

'*Skills.*'

'Ah.' She smiled. 'Are you sure? You might learn something.'

Seth planted his hands on his hips, offended.

'I'll have you know, I pleasure women just fine at the moment, thank you!'

Qattren laughed. The sound was musical.

'What?' he said, smiling despite himself. 'What are you laughing at?'

'You remind me of him.'

Her grin faltered slightly, but a shade of it still hung to her features as she remembered.

'He was also a little too comfortable around the opposite gender – until he found who he wanted. He wouldn't let anything come between him and what he wanted most. He'd cling to it, hard. And he wouldn't let it go.'

Her smile fell away completely.

'Even when it posed a threat to him.'

She examined her dress, impassive as ever.

'The fire was what made him let go of me,' she whispered. 'It was the last straw. Before that, I had been everything to him. Even his son – your father – wasn't as important as us. But now… I'd broken his country. Soiled his reputation. The only thing he loved more than me.

'I kept telling him to get rid of the deserters that tried to usurp him, but he wouldn't dismiss them. He hated them, but he wanted their favour. For Adem's sake.' She pursed her lips. 'Then they killed a friend of mine. And I didn't care. I was so naïve, I thought he would value my reasons for my actions, so I burned it up…'

Seth listened without a sound, his eyes fixed to his boots.

'I didn't know there were people in those houses. The streets were empty, I just assumed the families had fled into exile, but then they started *screaming*…'

She shuddered.

'I went to him after that. Told him what I had done. The way he looked at me… the *betrayal* in his eyes, I'd never seen him look so hurt… he told me he didn't want me anymore. Said we would remain allies for Adem's sake, but it wasn't what I wanted. I just wanted to forget it all and go back to the way we were.'

She took a breath and composed herself.

'It was my own doing. He acted with honour during the war, and I acted like a fool. He always put the majority before himself… and me. When it mattered.'

Seth hesitated. 'This friend they killed. Did they matter?'

Qattren met his gaze.

'She did to me,' she said hoarsely.

Seth fixed her a firm look. 'Then she should have to him, too.'

Qattren flinched and turned away, and her nonchalance was

back, the sadness replaced as suddenly as it had come.

'Vladimir should have arrived by now,' she said, staring out once more. 'The demons should have taken him into custody long ago. He's only a five-minute ride away.'

'Unless his mother has already dealt with them.'

'I doubt it. They're nearly powerful enough to harm me, never mind her.' Qattren blinked. 'But their owners, however.'

She whistled piercingly.

Seth winced as his ears stung.

Otherwise, nothing happened.

'They're gone, they would have come otherwise,' she said, stalking to the Stonekeep entrance. 'Wait here for me.'

She dematerialised.

Seth sighed heavily and leaned against the Stonekeep's fragile-looking wall. His mind strayed to Adrienne, kneeling in her own blood, the only thing left of Seth's child. It was the same, he realised. Qattren had destroyed the one thing Seb loved more than her. The betrayal in his eyes…

Betrayal. That's all he felt for Adrienne now. Betrayal.

Seth wondered if it would ever stop hurting him as the darkness shrouded him from view. Then he saw a horseman approach.

~

Qattren burst into the Stonekeep's massive throne room, shrouded in Sal'plae.

'What are you doing here?'

Geldemar slouched on the Stonethrone, waggling his fingers at her.

'Taking back what's mine, of course. You did say it would only take a day.'

Qattren sighed angrily. 'You knew I would bring them back when I was finished with them.'

'Ah, but you said that last time. Remember? On the Night of Raining Thorns, just before The Kill-Kill Song made its second appearance.'

Qattren scowled at him.

'We heard it starting again, so we decided to confiscate your weapons from you. Not that you need them now. Your newest adversary is on his way to you, so we decided to relieve him of his escorts.'

'And the dragon?'

'Round the back, waiting for your little plan.' He winked.

Qattren saw his expression. 'Ready and willing?'

'Willing and able,' he said.

'And the banshee?'

'Consider her already dealt with.'

Qattren smiled slightly. 'Very well.'

She left Sal'plae promptly.

~

XI

Queen Aaliyaa Horne stood outside the front portcullis, merely a black shadow in the darkness. Albeit a wobbly one: the head wound had taken a toll on her, along with the energy used to cast the curse.

She had been startled to see Qattren Meriangue alongside Seth Crey outside the Stonekeep. It was well known she avoided Crey affairs. However, Aaliyaa's disguise as a common crone seemed to have held her at bay.

Long enough for her to cast the curse on the new King of Adem.

Those you love will run from you screaming...

She was damned if she remembered what else the curse described – she'd been rather caught up in the moment. Betrayal figured in there somewhere. Some kind of hideous skin disease was probably another one. Black-hearted children of sinful descent was one of her favourites. Did she remember to give him a sexually transmitted disease like Vladimir asked her to? No, she'd forgotten that one. Oops.

Never mind. Screaming seemed to be the general gist of it.

She turned her gaze to the sky, her face scrunched in concentration.

But before she could cast her protection spell, a blue light shrouded her.

Her surroundings wavered, then changed as a large wooden palace materialised before her.

'Enter, Aaliyaa,' an amiable voice said.

She entered the double doors – not before blessing herself with water from the font beside her.

Inside, a huge circular hall welcomed her. Seven people looked benevolently upon her.

Aaliyaa was enraptured.

'The Seven,' she whispered.

'It is us,' the twins replied in unison.

Aaliyaa knelt in front of them, her head bowed. 'Seven lords, I am honoured by your presence.'

'And we are honoured by yours,' the golden-eyed one said. 'We have observed the work you have done to aid our will. We are proud of you, child.'

'Thank you, my lord,' she said, lifting her chin proudly.

'We have plans for you,' the one in green said. 'An ascension to demi-deity is on the cards, daughter.'

'But there is something you must do for us first,' said the golden-eyed one.

'Anything you wish is my command, my lord,' she said.

'Aaliyaa,' he said, 'your work is admirable… but you must hold back for now.'

Aaliyaa's head snapped up. 'Why, my lord?'

'Prince Vladimir must seal his fate himself. Events are due to happen that cannot happen with you present.'

She bowed her head. 'Anything you say, I shall obey, my lord.'

'Excellent. Travel to the Dead Cities to await your fate. We will let you know when we need you next.'

'Yes, my lords.'

The golden-eyed one nodded and held a hand over Aaliyaa's head.

The blue light surrounded her again and she disappeared.

A loud snort broke the serenity in her wake.

'Sucker,' said Geldemar.

'She shouldn't have touched the water,' said Gale, shaking his head.

~

Vladimir swayed blithely in the saddle.

His palfrey led herself up the steep path to the portcullis, having already decided that Vladimir's drunken instruction led them in a route far too long to the stables for her liking.

Vladimir gazed up at the keep fondly. It was cliché, but it had style.

He patted the wall on his way into the gaping portcullis. The forecourt was silent. *Where is everyone?* He craned his neck back to scrutinise the gatehouse, but there was no sign of life there either.

With a dismissive shrug, he swung himself to the ground and led his horse to the…

… vacant stable.

'Oh, for gods' sake,' Vladimir seethed, his tipsy good humour evaporating.

He pondered on the correct procedure to sort his horse out, decided he didn't know or indeed care and simply flung the reins over one shoulder.

The palfrey watched them bounce off her shoulder with a blank expression.

He tugged his cloak around himself and strode to the keep.

Followed by Seth, skulking in the shadows.

Vladimir entered the throne room, wondering at the desolation of the place.

'Mother?' he called, his voice the only sound in the building as it bounced from wall to wall. 'Are you here?'

A slam swung his attention to the entrance.

Seth Crey leaned against the doors with his hands in his pockets.

'Evening,' he said casually.

Vladimir simply frowned at him. He heard footfall on the stairs behind him.

'Mother,' he said, turning, 'why is there a Crey in our cas—'

Qattren Meriangue stood at the end of the stairs, her hands on her hips and her hair tied back loosely.

'Lost your mummy, have you?' said Seth.

Vladimir flung him a withering glance.

'She must have abandoned you,' said Qattren, stepping forward, 'after realising the folly of your actions.'

Vladimir grimaced at her. 'What actions?'

Seth closed in behind him.

'Your actions towards my wife.'

Vladimir burst out laughing.

'Oh, she told you about that, did she? Honestly, you can't say anything hypothetically to you people, can you?'

'Whatever,' Seth said, clearly not listening. 'What have you done with her?'

Vladimir pulled a face. 'Done with who?'

Seth's eyes rolled upward. '*My wife.*'

'I haven't done anything with her!' he said shrilly. 'Why?'

'The Emmetts claim that a group of men bearing your colours abducted Cienne Fleurelle from their coach on their way to Emmett Jr's manor house,' said Qattren. 'Do you want to call them liars?'

'Yes!' Vladimir shrieked. 'Emmett Jr told you this, is it? That's like him. Just you ask him what happened between him and my Cousin Tetzil in the flowerbed thirteen years ago, you'll soon see what he looks like when he's lying.'

'Your childhood argument with the Emmetts is irrelevant,' Seth said flatly. 'I haven't come to fight with anyone. I've come to propose a bargain.'

'If you agree to forfeit your claim to Stoneguard and return Queen Cienne to us, we will drop all animosity between us for this slight and allow you to govern Stoneguard as Lord Protector.'

'And if I refuse?'

'We explode the castle and all individuals therein.'

Seth pivoted. '*All* individuals therein?'

'We will be out by the time of the explosion, as you know, King Seth,' Qattren said pointedly.

Seth's eyes widened.

'Yes, obviously,' he said swiftly, swinging back to Vladimir. 'So just you, then.'

'But I haven't done anything!' Vladimir howled. 'I don't have the woman! You've clearly just done something to all of my staff, surely you would have found the woman in here somewhere if I had her?'

Seth snorted. 'Exactly what you'd like us to think.'

Vladimir flung his gaze to the ceiling. 'Look, we haven't done anything to her. We have our own lives to live, you know. I'll propose my bargain. Return my staff from wherever it is you've magicked them off to and I'll send out a search party.'

'And if I refuse?'

Seth drew his sword.

Vladimir sighed and drew his own. 'You tell me.'

Qattren held Seth back by one shoulder.

'If you want to have a sword fight, be my guest,' she said tiredly. 'But I need a decision, Vladimir. Do you yield Stoneguard?'

Vladimir's lip twitched.

'That's "your majesty" to you, your majesty,' he sneered. 'And I yield nothing. You'll soon regret toying with me when my lords hear about this folly.'

He thrust the sword point in Seth's direction.

'Go on, then!' he said. 'Do your worst.'

Seth looked to Qattren for guidance.

She whispered in his ear.

He conferred back.

She whispered again.

Vladimir jiggled his sword up and down in the air.

'Today!' he barked.

Seth smiled at Vladimir and lifted his sword. 'As you will, your majesty.'

'She has to leave,' added Vladimir, throwing a gesture at Qattren. 'I want a fair fight.'

'As you wish,' Qattren said.

She opened one of the doors behind them and slid out, giving Seth a meaningful glance.

Seth waited for the door to clap shut before sprinting forward.

Vladimir ducked to the right, missing Seth's blade by a foot.

Seth's back was turned, his hands fumbling with the sword.

Vladimir swung at his head.

Seth deflected, throwing him back.

Without missing a beat, Vladimir lunged again.

Seth leapt backwards, stumbling on the poorly set tiles beneath his feet.

Qattren jogged to the back of the castle, her skirts gathered in her hands. She rounded the corner and found Lyseria curled in the grass, gazing lazily at her.

Inside, the two men circled each other warily, swords raised.

'Do you know anything about sword fighting, your majesty?' Vladimir said mockingly.

'Nothing at all,' said Seth, both hands locked tightly around the hilt.

In retrospect, the crystal sword, it being as light as a feather, would have been much better suited to the task, Qattren, he thought bitterly.

'You?'

'As little as you do. My mother has cleaner ways to deal with the likes of you, but alas she seems to be elsewhere. Makes things much messier, but no matter.'

'Yield, then.'

Vladimir hurled himself at him in an apparent 'no'.

Seth fled upstairs, swiftly pursued by Vladimir.

Once the ground floor was empty, Qattren crept in silently, followed by Lyseria.

The dragon lay on her belly and watched Qattren. She cracked her knuckles and held the beast by her nose.

Upstairs, Seth burst into a bedchamber and spun in time to block a blow from Vladimir.

'Finished running, have we?' Vladimir snarled, swinging.

Seth deflected clumsily.

'What's wrong with your arms? Can't you hit me?'

Seth ignored his taunts, his attention focussed to Vladimir's blade.

'HIT ME!' Vladimir screamed, his blade over his shoulder. 'You're taking my entire livelihood, why not take my life as well? Go on! HIT ME!!'

Seth turned his head away, deflecting.

Vladimir shrieked at him, each word punctuated with a swing.

'Undeserving—'

Clang!

'—self-absorbed—'

Clang!

'—crown-stealing—'

Clang!

'—SWINE!'

Clang!

Seth's sword flew from his hands and skittered across the flagstones.

Teeth bared manically, Vladimir raised his weapon over his shoulder and swung for Seth's head.

It swept an inch above its target as Seth ducked. The blade exploded into the mortar between two bricks in the edge of the privy doorway with a crack.

The hilt came free in Vladimir's hand.

He gaped at it in astonishment.

The steel wobbled, the blade half-buried into the wall.

Vladimir stared at it with bulging eyes.

'It's broken!' he shrilled.

Seth snatched his own sword from the tiles and levelled it at Vladimir's throat.

'Shame when that happens,' he said with a smirk.

~

Lyseria whined.

'Good girl,' Qattren murmured, stroking her snout.

Lyseria arched her back, scales glinting red in the moonlight. A light shone from beneath her haunches and she flinched, releasing the white-hot egg.

Qattren caught it, concentrating.

It was crucial she did not touch the egg.

Summoning all the strength she possessed, she pushed back every lingering flashback of the Battle in the Orchard and, sucking in a breath, summoned her flames.

Cold blue tendrils enveloped the shining white sphere.

The memory of her former palace came into stark focus, the red smoke filling the halls, her sitting on the landing, looking down on the dead bodies below. Unfertilised dragon eggs were so volatile that so much as a jolt would explode them into flames. The insides of a dragon could withstand that – humans in the vicinity of an explosion, not so much.

She figured it would take a good two minutes for the egg to explode once in contact with the ground. Hopefully, they would not need that long.

Guiding the egg into the air via the flames from her palms, she stamped hard on one of the flagstones, shattering it instantly. A small sinkhole hid underneath.

My thanks to Gale, she thought with a smile.

Slowly, one foot on either side of the sinkhole, she lowered the egg inside.

Lyseria bolted from the hall, breaking the doors open in her haste.

The white orb hit the bottom.

The ground already began to tremble.

Qattren backed away.

'SETH!!'

~

'COMING!!'

Seth yanked both ends of the bed sheet in opposite directions. He dusted off his hands and patted Vladimir on the head.

'You won't get away, you know,' Vladimir seethed, wriggling in his bonds. 'I may be close to death, but I have allies, I—'

'Yeah, shut up.'

He stuffed Vladimir's mouth with a pair of woollen socks he'd found in a wardrobe.

Seth straightened up and glanced about listlessly.

Stay away from the ground floor, Qattren had whispered. Get upstairs and get away.

Stay away from the ground floor. That only left one option: out the window.

Seth rushed to the empty frame and his heart sank.

Only a Horne would organise for jagged rocks to be placed below the windows.

He could feel tremors beneath his feet. He had to hurry, or the floor would crumble away entirely.

A shape momentarily blotted out the moon in his peripheral vision.

Seth leaned over the windowsill.

Lyseria circled the castle, giving it a wide berth but waiting for him all the same.

Seth grinned and stood on the windowsill.

Then it dawned on him: he was only one floor up from ground level. She would have to be quick.

Vladimir mumbled something behind his socks.

Seth turned to face him.

Vladimir whined, whey-faced.

Seth weighed the chances of being able to get both him and Vladimir out of the keep safely. They were approximately as thin as the hair over Vladimir's forehead.

Lyseria shrieked, rounding the corner to his right.

'Well, good luck,' he said to him instead.

He saluted in his direction and dropped.

~

Qattren kept running until she was a few yards down the hill and looked back. She could see no one running after her. *What's he doing?*

Lyseria soared around a corner of the palace and over her head in an instant.

Qattren squinted at her back and was relieved to see a hand wave down at her.

Seth nursed his ribs, still sore from the fall onto her back.

Lyseria turned sharply right and flipped upside down.

Seth toppled into a pile of manure with a screech. He hauled himself upright and spat a lob of compost onto his lap. He glimpsed his pet soar to the east.

'Thanks,' he snarled, gagging.

Qattren stared in Seth's direction as he climbed down from the manure pile. Her brow furrowed.

Where's Vladimir?

She stalked up to him.

Seth brushed himself down with a disgusted expression as Qattren cleared her throat.

'Where is—'

Burchhh!

The Stonekeep exploded, casting a fireball of rubble into the stars.

The ground jolted, throwing Seth to the ground. Qattren,

however, stood as still as stone.

'Where is Vladimir?' Qattren asked as though nothing had happened.

Seth stared at the ball of flame and castle, on his hands and knees. It fell back onto the ground with a boom, throwing more dust and ash everywhere.

'I repeat,' she said patiently, ignoring the explosion and staring at Seth, 'where is Vladimir?'

Seth stuck his fingers into his ears and wriggled them up and down.

'Sorry, my ears just popped. Say that again louder?'

Qattren sighed and raised her voice. 'Did you save Vladimir?'

Seth frowned. 'Was I supposed to?'

'Yes!' she exclaimed, extending her arms in exasperation.

Seth made a face. 'Oops.'

Qattren's eyes and mouth widened in disbelief.

'You,' she said, holding her head, 'you absolute moron!'

Seth licked his lips carefully. 'Was that not the plan?'

She glared at him, shaking her head. 'What am I supposed to tell Ron?'

~

Cienne strode uphill and halted, ripping another petticoat from her dress in annoyance. She was down to five now after five minutes of tripping and stumbling. Her hand brushed a barb in the back.

She tugged out half a crossbow bolt, to her bewilderment. *How on earth—*

She decided she had bigger problems and stumbled on, disentangling the other half from the main skirt.

The ground beneath her shook. She thrust a hand against a nearby wall as the flames grew nearer and halted. Perhaps the church fire had reached the oil—

A great bang sounded from uphill.

Cienne fell onto the dusty road and anchored herself there until the tremors subsided. Her ears rang.

Seth better not have been in there, she thought in a panic, he'd better not have…

She rose to her feet and ran.

~

Residents of the city swarmed uphill, despite the lateness of the hour. The flames from the explosion had quickly tapered out, along with the church blaze, which had left superficial damage. Torchlight now highlighted Seth and Qattren as they stumbled downhill in silence, past crowds of nosy onlookers.

'What happened?' an elderly lady asked.

'There's been a terrible accident,' Qattren said in a monotone. They walked on.

'Where's the castle gone?'

'There's been a terrible accident,' said Seth as instructed.

They arrived back in the main city to see, to their surprise, Cienne, jogging to meet them in a mutilated dress with several petticoats hanging off the back.

'Looks like she saved herself,' Qattren commented.

'I wouldn't have expected any less,' Seth said with a half-smile.

Cienne caught sight of Seth and slowed to a weary walk, stopping a foot away from him. Her nose wrinkled.

'You smell like shit,' she said, uncharacteristically blunt.

He tilted his head to one side, observing her dust-stained appearance.

'You look like shit,' he said in retort.

She smiled.

He smiled back.

Cienne licked her lips. 'Shall we go home?'

Seth nodded, stepping forward.

'You'll have to carry me, though,' she added. 'My legs won't hold out for much longer.'

He half-smiled, slid a hand around her waist and another under her knees and hoisted her into his arms.

Something panged in Cienne's abdomen, despite his pungent stench.

'Qattren?'

Qattren looked at him in reply.

Seth strolled over to her and dumped Cienne in her arms.

'Carry her for me, would you?'

With that, he walked away.

Cienne giggled uncontrollably.

'Romance is lost on you, Seth Crey,' she called after him.

He turned his head to grin at her and even Qattren quirked a smile in amusement.

~

As morning began to dawn, Howie stirred. His head was killing him and appeared to have been bleeding as some point. He recalled the previous night's events and simply lay back on the cobblestones, letting the cool breeze wash over him.

A familiar voice caught his attention and he turned his head slowly to the left.

Standing in the road was Cienne, covered in a layer of grime. She was missing a considerable amount of petticoats but was still very much intact.

A shadow fell over him and his gaze met that of Seth Crey.

'Morning,' he greeted him.

Howie cleared his throat by way of reply.

'Just came by to give you this,' he said, dropping a bag of coins onto his chest. 'Should be enough for a journey to Serpus and back. She can pay her own way, but I can't have a Crey going without, even if he is a bastard.'

Howie squinted at him. 'What are you going on about?'

'You're going to Serpus to collect your stuff and your woman,' he said slowly, 'and then you're coming back here. For good. Would you like me to write that down?'

'Won't you miss her?' Howie asked bitterly.

Seth gazed out at Cienne. The hard looks he saved for Howie melted away, to be replaced with a smug half-smile. 'Nah.'

Howie glanced at her sullenly.

Seth spotted his expression and grinned at it. 'Glad you're as happy to see her as I am. Don't mind me, go on. Have a good look at her.'

Howie reluctantly turned his head.

Seth doubled over and pressed his lips to his ear.

'If you think of so much as looking at her after today,' he hissed with venom, 'I will make sure the rest of your unnatural little life is filled with pain. My son's passing will pale in comparison to what I'll do to you. Do you understand?'

'She's my mother. Are you sick in the head?'

Seth smirked. 'Good answer.'

He straightened up and beamed over the fence at Cienne, who smiled back uncertainly.

'See you around, Howard,' he said, strolling to the road, nonchalant.

Howie snorted. 'Not if I can help it, asshole.'

Seth smiled at himself, earning a bemused frown from Cienne.

Howie stared at them as Seth slipped an arm around her and, finally, realised that he didn't care. Cienne could be radiantly beautiful to someone else. If anyone deserved another shovel attack, it was him.

Howie thought of Adrienne, and her son – Seth's son. Was Howie worth the sacrifice, really?

He'd have to make sure he was.

He closed his eyes and relaxed for a while.

~

XII

Qattren sat at the head of Seth's dining table some days later. To her right sat Seth himself, beside Cienne, and to her left sat Ron, looking apprehensive.

She glanced at him, anxious. Under the circumstances, he'd taken his brother's death well. The abuse he'd suffered over the years had convinced Ron that the world was better off without Vladdy. Yet his expression still looked off. It appeared he had issues to work out.

Not least his new position as King of Stoneguard.

Also attending the sit-down were the Emmetts – Felicity, looking pale and horror-stricken; Gomez Sr, examining his daughter in concern; his son of the same name, sterilised and alien-looking as always; and Cienne's uncle Zephyr, the only member of the clan giving Cienne any kind regard this afternoon.

Qattren met the eye of each Emmett with a smile.

'Gentlemen, I thank you for travelling all this way so soon after returning from the Creys' celebrations.'

'We returned for our grieving kin, not your empty words,' Emmett Jr said coldly.

His father shot him a sharp glance.

'Forgive my son,' he said. 'He grieves for the prince, as do we all. We remained in my son's property in Osney after Lord Tetzel's untimely demise, it was not so long a journey.'

Qattren inclined her head.

'Now,' Emmett Sr announced, rubbing his hands together, 'back to business. We were told an accident involving your pet dragon led to the fate of our friend?'

'A dragon's reproductive system is… bizarre,' Qattren said. 'The eggs, if unfertilised, spontaneously combust when jolted or dropped. The prince tried to attack King Seth shortly before the accident and, to shield her master, Lyseria released the egg, allowing us barely enough time to escape with her assistance before it took the Stonekeep. The prince, sadly, fell behind.'

'A risk only too common to take with these creatures,' Zephyr said, nodding.

'My father did like to make a certain impression,' said Seth.

'Odd that Prince Vladimir was the only casualty,' Emmett Jr drawled.

Seth paused.

'Being aware of the trademark Crey temperament, I evacuated the palace before our confrontation with Vladimir,' Qattren said smoothly. 'My reputation makes tasks like this easy, as you can imagine.'

Gomez Emmett Sr smiled. 'Speaking of the Crey temperament, what of King Theo's untimely demise? Any ideas as to the culprit?'

'It cannot be proved now, of course,' said Qattren, 'but we suspected the late prince, which was why we came to Stoneguard, to arrest him.'

'Is that so?' Emmett Jr asked dully. 'I heard rumours his majesty was following our cousin the Lady Cienne after an "abduction".'

Cienne reddened.

'That too,' Seth said coldly. 'Misunderstanding it may have been, but when a relative by marriage appears to claim an abduction occurred, I take such events seriously.' He paused as Anna brought over a tray of goblets. 'I love my wife dearly.'

A goblet hit the table with force, splashing wine onto the surface.

The younger Emmett lifted a perceptive eyebrow.

'If you say so,' he said in a bored voice, waving Anna's offer of wine away.

'I wouldn't be surprised if your suspicions were correct,' his father said, accepting some wine with a handsome smile. 'The prince was prickly by nature: he and my son often came to blows when my children were fostered at the Stonekeep. And he was highly influenced by his mother.'

'Mmm,' Ron muttered. 'And we all know what she's like.'

There were murmurs of agreement.

'I fear we will not have seen the last of her,' Zephyr said darkly.

'No doubt,' his brother agreed. 'She will almost certainly return for her remaining son.'

'Probably,' Ron said bitterly.

'No doubt she will want young Ronald on the throne in Vladimir's place,' Emmett Sr continued.

There was a pause.

'Ronald is already on the throne,' Qattren said slowly.

'Actually, that is another matter we must discuss,' he said. 'We will be taking power of Stoneguard.'

Ron breathed a furtive sigh of relief.

'But Ronald is Vladimir's remaining heir,' Qattren said. 'Vladimir didn't produce a legitimate issue...'

Everyone looked at Felicity.

'Ah, but you see, he did,' Emmett Sr said with a sad smile.

'But I thought she had the mind of a five-year-oh...' Seth trailed off.

Cienne placed her fingers over her mouth.

Felicity stared at a spot on the tablecloth, her eyes glazed over.

'Alas,' Emmett Sr said, holding her hand, 'whether this child was agreed upon mutually or not, it remains within the laws of marriage. Thus, the child is an heir.'

'But if it's a girl—' Ron began.

'It is a boy,' he assured him. 'Queen Aaliyaa's black potions would have ensured that they conceived a male. The Hornes did all they could to prevent Ronald – and his loyal wife Qattren – grasping his throne.'

'Oh gods,' Ron said in horror, his eyes on Felicity.

She met his gaze and simply burst into tears.

Her father pulled her close to his side as she sobbed gently.

'As my attention is needed in Mellier,' he continued, 'I will be leaving my son Gomez in charge of the realm until the boy comes of age. I trust only him to look after his sister, and he will no doubt show the country the same due care and attention.'

Seth eyed the man's emotionless face and doubted it.

Emmett Sr led Felicity to her feet, and her kin rose with him.

'Now that we have said our piece,' he said, 'I think it is time for us to leave. Thank you for your co-operation, and your wine.'

He bowed to Seth and Cienne and left, his family behind him.

Zephyr halted, lingering by Cienne's side.

'If you need anything, my dear,' he said kindly, extending a hand, 'you let me know.'

She placed her hand in his, and he kissed it.

'Zephyr!' his brother called impatiently.

Zephyr inclined his head, taking his leave.

'They left quickly,' Seth commented.

'In case Ronald deigned to speak up for his claim,' Qattren said, giving him a sharp glance.

Ron did a double-take. 'I don't want it! If you want it, speak up for it yourself!'

Qattren rolled her eyes and rose also, jerking Ron's elbow up as she went.

'We had better leave also,' she said.

Ron straightened, giving her a black look.

'And we'll check on the Hole, to make sure it hasn't returned.'

'Alright,' Seth said, rising to accompany her to the door.

'And… thank you for everything,' Cienne added.

She curtsied politely, and Seth walked them out.

This left Cienne and Anna alone. Anna scowled at her hatefully, but Cienne didn't notice. She was thinking about Seth, as always.

'You must be grieving for the prince, your highness,' Anna commented, clearing the table.

Cienne frowned. 'Why should I be? I've only met him *once*.'

Anna frowned, feigning confusion. 'But I thought you and he were planning to elope?'

Cienne's eyes rolled upwards. 'So did he, but he was mistaken.'

'That isn't how your husband sees it,' said Anna, scrubbing the table.

Cienne turned slightly. 'What do you mean?'

'You hardly disappeared into thin air, did you?' she said idly. 'We all know where you really were shortly before conveniently appearing at the Stonekeep after the explosion.'

'What on earth,' Cienne drawled, 'do you think you're implying—'

Seth re-entered alone before Anna could reply.

'Ladies,' he greeted brightly.

'I'll let him explain himself,' Anna said coldly.

Seth blinked. 'Everything alright?'

'It will be once you've arrested the criminal sitting before you.'

Seth turned to Cienne quizzically.

'It's not true,' she protested. 'I told him no, I swear to you.'

Anna waited.

'Well, go on then!' she snapped, gesturing in her direction.

Seth frowned at Anna.

'Arrest her!' she exclaimed. 'What are you afraid of?'

'Seth, please,' Cienne said.

'Hang her, she betrayed you!' Anna demanded.

Cienne just looked at him, pleading.

He stared at her for a long moment. He turned his back to Anna and gestured at Cienne with one finger. 'Stand up.'

She did as he bid.

His face was impassive. 'I was going to let this go, considering who you are,' he told her, 'but I can't.'

Cienne paled. 'W-what?'

'Moat,' he said softly.

He entered the hall from the courtyard, evidently awaiting his call.

'Put her in the Tower.'

'Seth!' she shrilled, close to tears.

'Just go,' he said in disgust.

Then, glancing behind to ensure Anna's gaze was elsewhere, he gave Cienne a soft smile and winked.

Moat guided her by the waist and pulled her noiselessly from the hall.

'What's going on, Corporal, I don't understand—' she began.

Moat pressed a finger to his lips. 'Just come with me and watch the coach outside, your highness.'

He winked, just as Seth had, suppressing a smile.

Cienne let him lead her outside.

A carriage bearing the standard of the Creys waited on the path, beside an ornate gazebo. Cienne and Moat hid in the gazebo, waiting.

Anna came bounding out a couple minutes later, beaming.

'You head in, I'll just have a word with the coachman,' said Seth, strolling after her as she ran for the coach door eagerly.

He craned his neck to the gazebo to make sure Cienne was watching. After some whispered conversation with the man at the reins, Seth stood beside the coach door, a smirk creeping across his mouth.

Anna waited, her hands folded demurely on her lap. 'Aren't you coming in?'

'Nope,' he said. 'Changed my mind. Think I'll stay here.'

'What?' snapped Anna.

Seth slammed the door and waved her off.

The horses trotted downhill.

'Wait, stop!' wailed Anna as the coach rolled away. 'Seth!'

He waved again with a grin as Anna disappeared.

'Bitch,' he said under his breath.

Cienne paced forward to stand beside him.

'You seem to have run out of mistresses, your majesty,' she said playfully.

'I have, haven't I?' he said, facing her.

Cienne had taken to wearing a different style, Seth observed.

She'd done away with the petticoats and now wore a low-cut Truphorian gown in deep blue velvet. He preferred it. The fabric held her figure snugly, revealing every curve and shape all the way down to her—

He blinked.

'I don't think I need one at the moment,' he said.

Cienne grinned smugly.

~

Elliot jolted awake to the sound of Anna's screams of fury.

'What was that?'

'God knows,' Marbrand murmured, rolling over.

Marbrand didn't really care either at this present moment in time. He had just returned from their futile journey through the Wastelands, after Qattren hastily returned with the posh-person equivalent of 'Oh, yeah, we don't need to go to Stoneguard anymore, you can go home now'. All Marbrand wanted to do after that colossal waste of time was sleep, preferably forever.

Elliot paused. 'I've been wondering,' he said. 'Who do we work for now? Seth Crey or Ronald Horne?'

Marbrand paused also. That was a good question – one of the best Elliot had ever come up with.

'Whoever we want,' he decided. 'Personally, I prefer it here. Pay's good, the night watch is quiet, and the chance of his missus razing the place in a fit of rage is slim – well, slim*mer*. Job's a doddle here. We might as well be retired, we'll do such little work.'

'Until someone decides to kidnap or kill a member of a royal family and we have to go and rescue them,' said Elliot.

Marbrand paused.

'Nah, that'll never happen,' he said, rolling back towards the wall. 'King Theo's dead, remember?'

~

Howie entered Archie's workshop to find him packing away his things.

'You got my letter?' he asked Archie.

'Yep,' he confirmed. 'Past due time if you ask me. I'd swear another axe passed my bedroom window this morning.' He gazed wistfully to the window, at the bustling street outside. 'I've never had business as good in Stoneguard, mind you.'

'Not worth it, mate,' Howie sighed, clapping a hand on his shoulder. 'She upstairs?'

Archie nodded.

He found Adrienne on their bed – they shared one now – holding a toy horse Archie had made for her over a decade ago, before she and Howie had even met. She was crying. It was about time.

He sat on the bed and pulled her into his lap. 'I know.'

She sniffed. 'I wish I'd never gone into that chapel.'

Howie thought back to that day in Stoneguard, so long ago, to Father Toffer's chapel, the one that had started it all. 'Me too.'

She toyed with the little horse in her hands. She ran a thumb down a crack running down its back.

'D'you remember how this got here?' she said suddenly. 'You trod on it the day you arrived here, I'd left it in the front room. I nearly screamed at you, and then I saw your face.'

'You froze,' he said, remembering. 'I'm surprised you liked me at all. I trod on a lot of your things.'

She gave a soft laugh. 'I loved you from that moment,' she said. She trembled. 'I nearly asked Qattren to sacrifice the child on purpose. To save you. I don't know what I was thinking. I just wanted you out of that Tower.'

'You couldn't have done that, I wouldn't have let you,' he said, toying with a lock of her hair. '*You* wouldn't have let you. You're not a monster.'

'Aren't I?' she asked bitterly. 'The Duke of Osney sent people here while you were away. With money.'

'Oh, Christ,' he said, holding her closer.

'For my services to the realm,' she said in a dull voice. 'As if it was my idea and not his.'

'That fat old pig,' Howie growled under his breath. 'Just as well I wasn't here, I'd have shoved his money up his ass.'

'I shouldn't have taken it, should I?' she said in a small voice.

Something Seth had said drifted into Howie's mind at that note. *She can pay her own way…*

'It was from Seth,' he said. 'He mentioned something about it before, I just remembered.'

Adrienne stiffened. 'Seth sent it?'

A hot flush crept up Howie's chest. 'He paid you money like you were a whore.'

'Forget him,' Adrienne said immediately.

Howie released an angry breath.

'If *he* were a whore, I wouldn't have even deigned to pay him.'

They exchanged glances and burst out laughing.

'Was he that bad?' said Howie with a grin.

'He was *awful.*'

They laughed some more, leaning against one another. They wiped tears from their eyes, his of mirth and hers of grief. A few more giggles and they soon found themselves kissing passionately. It seemed a strange time to do that to Howie's mind, but it felt right. They hadn't locked lips since the night King Theo died.

They pulled apart with reluctance.

'D'you think I'll be as awful as he will?' he whispered.

'I don't think it will matter,' she said. 'D'you remember Qattren saying you had improvements brought on by the sorcery?'

He said he did.

She told him what else was a significant improvement.

They fell about laughing all over again.

~

Qattren and Ron stood in the pit where the Hole had been. Thankfully, it hadn't returned. Despite the lack of apparition, however, she still felt a presence, a sort of queer foreboding.

'No sign of anything strange,' Ron said, unaware of any sensations.

Qattren looked at him.

'No,' she agreed. Her imagination, she decided, shaking it off.

It began to rain softly as they returned to the trapdoor on foot. It reminded her of Seb, who had loved the rain. *It's cold mostly, but a refreshing change*, he would say. *Just like you.*

She smiled faintly.

Ron glanced at her. 'What's got you smirking?'

She caught his eye.

'Just remembering things,' she said softly.

He smiled at her before descending.

She watched her husband vanish down the ladder and turned her gaze upward, to where her lover was, somewhere.

'I miss you,' she said. 'Every day.' She blew him a kiss.

~

Seth entered the mausoleum, Cienne at his side.

'Are you sure you want to do this?'

'Very.'

They halted in front of King Theo Crey's crypt side by side, Seth with his hands behind his back, Cienne carrying a wooden plaque.

It had finally been finished not long after Anna's departure, and it was evident that the builders were improving. The ones next to the doors – belonging to Seth's ancestors – were half dust, and that was when they had been *made*. The entrance to King Theo's crypt was made of solid granite, with no decorations apart from a wooden plaque over their heads with 'Careful: Unstable As Yet' scraped on it. Seth saw merely an open door and a flight of stairs within, leading down into the king's final resting place.

Seth lowered himself to one knee, Cienne following suit. His father had been carted off for his ceremonial tour around the kingdom days earlier and wouldn't be laid to rest here until he returned, but Seth felt he needed to say a few words.

He cleared his throat.

'Recently,' he began, 'well, before your death, I know we had our... differences.' He could almost sense him snorting in defiance, but he ignored his conscience and moved on. 'And I know there were times when I hoped to see this door, knowing you were going to be in there, but...' He hesitated.

Cienne placed a hand on his shoulder.

'... I was stupid,' he continued. 'I've done a lot of stupid things where you're concerned, and...' He sighed and gave a shrug. 'No hard feelings?'

As if in response, a nail on the wooden plaque above them came loose, and one side of the plaque fell to hit Seth on the head.

'OW!'

Cienne looked around nervously for any priests, but no one heard his outburst.

'I'll take that as a no, then,' he muttered. 'I brought you a present, for all it's worth.'

He signalled to Cienne impassively and she handed him the plaque in her hands. He placed it in front of the door and gazed at it.

The Grim Reaper of Adem.

'King Theo Crey was never his real name, was it?' Cienne said amusedly.

Seth shook his head in reply

They rose to their feet together and he turned to gaze at her intently. Too intently, he realised as a hot flush washed up his back and over his head.

The long journey to the Mausoleum had been a nightmare: Lilly had insisted on coming with them, and Seth could hardly refuse her. That had left the three of them sitting in a wheelhouse for four days straight with nothing to look at but each other. Cienne's penchant for wearing tight bodices had driven Seth to such distraction that he nearly threw Lilly bodily from the wheelhouse and leapt on his wife then and there. He didn't know what had come over him. He couldn't keep his hands off her.

Lilly was at a nearby inn at the moment, lost in a drunken stupor, but a priest could come along at any moment…

He was still debating whether to risk it when Cienne took his hands.

'Seth,' she said, nervous. 'I need to tell you... I've never said it before, because I was afraid of humiliating myself, but… I've always…'

He nodded with a smile.

'Even though you're vile at times and you've given me so much grief and not enough reason to, I've... I've always just, despite...'

She shrugged.

'You know,' she said simply.

Seth snorted with a grin. 'Your insatiable lust for my body is entirely mutual.'

She grinned broadly and pulled him towards her.

He planted his mouth over hers and groaned as the kiss deepened. The flush washed against his back like an ocean wave on a cliff edge. He tightened his grip on her waist and made to kneel.

'Seth,' Cienne giggled as she landed on her knees. 'The priests… in front of your *father*'s crypt…'

'Oh, go on, it's what he would have wanted,' he said in between kisses.

Cienne cackled as they tumbled to one side.

An exaggerated cough sounded from the altar.

The two scrambled to their feet.

'This is a sacred place, my liege,' the priest said sternly. 'Fornication is a sin.'

'Why, I can only apologise for my wife, Father, she just can't keep her hands from me,' Seth said with a shrug.

Cienne giggled, her head on his shoulder. 'I apologise also, Father. It's just that the king had great hopes for our marriage. We wanted to show him that his last wish had been granted. Seth just…' A little sigh escaped her. 'Gets a bit carried away.'

The priest glared at them sullenly.

Probably jealous, Seth thought with satisfaction.

'You need to hold back from your urges,' he told them.

They sniggered like children.

'Sins from a king are not acceptable behaviour. Your father the good King Theo had never committed such abominations.'

'Never?' Seth said in shock. 'You mean to say my sister and I are...' He gasped. 'Another man's children?'

The priest's eyes widened. 'NO! No, no, of course I don't mean that, my liege—'

'Well then, he must have sinned at *some* point,' Cienne said.

'Well, well, yes, but—'

They sniggered again.

The priest frowned sternly. 'Do not desecrate the royal mausoleum with tomfoolery, my liege. Tone down your embraces when in Salator Crey's sight if you please.'

'Well, we did, because his actual request of us was to conceive—'

'ENOUGH!' the priest boomed desperately as they laughed aloud.

'Alright, alright, I'll leave,' Seth chuckled, disentangling himself from Cienne's grasp. 'Before I get struck by lightning or something. I'll see you later.' With that he left.

The priest eyed Seth's gift to the king with distaste as Seth shut the door behind him.

'Is his majesty aware that he left his gift to his own crypt?' he asked Cienne.

'No,' she replied. 'I think he would be offended if he learned you had installed his tomb early, even if it was King Theo's last wish.'

The man bowed his head.

As he left, Cienne heard one of the world's greatest examples of bad whispering mutter, 'Pity we aren't putting him *in* early, too.'

~

Vladimir opened his eyes.

A man looked down at him with golden eyes, and grinned.

Vladimir squeezed his eyes shut tightly and opened them again.

'Are you one of the Seven Gods?' he whispered in awe.

'Actually, no,' he said with a smile. 'But you're nearly right.'

Vladimir looked around at his surroundings. He was in a darkly lit room, on a wooden floor. And the two men weren't alone.

Standing next to the golden-eyed man was Cienne Fleurelle – and she was smiling at him.

'Oh,' he said in a high voice, staring at her. 'Lady Cienne! You're here... and you're not wearing anything...'

He wrung his hands and gave a little giggle.

Geldemar grinned broadly. 'Not even remotely right this time.'

He placed a hand on Vladimir's head, and Cienne's form changed. Suddenly she wasn't Cienne anymore... she was fully clothed, but she wasn't Cienne.

Vladimir stared wide-eyed at the thing in front of him and screamed.

'Yes, Liana is quite a sight to behold when in her true form,' Geldemar said jovially. 'Now tell me: why do you think you're here?'

Vladimir breathed heavily.

'I don't know,' he said in a whispery voice. 'The last thing I remember is...' His eyes widened. 'My home!'

'Yes, well, allow me to fill in the blanks.' He held out a hand. 'I am Geldemar, and this is Liana. We are two of the Seven Devils.'

Vladimir gulped fearfully. 'Oh no...'

'And you have sinned by succumbing to greed...' he gestured to himself, '... and lust.' He gestured to the thing that was apparently Liana. 'So now you belong to us.'

'No,' he stammered, 'no, I, I am king of Stoneguard, I, I cannot be here, I cannot be dead, I—'

'I'm afraid so,' Geldemar said piteously. 'Now I have a job for you. Put this on and stand in the path of those flaming arrows.'

Vladimir stared in horror at the scant amount of clothing in Geldemar's hands.

'Why?' he squeaked.

He leaned forward, smiling again. 'This is hell, remember? Why do you think?'

~

Lilly skipped to the Crook with a smile on her lips.

Keith held the door open for her greedily.

Seth had proclaimed openly that she could do whatever she wanted as long as she kept far away from him while doing it. She was glad to. 'My castle, my rules,' was his new catchphrase whenever she found him in interesting positions with Cienne on the dining room table. She missed her father every day, but at times like those, it was his axe she missed more.

However, all the money Seth was throwing at her to make her leave did ease the pain of his passing somewhat. Today she was going to splurge, in all senses of the word.

She hopped to a halt in front of Keith, dropped in his arms a heavy bag of gold Seth had given her to make her go away and entered eagerly.

It was here that she ran straight into Stan and head-butted him backwards onto the floor.

'OW!'

'OI! Get back inside! He keeps trying to do a runner today,' he told Lilly in annoyance before turning to Stan irritably. 'You've got work to do!'

'If I've said it once, I've said it a thousand times,' he snapped back, getting up grumpily, 'you can't fix a bed if it's being used! Especially the way it gets used here!'

'What, you want I should chuck people and their good money out to make your job easier?'

Stan stormed out.

'Where are you going?' his uncle snapped.

A light flashed behind Lilly's eyes.

'Keith?' she asked suddenly.

'Mmm?' he replied tiredly.

'D'you think I could buy him from you?'

'Lady, he ain't no use to you that way, he's disgusted by the notion—'

'No, no, not for that, for this.'

She took a map out of her pocket and handed it to him.

He unrolled it dubiously and his eyes widened. 'You're going *there?*'

'Thought I might go get a dragon,' she said brightly. 'Seth and Howard Rosethorn are hogging our one.'

'And you're taking Stan?'

'Thought I might use my natural feminine weakness as an excuse to make him carry my stuff,' she replied with a wink.

Keith looked at the bag in his hands. 'For this?'

Lilly nodded.

He held out a hand. 'Deal.'

~

EPILOGUE

lias deflated into a knitted armchair.

Candlelight bathed everything in the tiny cabin in a soft yellow glow as owls muttered outside. Qattren had left only ten minutes before, interrupting his meal to give him the good news – the Hole was gone, once and for all.

His relief was only tarnished by a deep feeling of sadness. The girl should not have suffered so. Qattren seemed convinced that her pain was suitable penance for the life she gave away, but Elias doubted the girl knew what she was doing. He had heard stories about Father Giery. He was too slippery by half. The snake emblem should have been allocated to him rather than the Creys.

And as for Manderly and the Duke of Osney…

A fist pounded on his front door, disturbing his thoughts.

His brow furrowed, Elias rose grouchily to answer it.

It was to be his downfall.

Literally.

From all directions.

A fair-haired man in black stood in the doorway, the remains of Elias falling around him like leaves.

He should have felt sick by what he'd just committed. It was his first murder, after all, and a bloody one at that. Mind you, he'd only been alive for a matter of weeks – the concept of guilt, or indeed the concept of human beings other than himself having feelings at *all*, was still a notion quite beyond his imagination. And being able to recall his own conception with startling clarity, this didn't bother him as much anyway. Things were generally more traumatic from the inside than the side-lines.

Rustling undergrowth alerted him to his companion's

presence.

Two voices spoke as one – a low monotonous drawl at the back of the man's trademark booming tones.

'IS IT DONE?'

'Done and dusted,' he said. 'Made a horrific mess, though.'

'EXCELLENT,' said his companion.

The murderer turned with a smile.

King Theo Crey's image stood before him, looking pleased.

'I'M MOST HAPPY I COULD RESTORE YOU,' he said. 'THE ONLY THING YOU NEED NOW IS A NAME. WE CAN'T JUST CALL YOU THE BASTARD, CAN WE?'

'Just don't name me Seth,' grimaced the man currently known rather unfairly as the Bastard. 'I'd rather stick with the insult than be named after my father. He's a disappointment to me.'

King Theo's face smiled broadly. 'I KNOW EXACTLY WHAT YOU MEAN.'

The Bastard smirked at his grandfather. The resemblance to Seth Crey was startling in all respects, apart from the eyes. His mother's eyes.

'They'll pay for that,' he vowed.

His voice took on an otherworldly timbre of its own.

'THEY'LL RUE THE DAY THEY GAVE ME TO THE HOLE.'

Dramatis Personae, for your reading convenience

Our Heroic Party:

Howard Rosethorn, an orphan born on the Night of Raining Thorns (see Historical Notes)

Archibald (Archie) Hart, his foster father who took him in as his carpentry apprentice

Adrienne Hart, Archie's niece and Howie's biggest admirer, training to be a surgeon and apothecary specialist

Prince Ronald Horne, second heir to Stoneguard, where they all live

Keith Large, a friend of Archie's who runs a chain of brothels

Dora, Keith's brief 'employee' whose favourite colour is yellow, by the way

The Holy Flying Cat, who briefly accompanies the group

The Faith of the Seven (who think Salator Crey is the devil):

Father George Toffer, head of the church of Stoneguard, the country's self-named capital city

The Seven Gods… or Devils, depending on your point of view:

- Geldemar, God of Greed
- Gale, god of nature
- Theo, god of war
- Rubena, goddess of rebellion
- Fortune and Misfortune, conjoined twins of fate
- Liana, goddess of desire

The Faith of Salator Crey (who thinks the Seven are devils):

His Eminence Father Abraham Furlong, Archpriest of the Faith of Salator Crey

Father Giery, head of the chapel of Creys' Keep.

Father Hope, head of the church of Serpus

Brother Daniel, briefly mentioned as a nuisance to Father Hope

Salator Crey, the world's creator

The three Christs, his demi-godly children come down onto earth to get everyone drunk or something

The Household of the Hornes

Prince Vladimir Horne, the prickly next in line to the throne of Stoneguard

Prince Ronald Horne, his younger brother

King Samuel Horne, their father

Queen Aaliyaa Horne, their mother and King Samuel's wife

Princess Felicity Horne (nee Emmett), Vladimir's wife

Lord Leroy Tetzel, Queen Aaliyaa's half-brother

Sir Sadie Marbrand, captain of the household guard

Elliot Maynard, who accompanies Marbrand to Adem later

Fred, the castle groundskeeper

The Crew of their ship to Adem:

Captain 'Legless' Hopkins

Sam, the first mate

Silas (Si/Two Finger Si) and Tully Beult, crewmates and general mischief-makers

Characters from Arthur Stibbons' Street, Serpus:

Petunia, manager of The Crook, Keith's brothel

Stanley Carrot, Keith's nephew and son of Hilary, briefly mentioned

The one-armed barman, landlord of the Prince Death, the street's main tavern

The Household of the Creys:

Prince Seth Crey, next in line to the throne of Adem

Princess Cienne Fleurelle, sole heir to the throne of Portabella and Seth's wife

King Theo Crey, Seth's father

Queen Eleanor Crey, Seth's mother

Princess Lilly-Anna (Lilly) Crey, Seth's younger sister

Lyseria, their dragon

James 'Jimmy' de Vil, the family butler

Anna Beult, the chambermaid

Duke Richard Crey of Osney, King Theo's younger brother

Father Giery, the palace priest

Cousin Elyse, Queen Eleanor's niece and the daughter of Uncle Fred, mentioned briefly by Lilly as being a 'bit of a man whore back in the day'

Cousin Mortimer, the Duke of Osney's son, missing and believed dead to all but King Theo

Captain Boris Necker, captain of the household guard

Corporal Moat, his nose-picking staff member

The Emmett Family:

Gomez Emmett, Lord Protector of the country of Mellier

Gomez Emmett Jr, his son

Felicity Horne nee Emmett, his daughter

Zephyr Emmett, Gomez Sr's younger brother

Queen Persephone Fleurelle nee Emmett, Gomez Sr's sister and Cienne's mother, deceased

In the Forest:

The Queen of the Forest, so formidable her name hasn't been spoken in Truphoria since the catastrophic Battle in the Orchard in 1320 (see Historical Notes)

Vhyn, a forest faerie

Cornelius Dali, a hermit sorcerer

Historical Events of Note:

The Night of Raining Thorns
1345 YM (Year of Mortality) – twenty years prior to the events of *Rosethorn*

The night the Queen of the Forest's castle was exploded by a dragon, starting a series of detonations across the Forest to the outskirts of Serpus. The name derives from the residents of Serpus, who spotted a flash in the distance and a shower of rose thorns from the foliage of the Forest, which had been blown in their direction.
It was also the night Prince Seth Crey was attacked by an assassin during the festivities for his upcoming wedding to Princess Cienne Fleurelle. Around the same time as this attack, Queen Persephone Fleurelle, Cienne's mother, was found murdered in the woods surrounding the Creys' Keep.

These events sparked a brief conflict between the Queen of the Forest and King Theo Crey, the supposed instigator of her palace's destruction, wherein she employed demonic beasts to attack his men. The conflict ended suddenly but uneasily, with both parties avoiding each other's territory and ensuring their subjects do the same.

~

The War for the Orchard
1315-1325 YM

A series of conflicts between King Seb Crey and Lord Janus Horne of Stoneguard for a series of provinces in Truphoria.

Truphoria once contained a series of provinces including Stoneguard and Adem, all ruled by the Creys – except for the forestry to the east, which had been conquered by the Queen of the Forest early in King Seb's reign. Lord Janus and a number of like-minded contemporaries decided to partition the rest of the continent into five independent countries – only for King Seb Crey to veto the decision in so flippant a fashion that it started a war – along with the then Prince Theo (aged 10) stealing an apple from King Janus's prized orchard.

One of these conflicts resulted in the involvement of the reclusive Queen of the Forest. In 1320 YM, she razed three of the six provinces in a fit of rage, consuming half of Truphoria in blue flames lasting several years afterwards. Everything from cities to countryside was completely destroyed in the blaze, including all wildlife, natural resources and people.

To hastily make amends for this catastrophe, King Seb reluctantly agreed to the partition, declaring Janus Horne King of Stoneguard, Truphoria's sole remaining province beside Adem and the Forest.

~

The Bloodthirsty Reign of King Rubeous Crey
1280-1295 YM

King Rubeous Crey came to the throne in 1280 upon the sudden disappearance of his father during Rubeous's coming of age ceremony. Following his coronation, he married thrice: to two women who lasted barely a year into the marriage before taking their own lives, and to his final wife Lilith, who bore him five children.

Only two of these lived past infancy. Using lack of dowry funds as an excuse for his actions, King Rubeous would murder and eat all children of his born female. Seb was the only child not subjected to this horror by lieu of being a viable heir.

When his younger sister was born, Lilith had a psychotic break shortly after labour. She dragged herself from the birthing bed seconds after bearing the child, hobbled to King Rubeous's chambers and bludgeoned King Rubeous to death before he had a chance to touch this newest victim.

His brother, the mild-mannered Gideon, was named King Regent until Seb, then two, came of age. He pardoned her immediately for the crime, given the tyranny of his brother's reign, and she would stand as King Seb's advisor during his reign in years to come.

Thanks for reading!

This book is self-published by Donna Shannon under the imprint DS Books. To help support the author, please leave a review on Goodreads, social media (@donnashandwich) or any online book retail outlet.

You can follow Donna Shannon on Wordpress, Goodreads, Facebook, Instagram, Threads and TikTok for all things books, art and general nonsense.

Many thanks for supporting an indie author in their journey!

Finding Retribution, Book 2 of the Raining Thorns Series, is coming soon!

Keep reading for a sneak peek! And don't forget, every purchase supports an indie author, so:

Do what the cat says!

Finding Retribution
Book 2 of the Raining Thorns Series

PROLOGUE

The Stonekeep, in the breakaway kingdom of Stoneguard on the third Tuesday of summer, 1345 YM.

aliyaa Horne, nee Ckerzi, glared at her youngest son through narrowed eyes. The toddler looked up from the block tower he was constructing and gave her a big four-toothed grin.

She had decided on the birthing bed that he was the Devil Incarnate.

His hair was like his father's – thick waves of pitch black, tumbling over wide brown eyes and a tiny button nose. His complexion was pale from his nocturnal inclinations, but he was an energetic and jolly child besides that. Time would tell whether he would have his father's square jaw and easy smile. Not that Aaliyaa was particularly taken with either.

A slam caused Aaliyaa to look up from the child.

Her husband Samuel entered, a bruised Vladimir following in his wake.

'What on earth happened to him?' snapped Queen Aaliyaa.

Vladimir, her eldest, was a wispy boy at twelve. Her heart nearly burst with pride all the same. He had the blood of the Far Isles.

Where the Hornes had common features and a tendency towards alcohol, Vladimir held himself with pride, his narrow face upturned in spite of its heavy bruising. He was dainty but dignified, his face set in a display of inner strength. His face still bore the roundness of childhood and was often sulky and petulant, but that would fade with maturity.

Vladimir kicked a couple of Ronald's wooden blocks.

It would fade, she told herself.

Ronald yelped in indignation.

Vladimir flicked the boy a hand gesture behind his father's back.

It would fade, she insisted again.

'The horse threw me off,' Vladimir said in reply to his mother, his thin voice breaking at points.

'Nonsense, you fell off,' Samuel said, harsh.

Samuel's broad shoulders bore a thick layer of muscle that was swiftly turning to fat. His plain brown garb was soaked with sweat and rainwater, and mud clung to the heels of his boots. He shook beads of sweat from his thinning hair and knelt before Ronald's creation.

'Excellent hand-eye coordination, this one,' he said, ruffling Ron's hair. 'Unlike his older brother.'

Vladimir scowled.

Ron giggled and said, 'Yap.' It was his only word as of yet.

'The boy's a heathen,' Aaliyaa spat.

Samuel slapped her across the face. Some people used corporal punishment to teach *children* a lesson, but King Samuel believed a child was only as good as his mother.

'Hold your tongue,' he said. 'Knowing that *you* awake in the daytime, I'd be nocturnal as well.' He flung a fond glance at Ronald. 'The child progresses well. Surely that's a better sign from the gods than an irregular sleeping pattern?'

Aaliyaa didn't respond. She had a feeling she would receive more than a slap for calling Ronald a light-fearing demon. In fact, it wasn't just a feeling, it was a conviction.

'Shame as much couldn't be said for Vladdy,' continued King Sam.

'Vladimir,' corrected Aaliyaa. 'His name is Vladimir.'

'Mmm,' he grunted. 'How on earth did you talk me into giving him that name? Vladimir Horne. Makes him sound like a damn vampire.' He eyed his eldest in distaste. 'He even looks like a vampire, thanks to your excessive prayer regime.'

'I need the prayer regime,' Vladimir snapped. 'The gods alone will give me what I need: my rightful throne and my rightful queen.'

Samuel rolled his eyes.

'The Fleurelle girl, loath as I am to inform you, is getting married as we speak.'

'Seth—'

Vladimir inserted a raspberry to substitute a middle name.

'—Crey will be dead before he can soil my woman. I'll make sure of that.'

'From the other side of the necropolis? Good luck, boy,' Samuel snorted. 'And I doubt the gods have time to take a child merely to serve the fantasies of a Far Isle banshee.'

Aaliyaa held her tongue at that, her cheek still smarting.

Instead, she held Vladimir by the shoulder.

'My boy will get what he wants,' she said with conviction.

'He bloody well won't. He'll get what he's given: the Emmetts' youngest scion and the deeds he was born for. I won't have you causing wars for your own selfish needs. I brought him up better than that.' He glanced back at Ron and ruffled his hair again. 'And I won't have you badmouthing Ronald either. He's a fine boy and there's nothing wrong with him.'

'Except that he's a light-fearing demon,' Vladimir muttered.

Samuel glared at him.

In accordance with his upbringing values, he slapped Aaliyaa across the face again, without looking away from Vladimir.

'Leave your brother alone,' he snarled. 'He'll outlive you by at least a decade, by my reckoning, so you'd better show him some respect. He's a fine boy,' he smiled down as Ron started a neighbour for his wooden tower, 'he'll make a fine man, and he'll make a fine husband for Lilly-Anna Crey.'

And he was right. Well… two out of three ain't bad for a drunkard.

Or so King Theo was thinking out of context, seven hundred and seventy-five leagues away in his keep just off Serpus, the capital of Adem.

He was currently observing the second most drunken leader in the world as Ambassador Krnk Bwl Xplsns (pronunciation undefined) slurred his way through a long congratulatory speech to the wrong Crey child.

Lilly, age three, snickered at him from her father's feet.

'No, Ambassador, it is Seth who is getting married, *Seth*,' Theo emphasised.

He gave Lilly a nudge to the shoulder in warning.

'Yuss, Seb, Seb, of course,' the Ambassador nodded.

'*Seth*,' he corrected, rolling his eyes.

'Yuss, yuss. Say, how is your father these days?'

'Smelly, I'd say, being dead for nearly a year and all,' Theo said in a dull voice.

Lilly giggled.

'Smelly,' she echoed, cracking up.

The king gave her shoulder another prod.

'Yes! He'll be down any minute, I imagine?'

Theo relented with a sigh. 'Yeah, why not?'

'Yes! Never seen a better swordsman in all my…'

'Yes, off you go, smelly,' Theo told his daughter.

He ushered his cackling daughter off and folded his arms, in wait for the Ambassador's reminiscing to cease.

Lilly wandered through the crowd listlessly, just one of a hundred little blond girls scurrying through the celebrations. She ignored the shrill exclamations of 'Aw! Look at the princess! How sweet!' and bolted for the front entrance. She had a hard time getting past her mother's doting ladies-in-waiting and punched a pair of nadgers belonging to a man trying to pull her in for a dance, but, stumbling on the hem of her dress, which she despised, she finally made it to the front of the keep…

And froze.

A dragon, a big, red one, rose above her imperiously, head tilted down to look at her.

'Ooh,' Lilly murmured.

The dragon lowered her head to Lilly's level and sniffed her. Upon establishing that the being before her did not smell at *all* edible, she opted to amuse it by throwing balls of fire into the air.

Red flame poured and burst high into the sky.

Lilly stared at the display, her mouth wide open.

A girl Lilly recognised as 'Seth's bed-warmer' – a term Theo had unwittingly passed on – hurried past with haste from the direction of the portcullis. Cienne skidded to a halt on the way to swiftly move the three-year-old away from the dragon, much to Lilly's irritation.

She was about to approach the dragon again when two big hands snatched her up by the ribs. A big reddish-brown beard came into view.

'Not for you, little one,' King Theo said sternly, hoisting her into his right elbow. 'Say, how much is that beast going for?'

'The Ambassador does not have this particular beast for sale,' said one of the Ambassador's attendants, 'but a similar breed and size could be acquired for a hundred thousand gold pieces, your majesty.'

'WHAT? That much for a dirty great lizard!'

Lilly gawked up at it. 'I want it.'

King Theo bellowed with laughter.

'I don't think so, little lady! Not after what you did to that cat!'

Lilly smiled sheepishly.

'If you tried that with a dragon, you'd be cooked alive! That would make you cry, wouldn't it?'

'It wouldn't!' Lilly exclaimed.

She never cried, not even once. She went through childbirth like it was a breeze, and when the want for night feeds came rumbling along, she climbed out of her swaddling blanket, onto her mother and was already breastfed by the time Queen Eleanor knew what was happening. Nothing made Lilly-Anna Crey cry. Nothing in the world.

Her father pinched her nose and placed her back on the ground.

'Back inside with you, little princess. There's a dirty great wedding cake inside with your name written all over it!'

'Cake!' exclaimed Lilly, running inside, all thoughts of the dragon forgotten.

King Theo watched his daughter go before turning back to the monster before him. Thinking of Seth, he swung back to the keep to drag his son out before the extortionist took the dragon away.

A minute later, all hell broke loose and palace gates were locked shut as the first rumours of the attempted assassination of Seth Crey made their fast descent to the city and beyond.

~

TO BE CONTINUED… SO DO WHAT THE CAT SAYS!

Acknowledgements

To everyone in the entire world apart from my god-awful Alexa Dot thing, who's a gobby incompetent little whore.

Not really (though she is a nuisance at best).

I want to start by thanking my family for putting up with me bursting into tears while trying to design the cover: namely Laura and my mum Sharon, who insisted I continue with it anyway. Also, my gran and Sinead, who read it, and Thomas, who read… well, something. I definitely don't remember writing that sex scene you read aloud to our parents from the first draft of *Rosethorn*'s sequel, but thanks anyway.

Many thanks to the Squid Squad: Roy Leon, Jae Waller, Rochelle Jardine, Lilah Souza and Beau Jones. Your advice, input and encouragement helped me become a better writer, and therefore helped *Rosethorn* become a better book. A gal couldn't ask for a better international beta group. Thank you always.

I could thank the myriad actors, comedians, writers and musicians who guided me through this story, but that would be cringe, so I won't.

Thank you to my hospital and college colleagues, particularly Ciaran Quirke, even if he did pester me for spoilers midway through reading *Rosethorn*. Also thanks to my former schoolmates David Bennett, Denis Bilo, Nicole Dwyer and Aaron Dwyer for the support you gave the entire decade it took to write this book – and special thanks to Kelly Taylor for the enthusiasm for *Rosethorn*, and also for dyeing my hair.

Final acknowledgements go out to the loved ones who couldn't be around to read it: my dad Tony, my sister Kelly and my uncle Steve. Love you always.

9 781739 433703